"I kn...
Ashle...
ambu...

She sto... ...ong moment, then bolted down the steps.

"What are you doing here?" she demanded.

Jack almost pitched out of the ambulance onto his face.

"Checking in," he said. "You're still in the bed-and-breakfast business, aren't you?"

Damn, the man had nerve.

"You belong in a hospital," she said evenly. "Not a bed-and-breakfast."

"I'm willing to pay double," Jack offered. His face, always strong, took on a vulnerable expression. "I need a place to lay low for a while, Ash. Are you game?"

The last thing in the world she wanted was Jack McCall under her roof again, but she couldn't afford to turn down a paying guest.

"Triple the usual rate," she said.

Jack squinted, probably not understanding at first, then gave a raspy chuckle. "Okay," he agreed. "Triple it is. Even though it is the off-season."

Ashley hesitated on the snowy sidewalk. First the cat. Now Jack.

Evidently, it was her day to be dumped on.

The daughter of a town marshal, **Linda Lael Miller** is a #1 *New York Times* and *USA TODAY* bestselling author of more than one hundred historical and contemporary novels, most of which reflect her love of the West. Raised in Northport, Washington, she now lives in Spokane, Washington.

Brenda Jackson is a *New York Times* and *USA TODAY* bestselling author of more than one hundred contemporary multicultural romance novels, including the Madaris Family series, the Westmorelands series and the Playas series. Many of her books have been adapted into movies. Brenda lives in Jacksonville, Florida, and divides her time between family, writing and traveling.

AT HOME
IN STONE CREEK

#1 *NEW YORK TIMES* BESTSELLING AUTHOR
LINDA LAEL MILLER

Harlequin

BESTSELLING AUTHOR COLLECTION

Harlequin®
BESTSELLING
AUTHOR
COLLECTION

Recycling programs
for this product may
not exist in your area.

ISBN-13: 978-1-335-62976-0

At Home in Stone Creek
First published in 2009. This edition published in 2025.
Copyright © 2009 by Linda Lael Miller

His to Claim
First published in 2019. This edition published in 2025.
Copyright © 2019 by Brenda Streater Jackson

For questions and comments about the quality of this book, please contact us at CustomerService@Harlequin.com.

TM and ® are trademarks of Harlequin Enterprises ULC.

Harlequin Enterprises ULC
22 Adelaide St. West, 41st Floor
Toronto, Ontario M5H 4E3, Canada
www.Harlequin.com

Printed in U.S.A.

CONTENTS

Visit the Author Profile page
at Harlequin.com for more titles!

AT HOME IN STONE CREEK

Linda Lael Miller

For Karen Beaty, with love.

Chapter 1

Ashley O'Ballivan dropped the last string of Christmas lights into a plastic storage container, resisting an uncharacteristic urge to kick the thing into the corner of the attic instead of stacking it with the others. For her, the holidays had been anything *but* merry and bright; in fact, the whole year had basically sucked. But for her brother, Brad, and sister Olivia, it qualified as a personal best—both of them were happily married. Even her workaholic twin, Melissa, had had a date for New Year's Eve.

Ashley, on the other hand, had spent the night alone, sipping nonalcoholic wine in front of the portable TV set in her study, waiting for the ball to drop in Times Square.

How lame was that?

It was worse than lame—it was *pathetic*.

She wasn't even thirty yet, and she was well on her way to old age.

With a sigh, Ashley turned from the dusty hodgepodge surrounding her—she went all out, at the Mountain View Bed and Breakfast, for every red-letter day on the calendar—and headed for the attic stairs. As she reached the bottom, stepping into the corridor just off the kitchen, a familiar car horn sounded from the driveway in front of the detached garage. It could only be Olivia's ancient Suburban.

Ashley had mixed feelings as she hoisted the ladder-steep steps back up into the ceiling. She loved her older sister dearly and was delighted that Olivia had found true love with Tanner Quinn, but since their mother's funeral a few months before, there had been a strain between them.

Neither Brad nor Olivia nor Melissa had shed a single tear for Delia O'Ballivan—not during the church service or the graveside ceremony or the wake. Okay, so there wasn't a greeting card category for the kind of mother Delia had been—she'd deserted the family long ago, and gradually destroyed herself through a long series of tragically bad choices. For all that, she'd still been the woman who had given birth to them all.

Didn't that count for something?

A rap sounded at the back door, as distinctive as the car horn, and Olivia's glowing, pregnancy-rounded face filled one of the frost-trimmed panes in the window.

Oddly self-conscious in her jeans and T-shirt and an ancient flannel shirt from the back of her closet, Ashley mouthed, "It's not locked."

Beaming, Olivia opened the door and waddled across the threshold. She was due to deliver her and Tanner's first child in a matter of days, if not hours, and from the looks of her, Ashley surmised she was carrying either quadruplets or a Sumo wrestler.

"You know you don't have to knock," Ashley said, keeping her distance.

Olivia smiled, a bit wistfully it seemed to Ashley, and opened their grandfather Big John's old barn coat to reveal a small white cat with one blue eye and one green one.

"Oh, no you don't," Ashley bristled.

Olivia, a veterinarian as well as Stone Creek, Arizona's one and only real-deal animal communicator, bent awkwardly to set the kitten on Ashley's immaculate kitchen floor, where it meowed pitifully and turned in a little circle, pursuing its fluffy tail. Every stray dog, cat or bird in the county seemed to find its way to Olivia eventually, like immigrants gravitating toward the Statue of Liberty.

Two years ago, at Christmas, she'd even been approached by a reindeer named Rodney.

"Meet Mrs. Wiggins," Olivia chimed, undaunted. Her china-blue eyes danced beneath the dark, sleek fringe of her bangs, but there was a wary look in them that bothered Ashley...even shamed her a little. The two of them had always been close. Did Olivia think Ashley was jealous of her new life with Tanner and his precocious fourteen-year-old daughter, Sophie?

"I suppose she's already told you her life story," Ashley said, nodding toward the cat, scrubbing her hands down the thighs of her jeans once and then heading for the sink to wash up before filling the electric kettle. At least *that* hadn't changed—they always had tea together, whenever Olivia dropped by—which was less and less often these days.

After all, unlike Ashley, Olivia had a life.

Olivia crooked up a corner of her mouth and began struggling out of the old plaid woolen coat, flecked, as always, with bits of straw. Some things never changed— even with Tanner's money, Olivia still dressed like what she was, a country veterinarian.

"Not much to tell," Livie answered with a slight lift of one shoulder, as nonchalantly as if telepathic exchanges with all manner of finned, feathered and furred creatures were commonplace. "She's only four- teen weeks old, so she hasn't had time to build up much of an autobiography."

"I do not want a cat," Ashley informed her sister.

Olivia hauled back a chair at the table and collapsed into it. She was wearing gum boots, as usual, and they looked none too clean. "You only *think* you don't want Mrs. Wiggins," she said. "She needs you and, whether you know it or not, you need her."

Ashley turned back to the kettle, trying to ignore the ball of cuteness chasing its tail in the middle of the kitchen floor. She was irritated, but worried, too. She looked back at Olivia over one stiff shoulder. "Should you be out and about, as pregnant as you are?"

Olivia smiled, serene as a Botticelli Madonna. "Preg- nancy isn't a matter of degrees, Ash," she said. "One either is or isn't."

"You're pale," Ashley fretted. She'd lost so many loved ones—both parents, her beloved granddad, Big John. If anything happened to any of her siblings, what- ever their differences, she wouldn't be able to bear it.

"Just brew the tea," Olivia said quietly. "I'm perfectly all right."

While Ashley didn't have her sister's gift for talking to animals, she *was* intuitive, and her nerves felt all twitchy, a clear sign that something unexpected was about to happen. She plugged in the kettle and joined Olivia at the table. "Is anything wrong?"

"Funny you should ask," Olivia answered, and though the soft smile still rested on her lips, her eyes were solemn. "I came here to ask *you* the same question. Even though I already know the answer."

As much as she hated the uneasiness that had sprung up between herself and her sisters and brother, Ashley tended to bounce away from any mention of the subject like a pinball in a lively game. She sprang right up out of her chair and crossed to the antique breakfront to fetch two delicate china cups from behind the glass doors, full of strange urgency.

"Ash," Olivia said patiently.

Ashley kept her back to her sister and lowered her head. "I've just been a little blue lately, Liv," she admitted softly. "That's all."

She would never get to know her mother.

The holidays had been a downer.

Not a single guest had checked into her Victorian bed-and-breakfast since before Thanksgiving, which meant she was two payments behind on the private mortgage Brad had given her to buy the place several years before. It wasn't that her brother had been pressing her for the money—he'd offered her the deed, free and clear, the day the deal was closed, but she'd insisted on repaying him every cent.

On top of all that, she hadn't heard a word from

Jack McCall since his last visit, six months ago. He'd suddenly packed his bags and left one sultry summer night, while she was sleeping off their most recent bout of lovemaking, without so much as a goodbye.

Would it have killed him to wake her up and explain? Or just leave a damn note? Maybe pick up a phone?

"It's because of Mom," Olivia said. "You're grieving for the woman she never was, and that's okay, Ashley. But it might help if you talked to one of us about how you feel."

Weary rage surged through Ashley. She spun around to face Olivia, causing her sneakers to make a squeaking sound against the freshly waxed floor, remembered that her sister was about to have a baby, and sucked all her frustration and fury back in on one ragged breath.

"Let's not go there, Livie," she said.

The kitten scrabbled at one leg of Ashley's jeans and, without thinking, she bent to scoop the tiny creature up into her arms. Minute, silky ears twitched under her chin, and Mrs. Wiggins purred as though powered by batteries, snuggling against her neck.

Olivia smiled again, still wistful. "You're pretty angry with us, aren't you?" she asked gently. "Brad and Melissa and me, I mean."

"No," Ashley lied, wanting to put the kitten down but unable to do so. Somehow, nearly weightless as that cat was, it made her feel anchored instead of set adrift.

"Come on," Olivia challenged quietly. "If I weren't nine and a half months along, you'd be in my face right now."

Ashley bit down hard on her lower lip and said nothing.

"Things can't change if we don't talk," Olivia persisted.

Ashley swallowed painfully. Anything she said would probably come out sounding like self-pity, and Ashley was too proud to feel sorry for herself, but she also knew her sister. Olivia wasn't about to let her off the hook, squirm though she might. "It's just that nothing seems to be working," she confessed, blinking back tears. "The business. Jack. That damn computer you insisted I needed."

The kettle boiled, emitting a shrill whistle and clouds of steam.

Still cradling the kitten under her chin, Ashley unplugged the cord with a wrenching motion of her free hand.

"Sit down," Olivia said, rising laboriously from her chair. "I'll make the tea."

"No, you won't!"

"I'm pregnant, Ashley," Olivia replied, "not incapacitated."

Ashley skulked back to the table, sat down, the tea forgotten. The kitten inched down her flannel work shirt to her lap and made a graceful leap to the floor.

"Talk to me," Olivia prodded, trundling toward the counter.

Ashley's vision seemed to narrow to a pinpoint, and when it widened again, she swayed in her chair, suddenly dizzy. If her blond hair hadn't been pulled back into its customary French braid, she'd have shoved her hands through it. "It must be an awful thing," she murmured, "to die the way Mom did."

Cups rattled against saucers at the periphery of Ashley's awareness. Olivia returned to the table but stood beside Ashley instead of sitting down again. Rested a hand on her shoulder. "Delia wasn't in her right mind, Ashley. She didn't suffer."

"No one cared," Ashley reflected, in a miserable whisper. "She died and no one even *cared*."

Olivia didn't sigh, but she might as well have. "You were little when Delia left," she said, after a long time. "You don't remember how it was."

"I remember praying every night that she'd come home," Ashley said.

Olivia bent—not easy to do with her huge belly—and rested her forehead on Ashley's crown, tightened her grip on her shoulder. "We all wanted her to come home, at least at first," she recalled softly. "But the reality is, she didn't—not even when Dad got killed in that lightning storm. After a while, we stopped needing her."

"Maybe *you* did," Ashley sniffled. "Now she's gone forever. I'm never going to know what she was really like."

Olivia straightened, very slowly. "She was—"

"Don't say it," Ashley warned.

"She drank," Olivia insisted, stepping back. The invisible barrier dropped between them again, a nearly audible shift in the atmosphere. "She took drugs. Her brain was pickled. If you want to remember her differently, that's your prerogative. But don't expect me to rewrite history."

Ashley's cheeks were wet, and she swiped at them with the back of one hand, probably leaving streaks in the coating of attic dust prickling on her skin. "Fair enough," she said stiffly.

Olivia crossed the room again, jangled things around at the counter for a few moments, and returned with a pot of steeping tea and two cups and saucers.

"This is getting to me," she told Ashley. "It's as if the earth has cracked open and we're standing on opposite sides of a deep chasm. It's bothering Brad and Melissa, too. We're *family*, Ashley. Can't we just agree to disagree as far as Mom is concerned and go on from there?"

"I'll try," Ashley said, though she had to win an inner skirmish first. A long one.

Olivia reached across the table, closed her hand around Ashley's. "Why didn't you tell me you were having trouble getting the computer up and running?" she asked. Ashley was profoundly grateful for the change of subject, even if it did nettle her a little at the same time. She hated the stupid contraption, hated anything electronic. She'd followed the instructions to the letter, and the thing *still* wouldn't work.

When she didn't say anything, Olivia went on. "Sophie and Carly are cyberwhizzes—they'd be glad to build you a website for the B&B and show you how to zip around the Internet like a pro."

Brad and his wife, the former Meg McKettrick, had adopted Carly, Meg's half sister, soon after their marriage. The teenager doted on their son, three-year-old Mac, and had befriended Sophie from the beginning.

"That would be…nice," Ashley said doubtfully. The truth was, she was an old-fashioned type, as Victorian, in some ways, as her house. She didn't carry a cell phone, and her landline had a rotary dial. "But you know me and technology."

"I also know you're not stupid," Olivia responded, pouring tea for Ashley, then for herself. Their spoons made a cheerful tinkling sound, like fairy bells, as they stirred in organic sugar from the chunky ceramic bowl in the center of the table.

The kitten jumped back into Ashley's lap then, startling her, making her laugh. How long had it been since she'd laughed?

Too long, judging by the expression on Olivia's face.

"You're really all right?" Ashley asked, watching her sister closely.

"I'm better than 'all right,'" Olivia assured her. "I'm married to the man of my dreams. I have Sophie, a barn full of horses out at Starcross Ranch, and a thriving veterinary practice." A slight frown creased her forehead. "Speaking of men…?"

"Let's not," Ashley said.

"You still haven't heard from Jack?"

"No. And that's fine with me."

"I don't think it *is* fine with you, Ashley. He's Tanner's friend. I could ask him to call Jack and—"

"No!"

Olivia sighed. "Yeah," she said. "You're right. That would be interfering, and Tanner probably wouldn't go along with it anyhow."

Ashley stroked the kitten even as she tried not to bond with it. She was zero-for-zero on that score. "Jack and I had a fling," she said. "It's obviously over. End of story."

Olivia arched one perfect eyebrow. "Maybe you need a vacation," she mused aloud. "A new man in your life. You could go on one of those singles' cruises—"

Ashley gave a scoffing chuckle—it felt good to engage in girl talk with her sister again. "Sure," she retorted. "I'd meet guys twice my age, with gold chains around their necks and bad toupees. Or worse."

"What could be worse?" Olivia joked, grinning over the gold rim of her teacup.

"Spray-on hair," Ashley said decisively.

Olivia laughed.

"Besides," Ashley went on, "I don't want to be out of town when you have the baby."

Olivia nodded, turned thoughtful again. "You should get out more, though."

"And do what?" Ashley challenged. "Play bingo in the church basement on Mondays, Wednesdays and Fridays? Join the Powder Puff bowling league? In case it's escaped your notice, O pregnant one, Stone Creek isn't exactly a social whirlwind."

Olivia sighed again, in temporary defeat, and glanced at her watch. "I'm supposed to meet Tanner at the clinic in twenty minutes—just a routine checkup, so don't panic. Meet us for lunch afterward?"

The kitten climbed Ashley's shirt, its claws catching in the fabric, nestled under her neck again. "I have some errands to run," she said, with a shake of her head. "You're going to stick me with this cat, aren't you, Olivia?"

Olivia smiled, stood, and carried her cup and saucer to the sink. "Give Mrs. Wiggins a chance," she said. "If she doesn't win your heart by this time next week, I'll try to find her another home." She took Big John's ratty coat from the row of pegs next to the back door and shoved her arms into the sleeves, reclaimed her purse from the end of the counter, where she'd set it on the way in. "Shall I ask Sophie and Carly to come by after school and have a look at your computer?"

Ashley enjoyed the girls, and it would be nice to bake a batch of cookies for someone. Besides, she was tired of being confronted by the dark monitor, tower and printer every time she went into the study. "I guess," she answered.

"Done deal," Olivia confirmed brightly, and then she was out the door, gone.

Ashley held the kitten in front of her face. "You're not staying," she said.

"Meow," Mrs. Wiggins replied.

"Oh, all right," Ashley relented. "But I'd better not find any snags in my new chintz slipcovers!"

The helicopter swung abruptly sideways in a dizzying arch, setting Jack McCall's fever-ravaged brain spinning. He hoped the pilot hadn't seen him grip the edges of his seat, bracing for a crash.

His friend's voice sounded tinny, coming through the earphones. "You belong in a hospital," he said. "Not some backwater bed-and-breakfast."

All Jack really knew about the toxin raging through his system was that it wasn't contagious—the CDC had ordered him into quarantine until that much had been determined—but there was still no diagnosis and no remedy except a lot of rest and quiet. "I don't like hospitals," he responded, hoping he sounded like his normal self. "They're full of sick people."

Vince Griffin chuckled at that, but it was a dry sound, rough at the edges. "What's in Stone Creek, Arizona?" he asked. "Besides a whole lot of nothin'?"

Ashley O'Ballivan was in Stone Creek, and she was a whole lot of somethin', but Jack had neither the strength nor the inclination to explain. Given the way he'd ducked out on her six months before, after taking an emergency call on his cell phone, he didn't expect a welcome, knew he didn't deserve one. But Ashley, being Ashley, would take him in, whatever her misgivings, same as she would a wounded dog or a bird with a broken wing.

He had to get to Ashley—he'd be all right then.

He closed his eyes, letting the fever swallow him.

There was no telling how much time had passed when he surfaced again, became aware of the chopper blades slowing overhead. The magic flying machine bobbed on its own updraft, sending the broth he'd sipped from a thermos scalding its way up into the back of his throat.

Dimly, he saw the ancient ambulance waiting on the airfield outside Stone Creek; it seemed that twilight had descended, but he couldn't be sure. Since the toxin had taken him down, he hadn't been able to trust his perceptions.

Day turned into night.

Up turned into down.

The doctors had ruled out a brain tumor, but he still felt as though something was eating his brain.

"Here we are," Vince said.

"Is it dark or am I going blind?"

Vince tossed him a worried look. "It's dark," he said.

Jack sighed with relief. His clothes—the usual black jeans and black turtleneck sweater—felt clammy against his flesh. His teeth began to chatter as two figures unloaded a gurney from the back of the ambulance and waited for the blades to stop so they could approach.

"Great," Vince remarked, unsnapping his seat belt. "Those two look like volunteers, not real EMTs. The CDC parked you at Walter Reed, and that wasn't good enough for you because—?"

Jack didn't answer. He had nothing against the famous military hospital, but he wasn't associated with the U.S. government, not officially at least. He couldn't see taking up a bed some wounded soldier might need, and, anyhow, he'd be a sitting duck in a regular facility.

The chopper bounced sickeningly on its runners, and Vince, with a shake of his head, pushed open his door and jumped to the ground, head down.

Jack waited, wondering if he'd be able to stand on his own. After fumbling unsuccessfully with the buckle on his seat belt, he decided not.

When it was safe, the EMTs came forward, following Vince, who opened Jack's door.

Jack hauled off his headphones and tossed them aside.

His old friend Tanner Quinn stepped around Vince, his trademark grin not quite reaching his eyes.

"You look like hell warmed over," he told Jack cheerfully.

"Since when are you an EMT?" Jack retorted.

Tanner reached in, wedged a shoulder under Jack's right arm, and hauled him out of the chopper. His knees immediately buckled, and Vince stepped up, supporting him on the other side.

"In a place like Stone Creek," Tanner replied, "everybody helps out."

"Right," Jack said, stumbling between the two men keeping him on his feet. They reached the wheeled gurney—Jack had thought they never would, since it seemed to recede into the void with every awkward step—and he found himself on his back.

Tanner and the second man strapped him down, a process that brought back a few bad memories.

"Is there even a hospital in this hellhole of a place?" Vince asked irritably, from somewhere in the cold night.

"There's a pretty good clinic over in Indian Rock," Tanner answered easily, "and it isn't far to Flagstaff." He paused to help his buddy hoist Jack and the gurney into the back of the ambulance. "You're in good hands, Jack. My wife is the best veterinarian in the state."

Jack laughed raggedly at that.

Vince muttered a curse.

Tanner climbed into the back beside Jack, perched on some kind of fold-down seat. The other man shut the doors.

"I'm not contagious," Jack said to Tanner.

"So I hear," Tanner said, as his partner climbed into the driver's seat and started the engine. "You in any pain?"

"No," Jack struggled to quip, "but I might puke on those Roy Rogers boots of yours."

"You don't miss much, even strapped to a gurney." Tanner chuckled, hoisted one foot high enough for Jack to squint at it and hauled up the leg of his jeans to show off the fancy stitching on the boot shaft. "My brother-in-law gave them to me," he said. "Brad used to wear them onstage, back when he was breaking hearts out there on the concert circuit. Swigged iced tea out of a whiskey bottle all through every performance, so everybody would think he was a badass."

Jack looked up at his closest and most trusted friend and wished he'd listened to Vince. Ever since he'd come down with the illness, a week after snatching a five-year-old girl back from her noncustodial parent—a small-time drug runner with dangerous aspirations and a lousy attitude—he hadn't been able to think about anyone or anything but Ashley. When he *could* think.

Now, in one of the first clearheaded moments he'd experienced since checking himself out of the hospital the day before, he realized he might be making a major mistake—not by facing Ashley; he owed her that much and a lot more. No, he could be putting her in danger, and putting Tanner and his daughter and his pregnant veterinarian wife in danger, as well.

"I shouldn't have come here," he said, keeping his voice low.

Tanner shook his head, his jaw clamped down hard, as though irritated by Jack's statement. Since he'd gotten married, settled down and sold off his multinational construction company to play at being an Arizona rancher, Tanner had softened around the edges a little, but Jack knew his friend was still one tough SOB.

"This is where you belong," Tanner insisted. Another grin quirked one corner of his mouth. "If you'd had sense enough to know that six months ago, old buddy, when you bailed on Ashley without so much as a fare-thee-well, you wouldn't be in this mess."

Ashley. The name had run through his mind a million times in those six months, but hearing somebody say it out loud was like having a fist close around his insides and squeeze hard.

Jack couldn't speak.

Tanner didn't press for further conversation.

The ambulance bumped over country roads, finally hit smooth blacktop.

"Here we are," Tanner said. "Ashley's place."

"I knew something was going to happen," Ashley told Mrs. Wiggins, peeling the kitten off the living room curtains as she peered out at the ambulance stopped in the street. "I *knew* it."

Not bothering to find her coat, Ashley opened the door and stepped out onto the porch. Tanner got out on the passenger side and gave her a casual wave as he went around back.

Ashley's heart pounded. She stood frozen for a long moment, not by the cold, but by a strange, eager sense of dread. Then she bolted down the steps, careful not to slip, and hurried along the walk, through the gate.

"What…?" she began, but the rest of the question died in her throat.

Tanner had opened the back of the ambulance, but then he just stood there, looking at her with an odd expression on his face.

"Brace yourself," he said.

Jeff Baxter, part of a rotating group of volunteers, like Tanner, left the driver's seat and came to stand a short but eloquent distance away. He looked like a man trying to brace himself for an imminent explosion.

Impatient, Ashley wedged herself between the two men, peered inside.

Jack McCall sat upright on the gurney, grinning stupidly. His black hair, military-short the last time she'd seen him, was longer now, and sleekly shaggy. His eyes blazed with fever.

"Whose shirt is that?" he asked, frowning.

Still taken aback, Ashley didn't register the question right away. Several awkward moments had passed by the time she glanced down to see what she was wearing.

"Yours," she answered, finally.

Jack looked relieved. "Good," he said.

Ashley, beside herself with surprise until that very instant, landed back in her own skin with a jolt. "What are you doing here?" she demanded.

Jack scooted toward her, almost pitched out of the

ambulance onto his face before Tanner and Jeff moved in to grab him by the arms.

"Checking in," he said, once he'd tried—and failed—to shrug them off. "You're still in the bed-and-breakfast business, aren't you?"

You're still in the bed-and-breakfast business, aren't you?

Damn, the man had nerve.

"You belong in a hospital," she said evenly. "Not a bed-and-breakfast."

"I'm willing to pay double," Jack offered. His face, always strong, took on a vulnerable expression. "I need a place to lay low for a while, Ash. Are you game?"

She thought quickly. The last thing in the world she wanted was Jack McCall under her roof again, but she couldn't afford to turn down a paying guest. She'd have to dip into her savings soon if she did, and not just to pay Brad.

The bills were piling up.

"Triple the usual rate," she said.

Jack squinted, probably not understanding at first, then gave a raspy chuckle. "Okay," he agreed. "Triple it is. Even though it *is* the off-season."

Jeff and Tanner half dragged, half carried him toward the house.

Ashley hesitated on the snowy sidewalk.

First the cat.

Now Jack.

Evidently, it was her day to be dumped on.

Chapter 2

"What *happened* to him?" Ashley whispered to Tanner, in the hallway outside the second-best room in the house, a small suite at the opposite end of the corridor from her own quarters. Jeff and Tanner had already put the patient to bed, fully dressed except for his boots, and Jeff had gone downstairs to make a call on his cell phone.

Jack, meanwhile, had sunk into an instant and all-consuming sleep—or into a coma. It was a crapshoot, guessing which.

Tanner looked grim; didn't seem to notice that Mrs. Wiggins was busily climbing his right pant leg, her infinitesimal claws snagging the denim as she scaled his knee and started up his thigh with a deliberation that would have been funny under any other circumstances.

"All I know is," Tanner replied, "I got a call from

Jack this afternoon, just as Livie and I were leaving the clinic after her checkup. He said he was a little under the weather and wanted to know if I'd meet him at the airstrip and bring him here." He paused, cupped the kitten in one hand, raised the little creature to nose level, and peered quizzically into its mismatched eyes before lowering it gently to the floor. Straightening from a crouch, he added, "I offered to put him up at our place, but he insisted on coming to yours."

"You might have called me," Ashley fretted, still keeping her voice down. "Given me some warning, at least."

"Check your voice mail," Tanner countered, sounding mildly exasperated. "I left at least four messages."

"I was out," Ashley said, defensive, "buying kitty litter and kibble. Because *your wife* decided I needed a cat."

Tanner grinned at the mention of Olivia, and something eased in him, gentling the expression in his eyes. "If you'd carry a cell phone, like any normal human being, you'd have been up to speed, situationwise." He paused, with a mischievous twinkle. "You might even have had time to bake a welcome-back-Jack cake."

"As if," Ashley breathed, but as rattled as she was over having Jack McCall land in the middle of her life like the flaming chunks of a latter-day Hindenburg, there was something else she needed to know. "What did the doctor say? About Olivia, I mean?"

Tanner sighed. "She's a couple of weeks overdue— Dr. Pentland wants to induce labor tomorrow morning."

Worry made Ashley peevish. "And you're just telling me this now?"

"As I said," Tanner replied, "get a cell phone."

Before Ashley could come up with a reply, the front door banged open downstairs, and a youthful female voice called her name, sounding alarmed.

Ashley went to the upstairs railing, leaned a little, and saw Tanner's daughter, Sophie, standing in the living room, her face upturned and so pale that her freckles stood out, even from that distance. Sixteen-year-old Carly, blond and blue-eyed like her sister, Meg, appeared beside her.

"There's an ambulance outside," Sophie said. "What's happening?"

Tanner started down the stairs. "Everything's all right," he told the frightened girl.

Carly glanced from Tanner to Ashley, descending behind him. "We meant to get here sooner, to set up your computer," Carly said, "but Mr. Gilvine kept the whole Drama Club after school to rehearse the second act of the new play."

"How come there's an ambulance outside," Sophie persisted, gazing up at her father's face, "if nobody's sick?"

"I didn't say nobody was sick," Tanner told her quietly, setting his hands on her shoulders. "Jack's upstairs, resting."

Sophie's panic rose a notch. "Uncle Jack is sick? What's wrong with him?"

That's what I'd *like to know*, Ashley thought.

"From the symptoms, I'd guess it's some kind of toxin."

Sophie tried to go around Tanner, clearly intending to race up the stairs. "I want to see him!"

Tanner stopped her. "Not now, sweetie," he said, his tone at once gruff and gentle. "He's asleep."

"Do you still want us to set up your computer?" Carly asked Ashley.

Ashley summoned up a smile and shook her head. "Another time," she said. "You must be tired, after a whole day of school and then play practice on top of that. How about some supper?"

"Mr. Gilvine ordered pizza for the whole cast," Carly answered, touching her flat stomach and puffing out her cheeks to indicate that she was stuffed. "I already called home, and Brad said he'd come in from the ranch and get us as soon as we had your system up and running."

"It can wait," Ashley reiterated, glancing at Tanner.

"I'll drop you off on the way home," he told Carly, one hand still resting on Sophie's shoulder. "My truck's parked at the fire station. Jeff can give us a lift over there."

Having lost her mother when she was very young, Sophie had insecurities Ashley could well identify with. The girl adored Olivia, and looked forward to the birth of a brother or sister. Tanner probably wanted to break the news about Livie's induction later, with just the three of them present.

"Call me," Ashley ordered, her throat thick with concern for her sister and the child, as Tanner steered the girls toward the front door.

Tanner merely arched an eyebrow at that.

Jeff stepped out of the study, just tucking away his cell phone. "I'm in big trouble with Lucy," he said. "Forgot to let her know I'd be late. She made a soufflé and it fell."

"Uh-oh," Tanner commiserated.

"We get to ride in an ambulance?" Sophie asked, cheered.

"Awesome," Carly said.

And then they were gone.

Ashley raised her eyes to the ceiling. Recalled that Jack McCall was up there, sprawled on one of her guest beds, buried under half a dozen quilts. Just how sick was he? Would he want to eat, and if so, what?

After some internal debate, she decided on homemade chicken soup.

That was the cure for everything, wasn't it?

Everything, that is, except a broken heart.

Jack McCall awakened to find something furry standing on his face.

Fortunately, he was too weak to flail, or he'd have sent what his brain finally registered as a kitten flying before he realized he wasn't back in a South American jail, fighting off rats willing to settle for part of his hide when the rations ran low.

The animal stared directly into his face with one blue eye and one green one, purring as though it had a motor inside its hairy little chest.

He blinked, decided the thing was probably some kind of mutant.

"Another victim of renegade genetics," he said.

"Meooooow," the cat replied, perhaps indignant.

The door across the room opened, and Ashley elbowed her way in, carrying a loaded tray. Whatever was on it smelled like heaven distilled to its essence, or was that the scent of her skin and that amazing hair of hers?

"Mrs. Wiggins," she said, "get down."

"Mrs.?" Jack replied, trying to raise himself on his pillows and failing. This was a fortunate thing for the cat, who was trying to nest in his hair by then. "Isn't she a little young to be married?"

"Yuk-yuk," Ashley said, with an edge.

Jack sighed inwardly. All was not forgiven, then, he concluded.

Mrs. Wiggins climbed down over his right cheek and curled up on his chest. He could have sworn he felt some kind of warm energy flowing through the kitten, as though it were a conduit between the world around him and another, better one.

Crap. He was really losing it.

"Are you hungry?" Ashley asked, as though he were any ordinary guest.

A gnawing in the pit of Jack's stomach told him he was—for the first time since he'd come down with the mysterious plague. "Yeah," he ground out, further weakened by the sight of Ashley. Even in jeans and the flannel shirt he'd left behind, with her light hair springing from its normally tidy braid, she looked like a goddess. "I think I am."

She approached the bed—cautiously, it seemed to Jack, and little wonder, after some of the acrobatics they'd managed in the one down the hall before he left—and set the tray down on the nightstand.

"Can you feed yourself?" she asked, keeping her distance. Her tone was formal, almost prim.

Jack gave an inelegant snort at that, then realized, to his mortification, that he probably couldn't. Earlier, he'd made it to the adjoining bathroom and back, but the effort had exhausted him. "Yes," he fibbed.

She tilted her head to one side, skeptical. A smile flittered around her mouth, but didn't come in for a landing. "Your eyes widen a little when you lie," she commented.

He sure hoped certain members of various drug and gunrunning cartels didn't know that. "Oh," he said.

Ashley dragged a fussy-looking chair over and sat down. With a little sigh, she took a spoon off the tray and plunged it into a bright-blue crockery bowl. "Open up," she told him.

Jack resisted briefly, pressing his lips together— he still had *some* pride, after all—but his stomach betrayed him with a long and perfectly audible rumble. He opened his mouth.

The fragrant substance turned out to be chicken soup, with wild rice and chopped celery and a few other things he couldn't identify. It was so good that, if he'd been able to, he'd have grabbed the bowl with both hands and downed the stuff in a few gulps.

"Slow down," Ashley said. Her eyes had softened a little, but her body remained rigid. "There's plenty more soup simmering on the stove."

Like the kitten, the soup seemed to possess some sort of quantum-level healing power. Jack felt faint tendrils of strength stirring inside him, like the tender roots of a plant splitting through a seed husk, groping tentatively toward the sun.

Once he'd finished the soup, sleep began to pull him downward again, toward oblivion. There was something different about the feeling this time; rather than an urge to struggle against it, as before, it was more an impulse to give himself up to the darkness, settle into it like a waiting embrace.

Something soft brushed his cheek. Ashley's fingertips? Or the mutant kitten?

"Jack," Ashley said.

With an effort, he opened his eyes.

Tears glimmered along Ashley's lashes. "Are you going to die?" she asked.

Jack considered his answer for a few moments; not easy, with his brain short-circuiting. According to the doctors at Walter Reed, his prognosis wasn't the best. They'd admitted that they'd never seen the toxin before, and their plan was to ship him off to some secret government research facility for further study.

Which was one of the reasons he'd bolted, conned a series of friends into springing him and then relaying him cross-country in various planes and helicopters.

He found Ashley's hand, squeezed it with his own. "Not if I can help it," he murmured, just before sleep sucked him under again.

Their brief conversation echoed in Ashley's head, over and over, as she sat there watching Jack sleep until the room was so dark she couldn't see anything but the faintest outline of him, etched against the sheets.

Are you going to die?

Not if I can help it.

Ashley overcame the need to switch on the bedside lamp, send golden light spilling over the features she knew so well—the hazel eyes, the well-defined cheekbones, the strong, obstinate jaw—but just barely. Leaving the tray behind, she rose out of the chair and made her way slowly toward the door, afraid of stepping on Mrs. Wiggins, frolicking at her feet like a little ghost.

Reaching the hallway, Ashley closed the door softly behind her, bent to scoop the kitten up in one hand, and let the tears come. Silent sobs rocked her, making her shoulders shake, and Mrs. Wiggins snuggled in close under her chin, as if to offer comfort.

Was Jack truly in danger of dying?

She sniffled, straightened her spine. Surely Tanner wouldn't have agreed to bring him to the bed-and-breakfast—to her—if he was at death's door.

On the other hand, she reasoned, dashing at her cheek with the back of one hand, trying to rally her scattered emotions, Jack was bone-stubborn. He always got his way.

So maybe Tanner was simply honoring Jack's last wish.

Holding tightly to the banister, Ashley started down the stairs.

Jack hadn't wanted to *live* in Stone Creek. Why would he choose to *die* there?

The phone began to ring, a persistent trilling, and Ashley, thinking of Olivia, dashed to the small desk where guests registered—not that *that* had been an issue lately—and snatched up the receiver.

"Hello?" When had she gotten out of the habit of answering with a businesslike, "Mountain View Bed and Breakfast"?

"I hear you've got an unexpected boarder," Brad said, his tone measured.

Ashley was unaccountably glad to hear her big brother's voice, considering that they hadn't had much to say to each other since their mother's funeral. "Yes," she assented.

"According to Carly, he was sick enough to arrive in an ambulance."

Ashley nodded, remembered that Brad couldn't see her, and repeated, "Yes. I'm not sure he should be here—Brad, he's in a really bad way. I'm not a nurse and I'm—" She paused, swallowed. "I'm scared."

"I can be there in fifteen minutes, Ash."

Fresh tears scalded Ashley's eyes, made them feel raw. "That would be good," she said.

"Put on a pot of coffee, little sister," Brad told her. "I'm on my way."

True to his word, Brad was standing in her kitchen before the coffee finished perking. He looked more like a rancher than a famous country singer and sometime movie star, in his faded jeans, battered boots, chambray shirt and denim jacket.

Ashley couldn't remember the last time she'd hugged her brother, but now she went to him, and he wrapped her in his arms, kissed the top of her head.

"Olivia…" she began, but her voice fell away.

"I know," Brad said hoarsely. "They're inducing labor in the morning. Livie will be fine, honey, and so will the baby."

Ashley tilted her head back, looked up into Brad's face. His dark-blond hair was rumpled, and his beard was growing in, bristly. "How's the family?"

He rested his hands on her shoulders, held her at a little distance. "You wouldn't have to ask if you ever stopped by Stone Creek Ranch," he answered. "Mac misses you, and Meg and I do, too."

The minute Brad had known she needed him, he'd been in his truck, headed for town. And now that he was there, her anger over their mother's funeral didn't seem so important.

She tried to speak, but her throat had tightened again, and she couldn't get a single word past it.

One corner of Brad's famous mouth crooked up.

"Where's Lover Boy?" he asked. "Lucky thing for him that he's laid up—otherwise I'd punch his lights out for what he did to you."

The phrase *Lover Boy* made Ashley flinch. "That's over," she said.

Brad let his hands fall to his sides, his eyes serious now. "Right," he replied. "Which room?"

Ashley told him, and he left the kitchen, the inside door swinging behind him long after he'd passed through it.

She kept herself busy by taking mugs down from the cupboard, filling Mrs. Wiggins's dish with kibble the size of barley grains, switching on the radio and then switching it off again.

The kitten crunched away at the kibble, then climbed onto its newly purchased bed in the corner near the fireplace, turned in circles for a few moments, kneaded the fabric, and dropped like the proverbial rock.

After several minutes had passed, Ashley heard Brad's boot heels on the staircase, and poured coffee for her brother; she was drinking herbal tea.

As if there were a hope in hell she'd sleep a wink that night by avoiding caffeine.

Brad reached for his mug, took a thoughtful sip.

"Well?" Ashley prompted.

"I'm not a doctor, Ash," he said. "All I can tell you for sure is, he's breathing."

"*That's* helpful," Ashley said.

He chuckled, and the sound, though rueful, consoled her a little. He turned one of the chairs around backward, and straddled it, setting his mug on the table.

"Why do men like to sit like that?" Ashley wondered aloud.

He grinned. "You've been alone too long," he answered.

Ashley blushed, brought her tea to the table and sat down. "What am I going to do?" she asked.

Brad inclined his head toward the ceiling. "About McCall? That's up to you, sis. If you want him out of here, I can have him airlifted to Flagstaff within a couple hours."

This was no idle boast. Even though he'd retired from the country-music scene several years before, at least as far as concert tours went, Brad still wrote and recorded songs, and he could have stacked his royalty checks like so much cordwood. On top of that, Meg was a McKettrick, a multimillionaire in her own right. One phone call from either one of them, and a sleek jet would be landing outside of town in no time at all, fully equipped and staffed with doctors and nurses.

Ashley bit her lower lip. God knew why, but Jack wanted to stay at her place, and he'd gone through a lot to get there. As impractical as it was, given his condition, she didn't think she could turn him out.

Brad must have read her face. He reached out, took her hand. "You still love the bastard," he said. "Don't you?"

"I don't know," she answered miserably. She'd definitely loved the man she'd known before, but this was a new Jack, a different Jack. The *real* one, she supposed. It shook her to realize she'd given her heart to an illusion.

"It's okay, Ashley."

She shook her head, started to cry again. "Nothing is okay," she argued.

"We can make it that way," Brad offered quietly. "All we have to do is talk."

She dried her eyes on the sleeve of Jack's old shirt. It seemed ironic, given all the things hanging in her closet, that she'd chosen to wear that particular garment when she'd gotten dressed that morning. Had some part of her known, somehow, that Jack was coming home?

Brad was waiting for an answer, and he wouldn't break eye contact until he got one.

Ashley swallowed hard. "Our mother died," she said, cornered. "Our *mother*. And you and Olivia and Melissa all seemed—relieved."

A muscle in Brad's jaw tightened, relaxed again. He sighed and shoved a hand through his hair. "I guess I *was* relieved," he admitted. "They said she didn't suffer, but I always wondered—" He paused, cleared his throat. "I wondered if she was in there somewhere, hurting, with no way to ask for help."

Ashley's heart gave one hard beat, then settled into its normal pace again. "You didn't hate her?" she asked, stunned.

"She was my mother," Brad said. "Of course I didn't hate her."

"Things might have been so different—"

"Ashley," Brad broke in, "things *weren't* different. That's the point. Delia's gone, for good this time. You've got to let go."

"What if I can't?" Ashley whispered.

"You don't have a choice, Button."

Button. Their grandfather had called both her and Melissa by that nickname; like most twins, they were used to sharing things. "Do you miss Big John as much as I do?" she asked.

"Yes," Brad answered, without hesitation, his voice still gruff. He looked down at his coffee mug for a second or so, then raised his gaze to meet Ashley's again. "Same thing," he said. "He's gone. And letting go is something I have to do about three times a day."

Ashley got up, suddenly unable to sit still. She brought the coffee carafe to the table and refilled Brad's cup. She spoke very quietly. "But it was a one-time thing, letting go of Mom?"

"Yeah," Brad said. "And it happened a long, long time ago. I remember it distinctly—it was the night my high school basketball team took the state championship. I was sure she'd be in the bleachers, clapping and cheering like everybody else. She wasn't, of course, and that was when I got it through my head that she wasn't coming back—ever."

Ashley's heart ached. Brad was her big brother; he'd always been strong. Why hadn't she realized that he'd been hurt, too?

"Big John *stayed*, Ashley," he went on, while she sat there gulping. "He stuck around, through good times and bad. Even after he'd buried his only son, he kept on keeping on. Mom caught the afternoon bus out of town and couldn't be bothered to call or even send a postcard. I did my mourning long before she died."

Ashley could only nod.

Brad was quiet for a while, pondering, taking the occasional sip from his coffee mug. Then he spoke again. "Here's the thing," he said. "When the chips were down, I basically did the same thing as Mom—got on a bus and left Big John to take care of the ranch and raise the three of you all by himself—so I'm in no position to judge anybody else. Bottom line, Ash? People are what they are, and they do what they do, and you have to decide either to accept that or walk away without looking back."

Ashley managed a wobbly smile. Sniffled once. "I'm sorry I'm late on the mortgage payments," she said.

Brad rolled his eyes. "Like I'm worried," he replied, his body making the subtle shifts that meant he'd be leaving soon. With one arm, he gestured to indicate the B&B. "Why won't you just let me sign the place over to you?"

"Would you do that," Ashley challenged reasonably, "if our situations were reversed?"

He flushed slightly, got to his feet. "No," he admitted, "but—"

"But what?"

Brad grinned sheepishly, and his powerful shoulders shifted slightly under his shirt.

"But you're a man?" Ashley finished for him, when he didn't speak. "Is that what you were going to say?"

"Well, yeah," Brad said.

"You'll have the mortgage payments as soon as I get a chance to run Jack's credit card," she told her brother, rising to walk him to the back door. Color suffused her cheeks. "Thanks for coming into town," she added. "I feel like a fool for panicking."

In the midst of pulling on his jacket, Brad paused. "I'm a big brother," he said, somewhat gruffly. "It's what we do."

"Are you and Meg going to the hospital tomorrow, when Livie…?"

Brad tugged lightly at her braid, the way he'd always done. "We'll be hanging out by the telephone," he said. "Livie swears it's a normal procedure, and she doesn't want everyone fussing 'as if it were a heart transplant,' as she put it."

Ashley bit down on her lower lip and nodded. She already had a nephew—Mac—and two nieces, Carly and Sophie, although technically Carly, Meg's half sister, whom her dying father had asked her to raise, wasn't really a niece. Tomorrow, another little one would join the family. Instead of being a nervous wreck, she ought to be celebrating.

She wasn't, she decided, so different from Sophie. Having effectively lost Delia when she was so young, she'd turned to Olivia as a substitute mother, as had Melissa. Had their devotion been a burden to their sister, only a few years older than they were, and grappling with her own sense of loss?

She stood on tiptoe and kissed Brad's cheek. "Thanks," she said again. "Call if you hear anything."

Brad gave her braid another tug, turned and left the house.

Ashley felt profoundly alone.

Jack had nearly flung himself at the singing cowboy standing at the foot of his bed, before recognizing him as Ashley's famous brother, Brad. Even though the room had been dark, the other man must have seen him tense.

"I know you're awake, McCall," he'd said.

Jack had yawned. "O'Ballivan?"

"Live and in person," came the not-so-friendly reply.

"And you're sneaking around my room because...?"

O'Ballivan had chuckled at that. Hooked his thumbs through his belt loops. "Because Ashley's worried about you. And what worries my baby sister worries *me*, James Bond."

Ashley was worried about him? Something like elation flooded Jack. "Not for the same reasons, I suspect," he said.

Mr. Country Music had gripped the high, spooled rail at the foot of the bed and leaned forward a little to make his point. "Damned if I can figure out why you'd come back here, especially in the shape you're in, after what happened last summer, except to take up where you left off." He paused, gripped the rail hard enough that his knuckles showed white even in the gloom. "You hurt her again, McCall, and you have my solemn word—I'm gonna turn right around and hurt *you*. Are we clear on that?"

Jack had smiled, not because he was amused, but because he liked knowing Ashley had folks to look after her when he wasn't around—and when he was. "Oh, yeah," Jack had replied. "We're clear."

Obviously a man of few words, O'Ballivan had simply nodded, turned and walked out of the room.

Remembering, Jack raised himself as high on the pillows as he could, strained to reach the lamp switch. The efforts, simple as they were, made him break out in a cold sweat, but at the same time, he felt his strength returning.

He looked around the room, noting the flowered wallpaper, the pale rose carpeting, the intricate woodwork on the mantelpiece. Two girly chairs flanked the cold fireplace, and fat flakes of January snow drifted past the two sets of bay windows, both sporting seats beneath, covered by cheery cushions.

It was a far cry from Walter Reed, he thought.

An even further cry from the jungle hut where he'd hidden out for nearly three months, awaiting his chance to grab little Rachel Stockard, hustle her out of the country by boat and then a seaplane, and return her to her frantic mother.

He'd been well paid for the job, but it was the memory of the mother-daughter reunion, after he'd surrendered the child to a pair of FBI agents and a Customs official in Atlanta, that made his throat catch more than two weeks after the fact.

Through an observation window, he'd watched as Rachel scrambled out of the man's arms and raced toward her waiting mother. Tears pouring down her face, Ardith Stockard had dropped to her knees, arms outspread, and gathered the little girl close. The two of them had clung to each other, both trembling.

And then Ardith had raised her eyes, seen Jack through the glass, and mouthed the words, "Thank you."

He'd nodded, exhausted and already sick.

Closing his eyes, Jack went back over the journey to South America, the long game of waiting and watching, finally finding the small, isolated country estate where Rachel had been taken after she was kidnapped from her maternal grandparents' home in Phoenix, almost a year before.

Even after locating the child, he hadn't been able to make a move for more than a week—not until her father and his retinue of thugs had loaded a convoy of jeeps with drugs and firepower one day, and roared off down the jungle road, probably headed for a rendezvous with a boat moored off some hidden beach.

Jack had soon ascertained that only the middle-aged cook—and he had reason not to expect opposition from her—and one guard stood between him and Rachel. He'd waited until dark, risking the return of the jeep convoy, then climbed to the terrace outside the child's room.

"Did you come to take me home to my mommy?" Rachel had shrilled, her eyes wide with hope, when he stepped in off the terrace, a finger to his lips.

Her voice carried, and the guard burst in from the hallway, shouting in Spanish.

There had been a brief struggle—Jack had felt something prick him in the side as the goon went down— but, hearing the sound of approaching vehicles in the distance, he hadn't taken the time to wonder.

He'd grabbed Rachel up under one arm and climbed over the terrace and back down the crumbling rock wall of the house, with its many foot- and handholds, to the ground, running for the trees.

It was only after the reunion in Atlanta that Jack had suddenly collapsed, dizzy with fever.

The next thing he remembered was waking up in a hospital room, hooked up to half a dozen machines and surrounded by grim-faced Feds waiting to ask questions.

Chapter 3

Ashley did not expect to sleep at all that night; she had too many things on her mind, between the imminent birth of Olivia's baby, lingering issues with her mother and siblings, and Jack McCall landing in the middle of her formerly well-ordered days like the meteor that allegedly finished off the dinosaurs.

Therefore, sunlight glowing pink-orange through her eyelids and the loud jangle of her bedside telephone came as a surprise.

She groped for the receiver, nearly throwing a disgruntled Mrs. Wiggins to the floor, and rasped out a hoarse, "Hullo?"

Olivia's distinctive laugh sounded weary, but it bubbled into Ashley's ear and then settled, warm as summer honey, into every tuck and fold of her heart. "Did I wake you up?"

"Yes," Ashley admitted, her heart beating faster as she raised herself onto one elbow and pushed her bangs back out of her face. "Livie? Did you—is everything all right—what—?"

"You're an aunt again," Olivia said, choking up again. "Twice over."

Ashley blinked. Swallowed hard. "Twice over? Livie, you had *twins*?"

"Both boys," Olivia answered, in a proud whisper. "And before you ask, they're fine, Ash. So am I." There was a pause, then a giggle. "I'm not too sure about Tanner, though. He's only been through this once before, and Sophie didn't bring along a sidekick when she came into the world."

Ashley's eyes burned, and her throat went thick with joy. "Oh, Livie," she murmured. "This is wonderful! Have you told Melissa and Brad?"

"I was hoping you'd do that for me," Olivia answered. "I've been working hard since five this morning, and I could use a nap before visiting hours roll around."

First instinct: Throw on whatever clothes came to hand, jump in the car and head straight for the hospital, visiting hours be damned. Ashley wanted a look at her twin nephews, wanted to see for herself that Olivia really was okay.

In the next instant, she remembered Jack.

She couldn't leave a sick guest alone, which meant she'd have to rustle up someone to keep an eye on him before she could visit Olivia and the babies.

"You're in Flagstaff, right?" she asked, sitting up now.

"Good heavens, no," Olivia replied, with another laugh. "We didn't make it that far—I went into labor at three-thirty this morning. I'm at the clinic over in Indian Rock—thanks to the McKettricks, they're equipped with incubators and just about everything else a new baby could possibly need."

"Indian Rock?" Ashley echoed, still a little groggy. Forty miles from Stone Creek, Meg's hometown was barely closer than Flagstaff, and lay in the opposite direction.

"I'll explain later, Ash," Olivia said. "Right now, I'm beat. You'll call Brad and Melissa?"

"Right away," Ashley promised. Happiness for her sister and brother-in-law welled up into her throat, a peculiar combination of pain and pleasure. "Just one more thing—have you named the babies?"

"Not yet. We'll probably call one John Mitchell, for Big John and Dad, and the other Sam. Even though Tanner and I knew we were having two babies—our secret—we need to give it some thought."

Practically every generation of the O'Ballivan family boasted at least one Sam, all the way back to the founder of Stone Creek Ranch. For all her delight over the twins' birth, Ashley felt a little pang. She'd always planned to name her own son Sam.

Not that she was in any danger of having children.

"C-congratulations, Livie. Hug Tanner for me, too."

"Consider it done," Olivia said.

Goodbyes were said, and Ashley had to try three times before she managed to hang up the receiver.

After drawing a few deep breaths and wiping away *mostly* happy tears, Ashley regained her composure, remembered that she'd promised to pass the news along to the rest of her family.

Brad answered the telephone out at the ranch, sounding wide-awake. The sun couldn't have been up for long, but by then, he'd probably fed all the dogs, horses and cattle on the place and started breakfast for Meg, Carly, Mac and himself. "That's great," he said, once Ashley had assured him that both Olivia and the babies were doing well. "But what are they doing in Indian Rock?"

"Olivia said she'd explain later," Ashley answered.

The next call she placed was to her own twin, Melissa, who lived on the other side of town. A lawyer and an absolute genius with money, Melissa owned the spacious two-family home, renting out one side and thereby making the mortgage payment without touching her salary.

A man answered, and the voice wasn't familiar.

A little alarmed—reruns of *City Confidential* and *Forensic Files* were Ashley's secret addiction—she sat up a little straighter and asked, "Is this 555-2293?"

"I think so," he said. "Melissa?"

Melissa came on the line, sounding breathless. "Olivia?"

"Your *other* sister," Ashley said. "Livie asked me to call you. The babies were born this morning—"

"Babies?" Melissa interrupted. "Plural?"

"Twins," Ashley answered.

"Nobody said anything about twins!" Being something of a control freak, Melissa didn't like surprises— even good ones.

Ashley smiled. "They do run in the family, you know," she reminded her sister. "And apparently Tanner and Olivia wanted to surprise us. She says all is well, and she's going to catch some sleep before visiting hours."

"Boys? Girls? One of each?" Melissa asked, rapid-fire.

"Both boys," Ashley said. "No for-sure names yet. And who is that man who just answered your phone?"

"Later," Melissa said, lowering her voice.

Ashley's imagination spiked again. "Just tell me you're all right," she said. "That some stranger isn't forcing you to pretend—"

"Oh, for Pete's sake," Melissa broke in, sounding almost snappish. She'd been worried about Olivia, too, Ashley reasoned, calming down a little, but still unsettled. "I'm not bound with duct tape and being held captive in a closet. You're watching too much crime-TV again."

"Say the code word," Ashley said, just to be absolutely sure Melissa was safe.

"You are so paranoid," Melissa griped. Ashley could just see her, pushing back her hair, which fell to her shoulders in dark, gleaming spirals, picture her eyes flashing with irritation.

"Say it, and I'll leave you alone."

Melissa sighed. "Buttercup," she said.

Ashley smiled. After a rash of child abductions when they were small, Big John had helped them choose the secret word and instructed them never to reveal it to anyone outside the family. Ashley never had, and she was sure Melissa hadn't, either.

They'd liked the idea of speaking in code—their version of the twin-language phenomenon, Ashley supposed. Between the ages of three and seven, they'd driven everyone crazy, chattering away in a dialect made up of otherwise ordinary words and phrases.

If Melissa had said, "I plan to spend the afternoon sewing," for instance, Ashley would have called out the National Guard. Ashley's signal, considerably less autobiographical, was, "I saw three crows sitting on the mailbox this morning."

"Are you satisfied?" Melissa asked.

"Are you PMS-ing?" Ashley countered.

"I wish," Melissa said.

Before Ashley could ask what she'd meant by that, Melissa hung up.

"She's PMS-ing," Ashley told Mrs. Wiggins, who was curling around her ankles and mewing, probably ready for her kitty kibble.

Hastily, Ashley took a shower, donned trim black woolen slacks and an ice-blue silk blouse, brushed and braided her hair, and went out into the hallway.

Jack's door was closed—she was sure she'd left it open a crack the night before, in case he called out—so she rapped lightly with her knuckles.

"In," he responded.

Ashley rolled her eyes and opened the door to peek inside the room. Jack was sitting on the edge of the bed, his back very straight. He needed a shave, and his eyes were clear when he turned his head to look at her.

"You're better," she said, surprised.

He gave a slanted grin. "Sorry to disappoint you."

Ashley felt her temper surge, but she wasn't about to give Jack McCall the satisfaction of getting under her skin. Not today, when she'd just learned that she had twin nephews. "Are you hungry?"

"Yeah," he said. "Bacon and eggs would be good."

Ashley raised one eyebrow. He'd barely managed chicken soup the night before, and now he wanted a trucker's breakfast? "You'll make yourself sick," she told him, hiking her chin up a notch.

"I'm already sick," he pointed out. "And I still want bacon and eggs."

"Well," Ashley said, "there aren't any. I usually have grapefruit or granola."

"You serve paying guests *health food*?"

Ashley sucked in a breath, let it out slowly. She wasn't about to admit, not to Jack McCall, at least, that she hadn't had a guest, paying or otherwise, in way too long. "Some people," she told him carefully, "care about good nutrition."

"And some people want bacon and eggs."

She sighed. "Oh, for heaven's sake."

"It's the least you can do," Jack wheedled, "since I'm paying triple for this room and the breakfast that's supposed to come with the bed."

"All right," she said. "But I'll have to go to the store, and that means *you'll* have to wait."

"Fine by me," Jack replied lightly, extending his feet and wriggling his toes, his expression curious, as though he wasn't sure they still worked. "I'll be right here." The wicked grin flashed again. "Get a move on, will you? I need to get my strength back."

Ashley shut the door hard, drew another deep breath in the hallway, and started downstairs, careful not to trip over the gamboling Mrs. Wiggins.

Reaching the kitchen, she poured kibble for the kitten, cleaned and refilled the tiny water bowl, and gathered her coat, purse and car keys.

"I'll be back in a few minutes," she told the cat.

The temperature had dropped below freezing during the night, and the roads were sheeted in ice. Ashley's trip to the supermarket took nearly forty-five minutes, the store was jammed, and by the time she got home, she was in a skillet-banging mood. She was an inn-keeper, not a nurse. Why hadn't she insisted that Tanner and Jeff take Jack to one of the hospitals in Flagstaff?

She built a fire on the kitchen hearth, hoping to cheer herself up a little—and take the chill out of her bones—then started a pot of coffee brewing. Next, she laid four strips of bacon in the seasoned cast-iron frying pan that had been Big John's, tossed a couple of slices of bread into the toaster slots, and took a carton of eggs out of her canvas grocery bag.

She knew how Jack liked his eggs—over easy—just as she knew he took his coffee black and strong. It galled her plenty that she remembered those details—and a lot more.

Cooking angrily—so much for her motto that every recipe ought to be laced with love—Ashley nearly jumped out of her skin when she heard his voice behind her.

"Nice fire," he said. "Very cozy."

She whirled, openmouthed, and there he was, standing in the kitchen doorway, but leaning heavily on the jamb.

"What are you doing out of bed?" she asked, once the adrenaline rush had subsided.

Slowly, he made his way to the table, dragged back a chair and dropped into the seat. "I couldn't take that wallpaper for another second," he teased. "Too damn many roses and ribbons."

Knowing that wallpaper was a stupid thing to be sensitive about, and sensitive just the same, Ashley opened a cupboard, took down a mug and filled it, even though the coffeemaker was still chortling through the brewing process. Set the mug down in front of him with a thump.

"Surely you're not *that* touchy about your décor," Jack said.

"Shut up," Ashley told him.

His eyes twinkled. "Do you talk to all your guests that way?"

As so often happened around Jack, Ashley spoke without thinking first. "Only the ones who sneaked out of my bed in the middle of the night and disappeared for six months without a word."

Jack frowned. "Have there been a lot of those?"

Jack McCall was the first—and only—man Ashley had ever slept with, but she'd be damned if she'd tell him so. After all, she realized, he hadn't just broken her heart once—he'd done it *twice*. She'd been shy in high school, but the day she and Jack met, in her freshman year of college at the University of Arizona, her world had undergone a seismic shift.

They talked about getting married after Ashley finished school, had even looked at engagement rings. Jack had been a senior, and after graduation, he'd enlisted in the Navy. After a few letters and phone calls, he'd simply dropped out of her life.

She'd gotten her BA in liberal arts.

Melissa had gone on to law school, Ashley had returned to Stone Creek, bought the B&B with Brad's help and tried to convince herself that she was happy.

Then, just before Christmas, two years earlier, Jack had returned. She'd been a first-class fool to get involved with him a second time, to believe it would last. He came and went, called often when he was away, showed up again and made soul-wrenching love to her just when she'd made up her mind to end the affair.

"I haven't been hibernating, you know," she said

stiffly, turning the bacon, pushing down the lever on the toaster and sliding his perfectly cooked eggs off the burner. "I date."

Right. Melissa had fixed her up twice, with guys she knew from law school, and she'd gone out to dinner once, with Melvin Royce, whose father owned the Stone Creek Funeral Home. Melvin had spent the whole evening telling her that death was a beautiful thing—not to mention lucrative—cremation was the way to go, and corpses weren't at all scary, once you got used to them.

She hadn't gone out with anyone since.

Oh, yes, she was a regular party girl. If she didn't watch out, she'd end up as tabloid fodder.

Not. The tabloids were Brad's territory, and he was welcome to them, as far as she was concerned.

"I'm sorry, Ashley," Jack said quietly, when they'd both been silent for a long time. She couldn't help noticing that his hand shook slightly as he took a sip of his coffee and set the mug down again.

"For what?"

"For everything." He thrust splayed fingers through his hair, and his jaw tightened briefly, under the blue-black stubble of his beard.

"Everything? That covers a lot of ground," Ashley said, sliding his breakfast onto a plate and setting it down in front of him with an annoyed flourish.

Jack sighed. "Leaving you. It was a dumb thing to do. But maybe coming back is even dumber."

The remark stung Ashley, made her cheeks burn, and she turned away quickly, hoping Jack hadn't noticed. "You arrived in an ambulance," she said. "Feel free to leave in one."

"Will you sit down and talk to me? Please?"

Ashley faced him, lest she be thought a coward.

Mrs. Wiggins, the little traitor, started up Jack's right pant leg and settled in his lap for a snooze. He picked up his fork, broke the yolk on one of his eggs, but his eyes were fastened on Ashley.

"What happened to you?" Ashley asked, without planning to speak at all. There it was again, the Jack Phenomenon. She wasn't normally an impulsive person.

Jack didn't look away, but several long moments passed before he answered. "The theory is," he said, "that a guy I tangled with on a job injected me with something."

Ashley's heart stopped, started again. She joined Jack at the table, but only because she was afraid her knees wouldn't support her if she remained standing. "A job? What kind of job?"

"You know I'm in security," Jack hedged, avoiding her eyes now, concentrating on his breakfast. He ate slowly, deliberately.

"Security," Ashley repeated. All she really knew about Jack was that he traveled, made a lot of money and was often in danger. These were not things he'd actually told her—she'd gleaned them from telephone conversations she'd overheard, stories Sophie and Olivia had told her, comments Tanner had made.

"I've got to leave again, Ashley," Jack said. "But this time, I want you to know why."

She *wanted* Jack to leave. So why did she feel as though a trapdoor had just opened under her chair, and she was about to fall down the rabbit hole? "Okay—why?" she asked, in somebody else's voice.

"Because I've got enemies. Most of them are in prison—or dead—but one has a red-hot grudge against me, a score to settle, and I don't want you or anybody else in Stone Creek to get hurt. I should have thought things through before I came here, but the truth is, all I could focus on was being where you are."

The words made her ache. Ashley longed to take Jack's hand, but she wouldn't let herself do it. "What kind of grudge?"

"I stole his daughter."

Ashley's mouth dropped open. She closed it again.

Jack gave a mirthless little smile. "Her name is Rachel. She's seven years old. Her mother went through a rebellious period that just happened to coincide with a semester in a university in Venezuela. She fell in with a bad crowd, got involved with a fellow exchange student—an American named Chad Lombard, who was running drugs between classes. Her parents ran a background check on Lombard, didn't like the results and flew down from Phoenix to take their daughter home. Ardith was pregnant—the folks wanted her to give the baby up and she refused. She was nineteen, sure she was in love with Lombard, waited for him to come and get her, put a wedding band on her finger. He didn't. Eventually, she finished school, married well, had two more kids. The new husband wanted to adopt Rachel, and that meant Lombard had to sign off, so the family lawyers tracked him down and presented him with the papers and the offer of a hefty check. He went ballistic, said he wanted to raise Rachel himself, and generously offered to take Ardith back, too, if she'd leave the other two kids behind and divorce the man she'd married. Naturally, she didn't want to go that route. Things were quiet for a while, and then one day Rachel disappeared from her backyard. Lombard called that night to say Phoenix P.D. was wasting its time looking for Rachel, since he had the child and they were already out of the country."

Although Ashley had never been a mother herself, it was all too easy to understand how frantic Ardith and the family must have been.

"And they hired you to find Rachel and bring her home?"

"Yes," Jack answered, after another long delay. The long speech had clearly taken a lot out of him, but the amazed admiration she felt must have been visible in her eyes, because he added, "But don't get the idea that I'm some kind of hero. I was paid a quarter of a million dollars for bringing Rachel back home safely, and I didn't hesitate to accept the money."

"I didn't see any of this in the newspapers," Ashley mused.

"You wouldn't have," Jack replied. He'd finished half of his breakfast, and although he had a little more color than before, he was still too pale. "It was vital to keep the story out of the press. Rachel's life might have depended on it, and mine definitely did."

"Weren't you scared?"

"Hell," Jack answered, "I was terrified."

"You should lie down," she said softly.

"I don't think I can make it back up those stairs," Jack said, and Ashley could see that it pained him to admit this.

"You're just trying to avoid the wallpaper," she joked, though she was dangerously close to tears. Carefully, she helped him to his feet. "There's a bed in my sewing room. You can rest there until you feel stronger."

His face contorted, but he still managed a grin. "You're strong for a woman," he said.

"I was raised on a ranch," Ashley reminded him, ducking under his right shoulder and supporting him as she steered him across the kitchen to her sewing room. "I used to help load hay bales in our field during harvest, among other things."

Jack glanced down at her face, and she thought she saw a glimmer of respect in his eyes. "*You* bucked bales?"

"Sure did." They'd reached the sewing room door, and Ashley reached out to push it open. "Did you?"

"Are you kidding?" Jack's chuckle was ragged. "My dad is a dentist. I was raised in the suburbs—not a hay bale for miles."

Like the account of little Rachel's rescue, this was news to Ashley. She knew nothing about Jack's background, wondered how she could have fallen so hard for a man who'd never mentioned his family, let alone introduced her to them. In fact, she'd assumed he didn't *have* a family.

"Exactly what *is* your job title, anyway?"

He looked at her long and hard, wavering just a few feet from the narrow bed. "Mercenary," he said.

Ashley took that in, but it didn't really register, even after the Rachel story. "Is that what it says on your tax return, under *Occupation*?"

"No," he answered.

They reached the bed, and she helped him get settled. Since he was on top of the blankets, she covered him with a faded quilt that had been passed down through the O'Ballivan clan since the days when Maddie and Sam ran the ranch.

"You do file taxes, don't you?" Ashley was a very careful and practical person.

Jack smiled without opening his eyes. "Yeah," he said. "What I do is unconventional, but it isn't illegal."

Ashley stepped back, torn between bolting from the room and lying down beside Jack, enfolding him in her arms. "Is there anything I can get you?"

"My gear," he said, his eyes still closed. "Tanner brought it in. Leather satchel, under the bed upstairs."

Ashley gave a little nod, even though he wouldn't see it. What kind of *gear* did a mercenary carry? Guns? Knives?

She gave a little shudder and left the door slightly ajar.

Upstairs, she found the leather bag under Jack's bed. The temptation to open it was nearly overwhelming, but she resisted. Yes, she was curious—*beyond* curious— but she wasn't a snoop. She didn't go through guests' luggage any more than she read the postcards they gave her to send for them.

When she got back to the sewing room, Jack was sleeping. Mrs. Wiggins curled up protectively on his chest.

Ashley set the bag down quietly and slipped out. Busied herself with routine housekeeping chores, too soon finished.

She was relieved when Tanner showed up at the kitchen door, looking worn out but blissfully happy.

"I came to babysit Jack while you go and see Olivia and the boys," he said, stepping past her and helping himself to a cup of lukewarm coffee. "How's he doing?"

Ashley watched as her brother-in-law stuck the mug into the microwave and pushed the appropriate buttons. "Not bad—for a mercenary."

Tanner paused, and his gaze swung in Ashley's direction. "He told you?"

"Yes. I need some answers, Tanner, and Jack is too sick to give them."

The new father turned away from the counter, the microwave whirring behind him, leaned back and folded his arms, watching Ashley, probably weighing the pros and cons of spilling what he knew—which was plenty, unless she missed her guess.

"He's talking about leaving," Ashley prodded, when Tanner didn't say anything right away. "I'm used to that, but I think I deserve to know what's going on."

Tanner gave a long sigh. "I'd trust Jack with my life—I trusted him with *Sophie's*, when she ran away from boarding school right after we moved here, but the truth is, I don't know a hell of a lot more about him than you do."

"He's your best friend."

"And he plays his cards close to the vest. When it comes to security, he's the best there is." Tanner paused, thrust a hand through his already mussed hair. "I can tell you this much, Ashley—if he said he loved you, he meant it, whatever happened afterward. He's never been married, doesn't have kids, his dad is a dentist, his mother is a librarian, and he has three younger brothers, all of whom are much more conventional than Jack. He likes beer, but I've never seen him drunk. That's the whole shebang, I'm afraid."

"Someone injected him with something," Ashley said in a low voice. "That's why he's sick."

"Good God," Tanner said.

A silence fell.

"And he's leaving as soon as he's strong enough,"

Ashley said. "Because some drug dealer named Chad Lombard has a grudge against him, and he's afraid of putting all of us in danger."

Tanner thought long and hard. "Maybe that's for the best," he finally replied. Ashley knew Tanner wasn't afraid for himself, but he had to think about Olivia and Sophie and his infant sons. "I hate it, though. Turning my back on a friend who needs my help."

Ashley felt the same way, though Jack wasn't exactly a friend. In fact, she wasn't sure how to describe their relationship—if they had one at all. "This is Stone Creek," she heard herself say. "We have a long tradition of standing shoulder to shoulder and taking trouble as it comes."

Tanner's smile was tired, but warm. "Go," he said. "Tuckered out as she is, Olivia is dying to show off those babies. I'll look after Jack until you get home."

Ashley hesitated, then got her coat and purse and car keys again, and left for the clinic in Indian Rock.

Chapter 4

Olivia was sitting up in bed, beaming, a baby tucked in the crook of each arm, when Ashley hurried into her room. There were flowers everywhere—Brad and Meg had already been there and gone, having brought Carly and Sophie to see the boys before school.

"Come and say hello to John and Sam," Olivia said gently.

Ashley, clutching a bouquet of pink and yellow carnations, hastily purchased at a convenience store, moved closer. She felt stricken with wonder and an immediate and all-encompassing love for the tiny red-faced infants snoozing in their swaddling blankets.

"Oh, Livie," she whispered, "they're beautiful."

"I agree," Olivia said proudly. "Do you want to hold them?"

Ashley swallowed, then reached out for the bundle

on the right. She sat down slowly in the chair closest to Olivia's bed.

"That's John," Olivia explained, her voice soft with adoring exhaustion.

"How can you tell?" Ashley asked, without lifting her eyes from the baby's face. He seemed to glow with some internal light, as though he were trailing traces of heaven, the place he'd so recently left.

Livie chuckled. "The twins aren't identical, Ashley," she said. "John is a little smaller than Sam, and he has my mouth. Sam looks like Tanner."

Ashley didn't respond; she was too smitten with young John Mitchell Quinn. By the time she swapped one baby for the other, she could tell the difference between them.

A nurse came and collected the babies, put them back in their incubators. Although they were healthy, like most twins they were underweight. They'd be staying at the clinic for a few days after Olivia went home.

Olivia napped, woke up, napped again.

"I'm so glad you're here," she said once.

Ashley, who had been rising from her chair to leave, sat down again. Remembered the carnations and got up to put them in a water-glass vase.

"How did you wind up in Indian Rock instead of Flagstaff?" Ashley asked, when Olivia didn't immediately drift off.

Olivia smiled. "I was on a call," she said. "Sick horse. Tanner wanted me to call in another vet, but this was a special case, and Sophie was spending the night at Brad and Meg's, so he came with me. We planned to go on to Flagstaff for the induction when I was finished, but the babies had other ideas. I went into labor in the barn, and Tanner brought me here."

Ashley shook her head, unable to hold back a grin. Her sister, nine and a half months pregnant by her own admission, had gone out on a call in the middle of the night. It was just like her. "How's the horse?"

"Fine, of course," Olivia said, still smiling. "I'm the best vet in the county, you know."

Ashley found a place for the carnations—they looked pitiful among all the dozens and dozens of roses, yellow from Brad and Meg, white from Tanner, and more arriving at regular intervals from friends and coworkers. "I know," she agreed.

Olivia reached for her hand, squeezed. "Friends again?"

"We were never *not* friends, Livie."

Olivia shook her head. Like all O'Ballivans, she was stubborn. "We were always *sisters*," she said. "But sisters aren't necessarily friends. Let's not let the mom-thing come between us again, okay?"

Ashley blinked away tears. "Okay," she said.

Just then, Melissa streaked into the room, half-hidden behind a giant potted plant with two blue plastic storks sticking out of it. She was dressed for work, in a tailored brown leather jacket, beige turtleneck and tweed trousers.

Setting the plant down on the floor, when she couldn't find any other surface, Melissa hurried over to Olivia and kissed her noisily on the forehead.

"Hi, Twin-Unit," she said to Ashley.

"Hi." Ashley smiled, glanced toward the doorway in case the mystery man had come along for the ride. Alas, there was no sign of him.

Melissa looked around for the babies. Frowned. She did everything fast, with an economy of motion; she'd come to see her nephews and was impatient at the delay. "Where are they?"

"In the nursery," Olivia answered, smiling. "How many cups of coffee have you had this morning?"

Melissa made a comical face. "Not nearly enough," she said. "I'm due in court in an hour, and where's the nursery?"

"Down the hall, to the right," Olivia told her. A worried crease appeared in her otherwise smooth forehead. "The roads are icy. Promise me you won't speed all the way back to Stone Creek after you leave here."

"Scout's honor," Melissa said, raising one hand. But she couldn't help glancing at her watch. "Yikes. Down the hall, to the right. Gotta go."

With that, she dashed out.

Ashley followed, double-stepping to catch up.

"Who was the man who answered your phone this morning?" she asked.

Melissa didn't look at her. "Nobody important," she said.

"You spent the night with him, and he's 'nobody important'?"

They'd reached the nursery window, and since Sam and John were the only babies there, spotting them was no problem.

"Could we not discuss this now?" Melissa asked, pressing both palms to the glass separating them from their nephews. "Why are they in incubators? Is something wrong?"

"It's just a precaution," Ashley answered gently. "They're a little small."

"Aren't babies *supposed* to be small?" Melissa's eyes were tender as she studied the new additions to the family. When she turned to face Ashley, though, her expression turned bleak.

"He's my boss," she said.

Ashley took a breath before responding. "The one who divorced his latest trophy wife about fifteen minutes ago?"

Melissa stiffened. "I knew you'd react that way. Honestly, Ash, sometimes you are such a prig. The marriage was over years ago—they were just going through the motions. And if you think I had anything to do with the breakup—well, you ought to know better."

Ashley closed her eyes briefly. She *did* know better. Her twin was an honorable person; nobody knew that better than she did. "I wasn't implying that you're a home-wrecker, Melissa. It's just that you're not over Daniel yet. You need time."

Daniel Guthrie, the last man in Melissa's life, owned and operated a fashionably rustic dude ranch between Stone Creek and Flagstaff. An attractive widower with two young sons, Dan was looking for a wife, someone to settle down with, and he'd never made a secret of it. Melissa, who freely admitted that she *could* love Dan and his children if she half tried, wanted a career—after all, she'd worked hard to earn her law degree.

It was a classic lose-lose situation.

"I didn't have sex with Alex," Melissa whispered, though Ashley hadn't asked. "We were just *talking*."

"I believe you," Ashley said, putting up both hands in a gesture of peace. "But Stone Creek is a small town. If some bozo's car was parked in your driveway all night, word is bound to get back to Dan."

"Dan has no claim on me," Melissa snapped. "*He's* the one who said we needed a time-out." She sucked in a furious breath. "And Alex Ewing is *not* a bozo. He's up for the prosecutor's job in Phoenix, and he wants me to go with him if he gets it."

Ashley blinked. "You would move to—to Phoenix?"

Melissa widened her eyes. "Phoenix isn't Mars, Ashley," she pointed out. "It's less than two hours from here. And just because you're content to quietly fade away in Stone Creek, quilting and baking cookies for visiting strangers, that doesn't mean *I* am."

"But—this is home."

Melissa looked at her watch again, shook her head. "Yeah," she said. "That's the problem."

With that, she walked off, leaving Ashley staring after her.

I am not *"content to quietly fade away in Stone Creek,"* she thought.

But wasn't that exactly what she was doing?

Making beds, cooking for guests, putting up decorations for various holidays only to take them down again? And, yes, quilting. That was her passion, her artistic outlet. Nothing wrong with that.

But Melissa's remarks *had* brought up the question Ashley usually avoided.

When was her *life* supposed to start?

Jack woke with a violent start, expecting darkness and nibbling rats.

Instead, he found himself in a small, pretty room with pale green walls. An old-fashioned sewing machine, the treadle kind usually seen only in antiques malls and elderly ladies' houses stood near the door.

The quilt covering him smelled faintly of some herb—probably lavender—and memories.

Ashley.

He was at her place.

Relief flooded him—and then he heard the sound. Distant—a heavy step—definitely *not* Ashley's.

Leaning over the side of the bed, which must have been built for a child, it was so short and so narrow, Jack found his gear, fumbled to open the bag, extracted his trusty Glock, that marvel of German engineering. Checked to make sure the clip was in—and full.

The mattress squeaked a little as he got to his feet, listening not just with his ears, but with every cell, with all the dormant senses he'd learned to tap into, if not to name.

There it was again—that thump. Closer now. Definitely masculine.

Jack glanced back over one shoulder, saw that the kitten was still on the bed, watching him with curious, mismatched eyes.

"Shhh," he told the animal.

"Meooow," it responded.

The sound came a third time, nearer now. Just on the other side of the kitchen doorway, by Jack's calculations.

Think, he told himself. He knew he was reacting out of all proportion to the situation, but he couldn't help it. He'd had a lot of practice at staying alive, and his survival instincts were in overdrive.

Chad Lombard couldn't have tracked him to Stone Creek; there hadn't been time. But Jack was living and breathing because he lived by his gut as well as his mind. The small hairs on his nape stood up like wire.

Using one foot, the Glock clasped in both hands, he eased the sewing room door open by a few more inches.

Waited.

And damn near shot the best friend he'd ever had when Tanner Quinn strolled into the kitchen.

"Christ," Jack said, lowering the gun. With his long outgoing breath, every muscle in his body seemed to go slack.

Tanner's face was hard. "That was my line," he said.

Jack sagged against the doorframe, his eyes tightly shut. He forced himself to open them again. "What the hell are you doing here?"

"Playing nursemaid to you," Tanner answered, crossing the room in a few strides and expertly removing the Glock dangling from Jack's right hand. "Guess I should have stuck with my day job."

Jack opened his eyes, sick with relief, sick with whatever that goon in South America had shot into his veins. "Which is what?" he asked, in an attempt to lighten the mood.

Tanner set the gun on top of the refrigerator and pulled Jack by the arm. Squired him to a chair at the kitchen table.

"Raising three kids and being a husband to the best woman in the world," he answered. "And if it's all the same to you, I'd like to stick around long enough to see my grandchildren."

Jack braced an elbow on the tabletop, covered his face with one hand. "I'm sorry," he said.

Tanner hauled back a chair of his own, making plenty of noise in the process, and sat down across from Jack, ignoring the apology. "What's going on, McCall?" he demanded. "And don't give me any of your bull crap cloak-and-dagger answers, either."

"I need to get out of here," Jack said, meeting his friend's gaze. "Now. Today. Before somebody gets hurt."

Tanner flung a scathing glance toward the Glock, gleaming on top of the brushed-steel refrigerator. "Seems to me, *you're* the main threat to public safety around here. Dammit, you could have shot Ashley—or Sophie or Carly—"

"I said I was sorry."

"Oh, well, that changes everything."

Jack sighed. And then he told Tanner the same story he'd told Ashley earlier. Most of it was even true.

"You call this living, Jack?" Tanner asked, when he was finished. "When are you going to stop playing Indiana Jones and settle down?"

"Spoken like a man in love with a pregnant veterinarian," Jack said.

At last, Tanner broke down and grinned. "She's not pregnant anymore. Olivia and I are now the proud parents of twin boys."

"As of when?" Jack asked, delighted and just a shade envious. He'd never thought much about kids until he'd gotten to know Sophie, after Tanner's first wife, Katherine, was killed, and then Rachel, the bravest seven-year-old in Creation.

"As of this morning," Tanner answered.

"Wow," Jack said, with a shake of his head. "It would *really* have sucked if I'd shot you."

"Yeah," Tanner agreed, going grim again.

"All the more reason for me to hit the road."

"And go where?"

"Dammit, I don't know. Just away. I shouldn't have come here in the first place—I was out of my mind with fever—"

"You were out of your mind, all right," Tanner argued. "But I think it has more to do with Ashley than the toxin. There's a pattern here, old buddy. You always leave—and you always come back. That ought to tell you something."

"It tells me that I'm a jerk."

"You won't get any argument there," Tanner said, without hesitation.

"I can't keep doing this. Every time I've left that woman, I've meant to stay gone. But Ashley haunts me, Tanner. She's in the air I breathe and the water I drink—"

"It's called *love*, you idiot," Tanner informed him.

"Love," Jack scoffed. "This isn't the Lifetime channel, old buddy. And it's not as if I'm doing Ashley some big, fat favor by loving her. My kind of romance could get her *killed*."

Tanner's mouth crooked up at one corner. "You watch the *Lifetime channel*?"

"Shut up," Jack bit out.

Tanner laughed. "You are so screwed," he said.

"Maybe," Jack snapped. "But you're not being much help here, in case you haven't noticed."

"It's time to stop running," Tanner said decisively. "Take a stand."

"Suppose Lombard shows up? He'd like nothing better than to take out everybody I care about."

Tanner's expression turned serious again, and both his eyebrows went up. "What about your dad, the dentist, and your mom, the librarian, and your three brothers, who probably have the misfortune to look just like you?"

Something tightened inside Jack, a wrenching grab, cold as steel. "Why do you think I haven't seen them since I got out of high school?" he shot back. "Nobody knows I *have* a family, and I want it to stay that way."

Tanner leaned forward a little. "Which means your name isn't Jack McCall," he said. "Who the hell are you, anyway?"

"Dammit, you *know* who I am. We've been through a lot together."

"Do I? Jack is probably your real first name, but I'll bet it doesn't say *McCall* on your birth certificate."

"My birth certificate conveniently disappeared into cyberspace a long time ago," Jack said. "And if you think I'm going to tell you my last name, so you can tap into a search engine and get the goods on me, you're a bigger sucker than I ever guessed."

Tanner frowned. He loved puzzles, and he was exceptionally good at figuring them out. "Wait a second. You and Ashley dated in college, and she knew you as Jack McCall. Did you change your name in high school?"

"Let this go, Tanner," Jack answered tightly. He had to give his friend something, or he'd never get off his back—that much was clear. And while they were sitting there planning his segment on *Biography*, Chad Lombard was looking for him. By that scumbag's watch, it was payback time. "I was one of those difficult types in high school—my folks, with some help from a judge, sent me to one of those military schools where they try to scare kids into behaving like human beings. One of the teachers was a former SEAL. Long story short, the

Navy tapped me for their version of Special Forces and put me through college. I never went home, after that, and the name change was their idea, not mine."

Tanner let out a long, low whistle. "Hot damn," he muttered. "Your folks must be frantic, wondering what happened to you."

"They think I'm dead," Jack said, stunned at how much he was giving up. That toxin must be digesting his brain. "There's a grave and a headstone; they put flowers on it once in a while. As far as they're concerned, I was blown to unidentifiable smithereens in Iraq."

Tanner glared at him. "How could you put them through that?"

"Ask the Navy," Jack said.

Outside, snow crunched under tires as Ashley pulled into the driveway.

"End of conversation," Jack told Tanner.

"That's what *you* think," Tanner replied, pushing back his chair to stand.

"I'll be out of here as soon as I can arrange it," Jack warned quietly.

Tanner skewered him with a look that might have meant "Good riddance," though Jack couldn't be sure.

The back door opened, and Ashley blew in on a freezing wind. Hurrying to Tanner, she threw her arms around his waist and beamed up at him.

"The babies are *beautiful*!" she cried, her eyes glistening with happy tears. "Congratulations, Tanner."

Tanner hugged her, kissed the top of her head. "Thanks," he said gruffly. Then, with one more scathing glance at Jack, he put on his coat and left, though not before his gaze strayed to the Glock on top of the refrigerator.

Fortunately, Ashley was too busy taking off her own coat to notice.

Jack made a mental note to retrieve the weapon before she saw it.

"You're up," she told him cheerfully. "Feeling better?"

He'd never left her willingly, but this time, the prospect nearly doubled him over. He sat up a little straighter. "I love you, Ashley," he said.

She'd been in the process of brewing coffee; at his words, she stopped, stiffened, stared at him. "What did you say?"

"I love you. Always have, always will."

She sagged against the counter, all the joy gone from her eyes. "You have a strange way of showing it, Jack McCall," she said, after a very long time.

"I can't stay, Ash," he said hoarsely, wishing he could take her into his arms, make love to her just once more. But he'd done enough damage as it was. "And this time, I won't be back. I promise."

"Is that supposed to make me feel better?"

"It would if you knew what it might mean if I stayed."

"What would it mean, Jack? If you stayed, that is."

"I told you about Lombard. He's the vindictive type, and if he ever finds out about you—"

"Suppose he does," Ashley reasoned calmly, "and you're not here to protect me. What then?"

Jack closed his eyes. "Don't say that."

"Stone Creek isn't a bad place to raise a family," she forged on, with a dignity that broke Jack's heart into two bleeding chunks. "We could be happy here, Jack. Together."

He got to his feet. "Are you saying you love me?"

"Always have," she answered, "always will."

"It wouldn't work," Jack said, wishing he hadn't been such a hooligan back in his teens. None of this would be happening if he hadn't ended up in military school and shown a distinct talent for covert action. He'd probably be a dentist in the Midwest, with a wife and kids and a dog, and his parents and his brothers would be dropping by for Sunday afternoon barbecues instead of visiting an empty grave.

"Wouldn't it?" Ashley challenged. "Make love to me, Jack. And then tell me it wouldn't work."

The temptation burned in his veins and hardened his groin until it hurt. "Ashley, don't."

She began to unbutton her blue silk blouse.

"Ashley."

"What's the matter, Jack? Are you chicken?"

"Ashley, *stop* it." It wasn't a command, it was a plea. "I'm not who you think I am. My name isn't Jack McCall, and I—"

Her blouse was open. Her lush breasts pushed against the lacy pink fabric of her bra. He could see the dark outline of her nipples.

"I don't care what your name is," she said. "I love you. You love me. Whoever you are, take me to bed, unless you want to have me on the kitchen floor."

He couldn't resist her any more than he'd been able to resist coming back every time he left. She was an addiction.

He held out his hand, and she came to him.

Somehow, they managed to get up the stairs, along the hallway, into her bedroom.

He didn't remember undressing her, or undressing himself.

It was as though their clothes had burned away in the heat.

Even a few minutes before, Jack wouldn't have believed he had the strength for sex, but the drive was deep, elemental, as much a part of him as Ashley herself.

There was no foreplay—their need for each other was too great.

The two of them fell sideways onto her bed, kissing as frantically as half-drowned swimmers trying to breathe, their arms and legs entwined.

He took her in one hard stroke, and found her ready for him.

She came instantly, shouting his name, clawing at his back with her fingernails. He drove in deep again, and she began the climb toward another pinnacle, writhing beneath him, flinging her hips up to meet his.

"Jack," she sobbed, *"Jack!"*

He fought to keep control, wondered feverishly if he'd die from the exertion. Oh, but what a way to go.

"Jack—"

"For God's sake, Ashley, lie still—"

Of course she didn't. She went wild beneath him.

Jack gave a ragged shout and spilled himself into her. He felt her clenching around him as she erupted in an orgasm of her own, with a long, continuous cry of exultant surrender.

Afterward, they lay still for a long time, spent, gasping for breath.

Jack felt himself hardening within her, thickening.

"Say it, Jack," she said. "Say you're going to leave me. I dare you."

He couldn't; he searched for the words, but they were nowhere to be found.

So he kissed her instead.

Ashley awakened alone, at dusk, naked and soft-boned in her bed.

The aftershocks of Jack's lovemaking still thrummed in her depths, even as panic surged within her. Damn, he'd done it again—he'd driven her out of her mind with pleasure and then left her.

She scrambled out of bed, pulled on her ratty chenille robe, and hurried downstairs.

"Jack?" She felt like a fool, calling his name when she knew he was already gone, but the cry was out of her mouth before she could stop it.

"In here," he called back.

Ashley's heart fluttered, and so did the pit of her stomach.

She followed the echo of his voice as far as the study doorway, found him sitting at her computer. The monitor threw blue shadows over the planes of his face.

"Hope you don't mind," he said. "My laptop came down with a case of jungle rot, so I trashed it somewhere in the mountains of Venezuela, and I haven't had a chance to get another one."

Ashley groped her way into the room, like someone who'd forgotten how to walk, and landed in the first available chair, a wingback she'd reupholstered herself, in pink, green and white chintz. "Make yourself at home," she said, and then blushed because the words could be taken so many ways.

His fingers flew over the keyboard, with no pause when he looked her way. "Thanks," he said.

"You've made a remarkable recovery, it seems to me," Ashley observed.

"The restorative powers of good sex," Jack said, "are legendary."

He was legendary. It had been hours since they'd made love, but Ashley still felt a deliciously orgasmic twinge every few moments.

"Answering email?" she asked, to keep the conversation going.

Jack shook his head. "I don't get email," he said. "After I booted this thing up and ran all the setups, I did a search. Noticed you didn't have a website. You can't run a business without some kind of presence on the Internet these days, Ashley—not unless you want to go broke."

"You're building a *website*?"

"I'm setting up a few prototypes. You can have a look later, see if you like any of them."

"You're a man of many talents, Jack McCall."

He grinned. He'd showered and shaved since leaving her bed, she noticed. And he was wearing fresh clothes—blue jeans and a white T-shirt. "I began to suspect you thought that while you were digging your heels into the small of my back and howling like a she-wolf calling down the moon."

Ashley laughed, but her cheeks burned. She *had* acted like a hussy, abandoning herself to Jack, body and soul, and she didn't regret a moment of it. "Pretty cocky, aren't you?" she said.

Jack swiveled the chair around. "Come here," he said gruffly.

Her heart did a little jig, and her breath caught. "Why?"

"Because I want you," he replied simply.

She stood up, crossed to him, allowed him to set her astraddle on his lap. Moaned as he opened her bathrobe, baring her breasts.

Jack nibbled at one of her nipples, then the other. "Ummm," he murmured, shifting in the chair. He continued to arouse delicious feelings in her breasts with his lips and tongue.

Her eyes widened when she realized he'd opened his jeans. He drew his knees a little farther apart, and she gave a crooning gasp when she felt him between her legs, hot and hard, prodding.

Just as he entered her, he leaned forward again, took her right nipple into his mouth, tongued it and then began to suckle.

Ashley choked out an ecstatic sob and threw back her head, her hair falling loose down her back. "Oh, God," she whimpered. "Oh, God, not yet—"

But her body seized, caught in a maelstrom of pleasure, spasmed wildly, and seized again. Taken over, possessed, she rode him relentlessly, recklessly, her very soul ablaze with a light that blinded her from the inside.

Jack waited until she'd gone still, the effort at restraint visible in his features, and when he let himself go, the motions of his body were slow and graceful. Ashley watched his face, spellbound, until he'd stopped moving.

He sighed, his eyes closed.

And then they flew open.

"You *are* on the pill, aren't you?" he asked.

She had been, before he left. After he was gone, there had been no reason to practice birth control.

Ashley shook her head.

"What?" Jack choked out.

Ashley closed her robe, moved to rise off his lap.

But he grasped her hips and held her firmly in place. "Ashley?" he rasped.

"No, Jack," she said evenly. "I'm not on the pill."

He swore under his breath.

"Don't worry," she told him, hiding her hurt. "I'm not going to trap you."

He was going hard inside her again—angry hard. His eyes smoldering, his hands still holding her by the hips, he began to raise and lower her, raise and lower her, along the growing length of his shaft.

She buckled with the first orgasm, bit back a cry of response.

Jack settled back in the chair, watching her face, already driving her toward another, stronger climax.

And then another, and still another.

When his own release came, much later, he didn't utter a sound.

Chapter 5

In some ways, that last bout of lovemaking had been the most satisfying, but it left Ashley feeling peevish, just the same. When it was over, and she'd solidified her sex-weakened knees by an act of sheer will, she tugged her bathrobe closed and cinched the belt with a decisive motion.

"Good night," she told Jack, her chin high, her face hot.

"'Night," he replied. Having already refastened his jeans, he turned casually back to the computer monitor. To look at him, nobody would have guessed they'd been having soul-bending sex only a few minutes before.

"I'll need a credit card," Ashley said.

Jack slanted a look at her. "I beg your pardon?" he drawled.

Ashley's blush deepened to crimson. "Not for the sex," she said primly. "For the room."

Jack's attention was fixed on the monitor again. "My wallet's in the bag with my other gear. Help yourself."

As she stormed out, she thought she heard him chuckle.

Fury zinged through her, like a charge.

Since she was no snoop, she snatched up the leather bag, resting on the sewing room floor, and marched right back to the study. Set it down on the desk with a hard thump, two inches from Jack's elbow.

He sighed, flipped the brass catch on the bag, and rummaged inside until he found his wallet. Extracted a credit card.

"Here you go, Madam," he said, holding it between two fingers.

Ashley snatched the card, unwilling to pursue the word *Madam*. "How long will you be staying?"

The question hung between them for several moments.

"Better put me down for two weeks," Jack finally said. "The food's good here, and the sex is even better."

Ashley glanced at the card. It was platinum, so it probably had a high limit, and the expiration date was three years in the future. The name, however, was wrong.

"'Mark Ramsey'?" she read aloud.

"Oops. Sorry." Jack took the card back.

"Is that your real name?"

"Of course not." Frowning with concentration, Jack thumbed through a stack of cards, more than most people carried, certainly.

"What *is* your name, then?" *Since I just had about fourteen orgasms straddling your lap, I think I have a right to know.*

"Jack McCall," he said sweetly, handing her a gold card. "Try this one."

"What name did you use when you rescued Rachel?"

"Not this one, believe me. But if a man calls here or, worse yet, comes to the door, asking for Neal Mercer, you've never heard of me."

Ashley's palms were sweaty. She sank disconsolately into the same chair she'd occupied earlier, before the lap dance. "Just how many aliases do you have, anyway?"

Jack was focused on the keyboard again. "Maybe a dozen. Are you going to run that card or not?"

Ashley leaned a little, peered at the screen. A picture of her house, in full summer regalia, filled it. Trees leafed out. Flowers blooming. Lawn greener than green and neatly mowed. She could almost smell sprinkler-dampened grass.

"Where did you get that?" she asked.

"The picture?" Jack didn't look at her. "Downloaded it from the Chamber of Commerce website. I'm setting you up to take credit cards next—the usual?"

She sighed. "Yes."

"Why the sigh?" He was watching her now.

"I have so much to learn about computers," Ashley said, after biting her lip. That was only part of what was bothering her, of course. She loved this man, and he claimed to love her in return, and she didn't even know who he was.

How crazy was that?

"It's not so hard," he told her, switching to another page on the screen, one filled with credit card logos. "I'll show you how."

"What's your name?"

He chuckled. "Rumpelstiltskin?"

"Hilarious. Do you even *remember* who you really are?"

He turned in the swivel chair, gazing directly into her eyes. "Jack McKenzie," he said solemnly. "As if it mattered."

"Why wouldn't it matter?" Ashley asked in a whisper.

"Because Jacob 'Jack' McKenzie is dead. Buried at Arlington, with full military honors."

She stared at him, confounded.

"Get some sleep, Ashley," Jack said, and now he sounded weary.

She was too proud to ask if he planned on sharing her bed—wasn't even sure she wanted him there. Yes, she loved him, with her whole being, there was no escaping that. But they might as well have lived in separate universes; she wasn't an international spy. She was a small-town girl, the operator of a modest B&B. Intrigue wasn't in her repertoire.

Slowly, she rose from the chair. She walked into the darkened living room, flipped on a lamp and proceeded to the check-in desk. There, she ran Jack's credit card.

It went through just fine.

She returned the card to him. "There'll be a slip to sign," she said flatly, "but that can wait until morning."

Jack merely nodded.

Ashley left the study again, scooped up a mewing Mrs. Wiggins as she passed and climbed the stairs.

Jack waited until he'd heard Ashley's bedroom door close in the distance, then set up yet another email account, and brought up the message page. Typed in his mother's email address at the library.

Hi, Mom, he typed. *Just a note to say I'm not really dead...*

Delete.

He clicked to the search engine, entered the URL of the website for his dad's dental office.

There was Dr. McKenzie, in a white coat, looking like a man you'd trust your teeth to without hesitation. The old man was broad in the shoulders, with a full head of silver hair and a confident smile—Jack supposed he'd look a lot like his dad someday, if he managed to live long enough.

The average web surfer probably wouldn't have noticed the pain in Doc's eyes, but Jack did. He looked deep.

"I'm sorry, Dad," he murmured.

His cell phone, buried in the depths of his gear bag, played the opening notes of "Folsom Prison Blues."

Startled, Jack scrabbled through T-shirts and underwear until he found the cell. He didn't answer it, but squinted at the caller ID instead. It read, "Blocked."

A chill trickled down Jack's spine as he waited to see if the caller would leave a voice mail. This particular phone, a throwaway, was registered to Neal Mercer, and only a few people had the number.

Ardith.

Rachel.

An FBI agent or two.

Chad Lombard? There was no way he could have it, unless Rachel or Ardith had told him. Under duress.

A cold sweat broke out between Jack's aching shoulder blades.

A little envelope flashed on the phone screen.

After sucking in a breath, Jack accessed his voice mail.

"Jack? It's Ardith." She sounded scared. She'd changed her name, changed Rachel's, bought a condo on a shady street in a city far from Phoenix and started a new life, hoping to stay under Lombard's radar.

Jack waited for her to go on.

"I think he knows where we are," she said, at long last. "Rachel—I mean, Charlotte—is sure she saw him drive by the playground this afternoon—oh, God, I hope you get this—" Another pause, then Ardith recited a number. "Call me."

Jack shuddered as he hit the call back button. Cell calls were notoriously easy to listen in on, if you had the right equipment and the skill, and given the clandestine nature of his life's work, Lombard surely did. If Rachel *had* seen her father drive past the playground, and not just someone who resembled him, the bastard was already closing in for the kill.

"H-hello?" Ardith answered.

"It's Jack. This has to be quick, Ardith. You need to get *Charlotte* and leave. Right now."

"And go where?" Ardith asked, her voice shaking. "For all I know, he's waiting right outside my door!"

"I'll send an escort. Just be ready, okay?"

"But where—?"

"You'll know when you get here. My people will use the password we agreed on. Don't go with them unless they do."

"Okay," Ardith said, near tears now.

They hung up without goodbyes.

Jack immediately contacted Vince Griffin, using Ashley's landline, and gave the order, along with the password.

"Call me after you pick them up," he finished.

"Will do," Vince responded. "I take it she and the kid are right where we left them?"

"Yes," Jack said. It was beyond unlikely that Ashley's phone was bugged, but Vince's could be. He had to take the chance, hope to God nobody was listening in, that his longtime friend and employee wouldn't be followed. "Be careful."

"Always," Vince said cheerfully, and hung up.

Jack heard a sound behind him, regretted that the Glock was hidden behind a pile of quilts in the sewing room.

Ashley stood, pale-faced, in the study doorway.

"They're coming here? Rachel and her mother?"

"Yes," Jack said, letting out his breath. *You could have shot Ashley*, he heard Tanner say. A chill burned through him. "They won't be here long—just until I can find them a safe place to start over."

"They can stay as long as they need to," Ashley said, but she looked terrified. "There's no safer place than Stone Creek."

It wouldn't be a safe place for long if Lombard tracked his ex-girlfriend and his daughter to the small Arizona town, but Jack didn't point that out. There was no need to say it aloud.

Jack shut down the computer and retired to the sewing room.

Knowing she wouldn't sleep, Ashley showered, put on blue jeans and an old T-shirt, and returned to the kitchen, where she methodically assembled the ingredients for the most complicated recipe in her collection— her great-grandmother's rum-pecan cake.

The fourth batch was cooling when dawn broke,

and Ashley was sitting at the table, a cup of coffee untouched in front of her.

Jack stepped out of the sewing room, a shaving kit under one arm. His smile was wan, and a little guilty. "Smells like Christmas in here," he said, very quietly. "Did you sleep?"

Ashley shook her head, vaguely aware that she was covered in cake flour, the fallout of frenzied baking. "Did you?"

"No," Jack said, and she knew by the hollow look in his eyes that he was telling the truth. "Ashley, I'm sorry—"

"Please," Ashley interrupted, "stop saying that."

She couldn't help comparing that morning to the one before, when she'd virtually seduced Jack right there in the kitchen. Was it only yesterday that she'd visited Olivia and the babies at the clinic in Indian Rock, had that disturbing conversation with Melissa outside the nursery? Dear God, it seemed as though a hundred years had passed since then.

The wall phone rang.

Jack tensed.

Ashley got up to answer. "It's only Melissa," she said. She always knew when Melissa was calling.

"I'm picking up twin-vibes," her sister announced. "What's going on?"

"Nothing," Ashley said, glancing at the clock on the fireplace mantel. "It's only six in the morning, Melissa. What are you doing up so early?"

"I told you, I've got vibes," Melissa answered, sounding impatient.

Jack left the kitchen.

"Nothing's wrong," Ashley said, winding the telephone cord around her finger.

"You're lying," Melissa insisted flatly. "Do I have to come over there?"

Ashley smiled at the prospect. "Only if you want a home-cooked breakfast. Blueberry pancakes? Cherry crepes?"

"You," Melissa accused, "are deliberately torturing me. Your own sister. You *know* I'm on a diet."

"You're five foot three and you weigh 110 pounds. If you're on a diet, I'm having you committed." Remembering that their mother had died in the psychiatric ward of a Flagstaff hospital, Ashley instantly regretted her choice of words. This was a subject she wanted to avoid, at least until she regained her emotional equilibrium. Melissa, like Brad and Olivia, had had a no-love-lost relationship with Delia.

"Cherry crepes," Melissa mused. "Ashley O'Ballivan, you are an evil woman." A pause. "Furthermore, you have some nerve, grilling me about Alex Ewing, when Jack McCall is back."

Ashley frowned. "How did you know that?"

"Your neighbor, Mrs. Pollack, works part-time in my office, remember? She told me he arrived in an ambulance, day before yesterday. Is there a reason you didn't mention this?"

"Yes, Counselor," Ashley answered, "there is. Because I didn't want you to know."

"Why not?" Melissa sounded almost hurt.

"Because I knew I'd look like an idiot when he left again."

"Not to be too lawyerly, or anything, but why invite me to breakfast if you were trying to hide a man over there?"

Ashley laughed, but it was forced, and Melissa probably picked up on that, though mercifully, she didn't comment. "Because I'm overstocked on cherry crepes and I need the freezer space?" she offered.

"You were supposed to say something like, 'Because you're my twin sister and I love you.'"

"That, too," Ashley responded.

"I'll be over before work," Melissa said. "You're really okay?"

No, Ashley thought. *I'm in love with a stranger, someone wants to kill him, and my bed-and-breakfast is about to become a stop on a modern underground railroad.*

"I will be," she said aloud.

"Damn right you will," Melissa replied, and hung up without a goodbye. Of course, there hadn't been a "hello," either.

Classic Melissa.

The upstairs shower had been running through most of her conversation with Melissa—Ashley had heard the water rushing through the old house's many pipes. Now all was silent.

Thinking Jack would probably be downstairs soon, wanting breakfast, Ashley fed Mrs. Wiggins and then took a plastic container filled with the results of her *last* cooking binge from the freezer.

A month ago she'd made five dozen crepes, complete with cherry sauce from scratch, when one of her college friends had called to say she'd just found out her husband was having an affair.

Before that, it had been a double-fudge brownie marathon—beginning the night of her mother's funeral. She'd donated the brownies to the residents of the nursing home three blocks over, since, in her own way, she was just as calorie-conscious as Melissa.

Baking therapy was one thing. Scarfing down the results was quite another.

Half an hour passed, and Jack didn't reappear.

Ashley waited.

A full hour had passed, and still no sign of him.

Resigned, she went upstairs. Knocked softly at his bedroom door.

No answer.

Her imagination kicked in. The man had *aliases*, for heaven's sake. He'd abducted a drug dealer's seven-year-old daughter from a stronghold in some Latin American jungle.

Maybe he'd sneaked out the front door.

Maybe he was lying in there, dead.

"Jack?"

Nothing.

She opened the door, her heart in her throat, and stuck her head inside the room.

He wasn't in the bed.

She raised her voice a little. "Jack?"

She heard the buzzing sound then, identified it as an electric shaver, and was just about to back out of the room and close the door behind her, as quietly as possible, when his bathroom door opened.

His hair was damp from the shower, and he was wearing a towel, loincloth style, and nothing else. He grinned as he shut off the shaver.

"I'm not here for sex," Ashley said, and then could have kicked herself.

Jack laughed. "Too bad," he said. "Nothing like a quickie to get the day off to a good start. So to speak."

A quickie indeed. Ashley gave him a look, meant to hide the fact that she found the idea more than appealing. "Breakfast will be ready soon," she said coolly. "And Melissa is joining us, so try to behave yourself."

He stepped out of the bathroom.

Her gaze immediately dropped to the towel. Shot back to his face.

He was grinning. "But we're alone *now*, aren't we?"

"I'm still not on birth control, remember?" Ashley's voice shook.

"*That* horse is pretty much out of the barn," Jack drawled. He was walking toward her.

She didn't move.

He took her hand, pulled her to him, pushed the door shut.

Kissed her breathless.

Unsnapped her jeans, slid a hand inside her panties.

All without breaking the kiss.

Ashley moaned into his mouth, wet where he caressed her.

He maneuvered her to the bed, laid her down.

Ashley was already trying to squirm out of her jeans. When it came to Jack McCall—McKenzie—*whoever*—she was downright easy.

Jack finally ended the kiss, proceeded to rid her of her shoes, of the binding denim, and then her practical cotton underpants.

She whimpered in anticipation when he knelt between her legs, parted her thighs, kissed her—*there*.

A shudder of violent need moved through her.

"Slow and easy," he murmured, between nibbles and flicks of his tongue.

Slow and easy? She was on fire.

She shook her head from side to side. "Hard," she pleaded. "Hard and fast, Jack. *Please...*"

He went down on her in earnest then, and after a few glorious minutes, she shattered completely, peaking and then peaking again.

Jack soothed her as she descended, stroking her thighs and murmuring to her until she sank into satisfaction.

She'd expected him to mount her, but he didn't.

Instead, he dressed her again, nipping her once through the moist crotch of her panties before tucking her legs into her jeans, sliding them up her legs, tugging them past her bottom. He even slipped her feet into her shoes and tied the laces.

"What about—the quickie?" she asked, burning again because he'd teased her with that little scrape of his teeth. Because as spectacular as her orgasm had been, it had left her wanting—*needing*—more.

"I guess that will have to wait," Jack said, sitting down beside her on the bed and easing her upright next to him. "Didn't you say your sister would be here for breakfast at any moment?"

She looked down at the towel—either it had miraculously stayed in place or he'd wrapped it around his waist again when she wasn't looking—and saw the sizable bulge of his erection. "You've got a hard-on," she said matter-of-factly.

Jack chuckled. "Ya think?"

Melissa's voice sounded from downstairs. "Ash? I'm here!"

Ashley bolted to her feet, blushing. "Coming!" she called back.

"You can say that again," Jack teased.

Smoothing her hair with both hands, tugging at her T-shirt, Ashley hurried out of the room.

"I'll be right down!" she shouted, from the top of the stairs.

Melissa's reply was inaudible.

Ashley dashed into her bathroom and splashed her face with cold water, then checked herself out in the full-length mirror on the back of the door.

She looked, she decided ruefully, like a woman who'd just had a screaming climax—and needed more.

Quickly, she applied powder to her face, but the tell-tale glow was still there.

Damn.

There was nothing to do but go downstairs, where her all-too-perceptive twin was waiting for cherry crepes. If she didn't appear soon, Melissa would come looking for her.

"You were having sex," Melissa said two minutes later, when Ashley forced herself to step into the kitchen.

"No, I wasn't," Ashley replied, with an indignant little sniff.

"Liar."

Ashley crossed the room, turned the oven on to pre-heat, and got very busy taking the frozen crepes out of their plastic container, transferring them to a baking dish. All the while, she was careful not to let Melissa catch her eye.

"Olivia and the twins are coming home today," Melissa said lightly, but something in her voice warned that she wasn't going to let the sex issue drop.

"I thought the babies had to stay until they were bigger," Ashley replied, still avoiding Melissa's gaze.

"Tanner hired special nurses and had two state-of-the-art incubators brought from Flagstaff," Melissa explained.

Once the crepes were in the oven, Ashley had no choice but to turn around and look at Melissa.

"You *were* having sex," Melissa repeated.

Ashley flung her hands out from her sides. "*Okay. Yes*, I was having sex!" She sighed. "Sort of."

"What do you mean, *sort of?* How do you 'sort of' have sex?"

"Never mind," Ashley snapped. "Isn't it enough that I admitted it? Do you want details?"

"Yes, actually," Melissa answered mischievously, "but I'm obviously not going to get them."

Jack pushed open the inside door and stepped into the kitchen.

"Yet," Melissa added, in a whisper.

Ashley rolled her eyes.

"Hello, Jack," Melissa said.

"Melissa," Jack replied.

Like Brad and Olivia, Melissa wasn't in the Jack McCall fan club. They'd all turned in their membership cards the last time he ditched Ashley.

"Just passing through?" Melissa asked sweetly.

"Like the wind," Jack answered. "Your brother already threatened me, so maybe we can skip that part."

Ashley raised her eyebrows. Brad had *threatened* Jack?

"As long as somebody got the point across," Melissa chimed.

"Oh, believe me, I get it."

"Will you both stop bickering, please?" Ashley asked.

Melissa sneezed. Looked around. "Is there a *cat* in this house?"

Jack grinned. "I could find the little mutant, if you'd like to pet it."

Melissa sneezed again. "I'm—*allergic*! Ashley, you *know* I'm all—all—*atchoo!*"

Ashley had completely forgotten about Mrs. Wiggins, and about her sister's famous allergies. Olivia insisted it was all in Melissa's head, since she'd been tested and the results had been negative.

"I'm sorry, I—"

Another sneeze.

"Bless you," Jack said generously.

Melissa grabbed up her coat and purse and ran for the back door. Slammed it behind her.

"Well," Jack commented, "that went well."

"Shut up," Ashley said.

Jack let out a magnanimous sigh and spread his hands.

Ashley went to the cupboard, got out two plates, set them on the table with rather more force than necessary. "You," she said, "are complicating my life."

"Are you talking to me or the cat?" Jack asked, all innocence.

"You," Ashley replied tersely. "I'm not getting rid of the cat."

"But you *are* getting rid of me? After that orgasm?"

"Shut up."

Jack chuckled, pressed his lips together, and pretended to zip them closed.

Ashley served the crepes. They both ate.

All without a single word passing between them.

After breakfast, Jack retreated to the study, and Ashley cleaned up the kitchen. Melissa called just as she was closing the dishwasher door.

"It wasn't the cat," Melissa said, first thing.

"Duh," Ashley responded.

"I mean, I thought it was, but I'm probably catching cold or something—"

"Either that, or you're allergic to Jack."

"He's bad news, Ash," Melissa said.

"I guess I could take up with Dan," Ashley said mildly. "I hear he's looking for a domestic type."

"Don't you dare!"

Ashley smiled, even though tears suddenly scalded her eyes. She was destined to love one man—Jack McCall—for the rest of her life, maybe for the rest of eternity.

And Melissa was right.

He was the worst possible news.

Chapter 6

"I'm going out to Tanner and Olivia's after work today," Melissa said. "Gotta see my nephews in their natural habitat. Want to ride along?"

By the time Melissa left her office, even if she knocked off at five o'clock—a rare thing for her—it would be dark out. Ardith and Rachel would surely arrive that night, and Ashley wanted to be on hand to welcome the pair and help them settle in.

She'd already decided to put the secret guests in the room directly across from Jack's; it had twin beds and a private bathroom. Jack would surely want to be in close proximity to them in case of trouble, and the feeling was undoubtedly mutual.

"I didn't sleep very well last night," she confessed. "By the time you leave work, I'll probably be snoring."

"Whatever you say," Melissa said gently. "Be careful, Ash. When the sex is good, it's easy to get carried away."

"Sounds like you're speaking from experience," Ashley replied. "Have you seen Dan lately?"

Melissa sighed. "We're not speaking," she said, with a sadness she usually kept hidden. "The last time we did, he told me we should both start seeing other people." A sniffle. "I heard he's going out with some waitress from the Roadhouse, over in Indian Rock."

"Is that why you're considering leaving Stone Creek? Because Dan is dating someone else?"

Melissa began to cry. There was no sob, no sniffle, no sound at all, but Ashley knew her sister was in tears. That was the twin bond, at least as they experienced it.

"Why do I have to choose?" Melissa asked plaintively. "Why can't I have Dan *and* my career? Ash, I worked so hard to get through law school—even with Brad footing the bills, it was *really* tough."

Ashley hadn't been over this ground with Melissa, not in any depth, anyway, because they'd been semi-estranged since the day of their mother's funeral. "Is that what Dan wants, Melissa? For you to give up your law practice?"

"He has two young sons, Ash. The ranch is *miles* from anywhere. In the winter, they get snowed in—Dan homeschools Michael and Ray from the first blizzard, sometimes until Easter, because the ranch road is usually impassable. Unless I wanted to travel by dogsled, I couldn't possibly commute. I'd go bonkers." Melissa pulled in a long, quivery breath. "I might even pull a 'Mom,' Ashley. If I got desperate enough. Get on a bus one fine afternoon and never come back."

"I can't see you doing that, Melissa."

"Well, *I* can. I love Dan. I love the boys—way too much to do to them what Delia did to us."

"Mel—"

"Here's how much I love them. I'd rather Dan married that waitress than someone who was always looking for an escape route—like me."

"Have you and Dan talked about this, Melissa? *Really* talked about it?"

"Sort of," Melissa admitted wearily. "His stock response was, 'Mel, we can work this out.' Which means I stay home and cook and clean and sew slipcovers, while he's out on the trail, squiring around a bunch of executive greenhorns trying to find their inner cowboys."

"How do you *know* that's what it means? Did Dan actually say so, Melissa, or is this just your take on the situation?"

"'*Just*' my 'take' on the situation?" Melissa countered, sounding offended. "I'm not some naive Martha Stewart clone like—like—"

"Like me?"

"I didn't say that!"

"You didn't have to, Counselor." *A Martha Stewart clone?* Was that how other people saw her? Because she enjoyed cooking, decorating, quilting? Because she'd never had the kind of world-conquering ambition Brad and Melissa shared?

"Ashley, I truly didn't mean—"

Ashley had always been the family peacemaker, and that hadn't changed. "I know you didn't mean to hurt my feelings, Melissa," she said gently. *Oh, but you did.* "And maybe it *is* time I had a little excitement in my life."

With Jack around, excitement was pretty much a sure thing.

Out-of-the-stratosphere sex and a drug dealer bent on revenge.

Who could ask for more?

There was a smile in Melissa's voice, along with a tremulous note of relief. "Kiss the babies for me, if you see them before I do," she said.

Ashley hadn't decided whether or not she'd make the drive out to Starcross Ranch that day. It wasn't so far, but the roads were probably slick. Although she had snow tires, her car was a subcompact, and it didn't have four-wheel drive.

"I'll do that," she answered, and the call was over.

Jack, she soon discovered, was in the study, working on potential websites for the bed-and-breakfast. He was remarkably cool, calm and collected, considering the circumstances, but Ashley couldn't help noticing that his nondescript cell phone was within easy reach.

She went upstairs, cast one yearning look toward her bed. Climbing into it wasn't an option—she might have another wakeful night if she went to sleep at that hour of the day.

Using her bedside phone, she placed a call to Olivia.

Her sister answered on the second ring. "Dr. O'Ballivan," she said, all business. Olivia had taken Tanner's name when they married, but she still used her own professionally.

Olivia was managing marriage, motherhood and a career, at least so far. Why couldn't Melissa do the same thing?

"You sound very businesslike, for someone who just

went through childbirth twice in the space of ten minutes," Ashley said.

Olivia laughed. "That's modern medicine for you. Have twins one day, go home the next. Tanner hired nurses to look after the babies round the clock until I've rested up, so I'm a lady of leisure these days."

"How are they?"

"Growing like corn in August," Olivia replied.

"Good," Ashley said. "Are you up for a visitor? Please say so if you're not—I promise I'll understand."

"I'd *love* to have a visitor," Olivia said. "Tanner's out feeding the range cattle, Sophie's at school, and of course the day nurse is busy doting on the two new men in the house. Ginger isn't in the mood for chitchat, so I'm at loose ends."

Ashley couldn't help smiling. Ginger, an aging golden retriever, was Olivia's constant companion, and the two of them usually had a lot to say to each other. "I'll be out as soon as I've showered and dressed," she said. "Do you need anything from town?"

"Nope. Loaded up on groceries over the weekend," Olivia answered. "The roads have been plowed and sanded, but be careful anyway. There's another snowstorm rolling in tonight."

Ashley promised to drive carefully and said goodbye.

She tried to be philosophical about the approaching storm, but for her, once Christmas had come and gone, snow lost its charm. Unlike her siblings, she didn't ski.

The shower perked her up a little—she used her special ginseng-and-rice soap, and the scent was heavenly. After drying off with the kind of soft, thick towel one would expect a "Martha Stewart clone" to have on hand, she dressed in a long black woolen skirt, a lavender sweater with raglan sleeves, and high black boots.

She brushed her hair out and skillfully redid her braid.

Frowned at her image in the steamy mirror.

Maybe she ought to change her hair. Get one of those saucy, layered cuts, with a few shimmery highlights thrown in for good measure. Drive to one of the malls in Flagstaff and have a makeover at a department-store cosmetics counter.

Jazz herself up a little.

The trouble was, she'd never aspired to jazziness.

Her natural color, a coppery-blond, suited her just fine, and so did the style. The braid was tidy, feminine, and practical, considering the life she led.

On the other hand, she'd been wearing that same French braid since college. Spiral curls, like Melissa's, might look sexy on her.

Did she *want* to be sexier?

Look how much trouble she'd gotten herself into with the same old hairdo and minimal makeup.

Quickly, she applied lip gloss and a light coat of mascara and headed downstairs. Pausing in the study doorway, she allowed herself the pleasure of watching Jack for a few moments before saying, "I'm going out to Olivia and Tanner's. Want to come along?"

Jack turned in the swivel chair. "Maybe some other time," he said. "I think I'd better stick around, in case Vince shows up with Ardith and Rachel sooner than expected."

Ashley didn't know who Vince was, though she had caught the name when she accidentally-on-purpose overheard Jack's phone conversation with Ardith the night before.

"Did he call?" She wanted to ask Jack if he was feeling ill again, but something stopped her. "Vince, I mean?"

Jack nodded. "They're on their way."

"No trouble?"

His gaze was direct. "Depends on how you define *trouble*," he replied. "Ardith has a husband and two other children besides Rachel. She's had to leave them behind—at least for the time being."

Ashley's heart pinched. She knew what it was to await the return of a missing mother. "Aren't the police doing anything?"

"They were willing to send a patrol car by Ardith's place every once in a while. Under civil law, unless Lombard actually attacks or kills her or Rachel, there isn't much the police can do."

"That's insane!"

"It's the law."

"The husband and the other children—aren't they in danger, too?" Wouldn't the whole family be better off together, Ashley wondered, even if they had to establish new identifies? At least they'd have each other.

"The more people involved," Jack told her grimly, "the harder it is to hide. For now, they're safer apart."

"A man like Lombard—wouldn't he go after the rest of the family, if only to force Ardith out into the open?"

"He might do anything," Jack admitted. "From what I've seen, though, Lombard is fixated on getting Rachel back and not much else. Ardith is in his way, and he won't hesitate to take her out to get what he wants."

Ashley hugged herself. Even inside, wearing warm

clothes, she felt chilled. "But *why* is he so obsessed? He wasn't around when Rachel was born—he couldn't have bonded with her the way a father normally would."

"Why does he run drugs?" Jack countered. "Why does he kill people? We're not dealing with a rational person here, Ashley. If I had to hazard a guess at his motive, I'd say it's pure ego. Lombard is a sociopath, if not worse. He sees Rachel as an object, something that *belongs* to him." He paused, and she saw pain in his eyes. "Do me a favor?" he asked hoarsely.

"What?"

"Don't come back here tonight. Stay with Tanner and Olivia. Or with Brad and his wife."

Ashley swallowed. "You think Lombard's coming— Here?" She'd known Jack thought exactly that, on some level, but it seemed so incredible that she had to ask.

"Let's just say I'd rather not take a chance."

"But you *will* be taking a chance, with your own life."

"That's one hell of a lot better than taking a chance with yours. Once I figure out what to do with Ardith and Rachel, make sure they're someplace Lombard will never find them, I'm going to draw that crazy son-of-a-bitch as far from Stone Creek as I can."

"This isn't going to end, is it? Not unless—"

"Not unless," Jack said, rising from the chair, approaching her, "I kill him, or he kills me."

"My God," Ashley groaned, putting a hand to her mouth.

Jack gripped her shoulders firmly, but with a gentleness that reminded her of their lovemaking. "I'll never be able to forgive myself if you get caught in the cross fire, Ashley. If you meant it when you said you loved me, then do what I ask. Take the cat, leave this house, and don't come back until I give the all clear."

"I *did* mean it, but—"

He brushed her chin with the pad of his thumb. "I understand that you come from sturdy pioneer stock and all that, Ashley. I know the O'Ballivans have always held their own against all comers, faced down any trouble that came their way. But Chad Lombard is no ordinary bad guy. He's the devil's first cousin. You don't want to know the things he's done—you wouldn't be able to get them out of your head."

Ashley stared into Jack's eyes, so deathly afraid for him that it didn't occur to her to be afraid for herself. "When you went looking for Rachel in South America," she said, her mouth so dry that she almost couldn't get the words out, "that wasn't your first run-in with Lombard, was it?"

"No," he said, after a long, long time.

"What hap—?"

"You don't want to know. I sure as hell wish *I* didn't." He slid his hands down her upper arms, squeezed her elbows. "Go, Ashley. Do this for me, and I'll never ask you for another thing."

"That's what I'm afraid of," she told him.

He leaned in, kissed her forehead. Took a deep breath, seeming to draw in the scent of her and hold it as long as possible. "Go," he repeated.

She agonized in silence for a long moment, then nodded in reluctant agreement. She'd wanted to meet Ardith and Rachel, but maybe it would be better—for them as well as for her—if that never happened.

"You'll call when you get to your sister's place?" Jack asked.

"Yes," Ashley said.

She turned away from Jack slowly, went back upstairs, packed a small suitcase.

She didn't say goodbye to Jack; there was something too final about that. Instead, she collected Mrs. Wiggins and set out for Starcross Ranch, though when she arrived at Tanner and Olivia's large, recently renovated house, she left her suitcase and the kitten in the car.

The last thing the Quinns needed, with new babies and incubators and three shifts of nurses already in residence, was a relative looking for a place to hide out. After the visit, she would drive on to Meg and Brad's, ask to spend the night in their guesthouse.

Although she knew she'd be welcome, Brad would want to know what was going on. After all, she had a perfectly good place of her own.

Lying wouldn't do any good—her brother knew Jack was there, knew their history, at least as a couple.

She would have to tell Brad the truth—but how much of it?

Jack hadn't asked her to keep any secrets. Given the situation, though, he might have thought that went without saying.

Tanner stepped out onto the porch as she came up the walk. He smiled, but his eyes were filled with unasked questions.

Ashley dredged up a tattered smile from somewhere inside, pasted it to her mouth. "Hello, Tanner," she said.

"Jack called," he told her.

Ashley stopped in the middle of the walk. A special system of wires kept the concrete clear of ice and snow, and she could feel the heat of it, even through the soles of her boots.

"Oh," she said.

He passed her on the walk without another word. Went to her car, reached in for the suitcase and the kitten.

"I was going to spend the night over at Brad and Meg's," she said, pausing on the porch steps.

"You're staying here," Tanner said. "It's not as though we don't have room, and I promise, the dogs won't eat your cat."

"But—the babies—Olivia—the last thing you need is—"

Beside her now, Tanner tried for a smile of his own and fell short. "Brad and Meg will be over later, with the kids. Melissa's stopping by when she's through at work. Time for a family meeting, kiddo, and you're the guest of honor."

Curiously, Ashley felt both deflated and uplifted by this news. "If it's about giving up Jack, you can all forget it," she said firmly.

Tanner didn't respond to that. Somehow, even with a protesting cat in one hand and a suitcase handle in the other, he managed to open the front door. "Olivia's in the kitchen," he told her. "I'll put your things in the guestroom. Cat included."

In that house, the "guestroom" was actually a suite, with a luxurious bath, a flat-screen TV above the working fireplace, and its own kitchenette.

Ginger rose from her cushy bed, tail wagging, when Ashley stepped into the main kitchen. Ashley bent to greet the sweet old dog.

Dressed in jeans and an old flannel shirt, Olivia sat in the antique rocking chair in front of the bay windows, a receiving blanket draped discreetly over her chest, nursing one of the babies. Seeing Ashley, she smiled, but her eyes were troubled.

Ashley went to her sister, bent to kiss the top of her head.

"Tell me what's going on, Ashley," Olivia said. "Tanner gave me a few details after he talked to Jack on the phone earlier, but he was pretty cryptic."

Ashley pulled one of the high-backed wooden chairs over from the table and sat down, facing Olivia. Their knees didn't quite touch.

Tanner came into the room, went to the coffeepot and filled a cup for Ashley. "You look like you could use a shot of whiskey," he commented. "But now that Sophie's a teenager, always having friends over, we decided to remove all temptation. This will have to do."

"Thanks," Ashley said, smiling a little and taking the cup.

Olivia was rocking the chair a little faster, her gaze fixed on Ashley. "Talk to us," she ordered.

Ashley sighed. When Brad and Meg and Melissa arrived, she'd have to repeat the whole incredible story—what little she knew of it, anyway—but it was clear that Olivia would brook no delay. So Ashley told her sister and brother-in-law what she knew about Rachel's rescue, and Chad Lombard's determination to, one, get his daughter back and, two, take revenge on Jack for stealing her away.

Tanner didn't look surprised; he probably knew more than she did, since he and Jack were close friends. Ashley didn't risk as much as a glance in Olivia's direction. She hated worrying her sister, especially now.

"Jack sent someone to bring Ardith and Rachel to Stone Creek," she finished. "And he wanted me out of the house in case Lombard managed to follow them somehow."

"It was certainly generous of Jack," Olivia said, with a bite in her tone, "to bring all this trouble straight to *your* door."

Tanner glanced at Olivia, grimaced slightly. "He was sick, Liv," he told her. "Out of his head with fever."

Olivia sighed.

"I'm in love with Jack," Ashley said bravely. "You might as well know."

Olivia and Tanner exchanged looks.

"What a surprise," Tanner said, one corner of his mouth tilting up briefly.

"You do realize," Olivia said seriously, her gaze boring into Ashley's face, "that this situation is hopeless? Even if Jack manages to get the woman and her little girl to safety, this Lombard character will always be a threat."

Tanner pulled up a chair beside Olivia and took her hand. "Liv," he said, "Jack is the best at what he does. He won't let anything happen to Ashley."

Tears filled Olivia's expressive eyes, then spilled down her cheeks. Ginger gave a little whimper and lumbered over to lay her muzzle on her mistress's knee. Rolled her brown eyes upward.

"I will *not* calm down," Olivia told the dog. "This is serious!"

This time, Tanner and Ashley looked at each other.

"I agree with Ginger," Tanner told his wife quietly. "You need to stay calm. We all do." By now, he was used to Olivia's telepathic conversations with animals. Ashley couldn't remember a time when her big sister didn't communicate with four-legged creatures of all species.

"How can I, when my sister is in mortal danger?" Olivia snapped, watching Ashley. "All because of *your* friend."

"Jack *is* my friend," Tanner responded, his voice still even. "And that's why I'm going to do whatever I can to help him."

Olivia turned her head quickly, stared at her husband. *"What?"*

"I can't just turn my back on him, Liv," Tanner said. "Not even for you."

"What about Sophie? What about John and Sam? They need their father, and *I* need my husband!"

Tanner started to speak, then stopped himself. Ashley saw a small muscle bunch in his jaw, go slack.

Ginger whimpered again, still gazing up at Olivia in adoring sorrow, her dog eyes liquid.

"That's easy for *you* to say," Olivia told the dog.

"This is why I didn't want to stay here," Ashley told Tanner sadly. "I've been in this house for five minutes, and I'm already causing trouble."

"You didn't do anything wrong," Olivia said, her voice and expression softening, her eyes still shining with tears. "Before Big John died, when Brad was away from home, busy with his career, I promised our grandfather I'd look after you and Melissa, and I intend to keep my word, Ashley."

"I'm not a little girl anymore," Ashley reminded her sister.

Olivia didn't answer. She was intent on tucking either John or Sam against her shoulder, patting his tiny back. The receiving blanket still covered her. When the burp came, Olivia smiled proudly.

Tanner stood up, gently took his son and carried him out of the kitchen.

Olivia straightened her clothing and laid the blanket aside. Gave Ginger a few reassuring strokes on the head before sending the animal back to her bed nearby.

"You are going to be the most amazing mother," Ashley said.

"Don't try to change the subject," Olivia warned. She was smiling, but her eyes remained moist and fierce with determination to protect her little sister. "So, you really are in love with Jack McCall?"

"Afraid so," Ashley replied. "And I think it's forever."

"Is he planning to stay this time?" Olivia's tone was kind, if wary.

Ashley raised her shoulders slightly, lowered them again. "He paid for two weeks at the B&B," she said.

Olivia's eyes narrowed, then widened. "Two weeks? That's all?"

"It's something," Ashley said, feeling like a candidate for some reality show about women trying to get over the wrong man. She made a lame attempt at a joke. "If we decide to make this permanent, I won't be charging him for bed and board."

Olivia didn't laugh, or even smile. "What if he leaves?"

"I think there's a good chance that he will," Ashley admitted. Then, without thinking, she rested one hand against her lower belly.

Olivia read the gesture with unerring accuracy. "Ashley—are you *pregnant*?"

"It's too early to know, doctor," Ashley said. "Unless there's a second-day test out there that I haven't heard about."

"*Unprotected sex?* Ashley, what are you *thinking*?"

"For once, I'm not. And it's kind of a relief."

"What if there's a baby? Jack might not be around to help you raise it."

"I'd manage, Olivia, as other women do, and *have* since cave days, if not longer."

"A child needs a father," Olivia said.

"Spoken like a very lucky woman with a husband who adores her," Ashley answered, without a shred of malice.

Tanner returned before Olivia could answer, took her by both hands, and gently hoisted her to her feet. "Time for your nap, Mama Bear," he told her.

Olivia didn't resist, but she did pin Ashley with a big-sister look and say, "We're not finished with this conversation."

Ashley simply spread her hands.

Shade by shade, shadow by shadow, night finally came.

Ashley had called from Olivia's place, as promised. They hadn't exchanged more than a few words, and those had been stiff and stilted.

It was no great wonder to Jack that Ashley was projecting a chill: She'd been banished from her own house by a man who had no damn business being there at all.

He was getting antsy.

He'd heard nothing about Ardith and Rachel since his first terse conversation with Vince Griffin, right after the pickup. On the bright side, the toxin seemed to be in abeyance, though he still broke out in cold sweats at irregular intervals, and spates of weakness invariably followed in their wake.

To keep from going crazy, or maybe to make sure he did, Jack logged on to his father's website again. Clicked to the Associates page.

There were his brothers, Dean and Jim. The last time Jack had seen them, they'd been in junior high, wannabe Romeos with braces and acne. Now, they looked like infomercial hosts.

He smiled.

A blurb at the bottom of the page showed a snapshot of Bryce, the youngest. In a wild break with McKenzie tradition, he was studying to be an optometrist.

There was no mention of Jack himself, of course. But his mother wasn't on the site, either, and that bothered him.

His dad had always been a big believer in family values.

What a disappointment I must have been, Jack thought, frowning as he left the website and ran another search. There might be a recent picture of his mom on the library's site. After all, she'd been the director when he'd left for military school.

The director's face beamed from the main page, and it wasn't his mother's.

Frowning, Jack ran another search, using her name.

That was when he found the obituary, dated three years ago, a week after her fifty-third birthday.

The picture was old, a close-up taken on a long-ago family vacation.

The headshot showed her beaming smile, the bright eyes behind the lenses of her glasses. Jack's own eyes burned so badly that he had to blink a few times before he could read beyond her name, Marlene Estes McKenzie.

She'd died at home, according to the writer of the obit, surrounded by family and friends. In lieu of flowers, her husband and sons requested that donations be made to a well-known foundation dedicated to fighting breast cancer.

Breast cancer.

Jack breathed deeply until his emotions were at least somewhat under control, then, against his better judgment, he reached for Ashley's phone, dialed the familiar number.

"Dr. McKenzie's residence," a woman's voice chimed.

Jack couldn't speak for a moment.

"Hello?" the woman asked pleasantly. "Is anyone there? Hello?"

He finally found his voice. "My name is—Mark Ramsey. Is the doctor around?"

"I'm so sorry," came the answer. "My husband is out of town at a convention, but either of his sons would be happy to see you if this is an emergency."

"It isn't," Jack said. Then, with muttered thanks, he quietly hung up.

He got out of the chair, walked to the window, looked out at the street. A blue pickup truck drove past. The house opposite Ashley's blurred.

All this time, Jack had imagined his mother visiting his grave at Arlington. Squaring her shoulders, sniffling a little, mourning her firstborn's "heroic" death in Iraq. Instead, she'd been lying in a grave of her own.

He rubbed his eyes with a thumb and forefinger.

How long had his dad waited, after his first wife's death, to remarry?

What kind of person was the new Mrs. McKenzie? Did Dean and Jim and Bryce like her?

Jack ached to call Ashley, needed to hear her voice.

But what would he say? *Hi, I just found out my mother died three years ago?* He wasn't sure he'd be able to get through the sentence without breaking down.

He moved away from the window. No sense making a target of himself.

The night grew darker, colder and lonelier.

And still Jack didn't turn on a light. Nor did he head for the kitchen to raid Ashley's refrigerator, even though he hadn't eaten since breakfast.

He'd done a lot of waiting in his life. He'd waited for precisely the right moment to rescue children and diplomats and wealthy businessmen held for ransom. He'd waited to be rescued himself once, with nearly every bone in his body broken.

Waiting was harder now.

In his mind, he heard the voice of a young soldier. "You'll be all right now, sir. We're United States Marines."

Jack's throat tightened further.

And then the throwaway cell phone rang.

Sweat broke out on Jack's upper lip. He'd spoken to Vince over Ashley's phone. He'd warned Ardith not to use the cell number again, in case it was being monitored.

It was unlikely that the FBI would be calling him up to chat. They had their own ways of getting in touch.

Holding his breath, he pressed the Talk button, but didn't speak.

"I'll find you," Chad Lombard said.

"Why don't I make it easy for you?" Jack answered lightly.

"Like, how?" Lombard asked, a smirk in his voice.

"We agree on a time and place to meet. One way or another, this thing will be over."

Lombard laughed. "I must be crazy. I kind of like that idea. It has a high-noon sort of appeal. But how do I know you'll come alone, and not with a swarm of FBI and DEA agents?"

"How do I know *you'll* come alone?" Jack countered.

"I guess we'll just have to trust each other."

"Yeah, right. When and where, hotshot?"

"I'll be in touch about that," Lombard said lightly. "Oh, and by the way, I've already killed you, for all intents and purposes. The poison ought to be in your bone marrow by now, eating up your red blood cells. Still, I'd like to be around to see you shut down, Robocop."

Jack's stomach clenched, but his voice came out sounding even and in charge.

"I'll be waiting to hear from you," he said, and hung up.

Chapter 7

Oh, and by the way, I've already killed you, for all intents and purposes. The poison ought to be in your bone marrow by now, eating up your red blood cells.

Lombard's words pulsed somewhere in the back of Jack's mind, like a distant drumbeat. The man was a skilled liar—and that was one of his more admirable traits, but this time, instinct said he was telling the truth.

Jack had never been afraid of death, and he still wasn't. But he was *very* afraid of leaving Ashley exposed to dangers she couldn't possibly imagine, even after all he'd told her. Tanner and her brother would *try* to protect her, and they were both men to be reckoned with, but were they in the same league with Lombard and his henchmen?

One-on-one, Lombard was no match for either of them.

The trouble was, Lombard never *went* one-on-one; he was too big a coward for that.

Coupled with the news of his mother's passing, *three years ago*, the knowledge that some concoction of jungle-plant extracts and nasty chemicals was already devouring his bone marrow left Jack reeling a little.

Suck it up, McCall, he thought. *One crisis at a time.*

It was after midnight when a local cab pulled up in front of Ashley's house.

Jack watched nervously from the study window as Vince got out of the front passenger seat, tucking his wallet into the back pocket of his chinos as he did so, and then opened the rear door, curbside.

Rachel scrambled out to the sidewalk, standing with her small hands on her hips like some miniature queen surveying her kingdom. She was soon followed by a much less confident Ardith, hunched over in a black trench coat and hooded scarf.

The cab drove away, and Vince steered Ardith and Rachel up the front walk.

Jack was quick to open the door; Rachel flashed past him, clad in jeans and a blue coat that looked like it might have been rescued from a thrift store, with Ardith slinking along behind.

"A *cab*?" Jack bit out, the minute he and Vince came face-to-face on the unlighted porch.

"Hide in plain sight," Vince said casually.

Jack let it pass for the moment, mainly because Rachel was tugging at the back of his shirt in a rapidly escalating effort to get his attention.

"My name is Charlotte now," she announced, "but you can still call me Rachel if you want to."

Jack grinned. He wanted to hoist the child into his arms, but didn't. After the conversation with Lombard, he couldn't quite shake the vision of his bones going hollow, caving in on themselves at the slightest exertion. He would need all his strength to deal with the inevitable.

Get over it, he told himself. If he lived long enough, he would check into a hospital, find out whether or not he was a candidate for a marrow transplant. In the meantime, there were other priorities, like keeping Rachel and Ashley and Ardith alive from one moment to the next.

"Are you hungry?" Jack asked, thinking of Ashley's freezer full of cherry crepes and other delicacies. God, what would it be like to live like a normal man—marry Ashley, live in this house, this Norman Rockwell town, for good?

"Just tired," Ardith said. Even trembling inside the bulky raincoat, she looked stick-thin, at least fifteen pounds lighter than the last time he'd seen her. And Ardith hadn't had all that much weight to spare in the first place.

"Yes!" Rachel blurted, the word toppling over the top of her mother's answer. "I'm *starved*."

"I wouldn't mind something to gnaw on myself," Vince said, his gaze slightly narrowed as he studied his boss, there in the dimness of Ashley's entryway.

"We rode in a helicopter!" Rachel sang out, on the way to the kitchen.

Jack stopped at the base of the stairs, conscious of Ardith's exhaustion. She seemed to exude it through every pore. The unseen energy of despair vibrated around her, pervaded Jack's personal space.

"You two go on to the kitchen," Jack told Vince and the little girl, indicating the direction with a motion of one hand. "Help yourselves to whatever you find." Although he kept his tone even, the glance he gave the pilot said, *We'll talk about the cab later.*

Jack did not regard himself as a hard man to work for—sure, his standards were high, but he paid top wages, provided health insurance and a generous retirement plan for his few but carefully chosen employees. On the other hand, he didn't tolerate carelessness of any kind, and Vince knew that.

Vince grimaced slightly, keenly aware of Jack's meaning, and shepherded Rachel toward the kitchen.

"Don't burn too many lights," Jack added, "and stay away from the windows."

Vince stiffened at the predictability of the order, but he didn't turn around to give Jack a ration of crap, the way he might have done in less dire circumstances.

Jack shifted his gaze to Ardith, but she'd turned her face away. He put a hand to the small of her back and ushered her up the stairs.

"Are you all right?" he asked quietly.

"I'm scared to death," Ardith replied, still without looking at him.

Even through the raincoat and whatever she was wearing underneath, Jack could feel the knobbiness of her spine against the palm of his hand.

"When is this going to be over, Jack?" she blurted, when they'd reached the top. She was staring at him now, her eyes huge and black with sorrow and fear. "When can I go back to my husband and my children?"

"When it's safe," Jack said, but he was thinking, *When Chad Lombard is on a slab.*

"When it's safe!" Ardith echoed. "You know as well as I do that 'when it's safe' might be *never*!"

She was right about that; unless he took Lombard

out, once and for all, she and Rachel would probably have to keep running.

"You can't think that way," Jack pointed out. "You'll drive yourself crazy if you do." He guided her toward the room across from his, the one Ashley had set aside for Ardith and Rachel.

Although he'd been the one to send Ashley away, he wished for a brief and fervent moment that she had stayed. Being a woman, she'd know how to calm and comfort Ardith in ways that would probably never enter his testosterone-saturated brain.

And he needed to tell *somebody* that his mother had died. He couldn't confide in Vince—they didn't have that kind of relationship. Ardith had enough problems of her own, and Rachel was a little kid.

Jack opened the door of the small but still spacious suite, with its flowery bedspreads, lace curtains and bead-fringed lamps. He'd closed the shutters earlier, and laid the makings of a fire on the hearth.

Taking a match from the box on the mantel, he lit the wadded newspaper and dry kindling, watched with primitive satisfaction as the blaze caught.

Ardith looked around, finally shrugged out of the raincoat.

"I want to call Charles," she said, clearly expecting a refusal. "I haven't talked to my husband since—"

"If you want to put him and the other kids in Lombard's crosshairs, Ardith," Jack said evenly, giving her a sidelong glance as he straightened, then stood there, soaking in the warmth of the fire, "you go right ahead."

She was boney as hell, beneath a sweat suit that must have been two sizes too big for her, and her once-beautiful face looked gaunt, her cheekbones protruding, her skin gray and slack. She'd aged a decade since gathering her small daughter close in that airport.

Ardith glanced toward the open door of the suite, then turned her gaze back to Jack's face. "I have two other children besides Rachel," she said slowly.

Jack added wood to the fire, now that it was crackling, and replaced the screen. Turned to Ardith with his arms folded across his chest.

"Meaning what?" he asked, afraid he already knew what she was about to say.

She sagged, limp-kneed, onto the side of one of the twin beds, her head down. "Meaning," she replied, after biting down so hard on her lower lip that Jack half expected to see blood, "that Chad is wearing me down."

Jack went to the door, peered out into the hall, found it empty. In the distance, he could hear Vince and Rachel in the kitchen. Pans were clattering, and the small countertop TV was on.

He shut the door softly. "Don't even tell me you're thinking of turning Rachel over to Lombard," he said.

A tear slithered down one of Ardith's pale cheeks, and she didn't move to wipe it away. Maybe she wasn't even aware that she was crying. Her eyes blazed, searing into Jack. "Are you judging me, Mr. McCall? May I remind you that you work for me?"

"May I remind you," Jack retorted calmly, "that Lombard is an international drug runner? That he tortures and kills people on a regular basis—for fun?"

Ardith dragged in a breath so deep it made her entire body quiver. "I wish I'd never gotten involved with him."

"Get in line," Jack said. "I'm sure your parents would agree, along with your present husband. The fact is, you *did* 'get involved,' in a big way, and now you've got a seven-year-old daughter who deserves all the courage and strength you can muster up."

"I'm running on empty, Jack. I can't keep this up much longer."

"Where does that leave Rachel?"

Misery throbbed in her eyes. "With you?" she asked, in a small voice. "She'd be safe, I know she would, and—"

"And you could go back home and pretend none of this ever happened? That you never met Lombard and gave birth to his child—*your* child?"

"You make me sound horrible!"

Jack thrust out a sigh. "Look, I know this is hard. It's *worse* than hard. But you can't bail on that little girl, Ardith. Deep down, you don't even want to. You've got to tough this out, for Rachel's sake and your own."

"What if I can't?" Ardith whispered.

"You can, Ardith, because you don't have a choice."

"Couldn't the FBI or the DEA help? Find her another family—?"

"Christ," Jack said. "You can't be serious."

Ardith fell onto her side on the bed, her knees drawn up to her chest in a fetal position, and sobbed, deeply and with a wretchedness that tore at the fabric of his soul. It was one of the worst sounds Jack had ever heard.

"You're exhausted," he said. "You'll feel different when you've had something to eat and a good night's sleep. We'll come up with some kind of solution, Ardith. I promise."

Footsteps sounded on the stairs, then in the hallway, and Rachel burst in. "Mommy, we found beef stew in the fridge and—" she stopped, registering the sight her mother made, lying there on the bed. Worry contorted the child's face, made her shoulders go rigid. "Why are you crying?"

Stepping behind Rachel so she couldn't see him, Jack glared a warning at Ardith.

Ardith stopped wailing, sat up, sniffled and dashed at her cheeks with the backs of both hands. "I was just missing your daddy and the other kids," she said. She straightened her spine, snatched tissues from a decorative box on the table between the beds, and blew her nose.

"I miss them, too," Rachel said. "And Grambie and Gramps, too."

Ardith nodded, set the tissue aside. "I know, sweetheart," she said. Somehow, she summoned up a smile, misty and faltering, but a smile nonetheless. "Did someone mention beef stew? I could use something like that."

Rachel's attention had shifted to the cheery fireplace. "We get our own *fireplace*?" she enthused.

Jack thought back to the five days he and Rachel had spent navigating that South American jungle after he'd nabbed her from Lombard's remote estate. They'd dealt with mosquitoes, snakes, chattering monkeys with a penchant for throwing things at them, and long, dark nights with little to cover them but the stars and the weighted, humid air.

Rachel hadn't complained once. When they were traveling, she got to ride on Jack's back or shoulders, and she enjoyed it wholeheartedly. She'd chattered incessantly, every waking moment, about all the things she'd have to tell her mommy, her stepfather, and her little brother and sister when they were together again.

"Your own fireplace," Jack confirmed, his voice husky.

He and Ardith exchanged glances, and then they all went downstairs, to the kitchen, for some of Ashley's beef stew.

Ashley waited until she was sure Olivia and Tanner were sound asleep, then crept out of the guest suite. The night nurse sat in front of the television set in the den, sound asleep.

Behind Ashley, Mrs. Wiggins mewed.

Ashley turned, a finger to her lips, hoisted the kitten up for a nuzzle, then carried the little creature back into the suite, set her down, and carefully closed the door.

Her eyes burned as the kitten meowed at being left behind.

Reaching the darkened and empty kitchen, Ashley let out her breath, going over the plan she'd spent several hours rehearsing in her head.

She would disable the alarm, then reset it before closing the door behind her. Drive slowly out to the main road, waiting until she reached the mailboxes before turning her headlights on.

Ginger, snoozing on her dog bed in the corner, lifted her golden head, gave Ashley a slow, curious once-over.

Ashley put a finger to her lips, just as she'd done earlier, with the kitten.

A voice bloomed in her mind.

"Don't go," it said.

Ashley blinked. Stared at the dog. Shook her head.

No. She had *not* received a telepathic message from Olivia's dog. She was still keyed up from the family meeting, and worried about Jack, and her imagination was running away with her, that was all.

"I'll tell," the silent, internal voice warned. *"All I have to do is bark."*

"Hush," Ashley said, fumbling in her purse for her car keys. "I'm not hearing this. It's all in my head."

"It's snowing."

Unnerved, Ashley tried to ignore Ginger, who had now risen on all four paws, as though prepared to carry out a threat she couldn't possibly have made.

Ashley went to the nearest window, the one over the sink, and peered through it, squinting.

Snowflakes the size of golf balls swirled past the glass.

Ashley glanced back at Ginger in amazement. "Well, it *is* January," she rationalized.

"You can't drive in this blizzard."

"Stop it," Ashley said, though she couldn't have said whether she was talking to the golden retriever or to herself. Or both.

The dog simply stood there, ready to bark.

Nonsense, Ashley thought. *Olivia hears animals. You don't.*

Still, either her imagination or the dog had a point. Her small hybrid car wouldn't make it out of the driveway in weather like that. The yard was probably under a foot of snow, and visibility would be zero, if not worse.

She had to think.

As quietly as possible, she drew back a chair at the big kitchen table and sat down.

Ginger relaxed a little, but she was still watchful.

Just sitting at that table caused Ashley to flash back to the family meeting earlier that evening. Meg and

Brad, Melissa, Olivia and Tanner—even Sophie and Carly and little Mac, had all been there.

As the eldest of the four O'Ballivan siblings, Brad had been the main spokesperson.

"Ashley," he'd said, "you're not going home until McCall is gone. And Tanner and I plan to make sure he is, first thing in the morning."

She'd gaped at her brother, understanding his reasoning but stung to fury just the same. Looking around, she'd seen the same grim determination in Tanner's face, Olivia's, even Melissa's.

Outraged, she'd reminded them all that she was an adult and would come and go as she pleased, thank you very much.

Only Sophie and Carly had seemed even remotely sympathetic, but neither of them had spoken up on her behalf.

"You can't hold me prisoner here," Ashley had protested, her heart thumping, adrenaline burning through her veins like acid.

"Oh, yeah," Brad had answered, his tone and expression utterly implacable. "We can."

She'd decided right then that she'd get out—yes, their intentions were good, but it was the principle of the thing—but she'd also kept her head. She'd pretended to agree.

She'd helped make supper.

She'd loaded the dishwasher afterward.

She'd even rocked one of the babies—John, she thought—to sleep after Olivia had nursed him.

The evening had seemed endless.

Finally, Meg and Brad had left, taking Mac and Carly with them. Sophie, having finished her homework, had given Ashley a hug before retiring to her room for the night.

Ashley had yawned a lot and vanished into her own lush quarters.

She'd taken a hot bath, put on her pajamas and one of Olivia's robes, watched a little television—some mindless reality show.

And she'd waited, listening to the old-new house settle around her, Mrs. Wiggins curled up on her lap, as though trying to hold her new mistress in her chair with that tiny, weightless body of hers.

Once she was sure the coast was clear, Ashley had quietly dressed, never thinking to check the weather. Such was her state of distraction.

Now, here she sat, alone in her sister's kitchen at one-thirty in the morning, engaged in a standoff with a talking dog.

"I can take the Suburban," she whispered to Ginger. "It will go anywhere."

"What's so important?" Ginger seemed to ask.

Ashley shook her head again, rubbed her temples with the fingertips of both hands. "Jack," she said, keeping her voice down because, one, she didn't want to be overheard and stopped from leaving and, two, she was talking to a *dog*, for pity's sake. "*Jack* is so important. He's sick. And something is wrong. I can feel it."

"You could ask Tanner to go into town and help him out."

Ashley blinked. Was this really happening? If the conversation *was* only in her mind, why did the other side of it just pop up without her framing the words first?

"I can't do that," she said. "Olivia and the babies might need him."

Resolved, she rose from her chair, crossed to the wooden rack where Olivia kept various keys, and helped herself to the set that would unlock and start the venerable old Suburban.

She jingled the key ring at Ginger.

"Go ahead," she said. "Bark."

Ginger gave a huge sigh. *"I'll give you a five minute head start,"* came the reply, *"then I'm raising the roof."*

"Fair enough," Ashley agreed, scrambling into Big John's old woolen coat, the one Olivia wore when she was working, hoping it would give her courage. "Thanks."

"I was in love once," Ginger said, sounding wistful.

Ashley moved to the alarm-control panel next to the back door. Racked her brain for the code, which Olivia had given to her in case of emergency, finally remembered it.

Grabbed her coat and dashed over the threshold.

The cold slammed into her like something solid and heavy, with sharp teeth.

Her car was under a mound of snow, the Suburban a larger mound beside it. Perhaps because of the emotions stirred by the family meeting, Tanner had forgotten to park the rigs in the spacious garage with his truck, the way he normally would have on a winter's night.

Hastily, she climbed onto the running board and wiped off the windshield with one arm, grateful for the heavy, straw-scented weight of her grandfather's old coat, even though it nearly swallowed her. Then she opened the door of the Suburban, got in and rammed the key into the ignition.

The engine sputtered once, then again, and finally roared to life.

Ashley threw it into Reverse, backed into the turn-around, spun her wheels for several minutes in the deep snow.

Swearing under her breath, she slammed the steering wheel with one fist, missed it, and hit the horn instead.

"Do. Not. Panic," she told herself out loud.

Just how many minutes had passed, she wondered frantically. Had Ginger already started barking? Had anyone heard the Suburban's horn when she hit it by accident?

She drew a deep breath, thrust it out in a whoosh.

No, she decided.

Lights would be coming on in the house if the dog were raising a ruckus. The howling wind had probably covered the bleat of the horn.

She shifted the Suburban into the lowest gear, tried again to get the old wreck moving. It finally tore free of the snowbank, the wheels grabbing.

As she turned the vehicle around and zoomed down the driveway, she heard the alarm system go off in the house, even over the wind and the noise of the engine.

Crap. She'd either forgotten to reset the system, or done it incorrectly.

Looking in the rearview mirror would have been useless, since the back window was coated with snow and frost, so Ashley sped up and raced toward the main road, praying she wouldn't hit a patch of ice and spin off into the ditch.

I'm sorry, she told Tanner and Olivia, the babies and Sophie and the night nurse, the alarm shrieking like a convention of angry banshees behind her. *I'm so sorry*.

* * *

Her kitchen was completely dark.

Shivering from the cold and from the harrowing ride into town, Ashley shut the door behind her, dropped her key into the pocket of Big John's coat and reached for the light switch.

"Don't move," a stranger's voice commanded. A *male* stranger's voice.

Flipping the switch was a reflex; light spilled from the fluorescent panels in the ceiling, revealing a man she'd never seen before—or had she?—seated at her table, holding a gun on her.

"Who are you?" she asked, amazed to discover that she could speak, she was so completely terrified.

The man stood, the gun still trained squarely on her central body mass. "The pertinent question here, lady, is who are *you*?"

A strange boldness surged through Ashley, fear borne high on a flood of pure, indignant rage. "I am Ashley O'Ballivan," she said evenly, "and this is my house."

"Oh," the man said.

Just then, the inside door swung open and Jack was there, brandishing a gun of his own.

What was this? Ashley wondered wildly. Tombstone?

"Lay it down, Vince," Jack said, his voice stone-cold.

Vince complied, though not with any particular grace. The gun made an ominous thump on the table-top. "Chill, man," he said. "You told me to stand watch and that's all I was doing."

Ashley's gaze swung back to Jack. She was furious and relieved, and a host of other things, too, all at once.

"I do not allow firearms in my house," she said.

Vince chuckled.

Jack told him to get lost, shoving his own pistol into the front of his pants. The move was too expert, too deft, and the gun itself looked military.

Vince ambled out of the room, shaking his head once as he passed Jack.

"What are you doing here?" Jack asked, as though *she* were the intruder.

"Do I have to say it?" Ashley countered, flinging her purse aside, fighting her way out of Big John's coat, which suddenly felt like a straightjacket. *"I live here, Jack."*

"I thought we agreed that you wouldn't come back until I gave you a heads-up," Jack said, keeping his distance.

Considering Ashley's mood, that was a wise decision on his part, even if he *was* armed and almost certainly dangerous.

"I changed my mind," she replied, tight-lipped, her arms folded stubbornly across her chest. "And who is that—that *person*, anyway?"

"Vince works for me," Jack said.

Another car crunched into the driveway. A door slammed.

Jack swore, untucking his shirt so the fabric covered the gun in the waistband of his jeans.

Tanner slammed through the back door.

"Well," Jack observed mildly, "the gang's all here."

"Not yet," Tanner snapped. "Brad's on his way. What the *hell* is going on, Ashley? You set off the alarm, the dog is probably *still* barking her brains out, and the babies are permanently traumatized—not to mention Sophie and Olivia!"

"I'm sorry," Ashley said.

A cell phone rang, somewhere on Tanner's person.

He pulled the device from his coat pocket, after fumbling a lot, squinted at the caller ID and took the call. "She's at her place," he said, probably to Olivia. A crimson flush climbed his neck, pulsed in his jaw. And his anger was nothing compared to what Brad's would be. "No, don't worry—I think things are under control..."

Ashley closed her eyes.

Brakes squealed outside.

Tanner's voice seemed to recede, and then the call ended.

Brad nearly tore down the door in his hurry to get inside.

Jack looked around, his expression drawn but pleasant.

"Cherry crepes, anyone?" he asked mildly.

Chapter 8

"I know a place the woman and the little girl will be safe," Brad said wearily, once the excitement had died down and Ashley, her brother, Jack and Tanner were calmly seated around her kitchen table, eating the middle-of-the-night breakfast she'd prepared to keep from going out of her mind with anxiety.

Vince, the man with the gun, was conspicuously absent, while Ardith and Rachel slept on upstairs. Remarkably, the uproar hadn't awakened them, probably because they were so worn-out.

Jack shifted in his chair, pushed back his plate. For a man who believed so strongly in bacon and eggs, he hadn't eaten much. "Where?" he asked.

"Nashville," Brad replied. Then he threw out the name of one of the biggest stars in country music. "She's a friend," he added, as casually as if just *anybody* could wake up a famous woman in the middle of the night and ask her to shelter a pair of strangers for an indefinite length of time. "And she's got more high-tech security than the president. Bodyguards, the whole works."

"She'd do that?" Jack asked, grimly impressed.

Brad raised one shoulder in a semblance of a shrug. "I'd do it for her, and she knows that," he said easily. "We go way back."

"Sounds good to me," Tanner put in, relaxing a little. Everyone, naturally, was showing the strain.

"Me, too," Jack admitted, and though he didn't sigh, Ashley sensed the depths of his relief. "How do we get them there?"

"Very carefully," Brad said. "I'll take care of it."

Jack seemed to weigh his response for a long time before giving it. "There's a woman's life at stake here," he said. "And a little girl's future."

"I get that," Brad answered. His gaze slid to Ashley, then moved back to Jack's face, hardening again. "Of course, I want something in return."

Ashley held her breath.

Jack maintained eye contact with Brad. "What?"

"You, gone," Brad said. "For good."

"Now, *wait just one minute*—" Ashley sputtered.

"He's right," Jack said. "Lombard wants me, Ashley, not you. And I intend to keep it that way."

"So when do we make the move?" Tanner asked.

"Now," Brad responded evenly, a muscle bunching in his jawline. He could surely feel Ashley's glare boring into him. "I can have a jet at the airstrip within an hour or two, and I think we need to get them out of here before sunrise."

"Can't you let Rachel and her mother rest, just for

this one night?" Ashley demanded. "They must be absolutely exhausted by all this—"

"It has to be tonight," Brad insisted.

Jack nodded, sighed as he got to his feet. "Make the calls," he told Brad. "I'll get them out of bed."

Things were moving too fast. Ashley gripped the table edge, swaying with a sudden sensation of teetering on the brink of some bottomless abyss. "Wait," she said.

She might as well have been invisible, inaudible. A ghost haunting her own house, for all the attention anyone paid her.

Brad was already reaching for his cell phone. "When I get back from Nashville," he said, watching Jack, "I expect you to be history."

Jack nodded, avoiding Ashley's desperate gaze. "It's a deal," he said, and left the room.

Ashley immediately sprang out of her chair, without the faintest idea of what she would do next.

Tanner took a gentle hold on her wrist and eased her back down onto the cushioned seat.

Brad placed a call to his friend. Apologized for waking her up. Exchanged a few pleasantries—yes, Meg was fine and Mac was growing like a weed, and sure there would be other kids. Give him time.

Ashley listened in helpless sorrow as he went on to explain the Ardith-Rachel situation and ask for help.

The singer agreed immediately.

Brad called for a private jet. He might as well have been ordering a pizza, he was so casual about it. Only with a pizza, he would at least have had to give a credit card number.

When Brad said, "jump," the response was invariably, "How high?"

Because she'd always known him as her big brother, the broad scope of his power always came as a surprise to her.

Things accelerated after the phone calls.

Resigned, Ashley got to work preparing food for the trip, so Ardith and Rachel wouldn't starve, though the jet probably offered catered meals.

Her guests stumbled sleepily into the kitchen just as she was finishing, herded there by Jack, their clothes rumpled and hastily donned, their eyes glazed with confusion, weariness and fear.

The little girl favored Ashley with a wan, blinking smile. "Have you been taking care of Jack?" she asked.

Ashley's heart turned over. "I've been trying," she said truthfully, studiously ignoring Brad, Tanner and Jack himself.

Vince had wandered in behind them. "Want me to go along for the ride?" he asked, meeting no one's eyes.

"No," Jack said tersely. "You're done here."

"For good?" Vince asked.

"For now," Jack replied.

Vince turned to Brad. "Catch a ride to the airstrip with you?"

Jack gave the man a quick glance, his eyes ever so slightly narrowed. "I'll take you there myself," he said, adding a brisk, "Later."

"You stopped trusting me, boss?" Vince asked, with an odd grin.

"Maybe," Jack said.

Some of the color drained from Vince's face. "Am I fired?"

"Don't push it," Jack answered.

In the end, it was decided that Tanner would drive

Vince back to his helicopter once Brad, Ardith and Rachel were aboard the jet, ready for takeoff. Later, Tanner would see that Jack boarded a commercial airliner in Flagstaff, bound for Somewhere Else.

Holding back tears, Ashley handed her brother the food she'd packed, tucked into a basket with a cheery red-and-white-checkered napkin for a cover.

Something softened in Brad's eyes as he accepted the offering, but he didn't say anything.

And neither did Ashley.

A gulf had opened between Ashley and the big brother she had always loved and admired, far wider than the one created by their mother's death. Even knowing he was doing what he thought was right— what probably *was* right—Ashley felt steamrolled, and she resented it.

Soon, Brad was gone, along with Ardith and Rachel.

Approximately an hour later, Tanner and the chastened Vince left, too.

Jack and Ashley sat on opposite sides of the kitchen table, unable to look at each other.

After a long, long time, Jack said, "My mother died three years ago. And I didn't have a clue."

Startled, Ashley sat up straighter in her chair. "I'm sorry," she said.

"Breast cancer," Jack explained gruffly, his eyes moist.

"Oh, Jack. That's terrible."

He nodded. Sighed heavily.

"I guess this is our last night together," Ashley said, at some length.

"I guess so," Jack agreed miserably.

Purpose flowed through Ashley. "Then let's make it count," she said. She locked the back door. She flipped off the lights. And then she took Jack's hand, there in the darkness, and led him upstairs to her bed.

Every moment, every gesture, was precious, and very nearly sacred.

Jack undressed Ashley the way an archeologist might uncover a fragile treasure, with a cherishing tenderness that stirred not only her body, but her soul. Head back, she surrendered her naked breasts to him, reveled in the sensations wrought by his lips and tongue.

A low, crooning sound escaped her, and she found just enough control to open his shirt, her fingers fumbling with the buttons. She needed to feel his flesh, bare and hard, yet warm against her palms and splayed fingers.

They kissed, long and deep, with a sweet urgency all the better for the smallest delay.

In time, Jack eased her onto the bed, sideways, and spread her legs to nuzzle and then suckle her until she was gasping with need and exaltation.

She whispered his name, a ragged sound, and tears burned in her eyes. How would she live without him, without this? How colorless her days would be, when he was gone, and how empty her nights. He'd taught her body to crave these singular pleasures, to need them as much as she needed air and water and the light of the sun.

But, no, she thought sorrowfully. She mustn't spoil what was probably their last night together by leaving the moment, journeying into a lonely and uncertain future. It was *now* that mattered, and only now. Jack's hands on her inner thighs, Jack's mouth on the very center of her femininity.

Dear God, it felt so good, the way he was loving her, almost too good to be borne.

The first climax came softly, seizing her, making her buckle and moan in release.

"Don't stop," she pleaded, entangling her fingers in his hair.

She hoped he would *never* cut his hair short again.

He chuckled against her moist, straining flesh, nipped at her ever so lightly with his teeth and brought her to another orgasm, this one sharp and brief, a sudden and wild flexing deep within her. "Oh, I'm a long way from finished," he assured her gruffly, before falling to her again.

Ashley could never have said afterward how many times she rose and fell on the hot tide of primitive satisfaction, flailing and writhing and crying out with each new abandoning of her ordinary self.

When he finally took her, she gloried in the heat and length and hardness of him, in the pulsing and the renewed wanting. Her body became greedier than before, demanding, reaching, shuddering. And Jack drove deep, eventually losing control, but only after a long, delicious period of restraint.

They made love time and again that night, holding each other in silence while they recovered between bouts of fevered passion.

"I'll come back if I can," Jack told her, at one point, barely able to breathe, he was so spent. "Give me a year before you fall in love with somebody else, okay?"

A year. It seemed like an eternity to Ashley, she was so aware of every passing moment, every tick of the celestial clock. At the same time, though, she knew it was safe to promise. She'd wait a lifetime, a dozen lifetimes, because for her, there *was* no man but Jack.

She nodded, dampening his bare shoulder with her tears, and finally slept.

* * *

Jack eased himself out of Ashley's arms, and her bed, around eight o'clock the next morning. It was one of those heartrendingly beautiful winter days, with sunlight glaring on pristine snow. Everything seemed to be draped in purity.

He dressed in his own room, gathered the few belongings he'd brought with him, and tucked them into his bag.

Given his druthers, he would have sat quietly in a chair, watching Ashley sleep, memorizing every line and curve of her, so he could hold her image in his mind and his heart until he died.

But Jack was the sort of man who rarely got his druthers.

He had things to do.

First, he'd meet with Chad Lombard.

If he survived that—and it was a crapshoot, whether he or Lombard or neither of them would walk away— he'd check himself into a hospital.

Feeling more alone than he ever had—and given some of the things he'd been through that was saying a lot—Jack gravitated to the computer in Ashley's study. He called up his dad's website, clicked to the Contact Us link, wrote an email he never intended to send.

Hello, Dad. I'm alive, but not for long, probably...

He went on to explain why he'd never come home from military school, why he'd let everyone in his family believe he was dead. He apologized for any pain they must have suffered because of his actions, and resisted the temptation to lay any of the blame on the Navy.

The mission had been a tough one, with a high price, but no one had held a gun to his head. He'd made the decision himself and, in most ways, he had never regretted it.

He went on to say that he hoped his mother hadn't had to endure too much pain, and asked for forgiveness. In sketchy terms, he described the toxin that was probably killing him.

In closing, he wrote, *You should know that I met a woman. If things were different, I'd love to settle down with her right here in this little Western town, raise a flock of kids with her. But some things aren't meant to be, and it's beginning to look as if this is one of them.*

No matter how it may seem, I love you, Dad.

I'm sorry.

Jack.

He was about to hit the Delete button—writing the piece had been a catharsis—when two things happened at once. His cell phone rang, and somebody knocked hard at the front door.

Simultaneously, Jack answered the call and admitted Tanner Quinn to the house he'd soon be leaving, probably forever.

No more cherry crepes.

No more mutant cat.

No more Ashley.

"Mercer?" Lombard asked affably, "is that you?"

Jack shifted to the Neal Mercer persona, because Lombard knew him by that name, gestured for Tanner to come inside, but be quiet about it.

Ashley was still sleeping, and Jack didn't want to wake her. Leaving was going to be hard enough, without a face-to-face goodbye.

On the other hand, didn't he owe her that much?

"What?" he asked Lombard.

"I've decided on a place for the showdown," Lombard said. "Tombstone, Arizona. Fitting, don't you think?"

"You're a regular John Wayne," Jack told him.

Tanner raised his eyebrows in silent question. Jack shook his head, pointed to his gear bag, waiting just inside the door.

Tanner picked up the bag, carried it out to his truck. The exhaust spewed white steam into the cold, bright air.

Leavin' on a jet plane… Jack thought.

"Tomorrow," Lombard went on. "High noon."

"High *drama*, you mean," Jack scoffed.

"Be there," Lombard ordered, dead serious now, and hung up.

Jack sighed and clicked the phone shut.

Glanced up at the ceiling.

Tanner returned from the luggage run, waiting with his big rancher's hands stuffed into the pockets of his sheepskin coat.

"Give me a minute," Jack said.

Tanner nodded, his eyes full of sympathy.

Jack turned from that. Sympathy wasn't going to help him now.

He had to be strong. Stronger than he'd ever been.

Upstairs, he entered Ashley's room, sat down on the edge of the bed, and watched her for a few luxurious moments, moments he knew he would cherish until he died, whether that was in a day, or several decades.

Ashley opened her eyes, blinked. Said his name.

For a lot of years, Jack had claimed he didn't have a heart. For all his money, love was something he simply couldn't afford.

Now he knew he'd lied—to himself and everyone else.

He had a heart, all right, and it was breaking.

"I love you," he said. "Always have, always will."

She sat up, threw her arms around his neck, clung to him for a few seconds. "I love you, too," she murmured, trembling against him. Then she drew back, looked deep into his eyes. "Thanks," she said.

"For—?" Jack ground out the word.

"The time we had. For not leaving without saying goodbye."

He nodded, not trusting himself to speak just then.

"If you can come back—"

Jack drew out of her embrace, stood. In the cold light of day, returning to Stone Creek, to Ashley, seemed unlikely, a golden dream he'd used to get through the night.

He nodded again. Swallowed hard.

And then he left.

He was boarding a plane in Flagstaff, nearly two hours later, before he remembered that he hadn't closed the email he'd drafted on Ashley's computer, spilling his guts to his father.

Ashley wasn't exactly a techno-whiz, he thought, with a sad smile, but if she stumbled upon the message somehow, she'd know most of his secrets.

She might even send the thing, on some do-gooder impulse, though Jack doubted that. In any case, she'd know about the damage the toxin was doing to his bone marrow and be privy to his deepest regrets as far as his family was concerned.

She'd know he'd loved her, too. Wanted to spend his life with her.

That shining dream could still come true, he supposed, but a lot of chips would have to fall first, and land in just the right places. The odds, he knew, were against him.

Nothing new there.

He took his seat on the small commuter plane, fastened his seat belt, and shut off his cell phone.

Tanner had been right there when he'd bought his ticket—he'd chosen Phoenix, said he'd probably head for South America from there, and gone through all the proper steps, checking his gear bag and filling out a form declaring that there was a firearm inside, properly secured.

What he *didn't* tell his friend was that he planned to charter a flight to Tombstone as soon as he reached Phoenix and have it out with Chad Lombard, once and for all.

Takeoff was briefly delayed, due to some mechanical issue.

During the wait, Jack switched his phone on again, placed a short call that drew an alarmed stare from the woman sitting next to him and smiled as he put the cell away.

"Air marshal," he explained, in an affable undertone.

The woman didn't look reassured. In fact, she moved to an empty seat three rows forward. A word to the flight attendants about the man in 7-B and he'd be off the plane, tangled in a snarl with a pack of TSA agents until three weeks after forever.

For some reason, she didn't report him. Maybe she didn't watch the news a lot, or fly much.

Jack settled back, closed his eyes, and tried not to think about Ashley and the baby they might have conceived together, the future they might have shared.

That proved impossible, of course, like the old game of trying not to think about a pink elephant.

The plane lifted off, bucked through some turbulence and streaked toward his destiny—and Chad Lombard's.

Carly McKettrick O'Ballivan watched her aunt with concern, while Meg, who was both Carly's sister *and* her adoptive mother—how weird was that?—puttered around the big kitchen, trying to distract Ashley.

Meg was expecting a baby, and the news might have cheered Ashley up, but Carly and her mother-sister had agreed on the way into town to wait until Brad-dad was back from wherever he'd gone.

Unable to bear Ashley's pale face and sorrowful eyes any longer, Carly excused herself and wandered toward the study. She'd set up the computer, she decided. Use this strange morning constructively.

School was closed on account of megasnow, but nothing stopped members of the McKettrick clan when they wanted to get somewhere. Meg had told Carly they were going to town, fired up her new Land Rover right after breakfast, acting all mysterious and sad, buckled a squirmy Mac into his car seat, and off they'd gone.

Carly, a sucker for adventure, had enjoyed the ride into town, over roads buried under a foot of snow. Once, Meg had even taken an overland route, causing Mac to giggle and Carly to shout, "Yee-haw!"

Even the plows weren't out yet—that's how deep the stuff was.

To Carly's surprise, someone had beaten her to the computer gig. The monitor was dark, but the machine was on, whirring quietly away in the otherwise silent room.

She sat down in the swivel chair, touched the mouse.

An email message popped up on the monitor screen.

Since Brad and Meg were big on personal privacy, Carly didn't actually read the email, but she couldn't help noticing that it was signed, "Love, Jack."

She barely knew Jack McCall, but she'd liked him. Which was more than could be said for Brad and Meg.

They clearly thought the man was bad news.

Carly bit her lower lip. If Jack had gone to all the trouble of writing that long email, she reasoned, her heart thumping a little, surely he'd intended to send it.

With so much going on—Carly had no idea what any of it actually was, except that it had obviously done a real number on Ashley, so it must be pretty heavy stuff—he'd probably just forgotten.

Carly took a deep breath, moved the cursor, and hit Send.

"Carly!" Meg called, clearly approaching.

Carly closed the message panel. "What?"

Meg appeared in the doorway of the study. "School's open after all," she said. "I just heard it on the kitchen radio."

Carly sighed. "Awesome," she said, meaning exactly the opposite.

Meg chuckled. "Get a move on, kiddo," she ordered.

"Are there snowshoes around here someplace?" Carly countered. "Maybe a dogsled and a team, so I can *mush* to school?"

"Hugely funny," Meg said, grinning. Like all the other grown-ups, she looked tired. "I'd drive you to school in the Land Rover, but I don't think I should leave Ashley just yet."

Carly agreed, with the teenage reluctance that was

surely expected of her, and resigned herself to the loss of that greatest of all occasions, a snow day.

Trudging toward the high school minutes later, she wondered briefly if she should have left that email in the outbox, maybe told Meg or Ashley about it.

But her friends were converging up ahead, laughing and hurling snowballs at each other, and she hurried to join them.

Ashley both hoped for and dreaded a call from Jack, but none came.

Not while Meg was there, and not when she left.

A ranch hand from Starcross brought Mrs. Wiggins back home, and Ashley was glad and grateful, but still wrung out. She felt dazed, disjointed, as though she were truly beside herself.

She slept.

She cooked.

She slept some more, and then cooked some more.

At four o'clock that afternoon, Brad showed up.

"He's gone," she said, meaning Jack, meeting her taciturn-looking brother at the back door. "Are you happy now?"

"You know I'm not," Brad said, moving past her to enter the house when she would have blocked his way. He helped himself to coffee and, out of spite, Ashley didn't tell him it was decaf. If he expected a buzz from the stuff, something to jump-start the remainder of his day, he was in for a disappointment.

"Are Ardith and Rachel safe?" she asked.

"Yes," Brad answered, leaning back against the counter to sip his no-octane coffee and study her. "You all right?"

"Oh, I'm just fabulous, thank you."

"Ashley, give it up, will you? You know Jack couldn't stay."

"I also know the decision was mine to make, Brad—not yours."

Her brother gave a heavy sigh. She could see how drained he was, but she wouldn't allow herself to feel sorry for him. Much. "You'll get over this," he told her, after a long time.

"Gee, thanks," she said, wiping furiously at her already-clean counters, keeping as far from Brad as she could. "That makes it all better."

"Meg's going to have a baby," Brad said, out of the blue, a few uncomfortable moments later. "In the spring."

Ashley froze.

Olivia had twins.

Now Meg and Brad were adding to their family, something she should have been glad about, considering that Meg had suffered a devastating miscarriage a year after Mac was born and there had been some question as to whether or not she could have more children.

"Congratulations," Ashley said stiffly, unable to look at him.

"You'll get your chance, Ash. The right man will come along and—"

"The right man *came* along, Brad," Ashley snapped, "and now he's gone."

But at least, this time, Jack had said goodbye.

This time, he hadn't wanted to go.

Small consolations, but something.

Brad set his mug aside, crossed to Ashley, took her shoulders in his hands. "I'd have done anything," he said hoarsely, "to make this situation turn out differently."

Ashley believed him, but it didn't ease her pain.

She let herself cry, and Brad pulled her close and held her, big brother-style, his chin propped on top of her head.

"O'Ballivan tough," he reminded her. It was their version of something Meg's family, the McKettricks, said to each other when things got rocky.

"O'Ballivan tough," she agreed.

But her voice quavered when she said it.

She felt anything *but* tough.

She'd go on, just the same, because she had no other choice.

Jack arrived in Earp-country at eleven forty-five that morning and, after paying the pilot of the two-seat Cessna he'd chartered in Phoenix, climbed into a waiting taxi. Fortunately, Tombstone wasn't a big town, so he wouldn't be late for his meeting with Chad Lombard.

Anyway, he was used to cutting it close.

There were a lot of tourists around, as Jack had feared. He'd hoped the local police would be notified, find some low-key way to clear the streets before the shootout took place.

Some of them might be Lombard's men.

And some of them might be Feds.

Because of the innocent bystanders and because both the DEA and the FBI had valid business of their own with Lombard, Jack had taken a chance and tipped them off while waiting for the commuter jet to take off from Flagstaff.

He stashed his gear bag behind a toilet in a gas station restroom, tucked his Glock into his pants, covered it with his shirt and stepped out onto the windy street.

If he hadn't been in imminent danger of being picked off by Lombard or one of the creeps who worked for the bastard, he might have found the whole thing pretty funny.

He even amused himself by wishing he'd bought a round black hat and a gunslinger's coat, so he'd look the part.

Wyatt Earp, on the way to the OK Corral.

He was strolling down a wooden sidewalk, pretending to take in the famous sights, when the cell phone rang in the pocket of his jean jacket.

"Yo," he answered.

"You called in the Feds!" Lombard snarled.

"Yeah," Jack answered. "You're outnumbered, bucko."

"I'm going to take you out last," Lombard said. "Just so you can watch all these mommies and daddies and little kiddies in cowboy hats bite the freaking dust!"

Jack's blood ran cold. He'd known this was a very real possibility, of course—that was the main reason he'd called in reinforcements—but he'd hoped, against all reason, that even Lombard wouldn't sink that low.

After all, the man had a daughter of his own.

"Where are you?" Jack asked, with a calmness he sure as hell didn't feel. Worse yet, the weakness was rising inside him again, threatening to drop him to the ground.

Lombard laughed then, an eerie, brittle sound. "Look up," he said.

Jack lifted his eyes.

Lombard stood on a balcony overlooking the main street, opposite Jack. And he was wearing an Earp hat and a long coat, holding a rifle in one hand.

"Gun!" Jack yelled. "Everybody out of the street!"

The crowd panicked and scattered every which way, bumping into each other, screaming. Scrambling to shield children and old ladies and little dogs wearing neckerchiefs.

Lombard raised the rifle as Jack drew the Glock.

But neither of them got a chance to fire.

Another shot ripped through the shining January day, struck Lombard, and sent him toppling, in what seemed like slow motion, over the balcony railing, which gave way picturesquely behind him, like a bit from an old movie.

People shrieked in rising terror, as vulnerable to any gunmen Lombard might have brought along as backup as a bunch of ducks in a pond.

Feds rushed into the street, hustling the tourists into restaurants and hotel lobbies and souvenir shops, crowd control at its finest, if a little late.

Government firepower seemed to come out of the woodwork.

Somebody was taking pictures—Jack was aware of a series of flashes at the periphery of his vision.

He walked slowly toward the spot where Chad Lombard lay, either dead or dying, oblivious to the pandemonium he would have enjoyed so much.

Lombard stared blindly up at the blue, blue sky, a crimson patch spreading over the front of his collarless white shirt. Damned if he hadn't pinned a star-shaped badge to his coat, just to complete the outfit.

The Feds closed in, the sniper who had taken Lombard out surely among them. A hand came to rest on Jack's shoulder.

More pictures were snapped.

"Thanks, McCall," a voice said, through a buzzing haze.

He didn't look up at the agent, the longtime acquaintance he'd called from the plane in Flagstaff. Taking the cell phone out of his pocket, he turned it slowly in one hand, still studying Lombard.

Lombard didn't look like a killer, a drug runner. Jack could see traces of Rachel in the man's altar-boy features.

"We had trouble spotting him until he climbed out onto that balcony," Special Agent Fletcher said. "By our best guess, he stole the gunslinger getup from one of those old-time picture places—"

"Why didn't you clear the streets earlier?" Jack demanded.

"Because we got here about five seconds before you did," Fletcher answered. "Are you all right, McCall?"

Jack nodded, then shook his head.

Fletcher helped Jack to his feet. "Which is it?" he rasped. "Yes or no?"

Jack swayed.

His vision shrank to a pinpoint, then disappeared entirely.

"I guess it's no," he answered, just before he lost consciousness.

Chapter 9

The first sound Jack recognized was a steady *beep-beep-beep*. He was in a hospital bed, then, God knew where. Probably going about the business of dying.

"Jack?"

He struggled to open his eyes. Saw his father looming over him, a pretty woman standing wearily at the old man's side. If it hadn't been for her, Jack would have thought he was hallucinating.

Dr. William "Bill" McKenzie smiled, switched on the requisite lamp on the wall above Jack's head.

The spill of light made him wince.

"I see you've still got all your hair," Jack said, very slowly and in a dry-throated rasp. "Either that, or that's one fine rug perched on top of your head."

Bill laughed, though his eyes glistened with tears. Maybe they were goodbye tears. "You always were a smart-ass," he said. "This is my real hair. And speaking of hair, yours is too long. You look like a hippie."

People still used the word *hippie*?

Obviously, his dad's generation did. For all he knew, Bill McKenzie had been a hippie, once upon a time. There was so much they didn't know about each other.

"How did you find me?" Jack asked. The things he felt were too deep to leap right into—there had to be a transition here, a gradual shift.

"It wasn't too hard to track you down. You were all over the Internet, the TV and the newspapers after that incident in Tombstone. You were treated in Phoenix, and then some congressman's aide got in touch with me—soon as you were strong enough, I had you brought home, where you belong."

Home, Jack thought. *To die?*

Jack's gaze slid to the woman, who looked uncomfortable. *My stepmother*, he thought, and felt a fresh pang of loss because his mom should have been standing there beside his dad, not this stranger.

"Abigail," Bill explained hoarsely. "My wife."

"If you'll excuse me," Abigail said, after a nod of greeting, and headed for the nearest exit.

Bill sighed, trailed her with his eyes.

Jack glimpsed tenderness in those eyes, and peace. "How long have I been here?" he asked, after a long time.

"Just a few days," Bill answered. He cleared his throat, looking for a moment as though he might make a run for the corridor, just as Abigail had done. "You're in serious condition, Jack. Not out of the woods by any means."

"Yeah," Jack said, trying to accept what was probably inevitable. "I know. And you're here to say good-bye?"

The old man's jaw clamped down hard, the way it used to when he was about to give one of his sons hell for some infraction and then ground him for a decade. "I'm *here*," he said, almost in a growl, "because you're my son, and I thought you were dead."

"Like Mom."

Bill's eyes, hazel like Jack's own, flashed. "We'll talk about your mother another time," he said. "Right now, boy, you're in one hell of a fix, and that's going to be enough to handle without going into all the *other* issues."

"It's a bone marrow thing," Jack recalled, but he was thinking about Ashley. She wasn't much for media, but even she had probably seen him on the news. "Something to do with a toxin manufactured especially for me."

"You need a marrow donor," Bill told him bluntly. "It's your only chance, and, frankly, it will be touch and go. I've already been tested, and so have your brothers. Bryce is the only match."

A chance, however small, was more than Jack had expected to get. He must have been mulling a lot of things over on an unconscious level while he was submerged in oblivion, though, because there was a sense of clarity behind the fog enveloping his brain.

"Bryce," he said. "The baby."

"He wouldn't appreciate being called that," Bill replied, with a moist smile. His big hand rested on Jack's, squeezed his fingers together. "Your brother will be ready when you are."

Jack imagined Ashley, the way she'd looked and smelled and felt, warm and naked beneath him. He saw her baking things, playing with the kitten, parking herself in front of the computer, her brow furrowed slightly with confusion and that singular determination of hers.

If he got through this thing, he could go back to her.

Swap his old life for a new one, straight across, and never look back.

But suppose some buddy of Lombard's decided to step up and take care of unfinished business?

No, he decided, discouraged to the core of his being. There were too many unknown factors; he couldn't start things up with Ashley again, even if he got lucky and survived the ordeal he was facing, until he was sure she'd be in no danger.

"So when is this transplant supposed to go down?" he asked his dad.

"Yesterday wouldn't have been too soon," Bill replied. "They were only waiting for you to stabilize a little."

"I'd like to see my brothers," Jack said, but even as he spoke, the darkness was already sucking him back under, into the dreamless place churning like an ocean beneath the surface of his everyday mind. "If they're speaking to me, that is."

Bill dashed at his wet eyes with the back of one large hand. "They're speaking to you, all right," he replied. "But if you pull through, you can expect all three of them to read you the riot act for disappearing the way you did."

If you pull through.

Jack sighed. "Fair enough," he said.

Reaching deep into her mind and heart in the days after Jack's leaving, Ashley had found a new strength.

She'd absorbed the media blitz, with Jack and Chad Lombard playing their starring roles, with a stoicism that surprised even her. After the first wave, she'd stopped watching, stopped reading.

Enough was enough.

Every sound bite, every news clip, every article brought an overwhelming sense of sorrow and relief, in equal measures.

Two days after the Tombstone Showdown, as the reporters had dubbed it, a pair of FBI agents had turned up at Ashley's door.

They'd been long on questions and short on answers.

All they'd really been willing to divulge was that she was in no danger from Chad Lombard's organization; some of its members had been taken into federal custody in Arizona. The rest had scattered to the four winds.

And Jack was alive.

That gave her at least a measure of relief.

It was the questions that fed her sorrow, innocuous and routine though they were. Something about the tone of them, a certain sad resignation—there were no details forthcoming, either in the media or from the visiting agents, but she sensed that Jack was still in trouble.

Had Jack McCall told her anything about his association with any particular government agencies and if so, what? the agents wanted to know.

Had he left anything behind when he went away?

If Mr. McCall agreed, would she wish to visit him in a location that would be disclosed at a later time?

No, Jack hadn't told her anything, beyond the things the FBI already knew, and no, he hadn't left anything

behind. Yes, she wanted to see him and she'd appreciate it if they'd disclose the mysterious location.

They refused, though politely, and left, promising
to contact her later.

After that, she'd heard nothing more.

Since then, Ashley had been seized by a strange and
fierce desperation, a need to do *something*, but she had
no idea where Jack was, or what kind of condition he
was in. She only knew that he'd collapsed in Tombstone—there had been pictures in the newspapers and
on the web.

Both Brad and Tanner had "their people" beating the
bushes for any scrap of information, but either they'd
really come up with nothing, as they claimed, or they
simply didn't want Jack McCall found. Ever.

Melissa was searching, too; even though she wasn't
any fonder of Jack than Brad and Olivia were, she and
Ashley had the twin link. Melissa knew, better than any
of the others, exactly what her sister was going through.

The results of that investigation? So far, zip.

After a week, Jack disappeared from the news, dis-
placed by accounts of piracy at sea, the president's latest budget proposal, and the like.

By the first of February, Ashley was very good at
pretending she didn't care where Jack McCall was, what
he was doing, whether or not he would—or could—
come back.

She'd decided to Get on with Her Life.

Carly and Sophie had spent hours with her, after
school, when they weren't rehearsing their parts in the
drama club's upcoming play, fleshing out one of the
websites Jack had created, showing her how to surf

the Net, how to run searches, how to access and reply to email.

In fact, they'd both managed to earn special credit at school for undertaking the task.

Slowly, Ashley had begun to understand the mysteries of navigating cyberspace.

She quickly became proficient at web surfing, and especially at monitoring her modest but attractive website, already bringing in more business than she knew what to do with.

The B&B was booked solid for Valentine's Day weekend, and the profit margin on her "Hearts, Champagne and Roses" campaign looked healthy indeed.

With two weeks to go before the holiday arrived, she was already baking and freezing tarts, some for her guests to enjoy, and some for the annual dance at the Moose Lodge. This year, the herd was raising money to resurface the community swimming pool.

She'd agreed to serve punch and help provide refreshments, not out of magnanimity, but because she baked for the dance every year. And, okay, partly because she knew everybody in town was talking about her latest romantic disaster—this one had gone national, with CNN coverage and an article in *People*, not that she'd been specifically mentioned—and she wanted to show them all that she wasn't moping. No, sir, not her.

She was O'Ballivan tough.

If she still cried herself to sleep once in a while, well, nobody needed to know that. Nobody except Mrs. Wiggins, her small, furry companion, always ready to comfort her with a cuddle.

As outlined in the piece in *People*, Ardith and Rachel were back home, in a suburb of Phoenix, happily reunited with the rest of the family.

Yes, Ashley thought, sitting there at her computer long after she should have taken a bubble bath and gone to bed, day by day, moment by moment, she was getting over Jack.

Really and truly.

Or not.

Glancing out the window, she saw Melissa's car, a red glow under the streetlight, swinging into her driveway.

"Good," Ashley said to Mrs. Wiggins, who was perched on her right shoulder like a parrot. "I could use a little distraction."

Melissa was just coming through the back door when Ashley reached the kitchen. Her hair was flecked with snow and her grin was wide. Looking askance at Mrs. Wiggins, now nestling into her basket in front of the fireplace, Ashley's twin gave a single nose twitch and carefully kept her distance.

"It happened!" she crowed, hauling off her red tailored coat. "Alex got the prosecutor's job, and I'm going to be one of his assistants! I start the first of March and I've already got a line on a condo in Scottsdale—"

"Wonderful," Ashley said.

Melissa narrowed her beautiful eyes in mock suspicion. "Well, *that* was an enthusiastic response," she replied, draping the coat over the back of one of the chairs at the table.

Ashley's smile felt wobbly on her mouth, and a touch too determined. "If this is what you want, then I'm happy for you. I'm going to miss you a lot, that's all. Except for when you were in law school, we've never really been apart."

Melissa approached, laid a winter-chilled hand on each of Ashley's shoulders. "I'll only be two hours away," she said. "You'll visit me a lot, and of course I'll come back to Stone Creek as often as I can."

"No, you won't," Ashley said, turning away to start some tea brewing, so she wouldn't have to struggle to keep that stupid, slippery smile in place any longer. "You'll be too busy with your caseload, and you know it."

"I need to get away," Melissa said, so sadly that Ashley immediately turned to face her again, no longer concerned about hiding her own misgivings.

"Because?" Ashley prompted.

Melissa rarely looked vulnerable—a good lawyer appeared confident at all times, she often said—but she did then. That sheen in her eyes—was she crying?

"Because," Melissa said, after pushing back her spirally mane of hair with one hand, "things are heating up between Dan and the waitress. Her name is Holly and according to one of the receptionists at the office, they've been in Kruller's Jewelry Store three times in the last week, looking at rings."

Ashley sighed, wiped her hands on her patchwork apron, her own creation, made up of quilt scraps. "Sit down, Melissa," she said.

To her amazement, Melissa sat.

Of the two of them, Melissa had always been the leader, the one who decided things and gave impromptu motivational speeches.

Forgetting the tea preparations, Ashley took the chair closest to her sister's. "That's why you're leaving Stone Creek?" she asked quietly. "Because Dan and this Holly person might get married?"

"'Might,' nothing," Melissa huffed, but her usually straight shoulders sagged a little beneath her very professional white blouse. "As hot and heavy as things were between Dan and me, he never said a *word* about looking at engagement rings. If he's shopping for diamonds, he's *serious* about this woman."

"And?"

Melissa flushed a vibrant pink, with touches of crimson. "And I *might* still be *just a little* in love with him," she admitted.

"You can't have it all, Melissa," Ashley reminded her sister gently. "No one does. You made a choice and now you either have to change it or accept things as they are and move on."

Melissa blinked. "That's easy for *you* to say!"

"Is it?" Ashley asked.

"What am I saying?" Melissa immediately blurted out. "Ash, I'm sorry—I know the whole Jack thing has been—"

"We're not talking about Jack," Ashley said, a mite stiffly. "We're talking about Dan—and you. He's probably marrying this woman on the rebound—if the rumors about the rings are even true in the first place—because he really cared about you. And he might be making the mistake of a lifetime."

"That's *his* problem," Melissa snapped.

"Don't be a bitch," Ashley replied. "You didn't want him, or the life he offered, remember? What did you expect, Melissa? That Dan would wait around until you retire from your seat on the Supreme Court someday, and write your memoirs?"

"Whose side are you on, anyway?" Melissa asked peevishly.

"Yours," Ashley said, and she meant it. "Just talk to Dan before you take the job in Phoenix, Melissa. Please?"

"*He's* the one who broke it off!"

"Don't you want to be sure things can't be patched up?"

"Have you been paying attention? It's *too late*, Ashley."

"Maybe it is, maybe it isn't," Ashley said, getting up to resume the tea making. "You'll never know if you don't talk things over with Dan while there's still time."

"What am I supposed to do?" Melissa demanded, losing a little steam now. "Drive out there to the back of beyond, knock on his door, and ask him if he'd like to live in a city and be Mr. Melissa O'Ballivan? I can tell you right now what the answer would be—and besides, what if I interrupted—well—*something*—?"

"Like what? Chandelier-swinging sex? Dan has kids, Melissa—he and Holly Hot-Biscuits probably don't go at it in the living room on a regular basis."

Melissa sputtered out a laugh, wholly against her will. *"Holly Hot-Biscuits?"* she crowed. "Ashley O'Ballivan, could it be that you actually have a *racy* side?"

"You'd be surprised," Ashley said, recalling, with a well-hidden pang, some of the sex she and Jack had had. A chandelier would have been superfluous.

"Maybe I wouldn't," Melissa teased. At least she'd cheered up a little. Perhaps that could be counted as progress. "You miss Jack a lot, don't you?"

"When I let myself," Ashley admitted, though guardedly, concentrating on scooping tea leaves into a china pot. "The other night, I dreamed he was—he was standing at the foot of my bed. I could see through him, because he was—dead."

Melissa softened, in that quicksilver way she had. Tough one minute, tender the next—that was Melissa O'Ballivan. "Jack can't be dead," she reasoned, looking as though she wanted to get up from her chair, cross the room, and wrap Ashley in a sisterly embrace, but wisely refraining.

Ashley wasn't accepting hugs these days—from anybody.

She felt too bruised, inside and out.

"Why not?" she asked reasonably, over the sound of the water she ran to fill the kettle.

"Because someone would have told Tanner," Melissa said, very gently. "Come to Scottsdale with me, Ash. Right now, this weekend. Help me decide on the right condo. It would be good for you to get away, change your perspective, soak up some of that delicious sunshine—"

The idea had a certain appeal—she was sick of snow, for one thing—but there was the B&B to think about. She had guests coming for Valentine's Day, after all, and lots of preparations to make. She'd even rented out her private quarters, planning to sleep on the couch in her study.

"Maybe after the holiday," she said. Except that she'd have skiers then, with any luck at all—she'd been pitching that on her new blog, on the website. And after that, it would be time to think about Easter.

"Can you handle Valentine's Day, Ash?" Melissa asked, with genuine concern. "You're still pretty raw."

"And you're not?" Ashley challenged, but gently. "Yes, I can 'handle' it, because I have to." She brought two cups to the table, along with milk and sugar cubes. "What is it with us, Melissa? Brad got it right with Meg, and Olivia with Tanner. Why can't we?"

"I think we're romantically challenged," Melissa decided.

"Or stubborn and proud," Ashley pointed out archly. Her meaning was clear: *Melissa* was stubborn and proud. *She* would have crawled over broken glass for Jack McCall, if it meant they could be together.

Not that she particularly wanted anyone else to know that.

All of which probably made her a candidate for an episode of *Dr. Phil*, during Unhealthy Emotional Dependency week. She would serve as the bad example. *This could happen to you.*

"Don't knock pride," Melissa said cheerfully. "And some people call stubbornness 'persistence.'"

"*Some* people can put a spin on anything," Ashley countered. "Are you going to clear things up with Dan before you leave, or not?"

"Not," Melissa said brightly.

"Chicken."

"You got it. If that man looks me in the eye and says he's in love with Holly Hot-Biscuits, I'll die of mortification on the spot."

"No, you won't. You're too strong. And at least you'd know where you stand." *I'd give anything for another chance with Jack.*

"I *know* where I stand," Melissa answered, pouring tea for Ashley and then for herself, and then warming her hands around the cup instead of drinking the brew. "Up the creek without a paddle."

"That's a mixed metaphor," Ashley couldn't help pointing out.

"Whatever," Melissa said.

And that, for the time being, was the end of the discussion.

A week after the transplant, the jury was still out on whether the procedure had been successful or not, but by pulling certain strings Jack had been reluctantly released from the hospital, partly on the strength of his well-respected father's promise to make sure he was looked after and did not overexert himself. He went home to Oak Park, Illinois, his old hometown, and let Abigail and the old man install him in his boyhood bedroom in the big brick Federal on Shady Lane.

Not that there were any leaves on the trees to provide shade.

Abigail, though shy around him, had taken pains to get his room ready for occupancy—she'd put fresh sheets on the bed, dusted, aired the place out.

The obnoxious rock-star posters, a reminder of his checkered youth, were still on the walls. The antiquated computer, which he'd built himself from scavenged components, remained on his desk, in front of the windows. Hockey sticks and baseball bats occupied every corner.

The sight of it all swamped Jack, made him miss his mother more acutely than ever.

And that was nothing compared to the way he missed Ashley.

Bryce, soon to be an optometrist, appeared in the doorway. He was in his mid-twenties, but he looked younger to Jack.

"You're going to make it, Jack," Bryce said, and he spoke in a man's voice, not a boy's.

So many things had changed.

So many hadn't.

"Thanks to you, maybe I will."

"No maybe about it," Bryce argued.

There was a brief, awkward pause. "What do you think of Abigail?" Jack asked, pulling back the chair at his desk and sitting down. He still tired too easily.

Bryce closed the door, took a seat on the edge of Jack's bed. Loosely interlaced his fingers and let his hands dangle between his blue-jeaned knees. "She's been good for Dad. He was a real wreck after Mom died."

"I guess that must have been a hard time," Jack ventured, turning his head to look out over the street lined with skeleton trees, waiting for spring.

"It was pretty bad," Bryce admitted. "Did Dad tell you the government is having your headstone removed from the cemetery at Arlington, and the empty box dug up?"

"Guess they need the space," Jack said, as an infinite sadness washed over him. Once, he'd been a hotshot. Now he was sick of guns and violence and war.

"Yeah," Bryce agreed quietly. "Who's the woman?"

Jack tensed. "What woman?"

"The one you mentioned in the email you sent to Dad's office."

Jack closed his eyes briefly, longing for Ashley. Wondering if she'd finally mastered the fine art of computing well enough to check out the Sent Messages folder.

"I'm getting engaged on Valentine's Day," Bryce

said, to fill the gap left by Jack's studied silence. "Her name is Kathy. We went to college together."

"Congratulations," Jack managed.

"I wanted to be like you, you know," Bryce went on. "Raise hell. Get sent away to military school. Maybe even bite the sand in Iraq."

Jack managed a tilt at one corner of his mouth, enough to pass for a grin—he hoped. "Thank God you changed your mind," he said. "Mom and Dad—after I disappeared—how were they?"

"Devastated," Bryce answered.

Jack shoved a hand through his hair. Sighed. What had he expected? That they'd go merrily on, as if nothing had happened? *Oh, well, Jack's gone, but we still have three sons left, don't we, and they're all going to graduate school.*

"I need to see Mom's grave," he said.

"I'll take you there," Bryce responded immediately. "After my last class, of course."

Jack smiled. "Of course."

Bryce rose, made that leaving sound by huffing out his breath. "Be nice to Abigail, okay?" he said. "Dad loves her a lot, and she's really trying to fit in without usurping Mom's place."

"I haven't been nice?"

"You've been…reserved."

"Staying alive has been taking up all my time," Jack answered. "Again, thanks to you, I've got a fighting chance. I'll never forget what you did, Bryce. No two ways about it, donating marrow hurts."

Bryce cleared his throat, reached for the doorknob, but didn't quite turn it. "It could take time," he said, letting Jack's comment pass. "All of us being a family again, I mean. But don't give up on us, okay? Don't just take off or something, because I can't even tell you how hard that would be for Dad. He's already lost so much."

"I'm not going anywhere," Jack promised. "I might need that grave at Arlington after all, you know. Maybe they shouldn't be too quick to lay the new resident to rest."

Bryce flushed. "Who's the woman?" he asked again.

Jack met his brother's gaze. "Her name is Ashley O'Ballivan. She runs a bed-and-breakfast in Stone Creek, Arizona. Do me a favor, little brother. Don't get any ideas about calling her up and telling her where I am."

"Why don't *you* call her?"

"Because I still don't know if I'm going to live or die."

Bryce finally turned the knob, opened the door to go. "Maybe she'd like to hear from you, either way. Spend whatever time you have left—"

"And maybe she'd like to get on with her life," Jack broke in brusquely.

After Bryce was gone, Jack booted up the ancient computer—or tried to, anyhow. The cheapest pay-as-you-go cell phone on the market probably had more power.

Giving up on surfing the web, catching up on all he'd missed since Tombstone, he tried to interest himself in the pile of high school yearbooks stacked on a shelf in his closet.

What a hotheaded little jerk he'd been, he thought. A throwback, especially in comparison to his brothers.

He revisited his junior year, flipping pages until he found Molly Henshaw, the love of his adolescent life. Although he hadn't been a praying man, Jack had begged God to let him marry Molly someday.

Looking at her class picture, he remembered that she'd had acne, which she tried to cover with stuff closer to orange than flesh tone. Big hair, too. And a come-hither look in her raccoonlike eyes. Even in the photograph, he could see the clumps of mascara coating her lashes.

Must have been the come hither, he decided.

And thank God for unanswered prayers.

Having come to that conclusion, Jack decided to go downstairs, where Abigail was undoubtedly flitting around the kitchen. Time to make a start at getting to know his father's new wife, though their acquaintance might be a short one if his body rejected Bryce's marrow.

For his dad's sake, because there were so many things he couldn't make up for, he had to give it a shot. Ironically, he knew it was what his mother would have wanted.

Later, he'd log on to his dad's computer, in the den.

See if Ashley's website was up and running.

With luck, there would be a picture of her, smiling like the welcoming hostess she was, dressed in something flowered, with her hair pulled back into that prim French braid he always wanted to undo.

For now, that would have to be enough.

Abigail was in the kitchen, the room where Jack had had so many conversations with his mother. Feminine and modestly pretty, Abigail wore a flowered apron, her hair was pinned up in a loose chignon at her nape, and her hands were white with flour.

She smiled shyly at Jack. "Your father likes peach pie above all things," she confided.

"I'm pretty fond of it myself," Jack answered, grinning. "You're a baker, Abigail?"

His stepmother shrugged. She couldn't have been more different, physically anyway, from his mom. She'd been tall and full-figured, always lamenting humorously that she should have lived in the 1890s, when women with bosoms and hips were appreciated. Abigail was petite and trim; she probably gardened, maybe knitted and crocheted.

His mother had loved to play golf and sail, and to Jack's recollection, she'd never baked a pie or worn an apron in her life.

"A baker and a few other things, too," Abigail said, with a quirky little smile playing briefly on her mouth. "I retired from real estate a year before Bill and I met. Sold my company for a chunk of cash and decided to spend the rest of my life doing what I love…baking, planting flowers, sewing. Oh, and fussing over my husband."

Jack swiped a slice of peach from the bowl waiting to be poured into the pie pan, and she didn't slap his hand. "Married before?" he asked casually. "Any kids?"

Abigail shook her head, and a few tendrils of her graying auburn hair escaped the chignon. "I was too busy with my career," she said, without a hint of regret. "Besides, I always promised myself I'd wait for the right man, no matter how long it took. Turned out to be Bill McKenzie."

He'd underestimated Abigail, that much was clear. She was an independent woman, living the life she chose to live, not someone looking for an easy life married to a prosperous dentist. In fact, Abigail probably had a lot more money than his dad did, and that was saying something.

"He's happy, Abigail. Thank you for that." Jack reached for a second slice, and this time, she did swat his hand, smiling and shaking her head.

She took a cereal bowl from the cupboard, scooped in a generous portion of fruit with a soup spoon, and handed him the works.

Jack decided he knew all he needed to know about Abigail—she loved his father, and that was as good as it got. Leaning in a little, he kissed her cheek.

"Welcome aboard, Abigail," he said hoarsely.

She smiled. "Thanks," she replied, and went back to building the pie.

Chapter 10

"Ms. O'Ballivan? My name is Bryce McKenzie and I—"

Ashley shifted the telephone receiver from her left ear to her right, hunching one shoulder to hold it in place, busy rolling out pie dough on the butcher's block next to the counter. "I'm sorry, Mr. McKenzie," she said, distracted, "but we're all booked up for Valentine's Day—"

The man replied with an oddly familiar chuckle. Something about the timbre of it struck a chord somewhere deep in Ashley's core. "Excuse me?" he said.

"The bed-and-breakfast—I guess I just assumed you were calling because of the publicity my website's been getting—"

Again, that sense of familiarity flittered, in the pit of Ashley's stomach now.

"I'm Jack McKenzie's brother," Bryce explained.

McKenzie. The name finally registered in Ashley's befuddled memory, the one Jack had admitted leaving behind so long ago. "Oh," she said, stretching the phone cord taut so she could collapse into a kitchen chair. *"Oh."*

"I probably shouldn't be calling you like this, but—well—"

"Is Jack all right?"

Bryce McKenzie sighed. "Yes and no," he said carefully.

Ashley put a floury hand to her heart, smearing her T-shirt with white finger marks. "Tell me about the 'no' part, Mr. McKenzie," she said.

"Bryce," he corrected. And then, after clearing his throat, he explained that Jack had needed a bone marrow transplant. The patient was up and around, and he was taking antirejection drugs, but he didn't seem to be recovering—or regressing—and his family was worried.

They'd had a family meeting, Bryce concluded, one Jack hadn't been privy to, and decided as a unit that seeing Ashley again might be the boost he needed to get better.

Ashley listened with her eyes closed and her heart hammering.

"Where is he now?" she asked, very quietly, when Bryce had finished.

"We live in Chicago, so he's here," he answered. "There's plenty of room at my dad's place, if you wanted to stay there. I mean, if you even want to come in the first place, that is."

Ashley's heart thrummed. Valentine's Day was a

week away and she had to be there to greet her guests, make them comfortable—didn't she? This was her chance to take the business to a whole new level, make some progress, stay caught up on her payments to Brad and fortify her faltering savings.

And none of that was as important as seeing Jack again.

"I think," she said shakily, "that if Jack wanted to see me, he would have called himself."

"He wants to make sure he's going to live through this first," Bryce answered candidly. Then, after sucking in an audible breath, he added, "Will you come? It could make all the difference in his recovery—or, at least, that's what we're hoping."

Ashley looked around her kitchen, cluttered now with the accoutrements of serious cooking. The freezer was full, the house was ready for the onslaught of lovers planning a romantic getaway.

How could she leave now?

How could she *stay*?

"I'll be there as soon as I can book a flight," she heard herself say.

"One of us will pick you up at O'Hare," Bryce said, his voice light with relief. "Just call back with your flight number and arrival time."

Ashley wrote down the cell numbers he gave her and promised to get in touch with him as soon as she had the necessary information.

"This is crazy," she told Mrs. Wiggins, as soon as she'd hung up.

"Meooow," Mrs. Wiggins replied, curling against Ashley's ankle.

Having made the decision, Ashley was full of sudden energy. She made airline reservations for the next day, flying out of Flagstaff, connecting in Phoenix, and then going on to Chicago. When that was done, she called Bryce back.

"You're sure Jack wants to see me?" she asked, having second thoughts.

"I'm sure," Bryce said, with a smile in his voice.

The next call was to Melissa, at her office, and Ashley was almost panicking by then. The moment Melissa greeted her with a curious "Hello"—Ashley never called her at work—the whole thing spilled out.

Ashley held her breath, after the spate of words, awaiting Melissa's response.

"I see," Melissa said cautiously.

"I might be back before Valentine's Day," Ashley blurted, anxious to assuage her sister's misgivings about Jack, "but I can't be absolutely sure, and I need you to cover for me if necessary."

"I don't know beans about running a bed-and-breakfast," Melissa said gamely, "much less *cooking*. But I'll be there, Ash. Get your bags packed."

Tears burned Ashley's eyes. She could always count on Melissa, on any member of her family, to come through in a pinch. Why had she doubted that, even for a moment? "Thanks, Melissa."

"You'll have to send the cat to Olivia's place," Melissa warned, though her tone was good-natured. "You know how my allergies flare up when I'm around anything with fur."

"I know," Ashley said sweetly, "that you're a hypochondriac. But I love you anyway."

"Gee, thanks," Melissa replied. "No cat," she clarified firmly. "The deal's off if Olivia won't take him."

"Her," Ashley said, smiling. "How many male cats do you know with the name 'Mrs. Wiggins'?"

"I don't know *any* cats, whatever the gender," Melissa answered, "and I don't want to, either."

Ashley grinned to herself. "I'm sure Olivia will cat-sit," she conceded. "One more thing. Could you serve punch at the Valentine's Day dance? I promised and I did all this baking and I'm not sure I'll be back in time—"

"Oh, for Pete's sake," Melissa said. *"Yes,* if it comes to that, but you'd better do your darnedest to be home before the first guests arrive. I mean well, but we're taking a risk here. I'm not the least bit domestic, remember, and I could put you out of business without half trying."

Ashley laughed, sniffled once. "I promise I'll do my O'Ballivan best," she said. "Have you seen Dan yet?"

"No," Melissa said, "and don't mention his name again, if you don't mind."

After the call ended, Ashley wrestled her one and only suitcase down from the attic—she rarely traveled—and set it on her bed, open.

Mrs. Wiggins immediately climbed into it, as though determined to make the journey with her mistress.

"Not this time," Ashley said, gently removing the furball.

The next dilemma was, what did a person pack for a trip to Chicago in the middle of winter?

She decided on her trademark broomstick skirts, lightweight tunic sweaters, and some jeans, for good measure.

When she called Starcross Ranch, hoping to speak to Olivia, Tanner answered instead. Ashley asked if Mrs. Wiggins could bunk in for a few days.

"Sure," Tanner said, as Ashley had known he would. But he also wanted an explanation. "Where are you off to, in such a hurry?"

Tanner was Jack's friend, and he'd surely been as worried about him as Ashley had. Although it was possible that the two men had been in touch, her instincts told her they hadn't.

Ashley drew a deep breath, let it out slowly, and hoped she was doing the right thing by telling Tanner. And by jetting off to Chicago when Jack hadn't asked her to come.

"Jack's in Chicago," she said. "He's had a bone marrow transplant—something to do with the toxin—and his family is worried about him. He's not getting worse, but he's not getting better, either."

Tanner murmured an exclamation. "I see," he said. "Jack didn't call you himself?"

"No," Ashley admitted, her shoulders sagging a little.

Tanner considered that, must have decided against giving an opinion, one way or the other. "You'll keep me in the loop?" he asked presently.

"Yes," Ashley said.

"I'll be there to get the cat sometime this afternoon. Do you want a ride to the airport?"

"I've got that covered," Ashley replied. "Thanks, Tanner. I really appreciate this."

"We're family," Tanner pointed out. "Brad could probably charter a jet—"

"I don't need a jet," Ashley interrupted, though gently. "And I'm not really ready to discuss any of this with Brad. Not just yet, anyhow."

"Is there a plan?" Tanner asked. "And if so, what is it?"

Ashley smiled, even though her eyes were burning again. "No plan," she said. "I'm not even sure Jack wants me there. But I have to see him, Tanner."

"Of course you do," Tanner agreed, sounding both relieved and resigned. "Brad is going to wonder where you've gone, though. He keeps pretty close tabs on his three little sisters, you know. But don't worry about that—I'll handle him."

She heard Olivia's voice in the background, asking what was going on.

"Let me talk to her," Ashley said, and told the whole story all over again.

"I don't like it that you're going alone," Olivia told her, a minute or so later. "I've got the babies to look after, and I think Sophie is coming down with a cold, but maybe Melissa could go along—"

"Melissa is going to house-sit," Ashley said. "And she'll have her hands full holding down the fort, especially if I'm not back before Valentine's Day. I'll be *fine,* Livie."

"You're sure? What if Jack—?"

"What if he doesn't want to see me? I'll handle it, Liv. I'm a big girl now, remember?"

Olivia's laugh was warm, and a little teary. "Godspeed, little sister," she said. "And call us when you get there."

"I will," Ashley said, thinking how lucky she was.

The next few hours passed in a haze of activity— there were project lists to make for Melissa, and dozens of other details, too.

As promised, Tanner showed up late that afternoon to collect a mewing Mrs. Wiggins in the small pet carrier Olivia had sent along.

"Tell Jack I said hello," Tanner said, as he was leaving.

Ashley nodded, and her brother-in-law planted a light kiss on the top of her head.

"Take care," he told her. And then he was gone.

Melissa showed up when she got off work, and she and Ashley went over the lists—which guests to put where, how to reheat the food she'd prepared ahead of time, frozen and carefully labeled, how to take reservations and run credit cards, and a myriad of other things.

Melissa looked overwhelmed, but in true O'Ballivan spirit, she vowed to do her best.

Knowing she wouldn't sleep if she stayed in Stone Creek that night, Ashley loaded her suitcase into the car and set out for Flagstaff, intending to check into a hotel near the airport and have a room-service supper.

Her flight was leaving at six-thirty the next morning.

Along the way, though, she pulled off onto the snowy road leading to the cemetery where her mother was buried, parked near Delia's grave, and waded toward the headstone.

There were no heartfelt words, no tears.

Ashley simply felt a need to be there, in that quiet place. Somehow, a sense of closure had stolen into her heart when she wasn't looking. She could let go now, move on.

The weather was bitterly cold, though, and she soon got back in her car and made her steady, careful way toward Flagstaff.

She would always love the mother she'd longed to have, she reflected, but it was time to go forward, appreciate the *living* people she loved, those who loved her in return: Brad and Meg, Olivia and Tanner, Melissa and little Mac and Carly and sweet Sophie and the babies.

And Jack.

She didn't obsess over what might happen when she arrived in Chicago. For once in her life, she was taking a risk, going for what she wanted.

And she wanted Jack McCall—McKenzie—who-ever he was.

Once she'd arrived in Flagstaff, she chose a hotel and checked in, ordered a bowl of cream of broccoli soup, ate it, and soaked in a warm bath until the chill seeped out of her bones. Most of it, anyway.

A part of her would remain frozen until she'd seen Jack for herself.

"You did *what*?" Jack demanded, after supper that night, when he and Bryce wound up the evening sitting in chairs in front of the fireplace. It had been a hectic thing, supper, with brothers and their wives, nieces and nephews, and even a few neighbors there to share in the meal celebrating Jack's return from the dead.

"I called Ashley O'Ballivan," Bryce repeated, with no more regret than he'd shown the first time. "She'll be here late tomorrow afternoon. I'm picking her up at O'Hare."

Jack sat back, absorbing the news. A part of him soared, anticipating Ashley's arrival. Another part wanted to find a place to hide out until she was gone again.

"You've got a lot of nerve, little brother," he finally said, with no inflection in his voice at all. "Especially considering that I told you I'm not ready to see her."

"Until you're sure you won't die," Bryce confirmed confidently. "Jack, *all* of us are terminal. Maybe you won't be around long. Maybe you'll live to be a hundred. But in the meantime, you need to see *this woman,* even if it's only to say goodbye."

Saying goodbye to Ashley the last time had been one of the hardest things Jack had ever had to do. Saying goodbye to her again, especially for eternity, might be more than he could bear.

His conscience niggled at him. What about what *Ashley* had to bear?

Jack closed his eyes. "I'll get you for this," he told his brother.

Bryce chuckled. "You'll have to get well first," he replied.

"You think you can take me?" Jack challenged, grinning now, both infuriated and relieved.

"I'm not a little kid anymore," Bryce pointed out. "I might be able to take you—even with all your paramilitary skills."

Jack opened his eyes, looked at his younger brother with new respect. "Maybe you could," he said.

Bryce stood, stretched and yawned mightily. "Better get back to my apartment," he said. "Busy day tomorrow."

Ashley, Jack thought, full of conflicting emotions he couldn't begin to identify. What was he so afraid of? Not commitment, certainly—at least as far as Ashley was concerned.

"After this," he told his departing brother, "mind your own business."

"Not a chance," Bryce said lightly.

And then he was gone.

The first signs of an approaching blizzard hit Chicago five minutes after Ashley's plane landed at O'Hare, and the landing had been so bumpy that her knuckles were white from gripping the armrests—letting go of them was a slow and deliberate process.

She was such a homebody, completely unsuited to an adventurer like Jack. If she'd had a brain in her head, she decided, gnawing at her lower lip, she would have turned right around and flown back to Arizona where she belonged, blizzard or no blizzard.

She waited impatiently while all the passengers in the rows ahead of hers gathered their coats and carry-ons and meandered up the aisle at the pace of spilled peanut butter.

They had all the time in the world, probably.

Ashley knew she might not.

She hurried up the Jetway when her turn finally came, having returned the flight attendant's farewell smile with a fleeting one of her own.

Finding her way along a maze of moving walkways took more time, and she was almost breathless when she finally stepped out of the secure area, scanning the waiting sea of strange faces. Bryce had promised to hold up a sign with her name on it, so they could recognize each other, but even standing on tiptoe, she didn't see one.

"Ashley?"

She froze, turned to see Jack standing at her elbow. A strangled cry, part sob and part something else entirely, escaped her.

He looked so thin, so pale. His eyes were, as Big John used to say, like two burned holes in a blanket.

"Hey," he said huskily.

Ashley swallowed, still unable to move. "Hey," she responded.

He grinned, resembling his old self a little more, and crooked his arm, and she took it.

"You're glad to see me?" she asked, afraid of the answer. His grin, after all, could have been a reflex.

"If I'd been given a choice," he replied, "I would have asked you not to come. But, yeah, I'm glad to see you."

"Good," Ashley said uncertainly, aware of the strangeness between them. And the ever-present electrical charge.

"My interfering brother is waiting over in baggage claim," he said. "Let's go find him, before this storm gets any worse and we get stuck in rush-hour traffic. It's a long drive out to Oak Park."

Ashley nodded, overjoyed to be there and, at the same time, wishing she'd stayed home.

Once she'd met Bryce McKenzie—he was taller than his brother, though not so broad in the shoulders—and collected her solitary, out-of-style suitcase, the three of them headed for the parking garage, Bryce carrying the bag.

Fortunately, Bryce drove a big SUV with four-wheel drive, and he didn't seem a bit worried about the weather. Ashley sat in the front passenger seat, while Jack climbed painfully into the back.

The snow was coming down so hard and so fast by then, and the traffic was so intense, that Ashley wondered if they would reach Oak Park alive.

They did, eventually, and all the McKenzies were waiting in the entryway of the large brick house when they pulled into the circular driveway out front.

Introductions were made—Jack's father and step-mother, his brothers and their wives, Bryce's fiancée,

Kathy—and most of their names went out of Ashley's head as soon as she'd heard them.

She could think of nothing—and no one—but Jack.

Jack, who'd sat silent in the backseat of his brother's SUV all the way from the airport. Bryce, bless his heart, had tried hard to keep the conversation going, asking Ashley if her flight had been okay, inquiring about Stone Creek and what it was like there.

Ashley, as uncomfortable in her own way as Jack was in his, had given sparse answers.

She shouldn't have come.

Just as she'd feared, Jack didn't want her there.

The McKenzies welcomed her heartily, though, and Mrs. McKenzie—Abigail—served a meat-loaf supper so delicious that Ashley made a mental note to ask for the recipe.

Jack, seated next to her, though probably not by his own choosing, ate sparingly, as she did, and said almost nothing.

"You must be tired," Jack's father said to her, when the meal was over and Ashley automatically got up to help clear the table. The older man's gaze shifted to his eldest son. "Jack, why don't you show Ashley to her room so she can rest?"

Jack nodded, gestured for Ashley to precede him, and followed her out of the dining room.

The base of the broad, curving staircase was just ahead.

Ashley couldn't help noticing how slowly Jack moved. He was probably exhausted. "You don't have to—"

"Ashley," he interrupted blandly, "I can still climb stairs."

She lowered her gaze, then forced herself to look at him again. "I'm sorry, Jack—I—I shouldn't have come, but—"

He drew the knuckles of his right hand lightly down the side of her cheek. "Don't be sorry," he said. "I guess—well—it's hard on my pride, your seeing me like this."

Ashley was honestly puzzled. Sure, he'd lost weight, and his color wasn't great, but he was still *Jack*. "Like what?"

Jack spread his arms, looked down at himself, met her eyes again. She saw misery and sorrow in his expression. "I might be dying, Ashley," he said. "I wanted you to remember me the way I was before."

Ashley stiffened. "You are *not* going to die, Jack McCall. I won't tolerate it."

He gave a slanted grin. "Is that so?" he replied. "What do you intend to do to prevent it, O'Ballivan?"

"Take a pregnancy test," Ashley said, without planning to at all.

Jack's eyes widened. "You think you're—?"

"Pregnant?" Ashley finished for him, lowering her voice lest the conversation carry into the nearby dining room.

"Yeah," Jack said, somewhat pointedly.

"I might be," Ashley said. This was yet another thing she hadn't allowed herself to think about—until now. "I'm late. *Very* late."

He took her elbow, squired her up the stairs with more energy than he'd shown since she'd come face-to-face with him at O'Hare. "Is that unusual?"

"Yes," Ashley whispered, *"it's unusual."*

He smiled, and a light spread into his eyes that hadn't

been there before. "You're not just saying this, are you? Trying to give me a reason to live or something like that?"

"If you can't come up with a reason to live, Jack Mc-Call," Ashley said, waving one arm toward the distant dining room, where his family had gathered, "you're in even sorrier shape than I thought."

He frowned. "Jack *McKenzie,*" he said, clearly thinking of something else. "I'm going by my real name now."

"Well, bully for you," Ashley said.

"'Bully for me'?" He laughed. "God, Ashley, you should have been born during the Roosevelt administration—the *Teddy* Roosevelt administration. Nobody says 'Bully for you' anymore."

Ashley folded her arms. "*I* do," she said.

His eyes danced—it was nice to know she was so entertaining—then went serious again. "Why are you here?"

She bristled. "You *know* why."

"No," Jack said, sounding honestly mystified. "I thought we agreed that I'd come back to Stone Creek after this was all over, and we'd stay apart until then."

Ashley's throat constricted as she considered the magnitude of what Jack was facing. "And *I* thought we agreed that we love each other. Whether you live or die, I want to be here."

Pain contorted his face. "Ashley—"

"I'm not going anywhere until I know what's going to happen to you," Ashley broke in. "When will you know whether the transplant worked or not?"

The change in him was downright mercurial; Jack's eyes twinkled again, and his features relaxed. He made a show of checking his watch. "I'm expecting an email from God at any minute," he teased.

"That isn't funny!"

"Not much is, these days." He took her upper arms in his hands. "Ashley, as soon as this blizzard lets up, I want you to get on an airplane and go back to Stone Creek."

"Well, here's a news flash for you: just because you *want* something doesn't mean you're going to get it."

He grinned, shook his head. "Strange that I never noticed how stubborn you can be."

"Get used to it."

He crossed the hall, opened a door.

She peeked inside, saw a comfortable-looking room with an antique four-poster bed, a matching dresser and chest of drawers, and several overstuffed chairs.

"I won't sleep," she warned.

"Neither will I," Jack responded.

Ashley turned, faced him squarely. Spoke from her heart. "Don't die, Jack," she said. "Please—whatever happens between us—don't just give up and die."

He leaned in, kissed her lightly on the mouth. "I'll do my best not to," he said. Then he turned and started back toward the stairs.

"Aren't you going to bed?" Ashley asked, feeling lonely and very far from home.

"Later," he said, winking at her. "Right now, I'm going to call drugstores until I find one that delivers during snowstorms."

Ashley's heart caught; alarm reverberated through her like the echo of a giant brass gong. "Are you running low on one of your medications?"

"No," Jack answered. "I'm going to ask them to send over one of those sticks."

"Sticks?" Ashley frowned, confused.

"The kind a woman pees on," he explained. "Plus sign if she's pregnant, minus if she's not."

"That can wait," Ashley protested. "Have you looked out a window lately?"

"I've got to know," Jack said.

"You're insane."

"Maybe. Good night, Ashley."

She swallowed. "Good night," she said. Stepping inside the guestroom, she closed the door, leaned her forehead against it, and breathed deeply and slowly until she was sure she wouldn't cry.

Her handbag and suitcase had already been brought upstairs. Sinking down onto the side of the bed, Ashley rummaged through her purse until she found the cell phone she'd bought on a wave of technological confidence, after she'd finally mastered her computer.

She dialed her own number at the bed-and-breakfast, and Melissa answered on the first ring.

"Ashley?" The twin-vibe strikes again.

"Hi, Melissa. I'm here—in Chicago, I mean—and I'm—I'm fine."

"You don't *sound* fine," Melissa argued. "How's Jack?"

"He looks terrible, and I don't think he's very happy that I'm here."

"Oh, Ash—I'm sorry. Was the bastard rude to you?"

Ashley smiled, in spite of everything. "He's not a bastard, Melissa," she said, "and no, he hasn't been rude."

"Then—?"

"I think he's given up," Ashley admitted miserably. "It's as if he's decided to die and get it over with. And he doesn't want me around to see it happen."

"Look, maybe you should just come home—"

"I can't. We're socked in by the perfect storm. I've never seen so much snow—even in Stone Creek." She paused. "And I wouldn't leave anyway. How's everything there?"

"It's fine. I've had to turn away at least five people who wanted to book rooms for Valentine's Day weekend." Melissa still sounded worried. "You do realize that you might be there a while? Do you have enough money, Ash?"

"No," Ashley said, embarrassed. "Not for a long haul."

"I can help you out if you need some," Melissa offered. "Brad, too."

Ashley gulped down her O'Ballivan pride, and it wasn't easy to swallow. "I'll let you know," she said, with what dignity she had left. "Do me a favor, will you? Call Tanner and Olivia and let them know I got here okay?"

"Sure," Melissa said.

They said their goodbyes soon after that, and hung up.

As tired as she was, Ashley knew she wouldn't sleep.

She took a bath, brushed her teeth and put on her pajamas.

She watched a newscast on the guestroom TV, waited until the very end for the weather report.

More snow on the way. O'Hare was shut down, and the police were asking everyone to stay off the roads except in the most dire emergencies.

At quarter after ten, a knock sounded on Ashley's door.

"It's me," Jack called, in a loud whisper. "Can I come in?"

Before Ashley could answer, one way or the other, the door opened and he stepped inside, carrying a white bag in one hand.

"Nothing stops the post office or pharmacy delivery drivers," he said, holding out the bag.

The pregnancy test, of course.

Ashley's hand trembled as she reached out to accept it. "Come back later," she said, moving toward her bathroom door.

Jack sat down on the side of her bed. "I'll wait," he said.

Chapter 11

Huddled in the McKenzies' guest bathroom, Ashley stared down at the plastic stick in mingled horror and delight.

A plus sign.

She was pregnant.

Ashley made some rapid calculations in her head; normally, if she hadn't been under stress, it would have been a no-brainer to figure out that the baby was due sometime in September. Because she was frazzled, it took longer.

"Well?" Jack called from the other side of the door. As a precaution, Ashley had turned the lock; otherwise, he might have stormed in on her, he was so anxious to learn the results.

Ashley swallowed painfully. She was bursting with the news, but if she told Jack now, she would, in effect, be trapping him. He'd feel honor-bound to marry her, whether he really wanted to or not.

And suppose he died?

That, of course, would be awful either way.

But maybe knowing about the baby would somehow heal Jack, inspire him to try harder to recover. To believe he could.

The knob jiggled. "Ashley?"

"I'm all right."

"Okay," Jack replied, "but are you *pregnant*?"

"It's inconclusive," Ashley said, too earnestly and too cheerfully.

"I read the package. You get either a plus or a minus," Jack retorted, not at all cheerful, but very earnest. "Which is it, Ashley?"

Ashley closed her eyes for a moment, offered up a silent prayer for wisdom, for strength, for courage. She simply wasn't a very good liar; Jack would see through her if she tried to deceive him. And, anyway, deception seemed wrong, however good her intentions might be. The child was as much Jack's as her own, and he had a right to know he was going to be a father.

"It's—it's a plus."

"Open the door," Jack said. Was that jubilation she heard in his voice, or irritation? Joy—or dread?

Ashley pushed the lock button in the center of the knob, and stepped back quickly to avoid being run down by a man on a mission. She was still holding the white plastic stick in one hand.

Jack took it from her, examined the little panel at one end, giving nothing away by his expression. His shoulders were tense, though, and his breathing was fast and shallow.

"My God," he said finally. "Ashley, *we made a baby*."

"You and me," Ashley agreed, sniffling a little.

Jack raised his eyes to hers. She thought she saw a quickening there, something akin to delight, but he looked worried, too. "You weren't going to tell me?" he asked. "I wouldn't exactly describe a plus sign as 'inconclusive.'"

"I didn't know how you'd react," Ashley said. She *still* couldn't read him—was he glad or sad?

"How I'd react?" he echoed. "Ashley, this is the best thing that's ever happened to me, besides you."

Ashley stared at him, stricken to silence, stricken by joy and surprise and a wild, nearly uncontainable hope.

"You do *want* this baby, don't you?" Jack asked.

"Of course I do," Ashley blurted. "I wasn't sure *you* did, that's all."

Jack looked down at the stick again, shaking his head and grinning.

"I peed on that, you know," Ashley pointed out, reaching for the test stick, intending to throw it away.

Jack held it out of her reach. "We're keeping this. You can glue it into the kid's baby book or something."

"Jack, it's not sanitary," Ashley pointed out. Why was she talking about trivial things, when so much hung in the balance?

"Neither are wet diapers," Jack reasoned calmly. "Sanitation is all well and good, but a kid needs good old-fashioned germs, too, so he—or she—can build up all the necessary antibodies."

"You don't have to marry me if you don't want to," Ashley said, too quickly, and then wished she could bite off her tongue.

"Sure, I do," Jack said. "Call me old-fashioned, but I think a kid ought to have two legal parents."

"Sure, you *have* to marry me, or sure, you *want* to?" Ashley asked.

"Oh, I want to, all right," Jack told her, his voice hoarse, his eyes glistening. "The question is, do you want to spend the rest of your life with me? You could be a widow in six months, or even sooner. A widow with a baby to raise."

"Not if you fight to live, Jack," Ashley said.

He looked away, evidently staring into some grim scenario only he could see. "There's plenty of money," he said, as though speaking to someone else. "If nothing else, I made a good living doing what I did. You would never want for anything, and neither would our baby."

"I don't care about money," Ashley countered honestly, and a little angrily, too. *I care about you, and this baby, and our life together. Our long,* long *life together.* "I love you, remember?"

He set the test stick carefully aside, on the counter by the sink, and pulled Ashley out into the main part of the small suite. "I can't propose to you in a bathroom," he said.

Ashley laughed and cried.

Awkwardly, Jack dropped to one knee, still holding her hand. "I love you, Ashley O'Ballivan. Will you marry me?"

"Yes," she said.

He gave an exuberant shout, got to his feet again and pulled her into his arms, practically drowning her in a deep, hungry kiss.

The guestroom door popped open.

"Oops," Dr. McKenzie the elder said, blushing.

Jack and Ashley broke apart, Jack laughing, Ashley embarrassed and happy and not a little dazed.

Bill looked even more chagrined than before. "I heard a yell and I thought—"

"Everything's okay, Dad," Jack said, with gruff affection. "It's better than okay. I just asked Ashley to marry me, and she said yes."

"I see," Bill said, smiling, and quietly closed the door.

A jubilant "Yes!" sounded from the hallway. Ashley pictured her future father-in-law punching the air with one fist, a heartening thought.

"I still might die," Jack reminded her.

"Welcome to the human race," Ashley replied. "From the moment any of us arrive here, we're on our way out again."

"I'd like to make love to you right now," Jack said.

"Not here," Ashley answered. "I couldn't—not in your dad's house."

Jack nodded slowly. "You're as old-fashioned as I am," he said. "As soon as this storm lets up, though, we're out of here."

They sat down, side by side, on the bed where both of them wanted to make love, and neither intended to give in to desire.

Not just yet, anyway.

"How soon can we get married?" Jack asked, taking her hand, stroking the backs of her knuckles with the pad of his thumb.

Ashley's heart, full to bursting, shoved its way up into her throat and lodged there. "Wait a second," she protested, when she finally gathered the breath to speak. The aftershocks of Jack's kiss were still banging around inside her. "There are things we have to decide first."

"Like?"

"Like where we're going to live," Ashley said, nervous now. She liked Chicago, what little she'd seen of the place, that is, but Stone Creek would always be home.

"Wherever you want," Jack told her quietly. "And I know that's the old hometown. Just remember that your family isn't exactly wild about me."

"They'll get over it," Ashley told him, with confidence. "Once they know you're going to stick around this time."

"Just *try* shaking me off your trail, lady," Jack teased. He leaned toward her, kissed her again, this time lightly, and in a way that shook her soul.

"Does that mean you won't go back to whatever it is you do for a living?" Ashley ventured.

"It means I'm going to shovel snow and carry out the trash and love you, Ashley. For as long as we both shall live."

Tears of joy stung her eyes. "That probably won't be enough to keep you busy," she fretted. "You're used to action—"

"I'm sick of action. At least, the kind that involves covert security operations. Vince can run the company, along with a few other people I trust. I can manage it from the computer in your study."

"I thought you didn't trust Vince anymore," Ashley said.

"I got a little peeved with him," Jack admitted, "but he's sound. He'd have been long gone if he wasn't."

"You wouldn't be taking off all of the sudden—on some important job that required your expertise?"

"I'm good at what I do, Ashley," Jack said. "But I'm not so good that I can't delegate. Maybe I'll hang out with Tanner sometimes, though, riding the range and all that cowboy-type stuff."

"Do you know how to ride a horse?"

Jack chuckled. "It can't be that much different from riding a camel." He grinned. "And I'd be a whole lot closer to the ground."

That last statement sobered both of them.

Jack might not be just closer to the ground, he might wind up *under* it.

"I'm going to make it, Ashley," he assured her.

She dropped her forehead against his shoulder, wrapped her arms around him, let herself cling for a few moments. "You'd better," she said. "You'd just better."

Three days later, the storm had finally moved on, leaving a crystalline world behind, trees etched with ice, blankets of white covering every roof.

A private jet, courtesy of Brad, skimmed down onto the tarmac at a private airfield on the fringes of the Windy City, and Jack and Ashley turned to say temporary farewells to Jack's entire family, gathered there to see them off.

The whole clan would be traveling to Stone Creek for the wedding, which would take place in two weeks. Valentine's Day would have been perfect, but with so many guests already booked to stay at the bed-and-breakfast, it was impossible, and neither Jack nor Ashley wanted to wait until the next one rolled around.

Bill McKenzie pumped his eldest son's hand, the hem of his expensive black overcoat flapping in a brisk breeze, then drew him into a bear hug.

"Better get yourselves onto that plane and out of this wind," Bill said, at last, his voice choked. He bent to kiss Ashley's cheek. "I always wanted a daughter," he added, in a whisper.

Jack nodded, then shook hands with each of his brothers. Every handshake turned into a hug. Lastly, he embraced Abigail, his stepmother.

Ashley looked away, grappling with emotions of her own, watched as the metal stairs swung down out of the side of the jet with an electronic hum. The pilot stood in the doorway, grinning, and she recognized Vince Griffin—the man who'd held a gun on her in her own kitchen, the night Ardith and Rachel arrived.

"Better roll, boss," he called to Jack. "There's more weather headed this way, and I'd like to stay ahead of it."

Jack took Ashley's arm, steered her gently up the steps, into the sumptuous cabin of the jet. There were eight seats, each set of two facing the other across a narrow fold-down table.

"Aren't you going to ask what I'm doing here?" Vince asked Jack, blustering with manly bravado and boyishly earnest at the same time.

"No," Jack answered. "It's obvious that you wangled the job so you could be the one to take us home to Stone Creek."

Home to Stone Creek. That sounded so good to Ashley, especially coming from Jack.

Vince laughed. "I'm trying to get back in your good graces, boss," he said, flipping a switch to retract the stairs, then shutting and securing the cabin door. "Is it working?"

"Maybe," Jack said.

"I hate it when you say 'maybe,'" Vince replied.

"Just fly this thing," Jack told him mildly, with mischief in his eyes. "I want to stay ahead of the weather as much as you do."

Vince nodded, retreated into the cockpit, and shut the door behind him.

Solicitously, Jack helped Ashley out of her coat, sat her down in one of the sumptuous leather seats and swiveled it to buckle her seat belt for her.

A thrill of anticipation went through her.

Not yet, she told herself.

Jack must have been reading her mind. "As soon as we get home," he vowed, leaning over her, bracing himself on the armrests of her seat, "we're going to do it like we've never done it before."

That remark inspired another hot shiver. "Are we, now?" she said, her voice deliberately sultry.

Jack thrust himself away from her, since the plane was already taxiing down the runway, took his own seat across from hers and fastened his belt for takeoff.

Four and a half hours later, they landed outside Stone Creek.

Brad and Meg were waiting to greet them, along with Olivia and Tanner, Carly and Sophie, and Melissa.

"*Thank God* you're back," Melissa said, close to Ashley's ear, after hugging her. "I thought I was going to have to *cook*."

Brad stood squarely in front of Jack, Ashley noticed, out of the corner of her eye, his arms folded and his face stern.

Jack did the same thing, gazing straight into Brad's eyes.

"Uh-oh," Melissa breathed. "Testosterone overload."

Neither man moved. Or spoke.

Olivia finally nudged Brad hard in the ribs. "Behave yourself, big brother," she said. "Jack will be part of the family soon, and that means the two of you have to get along."

It didn't mean any such thing, of course, but to Ashley's profound relief, Brad softened visibly at Olivia's words. Then, after some hesitation, he put out a hand.

Jack took it.

After the shake, Brad said, "That doesn't mean you can mistreat my kid sister, hotshot."

"Wouldn't think of it," Jack said. "I love her." He curved an arm around Ashley, pulled her close against his side, looked down into her upturned face. "Always have, always will."

Two weeks later
Stone Creek Presbyterian Church

"It's tacky," Olivia protested to Melissa, zipping herself into her bridesmaid's dress with some difficulty, since she was still a little on the pudgy side from having the twins. "Coming to a wedding with a U-Haul hitched to the back of your car!"

Melissa rolled her eyes. "I have to be in Phoenix bright and early Monday morning to start my new job," she said, yet again. The three sisters had been over the topic many times. Most of Melissa's belongings had already been moved to the fancy condo in Scottsdale; the rented trailer contained the last of them.

Initially, flushed with the success of helping Ashley steer the bed-and-breakfast through the Valentine's Day rush, Melissa had seemed to be wavering a little on the subject of moving away. After all, she liked her job at the small, local firm where she'd worked since graduating from law school, but then Dan Guthrie had suddenly eloped with Holly the Waitress. Now nothing would move Melissa to stay.

She was determined to shake the dust of Stone Creek off her feet and start a whole new life—elsewhere.

Ashley turned her back to her sisters and her mind to her wedding, smoothing the beaded skirt of her ivory-silk gown in front of the grainy full-length mirror affixed to the back of the pastor's office door. She and Melissa had scoured every bridal shop within a two-hundred-mile radius to find it, while Olivia searched the Internet, and the dress was perfect.

Not so the bridesmaids' outfits, Ashley reflected, happily rueful. They were bright yellow taffeta, with square necklines, puffy sleeves, big bows at the back, and way too many ruffles.

What was I thinking? Ashley asked herself, stifling a giggle.

The answer, of course, was that she *hadn't* been thinking. She'd fallen wholly, completely and irrevocably in love with Jack McKenzie, dazed in the daytime, *crazed* at night, when they made love until they were both sweaty and breathless and gasping for air.

The yellow dresses must have seemed like a good idea at the time, she supposed. Olivia and Melissa had surely argued against that particular choice—but Ashley honestly had no memory of it.

"We're going to look like giant parakeets in the pictures," Olivia complained now, but her eyes were warm and moist as she came to stand behind Ashley in front of the mirror. "You look so beautiful."

Ashley turned, and she and Olivia embraced. "I'll

make it up to you," Ashley said. "Having to wear those awful dresses, I mean."

Melissa looked down at her billowing skirts and shuddered. "I don't see how," she said doubtfully.

A little silence fell.

Olivia straightened Ashley's veil.

"I wish Mom and Dad and Big John could be here," Ashley admitted softly.

"I know," Olivia replied, kissing her cheek.

The church organist launched into a prelude to "Here Comes the Bride."

"Showtime," Melissa said, giving Ashley a quick squeeze. "Be happy."

Ashley nodded, blinking. She couldn't cry now. It would make her mascara run.

A rap sounded at the office door, and Brad entered at Olivia's "Come in," looking beyond handsome in his tuxedo. "Ready to be given away?" he asked solemnly, his gaze resting on Ashley in surprised bemusement, as though she'd just changed from a little girl to a woman before his very eyes. A grin crooked up a corner of his mouth. "We can always duck out the back door and make a run for it if you've changed your mind."

Ashley smiled, shook her head. Walked over to her brother.

Brad kissed her forehead, then lowered the front of the veil. "Jack McKenzie is one lucky man," he said gravely, but a genuine smile danced in his eyes. "Gonna be okay?"

Ashley took his arm. "Gonna be okay," she confirmed.

"We're supposed to go down the aisle first," Melissa said, grabbing Olivia's hand and dragging her past Brad and Ashley, through the open doorway, and into the corridor that opened at both ends of the small church.

"Is he out there?" Ashley whispered to Brad, suddenly nervous, as he escorted her over the threshold between one life and another.

"Jack?" Brad pretended not to remember. "I'm pretty sure I spotted him up front, with Tanner beside him. Guess it could have been the pastor, though." He paused for dramatic effect. "Oh, yeah. The pastor's wearing robes. The man I saw was in a tuxedo, tugging at his collar every couple of seconds."

"Stop it," Ashley said, but she was smiling. "I'm nervous enough without you giving me a hard time, big brother."

They joined Melissa and Olivia at the back of the church.

Over their heads, and through a shifting haze of veil, extreme anticipation, and almost overwhelming joy, Ashley saw Jack standing up front, his back straight, his head high with pride.

In just two weeks, he'd come a long way toward a full recovery, filling out, his color returning. He claimed it was the restorative power of good sex.

Ashley blushed, remembering some of that sex, and looking forward to a lot more of it.

The organist struck the keys with renewed vigor.

"There's our cue," Brad whispered to Ashley, bending his head slightly so she could hear.

"Go!" Melissa said to Olivia, giving her a little push.

Olivia moved slowly up the aisle, between pews jammed with McKenzies, O'Ballivans, McKettricks, and assorted friends.

Just before starting up the aisle herself, Melissa

turned, found Ashley's hand under the bouquet of snow-white peonies Brad had had flown in from God-knew-where and squeezed it hard.

"Go," Brad told Melissa, with a chuckle.

She made a face at him and started resolutely up the aisle.

Once she and Olivia were both in front of the altar, opposite Jack and Tanner, the organist pounded the keys with even more vigor than before. Ashley *floated* toward the altar, gripping Brad's strong arm, her gaze fixed on Jack.

The guests rose to their feet, beaming at Ashley.

Jack smiled, encouraged her with a wink.

And then she was at his side.

She heard the minister ask, "Who giveth this woman in marriage?"

Heard Brad answer, "Her family and I."

Ashley's eyes began to smart again, and she wondered if anyone had ever died of an overdose of happiness.

Brad retreated, and after that, Ashley was only peripherally aware of her surroundings. Her entire focus was on Jack.

Somehow, she got through the vows.

She and Jack exchanged rings.

And then the minister pronounced them man and wife.

Jack raised the front of Ashley's veil to kiss her, and his eyes widened a little, in obvious appreciation, when he saw that she'd forsworn her usual French braid for a shoulder-length style that stood out around her face.

She'd spent the morning at Cora's Curl and Twirl over in Indian Rock, Cora herself doing the honors, snipping and blow-drying and phoofing endlessly.

The wedding kiss was chaste, at least in appearance. Up close and personal, it was nearly orgasmic.

"Ladies and gentlemen," the minister said triumphantly, raising his voice to be heard at the back of the church, "may I present Mr. and Mrs. Jack McKenzie!"

Cheers erupted.

The organ thundered.

Jack and Ashley hurried down the aisle, emerging into the sunlight, and were showered with birdseed and good wishes.

The reception, held at the bed-and-breakfast, was everything a bride could hope for. Even the weather cooperated; the snow had melted, the sun was out, the sky cloudless and heartbreakingly blue.

"I ordered a sunny day just for you," Jack whispered to her, as he helped her out of the limo in front of the house.

For the next two hours, the place was crammed to the walls with wedding guests. Pictures were taken, punch and cake were served. So many congratulatory hugs, kisses and handshakes came their way that Ashley began to wish the thing would *end* already.

She and Jack would spend their wedding night right there at home, although they were leaving on their honeymoon the next day.

The sky was beginning to darken toward twilight when the guests began to leave, one by one, couple by couple, and then in groups.

Bill and Abigail McKenzie and their large extended family would occupy all the guestrooms at the bed-and-breakfast, so they lingered, somewhat at loose ends until Brad diplomatically invited them out to Stone Creek Ranch, where the party would continue.

Goodbyes were said.

Except for the caterers, already cleaning up, Melissa was the last to leave.

"I may never forgive you for this wretched dress," she told Ashley, tearing up.

"Maybe you'll get back at me one of these days," Ashley answered softly, as Jack moved away to give the twins room to say their farewells. Melissa planned to drive to Scottsdale that same night. "You'll be the bride, and I'll be the one who has to look like a giant parakeet."

Melissa huffed out a breath, shook her head. "I think you're safe from that horrid fate," she said wistfully. "I plan to throw myself into my career. Before you know it, I'll be a Supreme Court Justice, just as you said." She gave a wobbly little smile that didn't quite stick. "At least my memoirs will probably be interesting."

Ashley kissed her sister's cheek. "Take care," she said.

Melissa chuckled. "As soon as I swap this dress for a pair of jeans and a sweatshirt, and the heels for sneakers, I'll be golden."

With that, Melissa headed for the downstairs powder room, where she'd stashed her getaway clothes.

When she emerged, she was dressed for the road, and the ruffly yellow gown was wadded into a bundle under her right arm.

"Will you still love me if I toss this thing into the first Dumpster I see?" she quipped, as she and Ashley stood at the front door.

"I'll still love you," Ashley said, "no matter what."

Melissa gave a brave sniffle. "See you around, Mrs. McKenzie," she said.

And then she opened the front door, dashed across

the porch and down the front steps, and along the walk. She got into her little red sports car, which looked too small to pull a trailer, tossed the offending bridesmaid's dress onto the passenger seat and waved.

Jack was standing right behind Ashley when she turned from closing the door, and he kissed her briefly on the mouth. "She's an O'Ballivan," he said. "She'll be all right."

Ashley nodded. Swallowed.

"The caterers will be out of here in a few minutes," Jack told her, with a twinkle. "I promised to overtip if they'd just kick it up a notch. Wouldn't you like to get out of that dress, beautiful as it is?"

She stood on tiptoe, kissed the cleft in her husband's chin. "I might need some help," she told him sweetly. "It has about a million buttons down the back."

Jack chuckled. "I'm just the man for the job," he said.

Mrs. Wiggins came, twitchy-tailed, out of the study, where she'd probably been hiding from the hubbub of the reception, batted playfully at the lace trim on the hem of Ashley's wedding gown.

"No you don't," she told the kitten, hoisting the little creature up so they were nose to nose, she and Mrs. Wiggins. "This dress is going to be an heirloom. Someday, another bride will wear it."

"Our daughter," Jack said, musing. "If she's as beautiful as her mother, every little boy under the age of five ought to be warned."

Ashley smiled, still holding Mrs. Wiggins. "Get rid of the caterers," she said, and headed for the stairs.

Barely a minute later, she was inside the room that had been hers alone, until today—not that she and Jack hadn't shared it every night since they got back from Chicago.

The last wintry light glowed at the windows, turning the antique lace curtains to gold. White rose petals covered the bed, and someone had laid a fire on the hearth, too.

Their suitcases stood just outside the closet door, packed and ready to go. Tomorrow at this time, she and Jack would be in Hawaii, soaking up a month of sunshine.

Ashley's heart quickened. She put a hand to her throat briefly, feeling strangely like a virgin, untouched, eager to be deflowered, and a little nervous at the prospect.

The room looked the same, and yet different, now that she and Jack were married.

Married. Not so long ago, she'd pretty much given up on marriage—and then Jack "McCall" had arrived by ambulance, looking for a place to heal.

So much had happened since then, some of it terrifying, most of it better than good.

Mrs. Wiggins leaped up onto a slipper chair near the fireplace and curled up for a long winter's snooze.

Carefully, Ashley removed the tiara that held her veil in place and set the mound of gossamer netting aside. She stood in front of the bureau mirror and fluffed out her hair with the fingers of both hands.

Her cheeks glowed, and so did her eyes.

The door opened softly, and Jack came into the room, no tuxedo jacket in evidence, unfastening his cuff links as he walked toward Ashley. Setting the cuff links aside on the dresser top, he took her into his arms, buried his hands in her hair, and kissed her thoroughly.

Ashley's knees melted, just as they always did.

Eventually, Jack tore his mouth from hers, turned her around, and began unfastening the buttons at the back of her dress. In the process, he bent to nibble at her skin as he bared it, leaving tiny trails of fire along her shoulder blades, her spine and finally the small of her back.

The dress fell in a pool at her feet, leaving her in her petticoat, bra, panty hose and high heels.

She shivered, not with fear or cold, but with eagerness. She wanted to give herself to Jack—as his wife.

But he left her, untucking his white dress shirt as he went. Crouched in front of the fireplace to light a blaze on the hearth.

Another blaze already burned inside Ashley.

Jack straightened, unfastened his cummerbund with a grin of relief, and tossed it aside. Started removing his shirt.

His eyes smoldered as he took Ashley in, slowly, his gaze traveling from her head to her feet and then back up again.

As if hypnotized, she unhooked her bra, let her breasts spill into Jack's full view. His eyes went wide as her nipples hardened, eager for his lips and tongue.

It seemed to take forever, this shedding of clothes, garment by garment, but finally they were both naked, and the fire snapped merrily in the grate, and Jack eased Ashley down onto the bed.

Because of her pregnancy—news they had yet to share with the rest of the family, because it was too new and too precious—his lovemaking was poignantly gentle.

He parted her legs, bent her knees, ran his hands from there to her ankles.

Ashley murmured, knowing what he was going to do, needing it, needing him.

He nuzzled her, parted the curls at the juncture of her thighs, and his sigh of contented anticipation reverberated through her entire system.

She tangled her fingers in his hair, held him close.

He chuckled against her flesh, and she moaned.

And then he took her full in his mouth, now nibbling, now suckling, and Ashley arched her back and cried out in surrender.

"Not so fast," Jack murmured, between teasing flicks of his tongue. "Let it happen slowly, Mrs. McKenzie."

"I—I don't think I—can wait—"

Jack turned his head, dragged his lips along the length of her inner thigh, nipped at her lightly as he crossed to the other side. "You can wait," he told her.

"*Please,* Jack," she half sobbed.

He slid his hands under her bare bottom, lifted her high, and partook of her with lusty appreciation.

She exploded almost instantaneously, her body flexing powerfully, once, twice, a third time.

And then she fell, sighing, back to the bed.

He was kissing her lower belly, where their baby was growing, warm and safe and sheltered.

"I love you, Jack," Ashley said, weak with the force of her releases.

He turned her to lie full length on the bed, poised himself over her, took her in a slow, even stroke.

"Always have," she added, trying to catch her breath and failing. "Always will."

Epilogue

December 24
Stone Creek, Arizona

Jack McKenzie stood next to his daughter's crib, gazing down at her in wonder. Katie—named for his grandmother—was nearly three months old now, and she looked more like Ashley every day. Although the baby was too young to understand Christmas, they'd hung up a stocking for her, just the same.

The door of his and Ashley's bedroom opened quietly behind him.

"The doctor is on the phone," she said quietly.

Jack turned, took her in, marveled anew, the way he did every time he saw his wife, that it was possible to go to sleep at night loving a woman so much, and wake up loving her even more.

"Okay," he said.

She approached, held out the cell phone he'd left downstairs when he brought Katie up to bed. They'd been putting the finishing touches on the Christmas tree by the front windows, he and Ashley, and the place was decorated to the hilt, though there would be no paying guests over the holidays.

Busy with a new baby, not to mention a husband, Ashley had decided to take at least a year off from running the bed-and-breakfast. She still cooked like a French chef, which was probably why he'd gained ten pounds since they'd gotten married, and she was practically an expert on the computer.

So far, she didn't seem to miss running a business.

She'd been baking all day, since half the family would be there for a special Christmas Eve supper, after the early services at the church.

They'd stayed home, waiting for the call.

He took the cell phone, cleared his throat, said hello.

Ashley moved close to him, leaned against his side, somehow supporting him at the same time. Her head rested, fragrant, against his shoulder.

He kissed her crown, drew in the scent of her hair.

"This is Dr. Schaefer," a man said, as if Jack needed to be told. He and Ashley had been bracing themselves for this call ever since Jack's last visit to the clinic up in Flagstaff, a few days before, where they'd run the latest series of tests.

"Yes," Jack said, his voice raspy. Wrapping one arm around Ashley's waist. He felt fine, but that didn't mean he was out of danger.

And there was so very much at stake.

"All the results are normal, Mr. McKenzie," he heard

Dr. Schaefer say, as though chanting the words through an underwater tunnel. "I think we can safely assume the marrow transplant was a complete success, and so were the antirejection medications."

Jack closed his eyes. "Normal," he repeated, for Ashley's benefit as well as his own.

She squeezed him hard.

"Thanks, Doctor," he said.

A smile warmed the other man's voice. "Have a Merry Christmas," the doctor said. "Not that you need to be told."

"You, too," Jack said. "And thanks again."

He closed the phone, tucked it into the pocket of his shirt, turned to take Ashley into his arms.

"Guess what, Mrs. McKenzie," he said. "We have a future together. You and me and Katie. A long one, I expect."

She beamed up at him, her eyes wet.

Downstairs, the doorbell chimed.

Ashley squeezed Jack's hand once, crossed to the crib, and tucked Katie's blanket in around her.

"I suppose they'll let themselves in," Jack said, watching her with the same grateful amazement he always felt.

Ashley smiled, and came back to his side, and they went down the stairs together, hand in hand.

Brad and Meg, with Carly and Mac and the new baby, Eva, stood in the entryway, smiling, snow dusting the shoulders of their coats and gleaming in their hair.

Olivia and Tanner arrived only moments later, with the twins, who were walking now, and Sophie.

"Where's Melissa?" Olivia asked, looking around.

"She'll be here soon," Ashley said. "She called about

an hour ago—there was a lot of traffic leaving Scottsdale."

Ashley looked up at Jack, and they silently agreed to wait until everyone had arrived before sharing the good news about his test results.

The men spent the next few minutes carrying brightly wrapped packages in from the trucks parked out front, while the women and smaller children headed for the kitchen, where a savory supper was warming in the ovens.

Ashley and Meg and Olivia carried plates and silverware into the dining room, while Carly and Sophie kept the smaller children entertained.

A horn tooted outside, in the snowy driveway, and then Melissa hurried through the back door.

"It's cold out there!" she cried, spreading her arms for the rush of small children, wanting hugs. "And I think I saw Santa Claus just as I was pulling into town."

Soon, they were all gathered in the dining room, the grand tree in the parlor in full view through the double doors.

"I have news," Melissa said, just as Jack was about to offer a toast.

Everyone waited.

"I'm coming back to Stone Creek," Melissa told them all. "I'm about to become the new county prosecutor!"

The family cheered, and when some of the noise subsided, Ashley and Jack rose from their chairs, each with an arm around the other.

"The test results?" Olivia asked, in a whisper. Then, reading Jack's and Ashley's expressions, a joyous smile broke over her face. "They were good?"

"Better than good," Ashley answered.

Supper was almost cold by the time the cheering was over, but nobody noticed.

It was Christmas Eve, after all.

And they were together, at home in Stone Creek.

* * * * *

HIS TO CLAIM

Brenda Jackson

Acknowledgments

To the man who will always and forever be
the love of my life and the wind beneath my wings:
Gerald Jackson, Sr.

Special thanks to my readers who are
attending the Brenda Jackson Readers Reunion 2019
as we cruise to Aruba. Fun! Fun! Fun!
I always enjoy spending time with you!

To all my readers who requested Mac's story.
This book is for you.

Sending congratulations to my goddaughter,
Ty'ra Malloy, who is celebrating her graduation
from Florida State University.
Your Goddy is very proud of you!

Though thy beginning was small, yet thy latter end
should greatly increase.
—*Job* 8:7

Chapter 1

Thurston McRoy, called Mac by all who knew him, got out of his rental vehicle and slid the keys into the pocket of his jeans. There was a dark blue sedan parked in his driveway.

At two in the morning.

It looked like a brand-new luxury Lexus and had a Georgia license plate. The only people he knew who lived in Georgia were his parents. Was this their vehicle?

They would often visit Virginia to check on his wife, Teri, and the kids whenever he was away for long periods of time. With his work as a navy SEAL, he often took part in missions where he was out of communication with his family. He appreciated his parents for all they did to make his work easier on his family. However, he was surprised to see their car here, tonight.

Over the last year or so, they'd begun staying at a nearby hotel whenever they came to town. Unfortunately, there were no longer any spare rooms at the McRoy house.

The last time Mac had come home, he'd discovered Teri had given Tia, their oldest daughter of nine, her own room—namely the spare room. According to Teri, Tia was at the age where she now wanted privacy from her three younger sisters, Tatum, Tempest and Tasha. But did she have to take the only spare room in the house? The one that doubled as his man cave whenever he came home?

He and Teri had always talked about buying a bigger place. Frankly, he had more than enough means to make it happen thanks to the investments he'd made on the advice of his friend and teammate, Bane Westmoreland. However, over the past several years, he'd been gone a lot, sent on several missions, and he was too hands-on to even think of letting her make such a major purchase like that without him. He knew exactly what he wanted in a home and Teri knew what she wanted. And their wants were on the opposite ends of the spectrum. She wanted a two-story home and he wanted ranch style. The fewer stairs he had to climb, the better.

Tonight, he was returning home from an eight-month-long, highly classified covert operation near Libya. During that time, he hadn't been able to let anyone, not even Teri, know of his whereabouts. He had left home in the wee hours of the morning after making passionate love to his wife, without being able to tell her where he was going or when he would return.

As a toddler he recalled sitting on his maternal grandfather's knee and listening to stories of his military days, specifically as a SEAL. His paternal grandfather had been a military man, as well, an army ranger. Although Mac's father hadn't been in the military Mac had decided early in life protecting his country was something he wanted to do. Being a SEAL had always been his dream and he'd worked hard to make that particular dream come true. Now after almost twenty years whenever he thought it was time to retire, a part of him was convinced there was one more mission, one more opportunity to defend the country he loved.

The last operation had been brutal, but all the members of his team were alive and accounted for. Now he was glad to be back home with his wife and kids, and as much as he loved his parents, he hadn't counted on having any company. He needed a cold beer and his wife. Not necessarily in that order.

He figured everyone was in bed, yet an uneasy feeling crept over him as he entered his home. He paused in the foyer. Was that the television he heard coming from the living room? Typically, Teri would be in bed before ten because she got up around six to jump-start her day.

Tatum was seven and attended a different school than Tia. Tempest was five and attended kindergarten at the same school as Tatum. Tasha, their baby, who was barely three, attended day care. He hadn't liked the idea of Tasha in day care, but Teri claimed Tasha needed to be around kids her age at least a few days a week to start developing her social skills.

Mac hadn't wanted Teri to work outside the home, either, but she'd insisted that she needed to get out of the house for a while during the day. So now she was working part-time at one of the libraries in town.

Mindful of not waking the kids, while at the same time intent on not scaring his parents, he took out his phone and texted Teri. She practically slept with the phone beside her. When the message didn't immediately show as delivered, he frowned, wondering what was wrong with her phone. He'd tried calling her earlier, twice in fact, when his plane had landed in DC. He hadn't gotten an answer either time.

What was going on?

He placed his gear down and was headed toward his bedroom when his father rounded the corner. Carlton McRoy nearly jumped out of his skin when he saw his son.

"Damn it, Mac, you trying to give me heart failure?" his father asked. "I didn't hear you come in."

Mac crossed the floor to give his father a bear hug. "You weren't supposed to hear me. I'm a SEAL, Dad."

"Why didn't you ring the doorbell?"

Mac thought that was a crazy question. "I live here. I don't need to ring the doorbell. Besides, I didn't want to wake anyone. By the way, I like your new set of wheels."

His father beamed. "Thanks. It's your mom's car. I surprised her with it as an early anniversary gift. It's been almost forty years, you know."

Yes, Mac knew. He was the oldest of two and Carlton and Alexis Youngblood-McRoy hadn't wasted any time after their wedding to start a family. He'd been born a week shy of their first anniversary. He figured he was supposed to be one and done, but his sister Kylie had been born on his parents' tenth anniversary. "That's a nice gift."

"I thought so, and Lex was more than deserving," his father said.

Mac smiled. His parents were special. There weren't two adults he admired more and they had always been great role models for him and his sister. Their interracial marriage had worked for them because they'd always said love got them together and it would be love that kept them together.

"Thurston!"

Mac glanced around and chuckled when his mother practically threw herself into his arms. "Hey, Mom," he said, placing a kiss on her cheek.

"I heard voices and thought one of the girls had awakened."

"No, it's just me and Dad. He saw me when I was headed down the hall to my bedroom to let Teri know I was home."

He still had his arms around his mother's shoulders when he felt her tense up. "Mom? You okay?" he asked, looking down at her.

He thought the same thing now that he'd thought while growing up. His mother was a beautiful woman with eyes a unique shade of blue and ash-blond hair. His father had a dark chocolate complexion, which accounted for Mac and his younger sister's skin tone being a combination of the two.

When his mother still hadn't answered his question, he turned his eyes to his father, who had the same wary expression on his face that Mac's mother wore. Releasing his arm from around his mother's shoulder, Mac straightened to his full height of six feet three inches. "Okay, what's going on?"

When his parents glanced at each other, that uneasy feeling from earlier crept over him again. Not liking it, he turned to go down the hall toward his bedroom when his father reached out to stop him.

"Teri isn't here, Mac."

Mac turned back to his father. His mother had moved to stand beside his dad. "It's after two in the morning and tomorrow is a school day for the girls. So where is she?"

His mother reached out and touched his arm. "She needed to get away and she asked if we would come keep the girls."

Mac frowned. He knew his wife. She would not have gone anywhere without their daughters. "What do you mean she needed to get away? Why?"

"She's the one who has to tell you that, Thurston. It's not for us to say."

His mother looked up at him with an uncomfortable expression on her face. His gaze left his mother and moved over to his father, who was wearing the same look.

"What's going on, Dad? Mom? Why can't you tell me the reason Teri felt she had to get away?"

"Because it's not our place to do so, son."

Mac drew in a deep breath, not understanding any of this. Because his parents were acting so secretive, he felt his confusion and anger escalating. "Fine. Where is she?"

It was his father who spoke. "She left three days ago for the Torchlight Dude Ranch."

Mac's frown deepened. "The Torchlight Dude Ranch? In Wyoming?"

"Yes."

"What the hell did she go there for?"

His father didn't say anything for a minute and then gave Mac an answer. "She said she always wanted to go back there."

Mac rubbed his hand across his face. Yes, Teri had

always wanted to go back there, the place he'd taken her on their honeymoon a little over ten years ago. And he'd always promised to take her back. But between his covert missions and their growing family, there had never been enough time. Teri, who'd been raised on a ranch in Texas, was a cowgirl at heart and for a short while had competed on the rodeo circuit due to her roping and riding skills. She'd even represented the state of Texas as a rodeo queen before they'd met.

When they'd married, she had given it all up to travel around the world with her naval husband. She'd said she'd done so gladly. Why in the world would Teri leave their kids and go to a dude ranch by herself?

He knew the only person who could answer that question was Teri.

"I tried calling her twice from the airport and she's not answering her phone," he finally said, his tone truly filled with anger now.

"She probably couldn't. We talk to her every day when she calls to check on the girls. The reception at the dude ranch is not good and she has to drive into town to call out. Teri usually phones us around five every evening. I'm sure she'll be calling today as usual, so you'll get a chance to talk to her," his mother said, smiling.

He stared at his parents. Did they honestly think he intended to hang around and wait for Teri's call?

"I want to see the girls. I won't wake them, but I need to see them before I leave."

"Leave?" his father asked, looking at him strangely.

"Yes, leave."

"Where are you going?" his mother asked.

He met their gazes. "I'm going to the Torchlight Dude Ranch."

"Now?"

"Yes. Now."

Moments later, he slid open the door to his oldest daughter's room. Tia was asleep but he needed to look at her for himself to see that she was all right. He smiled as he studied her in sleep. She had her mother's mouth, but that was about it. Everything else was his. Her eyes didn't need to be open for him to know they were the exact color of his. A color so rich they looked like dark chocolate.

He'd been the one who'd chosen the name Tia for their first child and it had been Teri's decision to name all the other girls with the starting letter of *T* like his and Teri's names. Tia was determined to follow in her mother's footsteps and become a cowgirl, which was why she'd been taking horse-riding lessons since she turned five. He still didn't like the idea of her competing, though, not even in her age group, which was another thing he and Teri couldn't agree on.

Leaning down, he placed a kiss on Tia's cheek before leaving the room to check on Tatum and Tempest. Both had honey-brown eyes like Teri and favored their mother a lot. There was barely a two-year difference in Tatum's and Tempest's ages and the two were extremely close. They looked out for each other. He liked that about them. He figured that unlike Tia, they would never grow up and ask for separate rooms. They would enjoy being in each other's pockets for as long as they could. Placing kisses on their cheeks, as well, he moved to the room that was closest to his bedroom. The one where three-year-old Tasha slept.

Although he tiptoed into the room, he wasn't surprised when Tasha's eyes flew open and she stared at him a minute before a huge smile touched her lips. "Daddy!"

She threw himself into his arms and he held her. After three girls, he and Teri had been hoping for a boy, but when the nurse had placed Tasha in his arms, it hadn't mattered that he had gotten a fourth girl. Tasha looked more like him than any of the others. She was his Mini-Me.

Picking her up into his arms, he went over to the rocking chair he'd gotten for Tia, the one that had been passed down from daughter to daughter. He gazed down at his daughter and saw dark brown eyes staring back up at him.

"Tasha loves Daddy."

He smiled. "And Daddy loves Tasha."

Cradling her against his chest, he began rocking her back to sleep. Having come back from such a danger- ous mission, he needed peace in his life at that mo- ment, but he knew true peace wouldn't come until he went after Teri and found out what was going on with her. Why she'd called his parents to keep the girls so she could get away.

Other than him, his sister and his parents, Teri had no family. Her parents had died when she was young and her grandparents had raised her on their ranch in Terrell, Texas, which was a stone's throw from Dallas. When Mac had met her, the grandparents she'd adored had died and at twenty-three Teri was trying to run the ranch alone. After their whirlwind romance she'd made the decision—one that he knew had been hard for her, even though she'd never complained about it—to sell the ranch and accept his marriage proposal. She'd turned in her spurs to become a SEAL wife.

It had been her suggestion that they go to a dude ranch for their honeymoon, which would be her last hurrah as a cowgirl. That had been two weeks he'd totally enjoyed, and he'd gotten to show her how well he could handle a horse, thanks to his mother's family, who'd owned a horse ranch in Ocala, Florida.

The timing of their meeting had been perfect. He'd just graduated from the naval academy three years before and was enjoying being a SEAL. It had been his intention to remain a bachelor for quite a while, but all that had changed after he met Teri.

As he continued to rock his daughter back to sleep, Mac closed his eyes, recalling the day Teri Cantor walked into his life…

Ten years ago

"Damn, Lawton, will you slow down?"

Mac glanced over at the man walking beside him. Lawton was walking so fast you'd think he was rushing to put out a fire. Against his better judgment, Mac had let Lawton talk him into coming here of all places—a rodeo—just to see a woman.

"You shouldn't walk so slow," Lawton said, grinning, not breaking his stride.

"Whatever. Now, how did you and this woman meet again?"

"We met online three months ago and officially met last month when I flew to Atlanta for the weekend. She's a photographer for the Bill Pickett Rodeo circuit. LaDorria mentioned they would be in the DC area, so I figured this would be my chance to see her again."

As they neared the entrance to the arena Lawton

slowed down and so did Mac. "Is there a particular spot where the two of you plan to meet once we're inside?" Mac asked, looking around.

"Yes. She said to meet her at the booth that sells the commemorative booklets."

Ten minutes later they were there, and Lawton introduced Mac to LaDorria Clark. Mac had to admit she was an attractive woman, and just for the hell of it, he asked if she had a single friend. She quickly replied, "It just so happens I do. Her name is Teri and she's competing tonight."

LaDorria grabbed one of the commemorative booklets and flipped through to a certain page, pointed and said, "This here is Teri."

Mac figured if a man could fall in love with a photograph, then he had done so in that moment. The very beautiful woman in a cowgirl outfit was smiling for the camera and she captured his heart then and there.

"What event is she competing in?"

"Roping and barrel racing. She's the current champ in the women's division. She was also rodeo queen last year."

Mac looked at the photo again. He could definitely believe that. He figured her age was around twenty-two or twenty-three and she had the most gorgeous pair of honey-brown eyes. They were perfect for her high cheekbones and full, shapely lips. Her skin was the color of rich mocha and he loved the way the mass of curly hair fell around her shoulders.

He looked over at LaDorria. "And you'll introduce us?"

She laughed. "Yes, just as soon as the rodeo is over,

and only if you cheer for Teri tonight. Like I said, she's competing."

As far as Mac was concerned, Teri Cantor didn't need him cheering for her because she had her own fan section in the stands. And she was good. So good that she won both competitive events easily. He couldn't help admiring how well she handled a horse, how skillfully she rode the animal. Nor could he fight his attraction to her—she was a beautiful woman in person and in action in the ring. And he definitely liked the way she looked in her cowgirl outfits. She had changed into a couple of different ones and each one he would claim as a favorite.

He liked the way she handled a rope and how easily her lasso fell over the cow's head. He knew that sort of aptitude came from hours of practice. That meant she was well disciplined.

Mac had heard the comments from the men around him. Men who'd made it obvious they had the hots for Teri. Some had even admitted to hitting on her and striking out. He hoped he wouldn't be one of those men.

He thought about other women he'd dated in the past. Most liked the idea of dating a military man, but none ever fancied marrying one. They'd all heard the life of a SEAL's wife was too demanding. The thought of not knowing where their husband was and when he'd be returning was just something they couldn't tolerate.

Their attitude was something he hadn't been able to tolerate, either. Although he had no intention of acquiring a wife for years to come, it still bothered him how some women thought a relationship was all about them. They had no idea that a navy SEAL wife was, in a way, serving her country, as well.

"I just got a text from LaDorria," Lawton said at the end of the rodeo. "They asked us to give them thirty minutes and then they'll meet us by that souvenir table again."

"Okay, and it looks like you're kind of serious about LaDorria," he said to Lawton.

"I am. I just hope she's serious about me."

Mac hoped she was, as well, since Lawton was a pretty decent guy.

It was almost forty-five minutes later, but Mac was convinced it was worth every minute of waiting for LaDorria and Teri to arrive. When he saw Teri Cantor walking toward them, he thought she looked even better up close and in person.

She had changed out of her riding outfit into a pair of slacks and a blouse that made her look feminine as hell. Her hair was no longer tied back away from her face but hung in loose curls around her shoulders. He could tell the moment their gazes connected that there was interest between them and he didn't intend to let that interest go to waste.

"So, what do you think?" Lawton leaned over to ask before the two women had approached them.

Mac's response was quick and honest. "I think I'm in love."

Lawton laughed but Mac was totally serious. That was how his father claimed it had been for him when he'd seen Mac's mother for the first time, when the two had been attending classes together at Ohio State University.

Mac drew in a deep breath and didn't release it until the women had reached them. Introductions were being made by LaDorria. "Teri, I'd like you to meet a friend of Lawton's. Thurston McRoy."

Teri offered him her hand and the moment he took it, he felt…something flow through him. From the look in her eyes, he knew she'd felt it, as well.

"Nice meeting you, Thurston."

He smiled down at her. "My friends call me Mac."

She nodded. "Okay. It's nice meeting you, Mac."

"Same here." And he truly meant it.

That night they went to one of the bar-and-grills that stayed open late. He got to know her better but not as well as he wanted to. They exchanged phone numbers and stayed in touch, sometimes talking on the phone at night for hours.

They had their first official date a month later, when he'd flown to Montana to watch her perform in another rodeo. That was when he was about to be stationed in Spain and he'd wanted to see her again before leaving the country.

They exchanged texts and phone calls whenever they could, and it was two months later that she'd told him she was thinking about selling her ranch and moving to New York. She felt that maybe it was time to put her college degree in business to good use. He'd known it would be a tough decision for her to make. From their talks, he knew how much she'd enjoyed living on the ranch.

Once she made the decision to sell the ranch it had sold quickly, and before she could pack up and move to New York, he had persuaded her to visit him in Barcelona. When she said she would, he'd made all the arrangements and had sent her an airline ticket within twenty-four hours. He had been there to pick her up from the airport and the moment he saw her again he'd known he wanted to make her a permanent part of his life.

Teri had spent two wonderful weeks with him in Spain and it was during that time that they'd shared a bed for the first time. Making love to her had been just like he'd known it would be.

She'd literally rocked his world.

The intensity of their sexual joining was powerful. It was as if her body was made for him and his for her.

Before leaving to return to the States, he'd asked her to marry him, and she'd accepted.

A month later they were married.

Bringing his thoughts back to the present, Mac opened his eyes and glanced down at Tasha. She had gone back to sleep. Standing, he placed his daughter back in her bed and then he walked out of the room.

It was time to go find his wife.

Chapter 2

Teri McRoy sipped her coffee as she stood at the window and looked out.

For miles all she could see were beautiful plains, valleys and mountains. The Torchlight Dude Ranch, located in Torchlight, Wyoming, was a luxury guest ranch on over a thousand acres just west of Cheyenne. Mac had first brought her here for their honeymoon ten years ago and had promised that one day he would bring her back.

He never had.

Knowing she needed time alone to deal with a few issues, this was the first place she'd thought of coming due to the wonderful and lasting memories she had of the time spent here with Mac. Now she was glad she had come. She missed her girls more than anything and appreciated her in-laws for their quick response in coming to look after them. Her daughters couldn't ask for better grandparents. Mac's parents were the best. She couldn't imagine leaving the girls with anyone else right now. But still, she was compelled to check on them every day. She needed to hear their voices. As expected, they would tell her they missed her—and tell her how much fun they were having with Pop and Nana.

One of the things Teri liked most about this dude ranch was that you didn't have to stay in the main house. If you opted for more privacy, there were several small cabins spread out over the thousand acres. It was beautiful. Part of the package was that you got your very own horse to use daily and it was delivered to you each morning. Hers was a beautiful white stallion named Amsterdam. Over the past three days, she and Amsterdam had gotten to know each other well. She wasn't even put off by his spirited side. Being the horse expert that she was, she loved the challenge.

As she stood there thinking about just how idyllic this cabin was, she knew in her heart the one thing missing was her husband's presence. She missed Mac and always did whenever he was gone for long periods of time, although she tried hard not to let him know it. He had a dangerous job and she'd known that when she had married him. She'd also known he could be summoned away at a moment's notice without being able to inform her of where he was going or how long he'd be gone. The longest time he'd ever been gone was seven months. This time it had been almost nine and she was beginning to worry. What if…

Teri shook her head, refusing to go there. Mac expected her to be strong and handle things while he was gone. Unfortunately, this time around it was hard for her to do that. Things had happened that she hadn't counted on and her heart broke more and more each day.

Mac was a good man. A wonderful father and loving husband. He provided for his family, whatever their needs were. Financially, Mac's girls didn't want for anything. However, she was discovering that there were some things that money couldn't buy. Peace of mind. More good days than bad. And a marriage that was more blissful than stressful.

A part of her wanted Mac to not only be on the ranch with her to share in the beauty again, but to also just hold her and tell her everything was going to be all right. She needed him to not blame her for what had gone wrong. Even if it was the news of losing the very thing he would have wanted.

A son.

When she felt her tears fall again she drew in a deep breath. Her grief counselor had talked to her, told her that miscarriages were more common than most people even knew. She'd done nothing wrong.

The counselor didn't know the half of it.

She was not supposed to get pregnant. Mac had said that although he would have loved to have a son, when it didn't happen with Tasha that was it. He felt four kids were enough for her to handle on her own while he worked as a SEAL.

They'd talked to her doctor about getting her tubes tied, which could be done as an outpatient procedure. They'd scheduled the surgery, but he'd gotten called away. She was to keep the appointment for the procedure regardless. Then she'd gotten the call from the doctor saying results from presurgical blood work revealed she was already pregnant. There had been no way to reach out to Mac to let him know, but she figured he would eventually be happy about the news. Everything was going fine, but then four months later she'd miscarried.

She fought back the sob rattling her chest. When she was told she was having a boy she'd started thinking of names and in private moments called him TT. Tiny Thurston. She had wanted to share the news with Mac and had worried that by the time he returned, she would have had their son without him.

Wiping the tears from her eyes, she finished the rest of the coffee before forcing her mind to remember something else…namely that phone call she had received from the man who'd been her grandparents' attorney and the news he'd given her. The couple she'd sold her ranch to, close to twelve years ago now, were putting it on the market. According to the terms of the contract, they had to give her the first opportunity to buy it back. At the time she'd made that stipulation, she didn't think they would go for it, but the Jacobins had wanted to buy the ranch badly enough to agree with her terms. And of course, she'd thought they would never sell the ranch, but according to her grandparents' former attorney, because of Mr. Jacobin's failing health, they had no choice.

For her, that offer was a dream come true. She'd only been given ten days to take it and it had to be done in person. Unlike when she'd sold the ranch, she and Mac now had the means to buy it back. But the time frame meant the decision had to be made without Mac's input. So, she had.

She had weighed the advantages against the disadvantages and, in the end, she'd decided that buying the

ranch would be good for her family. A bigger house.
More land for their kids to spread out and enjoy. Getting
back to nature. A way to supplement their income after
Mac retired, if they decided to raise cattle for market.

Remembering her days spent on the ranch while
growing up, she wanted the same kind of memories
for her girls. There were good schools in the area and
although most of the neighbors who'd been her grandparents' friends had passed on, their heirs were people
Teri had grown up with and whom she looked forward
to sharing friendships with again.

Teri had figured she wouldn't be gone but for a day
and appreciated her neighbor and friend Carla for agreeing to watch the kids while Teri flew to Terrell, Texas,
to finalize the sale. The day after she returned to Virginia was when she began having stomach pains. Within
twenty-four hours, she'd lost the baby. Although the
doctor claimed her traveling had nothing to do with it,
she couldn't help wondering if it had.

She'd gained the ranch she'd thought lost to her for
good, but lost the baby she'd never expected to have.

Losing the baby had been hard and she appreciated
her in-laws for their love and support during a very difficult time for her. She'd tried pulling herself out of the
slump she'd felt herself slowly sinking into, and when
she'd been nearly at her wit's end, she'd called her in-
laws after her grief counselor suggested she get away
for a while.

Had the home she'd repurchased been empty she
would have gone there, but the sellers had asked to remain in the house three months before they were required to move out. She had no problem with that since
Mac was gone on a mission and she didn't want to move

their family to the ranch without letting him know what she'd done. She could just imagine Mac returning home to find a for sale sign on their home in Virginia without knowing all the details of why.

So here she was trying to deal with a number of things and wishing her husband was here with her. But then, maybe it was a good thing he wasn't. She believed he would understand how she felt about losing the baby and give her all the support and love she needed, but there was also the issue of the ranch she'd purchased. Would he understand that she'd done what she felt she had to do in the time limit she'd been given? They'd talked about getting a new house, but how would he feel about moving from Virginia to Texas? To the house that used to be her childhood home?

The other piece was that she'd paid a lot for the purchase, deciding to pay cash instead of getting a mortgage. How would Mac react when he found out she'd used their money to do so, without consulting him?

All those questions with no answers were issues that had kept her up at night.

She had endured long weeks of foreboding and her senses were filled with unease and worry about both situations. The surgery to have her tubes tied had been rescheduled and she was having apprehensions about that, and although a part of her wanted to believe that buying the ranch had been for the best, she wasn't sure how Mac would feel about it.

Being here at *this* ranch had helped soothe her mind and she didn't regret coming here, although she did miss the girls. There were so many activities to enjoy, and yesterday she'd even helped with the branding of the cattle and participated in a roundup. After today, she would only have four days left here and then she would return to Virginia, to her daughters and to wait for Mac to come home.

Mac.

Lately things hadn't been so great between them.

They seemed to argue more when he returned after being away. She didn't think it was related to PTSD; it was just a case of two strong-willed individuals not always agreeing on certain things. It was so hard for him to understand that while he was away, she was both mom and dad, and when he returned it wasn't easy for her to relinquish one of them. Usually by the time she did, he was gone again. Why was it becoming a vicious cycle that seemed to threaten their marriage to the point where she'd begun feeling that she was taken for granted?

There it was again.

Questions with no answers. Problems that needed solving.

She wanted, for the time being, to clear her mind of all of it and to recall a time when she didn't have any worries. Or at least not too many—for even back then she had been trying to decide how she would run a ranch without her grandparents. But all those years ago she had been a young girl who'd met a man she knew was meant to be a part of her life and she a part of his.

As she stood there sipping her coffee, her mind drifted back to that time...

Ten years ago

Less than an hour after her friend LaDorria had introduced them, Teri had known Thurston McRoy was a take-charge kind of man who was military through and through.

In addition to being breathtakingly handsome, he was also incredibly charming and outrageously kind. She'd discovered just how kind when they'd left the rodeo and they'd gone, along with LaDorria and Lawton, to this bar-and-grill for food and beer. He'd opened doors for her, pulled out chairs and hadn't tried taking control of their conversations.

He hadn't come on too strong, yet he'd managed to overwhelm her just the same. She had discovered he was someone easy to talk to, someone who had the ability to make her feel comfortable around him. It seemed LaDorria and Lawton had intentionally left them alone by staying on the dance floor. But she hadn't minded. It was during that time that she'd gotten to size him up. To see how he treated people, from the waiter who took their order to the busboy who'd come to clear off their table. He'd treated everyone with respect and gone out of his way to make their servers feel appreciated.

Although she had enjoyed that night with Mac, she hadn't been certain he would want to see her again. He'd asked for her phone number at the end of the night, but that didn't particularly mean anything. She'd long discovered that some men didn't care about dating a girl who not only loved horses but who was an ace on the back of one. Then there was her skill with a rope and her expertise with barrel racing. They preferred women who were all class and sophistication. Ones who wore expensive gowns rather than jeans and a Western shirt.

It didn't take long for her to see Mac wasn't that type of man. He had followed up their date with a number of phone calls. Her ability to rope a calf didn't bother him and he'd even said he liked how she looked in a pair of jeans. He'd told her that although he wasn't an expert on a horse like she was, he could ride and enjoyed riding because his grandparents owned a horse ranch.

Then there was the night he'd surprised her and shown up at one of her rodeos in Montana. She had won her competition that night and had felt good about it. After the rodeo she had seen him waiting on her, dressed as a cowboy with a Stetson on his head. She had found herself even more attracted to him and had offered no resistance when he'd taken her hand to lead her over to the SUV he'd rented.

"Where are we going?" she asked him when he opened the vehicle's door.

"I'm taking you somewhere to celebrate your win. You looked fantastic out there and you did an awesome job."

His words had made her feel good. Pretty darn special and she felt even more special in his company.

They'd had a lively discussion on their way to the restaurant for dinner. He'd told her more about both his grandfathers and how their time in the military had made him desire a military life of his own. She knew when his maternal grandfather had retired he and Mac's grandmother had purchased a ranch in Florida.

"I've never been to Florida."

He glanced over at her strangely when he brought the car to a stop in the restaurant's parking lot. "You haven't?"

"No. I heard the beaches there are beautiful."

He nodded. "They are, but then, Texas has beautiful beaches. I remember spending the weekend in Galveston one year."

She'd been tempted to inquire who he'd spent the weekend with but hadn't. Instead she said, "I bet you had a lot of fun."

"I did," he said, grinning over at her.

During the walk to the restaurant's door he told her more about himself and the more she got to know about him, the more she liked him. That night had pretty much established how things would be between them. She had accepted that he'd opted for a career as a navy SEAL and she knew any woman in his life would have to live with that choice. Since she'd been seriously considering selling her ranch, the idea of having a life with him, which would include traveling around the world, intrigued her.

When he invited her to Barcelona, she'd said yes right away, and those two weeks had been a game changer. She'd seen just what life with Mac would be like. As he showed her around Spain, she'd fallen in love with him. She had been a virgin and the night they'd made love for the first time was something she would never forget. He had made it special for her.

They had talked a lot, as well. Mac had told about his parents' interracial marriage and how dedicated they'd been to making it successful, remaining partners in all things. That was the kind of marriage he wanted for himself. One filled with love and commitment. She'd known that was the kind of marriage she wanted for herself, too, one where divorce would never be an option. The kind she was raised to believe her own parents had found, and the kind she knew her grandparents had shared.

Those had been the best two weeks of her life and

before she left to return to the United States, he'd asked her to marry him.

Not seeing any reason to have a long engagement, they'd gotten married a month later and she had no regrets.

Teri brought her thoughts back to the present. Lawton and LaDorria had gotten married a year after Mac and Teri and they were still together, living in New Mexico with their two kids. Lawton had gotten out of the military and had gone to work for the FBI. LaDorria had expanded her love of photography and opened her own shop. Teri and Mac heard from them from time to time, and she always looked forward to the Christmas photo card they sent each year. They always looked so happy. So perfect. She didn't want to think about how things weren't so photo perfect with her and Mac.

Placing the coffee cup aside, she moved toward the bedroom. It was time to get dressed for her daily morning ride on Amsterdam.

"I'm sorry, Mr. McRoy, but your name is not on the registration. Until Mrs. McRoy gives her permission for you to be added, we can't give you a key to her cabin."

Mac forced back his anger, trying to understand the man's position. He knew the rules were due to security measures, which he should appreciate. After all, for all the staff knew, he could very well be an ex-husband intent on doing bodily harm to his wife. That wasn't the case, although he would admit his anger had only grown on the flight here. It had been his fifth flight in less than twenty-four hours. His fifth flight since his commanding officer had told the team they were free to go home and, unless there was some type of international crisis that required their SEAL team to go into action, they had the next six months on leave.

It was six months all of them needed after their last operation. Because of the success of their mission, Americans would be able to sleep safe at night, and to him and his teammates, that was what truly mattered. But for him the battle wasn't over whenever he returned home. Those were the times he had to fight to reconnect with Teri. "That's fine," he finally said, seeing the man's features relax. He knew the clerk had expected an argument and a part of Mac was raring to give him one, but what would have been the use? "Do you have any idea where she is so she can give me permission?"

"We tried calling the cabin and she's not answering, so we can only assume she's out riding. I believe she does that every morning."

"Does she come here for breakfast?"

"No. She's in one of the cabins farthest away, one with a stocked kitchen." And then, as if realizing he might have provided too much information, he added, "That's all I can tell you. I left Ms. McRoy a voice-mail message. If you'd like to sit over there and wait, I'm sure she will be returning my call shortly."

"I'd rather wait outside. That way I can walk around a bit to stretch my legs. Can I leave my gear here while I do?"

"Yes, sir, you can."

Mac handed his duffel bag to the man before turning to walk out the door. He stepped out on the porch and drew in a deep breath, appreciating the moment of breathing in good American air. He'd been in Libya too long and was glad to be home. Only thing, he wasn't home. It wasn't even close enough to home to suit him. Getting on another plane within a few hours after getting off one hadn't made his day or his night, which he was yet to have. He hadn't slept in over thirty hours.

Glancing around, he saw the changes that had been made since the last time he'd been here on his honeymoon. There was a spanking new barn that was a lot bigger than the last one had been. Even the main ranch house had gotten a face-lift. It was three times the size it was before. He'd noticed the sign that read Under New Management the moment he'd walked into the place.

He was about to step off the porch when his cell phone rang. Recognizing the ringtone, he pulled the phone out of the back pocket of his jeans and clicked on. "Yeah, Bane?"

"You know the routine, Mac. You didn't touch base with any of us to let us know you'd gotten home."

He released a frustrated breath before saying, "I'm not home."

"Why the hell not?" That question came from another team member, Gavin Blake, whose code name was Viper. That meant in addition to Viper and Bane, Mac was on a call with the other two team members he was close friends with, as well: David Holloway, whose code name was Flipper, and Laramie Cooper, whose code name was Coop.

"Because when I got home, I discovered Teri was missing."

"Missing? What do you mean Teri was missing?" Flipper wanted to know.

"And your answer better be good, Mac. I hope she hasn't finally taken enough of your BS and left your ass," Coop added.

Mac rubbed his hand down his face. He didn't need his teammates to remind him that at times he wasn't the easiest man to get along with. "Will the four of you calm down?" Leaning against the porch post, he then told them what he knew. At least what his parents had told him. Which hadn't been much.

"And you haven't seen her yet?" Bane asked.

"No. I haven't been here but a few minutes. She's out riding and since my name isn't on her registration, they won't tell me which cabin she's staying in or give me a key."

"That's understandable," Viper said.

"Yes, but that doesn't mean I have to like it."

"Calm down, Mac," Bane warned.

Now they were the ones telling him to calm down. "I am calm. I haven't hit anything yet."

"And you won't. Listen to what Teri has to say. She must have had a good reason for taking off and leaving the kids with your folks," Coop was saying.

"Yes, and try to be understanding, no matter the reason," Viper suggested.

"And another thing," Flipper, the most recently married one of the team, spoke up to say, but Mac stopped him.

"Hold up. I don't need you guys giving me marital advice. I've been married a lot longer than any of you."

"That might be true, but you have a tendency to act like an ass at times, like you know everything," Coop said. "We've been gone awhile. Eight months, twelve days and fifteen hours to be exact. Show your woman how much you miss her, love her and appreciate her."

Mac shook his head. "Like I said, guys, I don't need your advice. I know how to handle my business."

"Your way of handling things doesn't work all the time, Mac," Viper said. "That's all we're saying."

Mac rubbed the back of his neck and felt a tension headache coming on. He never got headaches. "Duly noted. Now, goodbye."

"Hey, call us later to let us know things are okay," Bane said.

Mac rolled his eyes. "I'll think about it." He then clicked off the phone.

Teri had returned to the cabin after her morning ride and was about to go into the kitchen to prepare something to eat for breakfast when she noticed the blinking light on the cabin's telephone. She thought about ignoring it, thinking it was probably the resort manager giving her a rundown of that day's activities. However, she felt compelled to answer it anyway. Her cell phone was out of range and wasn't working. What if it was her in-laws trying to reach her?

Moving quickly to the phone, she picked it up to retrieve the message. "Ms. McRoy, this is Harold at the front desk. Please call me as soon as you get this message."

Teri pressed the number seven and Harold picked up immediately. "Harold, you called. Is something wrong?"

"No, ma'am. There's a man here who says he's your husband and has asked for a key to your cabin. Company policy restricts us from doing that. Said his name is Thurston McRoy."

Teri's heart suddenly began pounding hard in her chest. Mac was here? She drew in a deep breath. He must have returned and found she'd left and her in-laws had told him where she was? Had they also told him why she'd taken off? Did he know—

"Ms. McRoy? Is it okay to give him a key with directions on how to get to your cabin?"

She swallowed. "Is he there? If so, please let me talk with him."

"No, he's not here inside. He stepped outside."

Probably to cool off, she thought. Coming home and finding her gone had probably pissed him off. Coming after her would have made him angrier. Then being denied access to her cabin would have made the situation even worse.

"I can go outside and get him if you need to talk to him."

She drew in a deep breath. Knowing Mac, she figured that would agitate him even more. "No, that's not necessary. Please give him a key and directions on how to get here."

"Okay, I will."

When Teri hung up the phone, she drew in a deep breath.

She wouldn't have those additional three days alone here after all.

Chapter 3

Mac saw Teri the moment the SUV rounded a corner off a battered road lined with oak trees. It was in a secluded area and he wasn't sure he liked knowing she'd gotten a cabin so far from the main house. He didn't care one iota that the front desk guy had said someone from the office checked on her and all the other cabins every morning when they brought the horses.

She was dressed in Western attire and leaning against a post on a small porch. She looked good in a pair of jeans that fit perfectly over her curves, a long-sleeved shirt that, to his way of thinking, looked a little too snug over what he knew were beautiful breasts. A pair of riding boots were on her feet and a hat was covering that mass of gorgeous hair on her head.

It had been eight months since he'd seen her and at that moment his eyes couldn't help but drink in the sight of her. Damn. He'd missed her. She looked good but he couldn't let her looks and how deeply she'd been missed sway how upset he was with her right now. She owed him an explanation.

But still…

He couldn't help the flutter he felt in his heart or the yearning he felt in his soul. They might have their disagreements, some worse than others, but he knew he loved her. Always had and always would. He then thought about those disagreements. Lately there had been a lot of them. Too many. His teammates were right about him and his attitude. He tried working on it every time he returned home but Teri had a knack for making wild decisions about too many things at a time. He always looked at the whole picture. She didn't. If it was something she wanted, then she would find a way to justify them getting it. Then she would go on the defensive when he questioned her about it.

Mac didn't have a problem with her spending money—he just needed her to do so wisely. He remembered his parents' struggles over money and had sworn when he became an adult that wouldn't be him. Of course later he learned most of their struggles had been about sacrifices they'd made for him and Kylie.

Although his parents were pretty close to their own parents, during the earlier years of their marriage, neither liked hitting them up for loans when they'd encountered financial challenges. That wasn't the McRoy way. They had taught him early in life that if you make the bills, then you were responsible for paying them. That's one of the reasons he'd learned early to invest his money and had a nice bank account when he'd married Teri. He'd been intent on making sure she got all the things she needed, but not necessarily those things she wanted just for the sake of having them. There should always be money for rainy days, and then he was also focused on generational wealth to pass on to his daughters. Something his parents hadn't been able to do for him or his sister. So far the stock market had been good and those investments were better than he'd ever imagined.

Bringing the SUV to a stop in front of the cabin, he cut the ignition. She hadn't moved. She was still standing there, leaning against the post with one of those "I need to decipher your mood before I approach" looks on her face. Whether she knew it or not, usually that look told him more than what he wanted to know. Now he couldn't help wondering just what had gone on while he'd been away. He was also curious about how she had handled it and whether or not he would agree with the outcome.

He got out of the vehicle and closed the door behind him. "Teri." He suddenly felt his gut clench from the effect her honey-brown eyes had on him.

"Hi, Mac."

He tried not to focus on her lips but was powerless to do anything less. He loved her lips. The shape. The taste. And then because neither of them could help themselves after being separated for over eight months, they began moving toward each other as sexual tension sizzled between them. The moment she was there, standing directly in front of him, he pulled her into his arms. Explanations would come later. Right now, this was what he needed. The feel of her warm, feminine body pressed against his and the taste of her mouth.

He kissed her, long and deep, the woman he'd loved for over ten years. The woman who had rocked his world the first time he'd seen her. The woman who still managed to remind him what a damn lucky bastard he was even on those days when he felt like nothing was going right with her. She was the mother of his children and the reason he fought hard during every covert operation. He wanted to come back to her.

To this.

He deepened the kiss and she reciprocated in kind. He loved her taste. Always had and he figured he always would. She moaned into his mouth and he loved the sound. It had been a while since the last time he'd heard it. And he wanted more. More moans. More of her body pressed against his. He wanted her naked.

She could explain the reason she'd felt the need to come here later. He needed her now.

Sweeping her off her feet, he carried her into the house.

Teri felt them moving and knew they were headed for the bedroom. She had to stop him. More important, she had to stop herself from once again being totally overwhelmed by Mac. She wanted him and he wanted her and, in the past, knowing that had been enough.

But not this time.

She was tired of the off-the-chart-lovemaking followed by the questions and arguments. They needed to talk first.

When she yanked her mouth from his, he placed her on her feet, and she scrambled out of his arms. She looked up at him. Mac was tall, way over six feet. He had skin the color of café au lait, dark brown eyes, solid cheekbones, a sturdy neck and a pair of the sexiest lips any man had a right to own. And whether he was clean-shaven or sporting a beard on his masculine jaw like he was doing now, Mac was a hunk. A very sensuous and handsome hunk. He stood there, his focus entirely on her, and the desire she saw in his eyes wasn't helping the situation.

"What's wrong, Teri?"

If only he knew.

"We need to talk first, Mac." She needed to tell him everything. About the baby and about the purchase of her ranch. Not to mention all the doubts she'd been having.

He reached back out for her. "We can talk later."

That was his answer for almost everything. Whenever sexual need took over his mind on his return from a mission, the lovemaking would come first, followed by a good whole day of sleep. After that he'd spend quality time with the girls. Only then would he turn his well-rested, all-too-critical attention to her. He would ask how things had gone while he'd been away. She would tell him. Then the arguments would start. He would tell her how he would have handled the situation differently had he been there.

That "I know what's best" attitude would rattle her. It was what had driven them to seek marriage counseling when they'd reached the five-year mark in their marriage. He'd disliked Mr. Blum, the counselor. He hadn't like airing their dirty laundry to a total stranger, nor had he liked having that same person remind him that marriage was a partnership.

"No, Mac, we need to talk now."

He eyed her warily. "Why can't it hold, baby? I missed you. I love you and I need you, Teri. I need you bad."

She drew in a deep breath, knowing that was that. Those sentences got to her as much as the sight of him standing there.

Her Mac.

Because she knew from the look in his eyes that he did need her. She never knew what happened during those covert operations, the hell he went through, or how close he came to losing his life. Any information was highly classified and he couldn't tell her, so he held it inside. But she would know how hard it had been from the intensity of their lovemaking whenever he returned. And his words were always the key. The words he'd just spoken pretty much let her know that before they talked, he felt an urgency to let himself go. To reclaim his soul and hold on to his sanity. He wanted to forget all the anguish of the last eight months. Forget it and release it in her arms.

But what about her anguish? Wanting to reclaim her soul and hold on to her sanity? What about how she'd suffered in losing the baby she'd wanted and how she inwardly blamed herself…no matter what the doctor said. She would always wonder if traveling to Texas had been the cause.

"Teri?"

Mac saying her name made her realize that she'd just been standing there, staring at him. He had extended his hand out to her. Should she take it and find peace in his arms for a little while? Could they put off talking for later like he'd suggested?

Knowing no matter how much she wanted to, probably should, she couldn't deny Mac anything.

At that moment he was as crucial to her as she believed she was to him.

She took the couple of steps to him and placed her hand in his. He pulled her closer and swept her back into his arms to carry her into the bedroom.

When he placed her on the bed, at that moment everything felt good, right, so totally perfect. For now, she would put out of her mind any thoughts of those things that had driven her here. Instead she would give her full concentration to the man whose eyes were connected to hers. The man who was looking at her with intense, deep passion and desire.

And she was returning that gaze with the same need and longing. She knew her eyes were filled with the desire of a woman who loved and appreciated the man standing beside the bed, staring down at her. He'd removed his shirt and she thought the same thing now that she had when they'd met over ten years ago. Thurston McRoy was a very good-looking man. The six-foot-three-inch hulk of a navy SEAL could be one tough-as-nails badass but also a total pushover when it came to his girls. Although she might not know the details of the covert operation he'd just left, there was no doubt he and his teammates had been through hell and back and that they had left their mark on anyone who dared to threaten the country they loved.

"Like what you see, Teri Anne?"

He always asked her that question and her response would always be the same. Yes, she loved what she saw, especially his well-built body. He exercised often, and it showed. He was slightly older than most of his teammates and claimed he had to make sure he stayed in shape to keep up with them. Whatever the reason, he wore his age of thirty-nine well. She wondered if he was still thinking of retiring from military service at forty-one. He hadn't talked about retirement much lately. Her husband was a SEAL through and through and she couldn't imagine him being anything else. A lot of people assumed SEALs were paid a huge salary for the risks they took with their lives for their country, but they weren't. Most made under sixty thousand a year. She knew for most military men it wasn't about the salary but the service. She could say the same for Mac. The only reason they had everything they needed was because of his initiative in investing alongside his friend Bane Westmoreland.

Knowing he was still waiting on her response, she said, "Yes, I definitely like what I see, Thurston McRoy."

She mostly referred to him by his given name in the bedroom. She called him Thurston and he called her Teri Anne. They felt doing so created an even more intimate bond between them. Like they were using that time to not only deepen their connection but to get to know each other all over again. Something they felt they needed to do whenever he returned from his long excursions.

Smiling, he leaned down and captured her lips and she suddenly became drenched in passion of the most provocative kind. Eight months was a long time to be without each other and their bodies were letting them know it. The starvation and greed were evident.

Their tongues tangled and swirled, feasting on each other. For a minute it was hard to decipher which one was his and which was hers. Didn't matter. They shared the hunger, the persistence, the ravenousness. Everything about Mac was delectable—his taste, the way she fit in his arms, the way their bodies meshed together like that was the way they were supposed to be.

Finally, he snatched his mouth back and began undressing her with the urgency of a man who knew what he wanted but thought he might just die before getting it. When she was totally naked, he paused a moment and stared at her with the keen eyes of a husband. A lover. A man who knew her body in and out. Could he detect that something had been there that he hadn't known about? But was there no more?

"You're beautiful as ever. I am one hell of a lucky man."

His words made a knot in her throat thicken. He could say some of the most touching things. "And I'm a lucky woman."

Her head began whirling as he lowered his mouth to hers again and captured her mouth like he had before. Like he had every right to do so and intended to take full advantage of that fact.

Breaking off the kiss he moved back to remove the rest of his clothes and she got turned on just watching him. Jeans so tight they seemed imprinted on his flesh were slid down tight, masculine thighs. Then he stood there in sexy black briefs that clearly defined how well-endowed her man was.

Her man.

Yes, he was that and he would continue to be her man. Whatever issues they were dealing with were merely hiccups along the way. They would just have to deal with them later. She just hoped that when they did, they would remember this time when they pushed all thoughts, except for each other, aside, and put their love front and center.

She watched him ease his briefs down his legs and then he moved toward her with blazing hot desire burning in his eyes. "I want you," she whispered.

"I want you, too," he whispered back, placing a knee on the bed and then drawing her to him. He kissed her again, long and deep, before releasing her and moving back from the bed to stare at her nakedness.

She felt her stomach tighten and her navel tingle. Seeing him without clothes was making heat consume her from top to bottom. "I love undressing you. I've thought of doing it every single day I was gone."

His words sparked every cell within her. Mac had the ability to use words to take her to another level. That, combined with her physical attraction to him and the sexual chemistry that always seemed to radiate between them, made what they were sharing mind-blowingly extraordinary. The thought that he could desire her so deeply always did something to her.

He moved back to the bed and whispered erotic words in several different languages as he lowered her back against the pillows. And when he towered over her, she felt overwhelmed by the look she saw in his eyes.

She felt his hard shaft sliding inside her and she cried out his name, loving the feel of him stretching her. He kept going deep until he couldn't go any more. He began moving, slow at first, then faster, thrusting in and out, and she couldn't help crying out his name again and again. Then a climax struck her, ripping through her with an impact that nearly stopped her breathing.

She heard Mac's deep growl, the prologue to his orgasmic release. His thrusts kept coming, deeper and harder, and then she felt the instant his body began trembling above her, exploding inside of her.

"Teri…" He whispered her name seconds before leaning in and taking her mouth in his, kissing her as if to make up for the eight months they'd been apart.

She returned his kiss with just as much hunger and need. When he finally released her mouth she whispered, "Welcome back, Mac."

Then he reclaimed her mouth as if to start their love-making process all over again.

Chapter 4

Teri raced Amsterdam across the grassy plains with her hair blowing in the wind.

She loved this and hadn't realized how much she'd missed racing until this trip. With Tia taking riding classes, Teri had saddled up to ride, as well. But racing her horse was what she liked best. She needed this and she needed it now.

She had awakened that morning feeling somewhat dazed after making love to her husband most of yesterday and last night. Her pulse pounded every time she thought of all the things they'd done. At one point she'd thought he had fallen asleep from exhaustion and she had moved to ease out of bed.

Mac had awakened quickly and looked over at her. His eyes, laden with sleep, still managed to simmer with desire, and he had then proceeded to show her once again just how badly he wanted her.

She didn't have to go into town to call to check on the kids. Although her cell phone didn't work, Mac's special government issue security phone worked just fine. They'd talked to Mac's parents and the girls.

Late yesterday evening they had left the cabin to drive to Cheyenne for dinner and to shop at one of the Western outfitters. Mac had told her he would be staying with her for the rest of the week, which she'd figured he would. He had purchased several pieces of Western wear and he looked sexy as hell wearing a Stetson on his head.

She figured they would get the chance to have their talk during dinner but instead he steered the conversation, deliberately or otherwise, to other things. Such as the monstrosity of a house his teammate Bane Westmoreland and his wife, Crystal, were having built. They would be hosting a housewarming party when the house was completed and Mac and Teri were invited to attend.

She'd followed his line of conversation and brought him up to date on the girls, telling him how well Tia was doing with her horse-riding lessons and how Tatum had expressed an interest in gymnastics. And of course that meant Tempest was interested, too. She'd mentioned how she'd called in a plumber for the kitchen sink and about their yardman's illness. He'd listened as he always did and asked questions when he'd needed to do so.

She slowed Amsterdam down and headed back toward the cabin. This was the second time she'd ridden him today. As Mac usually did after returning from a long operation, he had slept through breakfast and lunch and there was no reason not to think he wouldn't sleep through dinner. He always said it was only when he was back on American soil he could let his guard down and sleep peacefully. Usually the girls, upon hearing their father had returned home, would camp outside the bedroom door waiting for him to wake up. He had a close relationship with their daughters and was a good dad.

As she trotted the horse back toward the cabin, she saw Mac. He was standing in the same spot on the porch where she'd been standing yesterday when he had arrived. He was leaning against the post, jeans riding low on his hips, shirtless and with a Stetson on his head.

She tightened her hands on the horse's reins. Her libido should be exhausted after the sexual activities she and Mac had participated in during the past twenty-four hours. Instead, however, it was flaring back to life. Why did he have to look so sexy standing there while sipping his coffee with his full attention on her?

She brought the horse to a stop and eased down, tying Amsterdam to the hitching post. "You're up, I see."

"Yes, and the first thing I noticed was that you were gone."

She came up the steps to him. "Did you honestly expect me to stay in bed and sleep as long as you did?"

"You used to."

She nodded, remembering. Yes, she had. That was before their first child. Whenever he came back from being gone on one of his operations, she'd been more than happy to spend her time lying in bed beside him for hours, days and nights.

She tilted her head back to look up at him. "That was the pre-babies days."

He chuckled. "You're right about that. In fact, I do believe it was during one of those sleep-ins that Tia was conceived."

It had been and him bringing that up reminded her of the reason she'd come to the dude ranch in the first place. "Yes, that's when Tia was conceived."

Neither one of them said anything for a minute and then Mac said, "I think it's time for us to talk, Teri. I need to know what drove you to come here."

As far as she was concerned it was past time. "Okay, let's talk."

She walked past him to go inside and he followed.

Mac watched his wife dust herself off before sitting down on the sofa. "Let me put this away," he said, before going into the kitchen to place the empty coffee cup in the sink.

She had wanted to tell him yesterday about whatever had driven her here and he should have been ready to hear it then. After all, he'd come home to find her gone, with his parents suddenly developing lockjaw about why she'd taken off. During the flight here, he'd been antsy about hearing what she had to say.

Then he'd seen her and the only thing he'd wanted was her. That had been pretty damn understandable since she was his wife and he hadn't seen or touched her in eight months. Teri would always be a desirable woman to him. In reality, she was a lot more. Whether she knew it or not, she was his life. He loved her so damn much. His teammates thought if she didn't know her value to him it was his damn fault for not telling her and saying it often.

Mac always felt he shouldn't have to tell her because she should know that she and the girls meant everything to him. He didn't take any chances with his life because of them. His goal for every covert operation was to come home alive and in one piece to Teri and the girls. He loved being a husband and father.

Returning to the living room, he took the seat across from her. It didn't take a rocket scientist to see that she was nervous. Why?

"So what is it, Teri? What big-ticket item did you buy while I was gone that was over-the-top enough to send you here?"

He could tell by the surprised look on her face that he'd been right. She had bought something and whatever it was, she knew it would be something he wouldn't like. Last year it had been a new bedroom set when they'd given Tia their old one. That didn't bother him as much as the price she'd paid for it. As far as he was concerned, a bed that cost that much should have the ability to sing them to sleep. They didn't have to worry about making ends meet, but it was the principle!

"That's not the reason I came here, Mac."

He nodded. "Okay, then, what's the reason?"

For a long moment, she didn't say anything and he watched her intently. When he saw the first sign of the tears that appeared in her eyes, he was out of his chair in a flash. He went over to the sofa and pulled her into his arms. His wife wasn't a crier unless she was truly upset about something.

"What is it, Teri? What's wrong?"

She looked up at him and took a deep breath, as if trying to find the courage to tell him whatever she had to say. He tensed, not knowing what would come next, and hoped he was prepared for whatever it was.

"We agreed that we wouldn't have any more children, and I was to have that surgery."

He watched her closely. "Yes, we did agree to that. I

wanted to be here with you for the surgery, but then I got that call from my commanding officer to leave immediately. You said you would have the surgery as scheduled and get the folks to come help out with the kids."

Mac watched her features and had an idea where this conversation was headed. "Are you trying to tell me that you didn't have the surgery after all, Teri?" He'd known that although they'd agreed the surgery was necessary, having another child would not have bothered her in the least.

"I couldn't."

He stared at her. "What do you mean you couldn't? We agreed that you would."

"I know, but—"

"Let me guess," he interrupted to say. "You changed your mind about having it done, right? It wouldn't be the first time you reneged on something we agreed to do, Teri. You had no right to take it upon yourself to do that. That was a decision we'd made together."

She pushed out of his arms, her features furious. "Damn you, Mac, don't you think I know what we agreed to do. I was going to have the procedure done, but like I said, I couldn't," she said, almost screaming at him, clearly getting emotional.

"Why?" he asked, crossing his arms over his chest.

"Because when I had my presurgical workup done, the doctor discovered I was pregnant."

Mac's head began spinning. He dropped his arms to his side. "Pregnant?"

"Yes, pregnant! Although a baby was something we hadn't planned, I figured you would want him."

"Him?"

"Yes, him. I carried our son for four months and then

I lost him. I lost my baby. Our baby." She then rushed from the house.

He stood there in shock. Teri had been pregnant? She'd gotten as far as four months and then miscarried? Their son? Oh, my God, what had happened? Snapping out of his shock, he quickly went to the door after her. He opened it in time to see Teri galloping off on that horse.

Teri kept riding, refusing to look back when Mac called after her and rebuffing the idea of going back to finish her conversation with him. At the moment she needed to get as far away as she could in order to pull herself together. Then she would go back. But not now.

She needed to be alone.

She knew Mac and truly believed that although they hadn't planned for a baby, he would have wanted their son. It would not have mattered if it had been a boy or girl. Mac would have wanted their baby. He loved kids. They both did. They had wanted three but had decided to try a fourth time for a boy. When it turned out to be a girl, they'd decided to have no more tries and had agreed four was enough.

Teri knew the only reason Mac had gone off like he had just now was because they were still at odds with each other. He believed she would defy him at every turn, and unfortunately, over the years, she had given him reason to think so. She never did anything deliberately, but it always seemed that way to him.

What he had to understand and what she'd tried explaining to him countless times was that when he was gone, she became the head of the household. That meant she had to make decisions without him. He claimed he didn't have a problem with that, yet he never agreed with any of the choices she made.

He would return home and begin questioning her decisions. On top of that he tried to control everything, as if he could just reappear after being gone for months and disrupt their lives. While he was gone, everything ran like a finely tuned machine. When he returned, that machine would break down. He would be so glad to see the girls that he would let them get away with murder. Then when he left it was up to her to implement martial law all over again and become what the girls thought of as the mean parent. She was sick and tired of him questioning what she did and why she did it. She wanted a marriage where she felt any decision she made wouldn't be questioned and ridiculed.

She slowed Amsterdam down to a trot and noticed she was in a different area from where she'd ridden before. Ahead she saw a large windmill and remembered that when they'd come here for their honeymoon this had been a coal miners' camp. Several mines were in the area and were now deserted, their openings boarded up.

Teri had been a history major in college and recalled that years ago several settlements in Wyoming had been considered mining towns. Even now Wyoming was the largest producer of coal in the country. She wondered when these particular mines had shut down since she recalled them being in operation when she'd been here on her honeymoon.

She nudged Amsterdam toward an area where she'd seen a huge lake the first day she'd ridden out this far. That particular area had reminded her of a section of her grandparents' property, which was now legally hers again. She wished she could be happy about that but knew she couldn't until she told Mac what she'd done.

It didn't take her long to reach the lake. Getting off Amsterdam, she tied him to a tree and decided to walk around awhile to calm her nerves before heading back. Before knowing all the facts, Mac had reacted pretty angrily to her not having that procedure done. If his re-action was an example of his mood, she wasn't in any hurry to tell him about her ranch. But she would tell him. It was best to tell him everything, let him get mad and then get over it.

And he would get over it, eventually.

She just hated this pattern they had to go through whenever he returned home. Should they seek marriage counseling again? She knew that was out of the ques-tion since he'd hated it the last time. Still, Teri couldn't discount the potential of another issue being added to the mix. Like she'd told him, she hadn't gotten that sur-gical procedure done. What she hadn't told him was that she hadn't been taking any type of birth control since. His arrival had been unexpected and when they'd made love, he hadn't used protection. What if she was pregnant again? Had he considered that possibility yet? Would he understand why she still hadn't gotten the procedure done three months later?

No, he wouldn't understand.

The more she thought about it, the more she felt she still needed time to herself. She'd told him what had happened with the baby and for now that was enough. At a later time she would go more into details, but for now she needed her time here to deal with things with-out him. The best way to handle Mac was to ask him to leave.

She wasn't sure how long she'd walked around the lake, deep in her thoughts, when suddenly she heard the sound of a horse approaching. When she glanced around, she saw it was Mac. He was racing his horse toward her. Unsurprisingly, he had a fierce frown on his face.

He barely brought the horse to a stop and was off the animal's back, looking every bit the cowboy in his jeans, Western shirt, boots and the Stetson on his head. Her husband was a gorgeous man, regardless of whether he was wearing navy attire or dressed as he was now. She could see him riding the range of the forty-acre ranch they now owned.

A ranch she had yet to tell him about.

He rushed over to her. "Why did you leave like that, Teri?"

She lifted her chin. "Honestly? What else was I to say, Mac?"

He reached out and pulled her into his arms. "I'm sorry, baby," he murmured brokenly. "I'm sorry you went through that alone. I'm sorry I wasn't there for you. And I would have wanted our baby, please know that."

She fought back tears when she lifted her head to look up at him. "I know that, Mac. I never doubted that you would. But what hurts more than anything is that I lost the son we wanted." And then she buried her face in his chest and sobbed.

Mac held his wife while she cried. The sound nearly broke his heart. He felt like an ass for saying what he had earlier without knowing all the facts. And now that he did know, he hurt right along with her.

He'd always wanted a big family and so had Teri.

Using sound judgment, they'd decided to stop at four. It was hard enough for Teri to handle everything alone when he was gone on his missions, without adding another child to their family. But that hadn't meant they would not have welcomed a fifth. She was a wonderful mother to his kids. He knew that. He also knew that after having four girls they'd entertained the idea of trying again for a son but had decided not to. There was no guarantee their fifth child would be a boy.

But it had been.

He gently stroked her back, wondering what had caused the miscarriage. He was about to ask when she pushed herself out of his arms. "I need time alone, Mac. Please leave."

He shook his head. "There's no way I'm going back to the cabin and leave you out here."

"No, I don't want you to do that. I want you to leave and go back to Virginia. I'll be home in a few days and we'll talk some more then."

Mac knew he had to be looking at her like she'd lost her mind. "I'm not going anywhere and leaving you here, Teri. Whatever happens in our marriage we're in this together. We—"

"No, Mac. With you it's never really 'we.' Not really. It's what you want and what you think, and like the good wife, I fall in line. But you know what, Mac? I didn't know how much I wanted another baby until I found out I was pregnant. Then I wanted it with everything within me. I didn't care about how difficult it would be, or how you and I can't seem to agree, because I knew we would make it work."

"Teri—"

"No, you always want me to do what you want, Mac. You never ask what I want. Like how I want to work."

"That's not fair. You knew how I felt about things before we married. Is it wrong for a man to want to take care of what's his?" he asked, not liking the way their conversation was going.

"Only when you start taking our marriage for granted."

He didn't say anything for a minute and then he asked her, "And you honestly think I've done that?"

"All I know is that I woke up yesterday morning feeling sad and depressed, and a part of me wished you were here with me."

"I am here with you now, Teri. I want to spend the rest of the week here with you. We can consider it a second honeymoon. We can—"

"No, I don't need a second honeymoon, Mac. I need a marriage with a husband who won't question everything I do when he returns home. If you stay here, we will only argue…especially when I tell you about the other thing."

Mac lifted a brow. Did that mean there was more? "What other thing?"

She shook her head. "I don't want to talk about it now. I need time alone, Mac. Please go home and stay with the girls until I return. When I get back on Sunday, I'll tell you everything."

"I am not leaving."

At that moment the sound of the horses caught their attention. Both animals were fidgeting, acting anxious and prancing about as if they were trying to get away.

"I wonder what's wrong with them," she said.

"I don't know," he replied, and they moved toward the animals to find out for themselves.

Mac glanced around. Had they picked up the scent of a wolf, coyote or some other wild animal? The closer he and Teri got to the horses, the more agitated the animals seemed to get.

"Oh, my God, Mac. Look!"

The frantic sound of Teri's voice had him looking over at her. She was pointing toward the sky. He saw it. Damn.

In the distance was a gigantic tornado. It had already touched down and was swirling right in their direction.

Chapter 5

"We need to get the hell out of here!" Mac said, pulling Teri toward the horses.

"And go where? We're not going to be able to outrun that, Mac."

"I know. I recall passing several abandoned mineshafts coming here," he said, untying her horse and handing her the reins.

"But we'll be headed toward the twister," Teri said, climbing on Amsterdam's back.

"We have no choice. If we stay here, we'll be out in the open. Our chances would be better trying to get to a mine before that damn tornado does. That means we'll need to ride like hell to get there."

Teri had no problem doing that and knew Mac didn't, either. "Then let's go."

She took off and Mac kept up with her. They had

to tighten their hold on the reins to control the horses. Animals had an instinct to avoid danger and they were forcing their steeds head-on toward it.

"It's okay, boy." She leaned in to whisper to Amsterdam. "It's okay."

As if the horse believed her, he picked up speed. And even through the sense of impending doom, Teri couldn't help smiling. From the moment Amsterdam had been selected as the horse for her during her stay, she believed they had bonded.

She glanced over at Mac and knew he had gone into SEAL mode, intent on keeping them alive, regardless of the danger. She doubted he'd talked to his horse, yet the animal seemed to accept the man on his back was master and wherever he led the horse had to go, regardless of whether he wanted to or not.

"We're almost there. I can see the windmill," Mac shouted over to her. She nodded against the wind that had picked up and she refused to look toward the sky. She just refused to do so.

They reached the area and quickly got off the horses. While Teri removed the saddlebags from the animals' backs, Mac grabbed a huge, thick limb off the ground and used it to knock some of the boards from one of the mineshaft openings. She released the horses, knowing their instinct for survival would have them running away to find refuge from the storm.

After the horses raced off, Teri rushed over to Mac. "Why did you decide on this particular mineshaft?" she asked him as she began helping to move the boards aside.

"The wider opening will afford more air to circulate. It also looks sturdier than the others and the ground

around here is damp. That means there's water somewhere in this shaft."

Teri glanced down at the ground. She hadn't noticed
that. At that moment she looked up to see several limbs
from a huge tree blown down near their feet.

"Get in. I'll take the saddlebags."

"I'll help."

Mac looked at her, opened his mouth as if he was
about to protest but then changed his mind, and said,
"Come on. We need to hurry."

Teri had never been in a mineshaft before and
glanced around. The area inside was dark. She could
barely see in front of her. When suddenly a light appeared, she saw it was the flashlight from Mac's cell
phone. It shone brighter than the one on hers.

"We need to get as far away from the opening as
possible."

Heeding Mac's advice, she followed him deeper and
deeper into the mineshaft, recalling horror stories of
miners who got trapped underground and died for lack
of air. "Let's place the saddles here," he said, placing
his on the ground, and she followed, placing hers there.

They walked farther into the mineshaft when suddenly the ground beneath their feet began to shake. At
the same time sediment began falling from the ceiling.
Mac grabbed for her and she clutched him tight while
he covered her body with his. Teri knew without being
told that the twister was practically above them.

Although they were midway in the mineshaft, they
could see debris flying around outside the mine's wide
opening. They actually saw a tree, the same one she'd
been standing under earlier, ripped from its roots to
tumble down to the ground. Appliances, from no tell-

ing where, had gotten caught up in the twister and were tossed effortlessly to the ground.

Mac tried to press her face into his chest so she wouldn't see the devastation happening around them, but she looked anyway. Suddenly, the opening was covered in tree limbs, boards and other flying debris. She glanced up at Mac, and he didn't have to tell her they were trapped inside.

As if he sensed her thoughts, he leaned in close and said, "We'll be fine, Teri. Once it passes, we'll get out of here." She wanted to believe him. She *had* to believe him. They had four little ones at home who needed them.

Five minutes later, when everything went still, they knew the twister had moved on and everything was calm again. "I'm going to remove whatever is blocking the entrance so we can get out of here," Mac said.

"And I'll help you."

Mac and Teri worked together a good twenty minutes before finally accepting the inevitable. Unblocking the entrance wasn't going to be as easy as they'd hoped. In addition to the flying debris, there seemed to be something large blocking the entry. Teri had a feeling that huge windmill had collapsed.

"What do we do now?" she asked Mac. "Can you use your phone to call for help?"

Mac shook his head, obviously frustrated. "No, but the flashlight has at least eight hours of battery life. Let's use it to see if there's another way out of here."

Teri wondered if Mac actually thought there was, or if he was saying that to calm her fears. "Okay."

He didn't say anything more as they walked farther and farther into the mineshaft. Mac would pause every so often to study the walls around them, reaching out to touch a rocky surface or a wooded wall covered with thick dust. He looked around for a long moment before turning to her. "Not certain how sturdy some of these planks are we're walking on, so watch your step."

"I'll be careful, Mac."

As if he assumed she wouldn't, he took her hand in his. She started to pull it back but figured doing such a thing would be childish. He was only making sure she was okay and wasn't going to take any chances. A part of her couldn't help appreciating his protectiveness; she knew that was an ingrained part of Mac and who he was.

When she'd met him, he'd been a SEAL and she had married him knowing what that kind of life meant for her. It hadn't mattered. She had loved him. They'd been different as day and night in how they dealt with life in general but they had always managed to work through it. As their marriage had grown, so had they. But lately it seemed they were encountering more and more roadblocks. He seemed to have less faith in her ability to handle things without his input. Was this what it meant for couples to grow apart?

She glanced over at him and saw how he was walking slowly and with purpose as he continued to take in their surroundings. There was a question she had to ask him. "Mac?"

He turned to her. "Yes?"

"Is our air supply limited in here?"

He held her gaze as if he was trying to decide how much to tell her. He then said, "Yes, somewhat, but not as much as I figured it would be."

"Why do you say that?"

"Because vegetation is covering some of the rocks."

She'd noticed it, too, but hadn't thought much about it. "And?"

"And in order for anything to grow in here it would need a sufficient amount of air, water and sunshine. I figure there is water coming from somewhere, probably some underground canal. But I'm not sure about the sunshine. This mineshaft shouldn't be anything more than a black hole in the earth's surface, and I haven't figured out the atmospheric piece yet."

She nodded. "I wonder how long it's been boarded up."

He shrugged massive shoulders that she had to admit looked good in his Western shirt. "There's no telling."

They continued walking and he held tight to her hand. When was the last time they'd held hands? Honestly, she shouldn't be wondering about that now, but she couldn't help doing so. When was the last time they'd taken time to just spend together? Just the two of them, away from the kids? Whenever he returned home, he slept the first day off. After that he had to readjust to the role of husband and father and would immediately want to become king of the castle. When that happened, his attitude would clash with hers.

Then there were always the numerous activities the kids were involved with, too many for them to set aside "daddy and mommy" time. All four girls were active in something. Even Tasha had started taking piano lessons at an early age. Several people had told them they thought their youngest daughter would grow up to be a gifted pianist one day. While Mac was home it was important to him to be there and share in their training, progress and achievements. Their daily schedules were full and to take off in search of time for each other seemed like a selfish act. Now more than ever she saw how such togetherness was needed for couples.

Dr. Blum had tried to encourage them during their counseling sessions to carve out periods for themselves. They'd said they would and it was then that Mac had promised to take her on a second honeymoon to Torchlight. But they had never found the opportunity and at some point had stopped making the effort to try. Now they were here, a couple still in the same predicament they'd been when they sought Dr. Blum's services.

"Well, what do we have here?"

Skirting around boards and makeshift walls, they came upon what had once been a storage room. Shelves were stocked with several kinds of canned goods. Teri moved closer to see tuna, peaches and dry milk. There were also several huge water barrels.

Mac checked out the barrels, smiled and gave a thumbs-up. "They are full, but I suspect there's an additional water channel somewhere in here, which is even better."

Teri nodded. "What type of place do you think this was?"

He glanced over at her. "I would guess it's what they thought of as their shelter—where food, water and supplies were kept. Usually, it's where they would bed down for the night when they weren't in the productive mines. I wouldn't be surprised if there are sleeping quarters somewhere in here."

Teri studied Mac. "You seem knowledgeable about mines."

He nodded. "Not as much mines as caves. Part of my duties as a SEAL is to scout and find the best place for us to hunker down whenever we're in hostile territory. A cave is where we were holed up most of the time while in Syria. Being out in the open in a camp is too risky."

He glanced around before saying, "SEALs have a knack of making caves appear uninhabitable. You wouldn't believe how many times our enemies were right there, outside the entrance of the cave, and we were able to listen to their every word. Once we overheard them strategize their entire plan of attack against us."

Teri wondered if Mac realized this was the first time he'd ever talked about his work as a navy SEAL and the danger he faced. Whenever he returned home it was as if he needed to put out of his mind whatever mission he'd gone through. Like that time a couple of years ago, when he'd assumed his teammate Laramie "Coop" Cooper had gotten killed, and Mac had shut up his emotions. No matter how she'd tried, she hadn't been able to tear through the grieving wall he'd erected.

"Ready to move on?"

She looked up at him. "Ready whenever you are."

Teri didn't want to think about how differently things might have turned out if he'd left when she'd asked him to leave earlier. Or if he hadn't come after her at all. She would have tried to outrun the twister and would probably have died doing so. She had begun resenting Mac's presence, but now she appreciated it.

She tightened her hold on his hand and they moved forward, going deeper and deeper toward the back of the mine.

Teri had stopped asking questions and Mac thought that was a good thing. He hadn't given her a straight answer when she asked about how much air they had.

In addition to his concern regarding lack of oxygen, he was worried about the possibility of poisonous gases in the air.

Knowing this particular mineshaft had been used as a shelter facility was a good thing. He couldn't tell for sure just how good until they checked out the place more. At least they had water and food for a while. But the uncertainty about the air component bothered him.

Nowadays most mineshafts were equipped with emergency kits that included portable devices providing a supply of breathable oxygen in case anyone got trapped underground, or should any type of poisonous gases leak into the air. Other kits contained small tanks filled with oxygen to which a miner had immediate access. He would love having either about now.

He figured this particular mine had undergone its share of digging and blasting, which accounted for the worn-looking internal structure. Typically mines, especially those used as shelters, had escape tunnels. If this one had such a thing, he was determined to find it.

He suddenly stopped when he heard a sound and immediately placed Teri behind him.

"Mac? What is it?" she asked, whispering close to his ear.

"I thought I heard something."

It wasn't uncommon for wild animals to take refuge in deserted mines. With that thought in mind, he eased his hunting knife from his pocket and immediately his stance went into an attack mode. He waited and when he didn't hear the sound again, he relaxed somewhat.

"False alarm."

"What do you think the sound was?" Teri asked him.

"Probably the shifting of the foundation. There's no

telling what all has fallen in on top of us." He glanced up and wondered if there was a chance the ceiling might collapse down on them. It didn't look too solid.

Checking his watch, Mac saw it was late afternoon. Chances were the authorities were out trying to assess damage in the region. Because of the magnitude of that tornado he figured there had been extensive destruction over a wide area. He hoped everyone had time to take shelter and that there weren't any casualties. But he'd seen that tornado, had witnessed its power and knew a number of places were flattened to the ground by now.

Because the cabin Teri had reserved was so far from the main house, there was no telling how long it would take before they were missed. Would the authorities assume they were in the house and look for them there? If the horses returned without riders would that clue them in? He knew that wouldn't necessarily be the case since they'd removed the saddles from the horses' backs.

Mac knew that meant they had to assume no one would be looking for them. Not totally true. He knew a certain group would come looking for him eventually. Namely his SEAL teammates. They would know he was alive and wouldn't give up until they found him.

When he heard Teri's stomach growl he remembered how late it was and realized they'd missed a meal. They wouldn't be eating by candlelight but at least they would be sharing a meal together.

Tightening his hand on hers, he said, "Come on, let's go back to where those canned goods were and get something to eat."

Bane Westmoreland heard the beeping of his phone and recognized it for what it was. It was an alert from one of his teammates. He eased away from his wife's side, hoping not to wake her, but he wasn't surprised when her eyes flew open. He should have known that with three-year-old triplets she didn't know the meaning of sound sleep, especially since it was four in the afternoon. Early on they had learned to take a nap whenever the triplets took theirs.

"That's my SEAL phone," he said, leaning over to kiss her on the lips.

"Do you think they're calling you back for another assignment this soon? You haven't been home but two days," Crystal said, pulling up beside him in bed.

"No, that's not it. That ringtone is from one of the guys. I'll be back in a minute."

He left his bedroom to go into the kitchen, walking over several toys to do so. Glancing out the window, he could see the structure of his home that was still under construction in the distance. He and Crystal had met with the builders that day and had been told their home would be ready in a few months. They were looking forward to moving in. There would definitely be more room for their three-year-old triplets. His cousin Gemma, the interior designer in the family, would be coming all the way from Australia to decorate.

He sat down at the kitchen table and called Coop when he saw the alert had come from him. "What's up, man? I know you aren't calling again for tips on how to get your daughter to sleep." Coop and his wife, Bristol, had a four-year-old son named Laramie and a one-and-a-half-year-old daughter named Paris.

"No, that's not it. Teri and Mac are missing."

Bane sat up straight. "What do you mean they are missing?"

"I take it you haven't been watching the news."

Bane rubbed a hand down his face. "No. Crystal and I decided to grab a nap while the kids took theirs."

"Then you wouldn't know about that tornado that ripped through the outskirts of Cheyenne, namely the town of Torchlight, a little more than an hour ago. And it was a bad one. Already the death toll has reached double digits."

Bane released a whistle, as he stood to his feet. "Mac is still alive," he said with certainty.

"Yes, our tracker says he is, but they're listed as missing for now. Mac's parents called our commanding officer after they were notified Mac and Teri are among those unaccounted for. I'm letting the others know we need to head out for Wyoming."

Bane nodded. "I'll see you in Torchlight."

David Holloway, known by family and friends as Flipper, glanced around the table. He was with his family, dining at their favorite restaurant in Dallas as they celebrated his brother's announcement that he would be remarrying in a few months. The woman his brother was marrying was none other than a cousin of Swan, Flipper's wife. His brother Liam had met Jamila Fairchild at his and Swan's wedding a year and a half ago.

Everyone was happy for the couple, especially his parents, Colin and Lenora Holloway. He knew they'd been worried about Liam, especially after his split with Bonnie over five years ago. He hadn't dated anyone seriously since then. He'd concentrated on being the perfect dad to his little girl.

Flipper noted the size of the Holloway family was growing. Now it included his parents, their five sons and four of those sons' wives, their grandkids, and Jamila, soon to be the newest addition to the family. Flipper and his brothers were close to his parents. Their loving and tight-knit relationships had been the reason none of their sons had had any qualms about settling down and marrying. Unfortunately, the woman his brother Liam had married the first time around had been bad news. The only good thing that had come from the union was their little girl.

Something else others found unique about his family was that his father had retired as a SEAL commander-in-chief. All five of his sons had followed in his footsteps to become SEALs, as well.

After congratulations were said by all, his father made a toast to welcome Jamila to the family. Flipper could tell from the huge smile on Swan's face that she was happy for the cousin with whom she shared a very close relationship. Although he and Swan made their home in Key West, they visited the family in Dallas every chance they got.

His cell phone went off and he recognized the ringtone. Excusing himself from the table, he moved to a different area to take Coop's call. He returned a few minutes later with a grim look on his face.

"What's wrong, Flipper?" his father asked him.

When all eyes went to him, he said, "That was Coop. A tornado went through Wyoming a few hours ago, not far from Cheyenne. The media is saying it's one of the deadliest to hit the area. Coop got a call from our commander-in-chief. Mac and Teri were there and now they're missing."

"Missing?" It seemed everyone at the table asked all at once.

"Yes, he and Teri were on a dude ranch there. The entire ranch was destroyed, and Mac and Teri can't be found. So they're listed as missing."

He turned to Swan. "I'm leaving tonight to go help find Mac."

"I'm joining you. I can leave tomorrow," Liam said.

"Don't leave us out." His other three brothers agreed to join them.

Flipper wasn't surprised. Because Mac had been a part of his life since his first day as a SEAL—as a teammate, another older brother and a mentor—he had won a special place in the hearts of Flipper's family members.

"Great. We'll need all the help we can get."

"What do you mean Mac is missing?" Viper asked Coop, struggling to prop his cell phone on his shoulder close to his ear, while handing their two-year-old son to his wife, Layla. His words, he noticed, had given her pause, as well.

He'd been out teaching his son, Gavin Blake IV, how to ride a pony. Gavin was at the same age Viper had been when he'd been taught to ride. He listened as Coop gave him the details about the tornado that had touched down near Wyoming, destroying the dude ranch where Mac and Teri had been staying.

"I'm calling everyone so we can get together and find Mac," Coop informed him.

"That's good. I'm leaving tonight."

"Okay. I'll see you then." Coop clicked off the phone knowing they never ceased being a team whether they were on duty or off. That was the SEAL way and for them, the only way.

Chapter 6

Mac used his knife to open the cans of tuna and thought the tin mugs from the saddlebags came in handy for water. They had turned over empty water barrels to sit on. Being the ever-efficient mom that she was, Teri never left home without a travel-size bottle of hand sanitizer and pulled it out of her saddlebag.

"This is all we have to eat for now. At least until I scope out the place to find what else might be here."

Teri glanced over at her husband. "No problem. Tuna and water are okay. Besides, I need to lose a few pounds."

"No, you don't. You look good. You always look good."

Teri smiled at her husband's compliment. He would tell her that often enough, but always when they were naked and about to make love. Never when she'd been fully dressed. "Thanks, but losing a few pounds won't hurt."

"If you say so."

She glanced over at him to see what changes she could notice since he'd left eight months ago. There were always invisible changes she wouldn't know about, so for now she would concentrate on the visible ones. He looked more built than ever. Even more alluring. She thought the same thing now that she'd thought when she'd first seen him that night at the rodeo: Thurston McRoy was a handsome man with rakish good looks.

Ten and a half years of marriage hadn't lessened her desire for him, not when he took such good care of himself. But then, he really didn't have a choice. Being a SEAL, especially a member of Team Six, the most highly trained elite forces in the US military, meant being physically fit at all times, and he was certainly that.

Facial hair used to annoy him, but because of the covert operations he'd been involved in lately, a beard had become the norm. However, as soon as he returned home, he would shave. Evidently, coming directly after her had robbed him of the time to do so.

"Is something wrong, Teri? You're staring at me."

She met his gaze. "No. I didn't mean to stare. Just trying to see any changes."

He shrugged. "Why do you expect there will be any?"

Now it was her time to shrug, although she could tell him of a few reasons. Like the time he'd gotten stabbed and hadn't told her until she'd seen the wound for herself. Or that time a bullet had grazed his ear. However, she wouldn't bring any of that up. "No reason."

Things got quiet between them as they ate and she

was determined not to let him catch her staring again. But then she could feel him staring at her and she was tempted to glance over at him and ask why he was staring, just like he'd asked her.

It was hard, nearly impossible, not to remember all those sexual fantasies she had about him whenever he was gone. Fantasies he was usually accommodating to play out when he returned and she told him about them. So why was she not telling him about those fantasies now when she'd definitely had a few? Actually, there had been more than a few.

"What happened, Teri? How did you lose the baby? Please tell me what happened."

His words intruded into her thoughts. A part of her didn't want to talk about it, especially not now. But then, she knew he deserved to know and that now was probably the best time to tell him. They had this time alone, where neither of them could walk out. They needed to use it to talk, and she meant really talk about issues that concerned them and their marriage.

Teri wasn't sure what to say. She could tell him just what the doctor said, or she could talk about what she suspected, which the doctor claimed was just guilt and not fact. She had not been restricted from flying. And she'd given birth to four kids with no problem. The only difference between those pregnancies and her recent fifth was that she'd gotten on a plane to travel somewhere during her first four months.

She glanced over at Mac. "The doctor said it was just one of those things, that up to one in five pregnancies end in miscarriage before twenty weeks."

"And you didn't do anything different?"

Was that accusation she heard in his voice? She didn't want to believe that it was and knew she was allowing her feelings of guilt to make her defensive. "I hadn't done anything that Dr. Gleason felt would have had a bearing on the pregnancy. I told him everything I'd been doing, and according to him none of it mattered. Like I told you, he said it was just one of those things and nothing I did contributed to it."

What she'd told him was the truth. He didn't have to know about the inner turmoil within her.

"Did you see the girls while you were home?" she asked, hoping to change the subject.

Mac knew his wife well enough to know when she wasn't being totally forthcoming about something. What was it that she wasn't telling him? And why? He intended to find out in due time. He wouldn't press her about it now.

"Yes, I saw the girls. Everyone was asleep except for Tasha. I think her eyes opened the moment I walked into the room. It was as if she knew I was home."

Teri chuckled. "Figures. I think she has a built-in radar where you're concerned."

"Just like her mama has a built-in radar whenever I'm home?"

Teri didn't say anything because that much was true. Whenever Mac was home it was as if her senses needed to know where he was every second. She tried not to worry about him while he was away on an assignment, instead depending on Bane, Viper, Coop and Flipper, the four SEAL teammates he was close to, to keep him safe. She wouldn't even discount Nick Stover. Although

Nick was no longer a SEAL and now worked for Homeland Security, Mac still spoke of him often and included him in the mix even now.

As far as she was concerned, those five looked up to Mac and considered him an older brother since Mac had been a SEAL a few years before them. To hear Mac tell it, he looked out for them, but she was sure it worked the other way around, as well. She was counting on it because she knew her husband could be a hothead at times, although he claimed he wasn't. But still, as much as she tried not to worry, as much as she assured herself she really didn't have to, she always did anyway.

"Yes, just like her mama has her radar," she finally said.

"So, tell me about your radar, Teri McRoy. Why are you so tuned in to me whenever I'm home?"

Teri thought that in all the years of their marriage, he'd never asked her to explain her actions whenever it came to him. Now she could speak freely and share her inner feelings about this particular topic. "I worry about you when you're home, Mac."

She knew it was silly because if anyone could take care of themselves, it was Mac. But because of her deep, unyielding need to protect him, she was very much tuned in to him. She could sense his movements. She knew it used to drive him crazy but now he'd gotten accustomed to it.

"You don't have to worry about me, Teri."

"Easier said than done. I worry about you not getting enough rest before you have to be gone again. As your wife I want to make your life better, less stressful when you come home, but it seems all I do is make it more taxing. You always concentrate on what you think I've done wrong while you were gone and not anything I might have done right."

Did he?

Mac didn't say anything as he thought about what she had said. Were her feelings of being taken for granted justified? He rubbed his hands down his face. When was the last time he'd told her how proud he was of the way she was raising their kids? Or how he appreciated how she made their house into the home he looked forward to returning to? Or better yet, how much he loved her?

Instead, he would come home and start finding fault in the changes or additions she'd made without his input, knowing there were some decisions she had no choice but to make without him.

He looked over at her. "I see what you've done right every time I return home and walk into the house, Teri. The girls are beautiful, well behaved, respectful and doing great in school. My home is my castle and you make it so. I teased you about your radar but I love your attentiveness to me."

Mac paused a moment and then added, "Even with all we have, I worry a lot about our finances. It's something I can't help doing."

She lifted her chin. "I can understand that due to your background, but do you have to be so critical? So obsessive about my decisions, Mac? Do Bane, Viper, Coop and Flipper question every single penny their wives spend?"

In a way her question irritated him because she knew the answer. "No, but then, they don't have to. Bane and

Coop were born to wealth and Viper's and Flipper's families aren't exactly poor, Teri. My parents were still paying for student loans when me and my sister were born. There was no money for my parents to inherit or to pass on to their offspring. They worked hard, provided for me and my sister, but there was never any extra money to invest in generational wealth. I'm not complaining, and I don't resent my friends, trust me. They've helped me make more out of the little I started with. I have no problem making my own way."

As a SEAL he got bonuses, and for years he'd used a portion of those bonuses toward investments that were paying off. His daughters' college funds looked pretty damn good and he was proud of that. In truth, they had more than they needed. But he couldn't escape the feeling that it was never enough to feel secure. Though now he was feeling comfortable about getting that new house they wanted. He'd intended for that to be his surprise to her on his trip back home this time around.

"Trust me, I know, Mac." Then, as if she was ready to change the conversation to something else, she asked, "Are we ever going to get out of here? For all anyone knows we're at that cabin and may not have been missed."

He could hear the worry in her voice. "When they find out we aren't there, they'll come looking for us."

"Yes, but will they know to look for us here?"

If she meant the authorities, then no, they wouldn't know. But he knew of four men, with the help of a fifth, who would. And he felt certain they would find them. He could arrest her fears about them being found but then he would have to explain why he was so certain of it, and he couldn't do that. It was a pact the six of them had made after that time when they'd thought they had lost Coop, whose captors led everyone to believe they had killed him. Instead he'd been held as prisoner in the Syrian mountains for nearly a year. That had been the hardest year of their lives, believing Coop was dead. When they'd gotten word he was alive, their SEAL team had gone in and rescued him. Their enemies had tried breaking his body but they couldn't break his spirit. Coop had said that what had kept him going was his belief that his teammates would eventually come and rescue him. And they had.

After that, Mac and his teammates had decided they never wanted to experience again what they'd gone through with Coop. So, when Nick had told them of this microchip tracking device that was more technologically advanced than any on the consumer market, they'd signed up to be the first to try it. The microchip was inserted under the skin of their right hands and no one knew of the implant other than their commanding officer, who had to approve the procedure. With the microchip, if any of the six of them went missing, they could be tracked to their precise location by latitude, longitude and altitude. Not only that, their body movement could be detected and studied to determine pain level due to the possibilities of injuries. The chip could also sense any other life-threatening symptoms emitted through brain waves. He knew his teammates would be testing the tracker's abilities for the first time with him.

He and Teri were fine for now with enough food and water to last a couple of days. His biggest concern was oxygen—how long would they be able to breathe, shut up underground like this? He wouldn't talk to Teri about it for fear she would worry.

"Mac, will they know to look here?"

His thoughts were pulled back to Teri when she repeated what she'd asked him earlier. A question he hadn't answered. "Not sure, but it doesn't matter."

She frowned. "Why doesn't it matter?"

"Because once Bane, Coop and the others get wind that I'm missing, they'll come looking for us."

She nodded. "You're certain of that?"

"Yes."

"But will they be able to find us, or will they assume we're somewhere in the vicinity of the cabin?"

He smiled over at her. "They are SEALs, Teri. They will figure things out."

"But will they do it in time?"

"They will find us in time."

He saw uncertainty in her eyes. Reaching out, he slid her hand into his and entwined their fingers. "Trust me, baby. I won't let anything happen to you."

She lifted her chin. "And I won't let anything happen to you, either."

He wanted to laugh at that, knowing he could do a better job of protecting her than she could of him. However, if thinking that way made her feel better and worry less he would give her that moment.

Smiling over at her, he said, "Okay, that's a deal. We won't let anything happen to each other. Now let's get rid of this trash and then figure out how and where we need to bunk down for the night."

"Mac's alive and his brain waves aren't showing any signs of distress," Nick said, reading Mac's tracking data off his computer. The tracking devices the six of them wore were manned by Nick since he was the most computer savvy of the group. Any of the others could step in to be Nick's backup if it came to that, but Nick knew they were all hoping it never did.

"That's good to hear. I talked to Bane, Flipper and Viper earlier. We're all heading to Wyoming," Coop said.

"And I'm joining all of you. I'll be able to pinpoint his exact location once I get to the area and study maps of the surroundings."

"How soon do you think you'll get there?" Coop asked.

"Sometime tomorrow. I'll let Natalie know I'll be leaving and that she'll be on her own with the triplets for a while. In the meantime, I'll get periodic readings on Mac to relay to everyone."

"Thanks, Nick, and we'll see you in Wyoming."

Mac had taken her hand again and Teri didn't mind.

He did seem more capable of handling this sort of thing than she, but that didn't mean she wouldn't protect him if it came to that. She'd meant what she'd said about not letting anything happen to him, just like she knew he had meant what he'd said regarding protecting her.

"What if we don't find anything, Mac?"

He looked down at her. "There are blankets in the saddlebags."

She lifted a brow. "How do you know?"

"I checked."

When had he done that? "If we have blankets, then what are we looking for?"

"Something that could possibly serve as a cushion on the floor."

"Oh." He stopped walking and she glanced around. "This place is kind of messy, isn't it?"

He chuckled. "It's a mineshaft, Teri. Not a luxury condo."

"I know that but still you would think it could look better. A lot neater."

Mac checked the time on his watch. She'd noticed him doing that a lot. "What time is it now?" she asked him.

"Eighteen o eight."

She knew that meant 6:08 p.m. You couldn't be married to a military man without adjusting to their time, as well. Even the girls knew to convert to military time whenever he came home. It was dinnertime for most folks. She had a feeling dinner wouldn't be the same for a lot of people tonight.

"I was hoping to come across something like this sooner or later."

They had stumbled upon several horse troughs filled with hay. She was a cowgirl at heart so she understood the excitement that she heard in his voice. "Now I don't have to worry about sleeping on the hard ground tonight."

He glanced over at her. The intensity in his gaze nearly made her knees buckle. "There was never a time you would have had to sleep on the ground tonight or any night."

She lifted a brow. "So where would I have slept?"

He gave her that crooked smile she'd always thought was irresistible when he said, "I would have taken the floor and you would have slept on top of me. Granted we would have gotten little sleep."

The serious look on his face made her heart pound because she believed what he said to be true. If their bodies touched in that way, fire would consume them and they would end up making love all over the place. Finding this hay was a good thing because the thought of sleeping on top of him gave her body sensuous shivers. Had she been tempted to sleep on him, she would be pregnant by the time they woke up tomorrow.

In the back of her mind, and slowly coming to the front, were memories of past lovemaking sessions with him. They would start off mating like rabbits because of the length of time they'd been apart. Then, after getting an hour or two of exhausted sleep, they would start another bout of lovemaking, proving how obsessed they were with each other and just how much they had missed each other.

It was during that second, slower time that they would try the positions their creative minds came up with. Just thinking of a few of those positions now actually brought color to her cheeks.

Mac thought it was rather cute that he could make his wife blush after ten years and four kids. No…five kids, he thought, feeling the loss of the one he hadn't known. His son. She had carried him inside her for four months, which meant she had gotten to spend time with him, develop a bond. Mac regretted he hadn't even been there to give her a tummy rub or to place his ear to her belly to hear his child moving inside her.

He had missed out on all those things.

"Well, now that won't be necessary."

He glanced back over at her and forced a wry smile to his lips. "You can still lie on top of me, though."

She met his gaze. "Like I said, that won't be necessary."

"Maybe not necessary but better."

Although the flashlight from his cell phone was holding its own, there wasn't a lot of light. But it was enough to see her. He thought now what he'd thought the first time he'd seen Teri. His wife was a stunner.

Not only that, she was a pretty damn intelligent woman to boot. And he couldn't forget what a great body she had. Slim waist, luscious hips, mouthwatering breasts and one hell of an ass. Whether she knew it or not, thoughts of her kept him going. Made him appreciate being a man.

A man who always returned home to her.

Then why did they argue so much when he got there?

He remembered what that marriage counselor had told him. He was a man who seemed programmed to sweat the small stuff. He knew that was true. He'd tried to change and for a little while he had. Just until his next assignment. When he'd returned home, he'd slowly slipped back into his old ways.

"Better for what, Mac?"

It was hard to stay focused around her. "Better when we make love again." He couldn't think of any better way to pass the time. He glanced over at all that hay. It would certainly serve a good purpose.

"We won't be making love again."

His head snapped around to look at her. "Excuse me?"

She drew in a deep breath and those luscious breasts moved in a tantalizing way when she did so. "I said we won't be making love again. We can't."

Hmm, maybe he needed to refresh her memory.

"We did. Yesterday. Last night. Before daylight this morning."

She nervously nibbled on her bottom lip. That delicious bottom lip. Intrigued, he studied her. He hadn't seen her do that in a while. She was uptight about something. What?

"I know but we can't do it again."

He lifted a brow. "Why? Last time I looked we were married, which means we can do just about anything, Teri."

"But we shouldn't have."

He heard the agitation in her brusque tone. What the hell was going on here? An awkward silence ensued between them as he looked at her. He was tempted to check her forehead for a possible fever. He'd never, ever recalled a time when they had to put the brakes on making love. They both enjoyed it.

"There must be a reason you think that, Teri," he said in what he hoped was his calmest voice. "You want to explain it to me?"

She didn't say anything for a minute. "There are two reasons, Mac. First, making love only serves as a Band-Aid on a festering wound between us. It's time to stop resorting to temporary solutions and try to heal the wound."

She made it sound like what was going on between them was something they couldn't work out. She had committed herself to his way of life when they married. It had been her choice to agree to move around the world whenever he got a new assignment, her choice to forgo her career to advance his. She'd always seemed understanding of those times he hadn't been there for special occasions and holidays and had done a great job of holding it together for him and their family.

"We'll get through this, Teri."

"How? By making love? I'm tired of you thinking

that's all it will take. What about my feelings, Mac? I need more from you than sex. I need for you to understand my feelings, trust my decisions, respect my role not only when you're gone but also when you return home. I need to feel appreciated and like I'm not being taken for granted."

He took in everything she'd said. "Okay, now what's the other reason?"

She nibbled on her bottom lip again before saying, "The reason is something I should have told you yesterday…before we made love."

"Then tell me now," he said, trying to keep the frustration out of his voice.

"It's me."

His gaze roamed all over her, and in his mind, she was still the sexiest woman on a pair of gorgeous legs. "What about you?"

She began nibbling on those lips once again. "Teri," he said in an impatient voice. "What about you?"

She met his gaze and held it. "I'm not on any type of birth control."

Chapter 7

Teri watched Mac go still, as if he'd been frozen in place. He was probably standing there remembering how many orgasms they'd shared within the last twenty-four hours. Enough to make a lot of babies if science worked that way. It didn't. But it had been more than enough times to make one.

"Any reason you didn't tell me before now?"

She could give him plenty of reasons, but they would all come back to one. The main one. "I had missed you and at the time I desperately needed to connect with you."

"Okay, I can understand that."

She knew he could understand because that was the reason they would make love often whenever he came home. Time apart always made them miss each other and want each other more. They couldn't wait to connect intimately. But then when their mating frenzies were over, they would be at odds with each other over one thing or another…like they were now.

"So why didn't you restart the pill after your pregnancy? You knew I was coming home sooner or later."

Whether he realized it or not, he was questioning her actions. Again. It bothered her whenever he did that. "I had rescheduled the surgery and figured I would have it done before you returned."

"You rescheduled the surgery?"

"Yes, it's scheduled for next week. That's one of the reasons I came here. I needed to come to terms with losing the baby and to stay focused on what we'd agreed to do and what it would mean to me."

He didn't say anything for the longest time and then he said, "Did it ever occur to you after losing the baby that proceeding with the surgery was something we needed to talk about?"

She raised an eyebrow. "No, that never occurred to me, Mac. The decision had already been made by us, and I honestly didn't think it would be back up for discussion, regardless of my pregnancy. I know how you can act when I go back on any decisions we've made together."

He stared at her for a long moment without saying anything. Then he turned and grabbed a huge armful of hay before walking off.

I know how you can act when I go back on any decisions we've made together.

Teri's words hit him hard in the gut. As he made several trips back to the trough for hay, he couldn't say anything but he did dwell on what she'd said. She had done a good job of reminding him just what an ass he could be at times. An inflexible ass.

Why was it so hard for him to loosen his grip on control? Mainly because he didn't see it as control but as looking out for someone. In this case, Teri and the girls.

He'd never intended for Teri to work outside the home once they started having kids. She'd known it and had seemed fine with the thought of being a stay-at-home mom. She'd loved children as much as he did, and they wanted a houseful. Only, things were hard with a household. He didn't want to add to Teri's burden while he was away, and they'd decided to call it quits at three. Then they'd agreed for a fourth, hoping it would be a boy, but regardless, a fourth child was the limit. They had enough love and money for four, but part of him couldn't help remembering how he'd grown up. The hardship. Mentally, the cost felt high, especially with all the activities in their children's futures and the rising cost of college educations.

The decision not to have any more kids had been one they'd both been okay with. For him her unexpected pregnancy was a game changer. Maybe it should not have been, but it was. At least for him, and he felt bad that she couldn't see that.

What if he'd come home two weeks from now instead of two days ago? She would have had the surgery by then. And what bothered him more than anything was that she felt that was what he would have expected. He wished he could claim that she didn't know him at all, if she believed that, but all he could say was that she thought it because she *did* know him.

When Mac returned with the last load of hay, he glanced over at Teri and saw what she'd done. She had separated the hay into two stacks to make separate beds for them. That was quite obvious now that she'd spread the blankets over the hay. Did she honestly think they wouldn't be sleeping together?

"What are you doing, Teri?"

Without looking up she said, loud enough for him to hear, "What does it look like I'm doing?"

Mac rubbed a hand down his face in frustration. "We aren't going to have separate beds. It's going to get cold tonight."

She looked up at him. "It won't be the first time I've had to keep myself warm, Mac."

That was a low blow, he thought. Was she itching for a fight? If so, one quick way to do it was to start complaining about the time he was gone from home as a SEAL. She'd known the score when she married him.

"Fine. Suit yourself."

She would discover soon enough just how cold it got in here at night. It didn't matter one iota what season it was—autumn, winter, spring or summer—since they were practically buried beneath the earth.

"I'm turning out the light now," he said, just seconds before he did it.

"Why did you do that?" she asked and he could hear the near hysteria in her voice.

"To save the battery," he said. He figured the answer was obvious.

"I haven't gotten ready for bed."

What was there to get ready for? It wasn't as if they were at some hotel. They would be sleeping in their clothes. Tomorrow, when he hoped there would be more light, he would move around and explore. If there was another opening out of this place, he intended to find it.

He had dropped down to the bed of hay and covered up with the blanket. He could hear movement where Teri was and wondered what she was doing but decided not to ask. He was following the advice of the marriage counselor they had gone to that time. He'd said, *When you feel yourself getting angry, allow yourself time to calm down and reflect and remember. Definitely remember. You have to force your mind to recall what drew the two of you together in the first place.*

His answer to that question was simple. It had been Teri's smile. It didn't just touch her lips but extended to her eyes, as well. Then it had been her body. It was definitely a body any man would love looking at. Then it had been her warm sense of humor.

It suddenly occurred to him that he saw less and less of that sense of humor each time he returned home. Why? Was any of that his fault? Probably. Just like it was his fault that she believed she had to have that surgical procedure done despite her unexpected pregnancy. He shifted in bed, thinking it was a damn shame he and Teri were doing something tonight they'd never done in the years they'd been married, which was to sleep in separate beds while he was home.

He figured she had a lot to think about and so did he. Tomorrow they would talk. When he heard the even sound of her breathing, he knew she'd drifted off to sleep and he allowed his eyes to drift closed to do the same. And he dreamed about how he'd made love to her that morning before she'd left to go riding.

How he'd kissed her awake with a desperation he wasn't aware he could experience. And how she had reciprocated, letting her tongue duel with his. He'd pulled her closer to him, not only needing to taste her but needing to feel her all over. His hands ran all over her naked body, down her back, before cupping her backside. He'd always loved the feel of her in his arms and this morning hadn't been an exception. He'd been gone for long periods of time before, but this had been one of the longest in years. He hadn't realized just how much he'd missed her until he'd begun making love to her.

And when he'd straddled her, the moan she'd emitted when his hard erection had slid inside of her, pressing her into the mattress, spurred him to go deeper. The moment he was buried inside her he went still, savoring the feel of his engorged flesh held tight in her warm, wet body.

It took everything he had within, his total control as a SEAL, every ounce of restraint he possessed, not to explode inside of her at that moment. He'd fought the urge to do so. It had been the questioning look in her eyes, and then her question of, "What are you waiting for?" that had made him start moving. Made him thrust hard and then harder. It was that question that had made him tip his head back and growl while appreciating how it felt to sink deeper still into her body.

More than once he had to make sure she was right there with him, especially those times when he was a mere heartbeat away from climaxing. The room had been filled with her moans as he continued to stroke nonstop inside of her. Those moans of pleasure had driven him to kiss her harder and longer, and to thrust repeatedly inside her body.

As he drifted deeper and deeper into sleep in the recesses of his dreams, he could still hear those moans.

Teri woke up. No matter how much she tried, she couldn't get warm. She shifted her position again and had a feeling her toes were frozen. She needed Mac's body heat. Point-blank, she needed Mac. Besides, she owed him an apology.

She should not have made that wisecrack about being used to keeping herself warm. That hadn't been fair to him. She'd known what he did for a living when she married him but she couldn't imagine living without him. He couldn't keep her warm when he was gone and that wasn't his fault. And whenever he was home, he not only kept her warm on cold nights, but he also made her feel loved and protected. So why was he over there and she over here?

Because they'd had one of their disagreements, the ones that were happening way too often. But this time it was serious—it had included another life, one they'd shared in making. And she knew that, like always, any decisions on how they moved forward would be shared by them, as well.

Not able to stop shivering, she stood and grabbed her cover and moved over to where Mac lay. As if he'd been expecting her, Mac pulled himself up in a sitting position and reached out a hand to her. She grasped it and he drew her close to ease down beside him. He didn't say anything. Not even "I told you so." But then, that was Mac's way whenever he was proven right. He wouldn't dig it in. He probably figured swallowing her pride was enough humiliation.

When he practically wrapped his body into hers, she immediately felt warm and couldn't help sighing. "Thanks, Mac."

"Don't ever thank me for taking care of what's mine, Teri," he whispered close to her ear, causing her body to shiver again. However, this time it was for a different reason.

Teri knew that to anyone else, his words would sound too possessive, as if she was an object he owned. She knew that wasn't the case. He was merely stating what was the truth. She was his—heart, body and soul—like he was hers. But still, that made her wonder how two people so into each other the way they were could be at odds with each other as much as they were.

They had different personalities. She got that. The marriage counselor they'd met with for an entire three months had made sure they understood that. They'd been backsliding and now it was up to the both of them to get back on track. But the issues they were dealing with now were pretty major and he didn't know the half of it.

"Mac?"

"Yes."

"I'm sorry about what I said about you not being home to keep me warm on cold nights. I didn't mean it the way it sounded."

"No harm done."

She had found a comfortable position and was about to drift off when Mac's voice stopped her. "Teri?"

He shifted his body around to face her and automatically, she threw her leg over his thigh. Too late she realized that wasn't a good move. "Yes?"

"I'm sorry you thought I would not have understood or supported your decision to delay having the surgery. I would have."

She didn't say anything for a minute. "Dr. Gleason told me I could reschedule the surgery a month ago but emotionally, I couldn't do it. I just wasn't ready. That's why it's scheduled for next week. At least it *was*."

There was no reason to tell him that it wouldn't be happening for a couple of reasons. First of all, even if they were rescued, there was no way she would feel up to having any type of surgery done. But the most important reason was that when they'd made love they hadn't used protection. That meant there was a possibility she could be pregnant now. Why didn't the thought of that bother her? In fact, the thought of having another baby lifted her spirits.

"And now you could be pregnant again."

His words had her looking over at him. So that possibility did occur to him. "Yes. How do you feel about that, Mac?"

"How would any man feel when the woman he loves carries his child? I just worry about your burden while I'm away. And I don't want our children to want for anything."

"You have always provided for us. The girls and I have never wanted for anything."

"But I want to give you more."

She wondered if he would ever realize that "more" wasn't everything and having each other was enough. "You can only do so much, Mac."

"How do you feel about us having another child, Teri?"

"Do you want me to be truthful?"

"No, Teri. I *expect* you to be truthful."

Yes, he would. "Then my answer is that I love the idea, Mac. Tasha is getting more independent and she doesn't want to be thought of as a baby anymore. She wants to be a big girl like Tatum and Tempest. I hate seeing my babies grow up."

"But they do," he said, being the voice of reason as usual.

"Yes, they do, and I know I can't replace one baby with another when that happens, Mac."

He didn't say anything for a minute. "I just worry about you, when I'm away. And I still think about how hard I had it growing up. I know that although we agreed not to have any more kids, deep down you would have been happy having a houseful."

He was right about that. She would love to have a houseful. Being the only child had been the pits.

"Yes, but I understood, Mac."

She loved her husband and knew carefully watching their finances was something he felt responsible for doing because of his background. Even though they had plenty. That made telling him about her purchase of the ranch that much harder.

"You said you have something else to tell me. What is it?"

Since they were talking, this would be the perfect opportunity to come clean and tell him everything. But she couldn't. It was lousy timing and she wasn't ready. However, she would be ready in the morning. She promised herself.

"Let's talk tomorrow, okay? I'm feeling sleepy, Mac."

He was quiet for a long moment and then he said, "All right, we'll talk tomorrow. Go to sleep."

Teri closed her eyes, appreciating her husband's body keeping her warm.

Chapter 8

Mac woke up the next morning and immediately noticed two things. First and foremost, his wife was sleeping soundly in his arms and her too-tempting body was pressed close to him. Second, the level of oxygen in the air had changed. He didn't need a barometer to detect that. The pressure wasn't at an alarming level; it was even one he'd expected, but he was fully aware of the change. In fact, he had even predicted the level to be lower than what it was. That meant air was seeping into the mine from somewhere, and he was determined to find where.

He figured his teammates had heard he was missing about now and would be looking for them. He believed that. He had to believe that.

He glanced down at Teri. Why did he have a feeling there was something she wasn't telling him, something she was stalling? He wouldn't bring it up again but would let her decide when the best time would be. Hopefully, they would talk this morning as she'd said they would do. But now, while she slept, he would explore the mine without her. When he'd walked yesterday to where all that straw had been, he had felt moisture in the air. Today he would investigate where it was coming from.

Untangling their limbs, he eased from Teri's side, immediately missing the feel of her body. But separating himself from her was a good idea, especially since he'd maintained an erection all night. It wouldn't have taken much for him to break down and try coaxing her into making love with him. They'd taken a few chances already and she could very well be carrying his child.

Stretching the kinks out of his body he glanced back down at Teri again before moving away to explore the mine without her. It didn't take long for him to come to the area where they'd found all that hay. He kept moving. The deeper he went into the mineshaft, the more the air changed, and he could feel moisture, to the degree that the rock walls around him were damp in some places.

He smiled when he came across the small pool of crystal clear water. Nature never ceased to amaze him. He figured the water was a spill-off from that lake a few miles back. From the steam it generated he knew it was connected to some kind of underground heated spring.

He couldn't wait to bring Teri here. With that thought in mind, he headed back.

Laramie Cooper observed from beneath hooded lashes the man, a first responder, who was talking to

Bane, Viper and Flipper. Coop had decided to hang back and check out their surroundings. He was certain that before the tornado had hit, this had been a pretty nice area. It reminded him of his spread in Texas. Now all he saw was devastation for miles. The majority of the trees were down and those left standing were barely doing so.

He suddenly turned his full concentration to the man because he'd offered his condolences, saying there was a chance Mac and Teri had not survived. The cabin where they'd been staying, as well as many others in the vicinity, had been flattened. A number of bodies had already been recovered, but not the McRoys'.

"And you won't recover them," Coop decided to say. "Thurston McRoy isn't dead."

The first responder, with an overly tired look, was about to reply to what Coop said when an approaching voice stopped the man. "I'll take over here, Floyd."

The man glanced over his shoulder, and then nodded. "Okay, Sheriff." He then walked off, his exhaustion apparent. The newcomer, who looked a little older but just as tired, faced them now and Coop quickly assessed him and concluded he was ex-military. It was his stance even under extreme fatigue. Before the man began speaking, Coop asked, "What branch of the military?"

The man turned his gaze to Coop, who'd moved to stand beside Bane, Viper and Flipper. As if he'd sized them up, he said, "I'm Sheriff Derwin Corilla, former marine." He then asked, "And you guys?"

It was Flipper who answered. "SEALs."

The man nodded, smiling. "I should have figured as much."

No one asked why. There had always been this rivalry between the navy and the marines but when it came to a mission and they were called to work together, they did. Most military men respected anyone who was willing to serve their country, no matter the branch.

Introductions were made, and Viper spoke up. "We share Coop's sentiments, Sheriff Corilla. Mac isn't dead."

Coop expected the man to ask why they were so certain. Instead he said, "I'm not going to go so far and say he isn't dead, but I don't think he or his wife were in that cabin when it came down."

"And why do you think that?" Bane asked.

Sheriff Corilla shifted his gaze to Bane. "Because we used the dogs and they didn't sniff out any bodies at the cabin. Then yesterday the two horses assigned to them to ride while they were here were found wandering the range, after having found refuge somewhere during the storm."

"They were saddled?" Viper asked.

"No, but one of my men, who is a trained horseman, checked them over and it looked as if they'd been ridden. I believe the McRoys had been out riding somewhere when the tornado hit. They must've set the horses free and hopefully found cover somewhere."

He paused and then said, "That tornado hit a vast area and we're still looking for survivors. I'm not giving up on anyone."

Coop nodded. "Not enough manpower." It was a statement and not a question.

Sheriff Corilla shook his head. "Is there ever? Right now, we're forming a search party to look for a seven-year-old kid who survived but somehow got away from his parents. So far we haven't found him."

"We're here to find Mac, but we'll be glad to help your guys out any way we can."

The man lifted a brow. "All four of you?"

Flipper grinned. "For now. To help find Mac we've called in the cavalry. A former teammate who now works for Homeland Security is on his way here, and then my four brothers who are SEALs are coming, as well. Mac's kind of special to all of us."

"Even when we have to do our best to tolerate him," Viper added, grinning, as well.

"We'll be glad to help look for that kid," Bane offered.

Corilla looked at Bane oddly, but he didn't question what he said, evidently accepting the SEALs had the rescue of the McRoys well under control. "In that case, thanks for the offer and I'll take any extra help we can get."

Viper nodded. "Then you got it."

Sheriff Corilla walked off.

Coop, Bane, Viper and Flipper glanced at each other. From their last phone conversation with Mac, they concluded that as usual, he was in need of an attitude adjustment when it came to Teri. Maybe with them stranded together they could use that time to hash out a few issues plaguing their marriage.

Nick had been monitoring Mac's brain waves via the tracker and at present, there was no reason to think he was in immediate danger. When Nick arrived later that day, he would be able to pinpoint Mac and Teri's exact location.

In the meantime, they would join that search party.

Teri woke up to the sounds of Mac and glanced around to focus directly on him. The flashlight from his cell phone illuminated the area. He was shirtless, down to his briefs and exercising. Running in place. As she watched him her blood began running in place, as well, rushing like crazy through her veins.

Although the air was cool, he'd worked himself into a hefty amount of sweat. It covered his chest and drenched his hair. She had a workout routine, as well, but her regimen was definitely not as intense as his. She would join him sometimes when he was home and knew to stick to her own pace and not try to keep up with him. That attempt would be impossible.

As she lay there, she recalled she had slept in his arms and they hadn't made love. That was a miracle in itself since she and Mac were two people with high sexual energy. But that meant he'd accepted what she'd told him. Not only did they have issues to resolve, there was a chance those issues were now compounded by a possible pregnancy.

Mac finished his sets of running in place and bent over to draw in deep breaths. She loved watching him do that, as well. She pulled herself up. "Good morning, Mac."

He glanced over at her and when he did so, those dark, piercing eyes captivated her. As usual. "Good morning, Mrs. McRoy."

Teri smiled at him. She loved it when he called her that. It was a reminder that he'd chosen her, had given her that name to wear proudly and that made her his to claim. And she liked whenever he claimed her.

"Isn't exercising wasting air that we need?"

"Air has the ability to get in and out of places where people can't. I've noticed a fluctuation in oxygen levels in here, but never anything to be concerned about.

It appears higher now than when I woke this morning, so I decided to take advantage of it and work out."

"I would join you, but I don't want to get all sweaty."

He chuckled. "A little sweat never hurt anyone."

"In my case it wouldn't be a little sweat. Whenever I work out with you, I tend to sweat a lot."

He chuckled. "That's what you get for trying to keep up with me."

"Trust me, Mac. I don't try keeping up with you. I'd be crazy to try, believe me. I work at my own pace."

He gave her an admiring nod and a sensuous smile that caught her low in her stomach. "In that case, you do a pretty good job of holding your own."

"I try."

"Then come try with me. You'll be glad to know you don't have to worry about the sweat. I'll wash it off you."

She lifted a brow. "Do we have that much water to waste?"

"Yes. I found a pool of clear water on the west end of this mineshaft."

Excitement filled her. "You did?"

The corners of his mouth lifted in another smile. "I did. Come join me."

She hesitated for a minute, remembering other times they'd exercised together and how they would shower together afterward. That always led to other things. Things they were better off not doing. He knew that, yet he was inviting her to work out with him anyway, with the promise of a shower afterward. He evidently had more willpower than she did. But then, she knew he honestly did.

"Okay. My muscles are kind of sore after a few days of riding Amsterdam."

He crossed the floor and offered her his hand to help her up from the bed of hay. "You sure it's Amsterdam that has you sore and not me?"

She couldn't help the blush that spread across her features. She'd been married to this man for over ten years, yet he could still do this to her. "Now that you mention it…"

He pulled her to him when she was on her feet and wrapped his arms around her waist. Her chest was pressed against his solid one, which was drenched in perspiration. "I hope you weren't teasing about finding that pool of water."

He held her gaze. "I kid you not. When was the last time we went swimming together alone?"

"In case you've forgotten, I believe that's how I got pregnant with Tatum." She studied his features to see if her reminder would squash the desire she saw in his eyes. It didn't. In fact, she could feel the lower part of his body harden.

To further confuse her, he smiled. "I remember now. The folks kept Tia so you could join me that time in Germany."

So, he had remembered his R and R time, when he'd rented a house with a pool. She had stayed two weeks. When she'd left, she was pregnant. They had hoped for that, thinking it was time for Tia to have a sibling.

"Now we work out," she said, trying to ease from his arms.

"Not yet. I haven't kissed you good-morning yet. Do you have any idea how often I wake up whenever I'm on an operation, wishing it was your face I was waking up to see, and not my teammates'. I would give anything to be able to kiss you when it's a real kiss and not a dream. So, Teri McRoy, I hope you don't mind indulging me right now."

She swallowed while gazing up at him. They were supposed to talk this morning. She knew that. But a kiss, exercise and a swim sounded a whole lot better.

For now.

"Not at all, Mac, as long as you promise that's all it will be, a kiss."

As he lowered his head to her lips, he whispered, "I promise."

Chapter 9

Mac was convinced he could stand there and kiss his wife forever since he enjoyed doing it just that much. He intended to make sure she enjoyed it, as well, and from the way she was kissing him back, she was.

It was times like these when he missed her the most. Times like these when he regretted being away from her and the girls as much and as often as he was. Losing the baby had been hard on her, and he of all people knew it. A part of him knew she was still going through a grieving period, a period he'd yet to share with her.

Yet, he grieved regardless. For the son he'd lost and for the wife a part of him felt he was losing.

His concentration was pulled back to her when she began wiggling her tongue all around in his mouth, something he had taught her to do years ago. It was during those times when pleasuring him was the only thing she wanted to do, and he'd been all in.

But not now. Although it might kill him, he would keep his promise. If nothing else, he now understood what she needed and he knew what he needed. There were a number of issues on the table. First and foremost, he needed to prove to his wife that she mattered. If he had made the mistake of taking her for granted, taking their marriage for granted, it was time he shaped up or shipped out. Mac had no intentions of calling it quits where his wife and family were concerned. He needed them as much as he wanted them to need him.

He reluctantly broke off the kiss and pulled his mouth back. He had to take control, both mentally and physically…especially physically. He couldn't take care of the latter until they wrapped themselves around the problems that could eventually destroy their marriage if they went unchecked.

His wife could be pregnant. He knew how she felt about that possibility because he'd asked, and she'd had no problem telling him. The one thing she hadn't asked was how he felt about it. Why? Did she think he wouldn't feel the same way?

He knew they had a lot of emotions to deal with. They were emotions he had conditioned himself not to feel.

But not anymore.

"Come on, time to join me and work out."

"You did good, kiddo."

Totally out of breath and bending over with hands resting on her knees, Teri glanced up at Mac. "Thanks. Glad you approve." She'd worked out in moderation. It was too early to tell if she was pregnant but just in case, she'd decided not to overdo anything. "I'm ready for my swim now."

"Then come with me." He took her hand in his and she tried not to think about how good it felt whenever he did that.

They didn't say anything and she wondered what he was thinking. He hadn't put his jeans and shirt back on but seemed perfectly at ease to walk through the mine-shaft in just his briefs and carrying his clothes in one hand while holding her hand with the other.

Glancing down, he asked, "How did you sleep last night?"

She smiled up at him. "Great. You kept me warm and I appreciated that. You took good care of me, Mac."

"And I always will."

For some reason his words touched her. Now if she could only get him to believe in her. But then, was she being fair wanting him to do that when she hadn't been totally forthcoming with him about what she'd done? She still had the issue of her buying the ranch between them. She still intended to tell him about it today like she had promised. But she wanted to find the right time to do so.

"So what do you think?"

She glanced up and saw the inlet, a small pool of crystal clear water. This was better than she expected. "How is this possible?" she turned to asked him.

"I figure it's part of that lake we saw a mile or so back and is a spill-off running underground. Because the water is warm, it must be connected to a hot spring, as well. I checked it out to make sure it's not a whirlpool. It doesn't look deep. You can swim, so you'll be fine."

Yes, she could swim. There had been a number of

swimming holes on her grandparents' ranch. "Are you swimming, as well?" she asked, unbuttoning her shirt. She paused and glanced over at him upon realizing what she was doing. She was about to strip in front of him. He was her husband, so honestly, there shouldn't be an issue in her doing that. But there was. Could she honestly expect him not to touch her if he saw her naked? She'd never placed restrictions or limitations on their lovemaking before.

She looked over at him. "Mac?"

"Go ahead and take off your clothes, Teri. I understood what you said about us not making love until we get some issues in our marriage resolved. I won't touch you, no matter what. I do have control, you know."

Yes, she knew about his control, but he'd never had to exercise restraint when it came to her. She nodded and then, while he watched, she stripped down to her bra and panties.

She glanced over at him, saw the heat in his gaze. He gave her one of his sexy smiles and said, "Maybe I shouldn't have encouraged you to remove your clothes after all."

She returned his smile. "Too late to call it back now."

He shrugged massive shoulders before shoving away from the wall to move toward her. "I guess so. Come on, let's swim."

When they got close to the water, they dived in.

As Mac watched Teri glide through the water, he realized he had forgotten just what a skilled swimmer she was. She looked good and he was fighting every part of his desirous body. He'd done several laps and now just preferred hanging back while she did hers.

Her body was perfectly arched as she progressed through the water, moving her head from side to side as she concentrated on her strokes.

It dawned on him then how relaxed she appeared, so carefree. Today she didn't have to be the mommy in control or the wife in demand. She could be Teri. It had been years since he'd seen her this…at peace. It was then he blamed himself for a lot of things. For not recognizing that she needed downtime. As her husband he should have taken her away somewhere, and often. Just the two of them.

They could have not only stimulated their minds but talked about a lot of things that bothered them. Parents needed "me" time, and he could see that now. She'd held a part-time job at a library for a couple of years now and he'd never even asked how she liked it. Mainly because he hadn't wanted her to work. He now saw just how unfair that was to her.

"I enjoyed that, Mac."

He blinked, realizing Teri had swum over to him. He'd been so caught up in his thoughts that he hadn't noticed her approach. "I'm glad you did." He pulled himself up over the edge and then reached his hand to help her out, as well.

"Thanks."

"You're welcome." He stepped back since standing too close to her could affect his self-control. "No towels, so we'll have to air our bodies dry."

"And risk catching pneumonia?" she asked, ringing the water out of her hair. "Do this."

He lifted a brow. "Do what?"

"This." She then demonstrated using her hands to

wipe off excess water from her body and doing it in such a way that her palms appeared to act as a sponge.

Mac doubted Teri had any idea how turned on he was getting just watching her rub her hands all over herself. It was a definite turn-on, which was something he could do without right now. Not to call attention to his growing erection, he followed her lead and saw her technique was working. "How do you know about this?"

She chuckled. "Nothing top secret here. Just one of those 'mommy knows it all' things."

"I see." And in a way, he was at least beginning to see. It wasn't that he hadn't appreciated her role as the mother of his kids before because he had. However, he would admit he'd never been privy to those 'mommy things' and just how good she was at them before now.

He didn't say anything as they put their clothes back on and he didn't try to be discreet in watching her.

He'd said he wouldn't touch her; he hadn't promised he wouldn't get his fill of admiring how her body looked.

"I'm hungry now."

He smiled. "Tuna and water again. This time with peaches."

"I'll take it. My grandparents used to say beggars can't be choosers."

He laughed. "That's funny. My parents would often say the same thing. Come on, let's eat."

Sheriff Corilla smiled appreciatively. "I can't thank you men enough for what you did. I doubt little Larry Johnson will be wandering off again anytime soon."

"We were glad to help, Sheriff," Bane said. The little boy had been found alive and well, although hungry, and had been returned to his parents. "Now we could use your help."

"Certainly. What can I do?"

"This is our former SEAL team member, Nick Stover. He was able to pinpoint Mac's location."

Sheriff Corilla lifted a brow. "You did?" he asked, shaking Nick's hand.

Nick nodded. "Yes, and that's where I need your help," he said, clicking on his laptop, which immediately flared to life. Within seconds an aerial view came on the screen. "Based on the latitude, longitude and altitude I've documented, Mac's location has been pinpointed to this area."

"Information you've documented?" Corilla asked, rubbing his chin. It was obvious he was trying to figure out just how Nick had managed that. But they figured he knew it was something for which he wouldn't be getting answers, so he turned his attention to the laptop screen.

"That's Martinsville," he said. "It's a mining site that's been deserted for over five years now. I had my men check out the area and they said the tornado ripped through there pretty bad. Since the place has been deserted we had no reason to hang around."

"Evidently Mac and Teri were in the area and sought refuge in one of those mineshafts. That's where we're headed," Coop said.

"We figure there's a lot of debris in the area, so my four brothers are on their way with heavy equipment and machinery to help plow our way through," Flipper added.

Sheriff Corilla nodded. "You're going to need it. There are three shafts there, within several feet of each other. And according to my men, the windmill came down in that area and several trees were uprooted and landed on them, as well. I don't know which one your friend and his wife might be holed up inside, but I'm hoping it's not this one," he said, pointing at the mine-shaft on the right.

"Why?" Viper asked.

Sheriff Corilla glanced over at him. "It contains a pool of water, a hot spring, so to speak."

Bane lifted a brow. "We have several of those on my property in Denver. Why would that pose a threat?"

"Because it's a spill-off from McKevor Lake and I understand that the runoff from the lake is blocked with fallen trees and limbs acting like a dam, impeding natural flow. That means the water has nowhere to go."

Nick stared at the sheriff. "You believe there will be flooding in the area?"

"Yes, and it's already started. But what causes grave concern with this particular mineshaft is that because of the spring inside, it will start flooding when the spring overflows, with no warning. Unfortunately, there is no high section within the mineshaft to escape the rising water. It's happened before, and a couple of unsuspect-ing miners lost their lives. If you honestly think this is where the McRoys are, then I suggest you get them out as soon as possible."

Chapter 10

"Tell me about your job at that library, Teri."

She glanced over at Mac, wondering why he wanted to know more about it when her working there had been a sore point with him. Besides, he'd never before asked her about what she did at the library. Was this his lead-in question before they argued about her keeping her job?

"What do you want to know about it?"

"Anything you want to tell me."

Honestly? Did he? There was only one way to find out. "I only work three days a week, four hours a day, but I love what I do."

"Which is?"

"I'm in charge of the history section. That's great for me because of my degree in history. I get to sug-gest good books to the people who come to the library, about whatever part of history they are interested in.

You won't believe the number of young people who come to the library wanting books on the World Wars, specifically World War II."

"Why do you think that is?"

"Not sure, but I'm just glad they are interested in it. I believe you can't fully appreciate your present until you know your past. At least that's what's my grand-dad used to say."

"I wish I could have met your grandparents. They sound like swell people."

He'd told her that several times before, when she'd told him something her grandparents had passed on to her. "And there's no doubt they would have wanted to meet you." Sadly, her mother had died when she'd been two and her father before her tenth birthday, leaving her to be raised by her grandparents.

They had been the best and when they'd died not long after she'd finished college, within the same year, it had been hard for her. Selling the ranch they'd loved had been even harder and a part of her felt she'd let them down by doing so. Now she owned it again. Would Mac understand her need to atone for those feelings of guilt? Would he understand that was one of her reasons for doing what she'd done?

"I'm glad you're doing something that you enjoy, Teri."

She looked over at him. Did he really? If he did, then that was a switch. "Why, Mac? Why are you glad now when you've always been resentful?"

"I've never been resentful, not really. I just never understood your need to work outside the home."

"And you do now?" she asked, staring at him.

He nodded. "Yes, I'm beginning to. In a way, it's

no different than my need to do something I love. I wanted to be a SEAL since listening to my maternal grandfather tell me of all the things he did as one. I wanted that kind of life. The adventure. The need to protect my country. Mom and Dad didn't understand why I would pass on a football scholarship to apply to the naval academy instead."

He didn't say anything for a minute and then added, "The only other thing I needed to make my life complete was something I thought I'd never find, and that was a mate who was willing to put up with it. But then I found you. However, in creating the life I wanted, I failed to realize something."

"What?"

He studied her for a moment. "That you had dreams of your own. Dreams I expected you to forgo for mine."

Teri didn't say anything, realizing this was the first time they'd had a heart-to-heart talk on things that bothered her and that had affected their marriage. Yes, they'd sought counseling, but even then she'd felt Mac had never given those sessions his absolute all. He'd merely been placating her at the time.

"And do you know what's obvious to me now, Teri?"

"No, what?"

"That you did forgo them. And instead of appreciating your sacrifice, I scorned you every time I returned from a mission for decisions you made in my absence."

Teri couldn't let him take full blame. There were some decisions she could have given more in-depth thought to before making them. But then there were some decisions, like the purchase of the ranch, that, although made on the spur of the moment, had been a dream come true for her.

"It wasn't always that way, Mac. Even I admit there were some things I could have done differently." She paused. It was time to tell him about the ranch. She'd withheld it from him long enough. "Mac, I—"

"Wait," he said, holding up his hand. She saw his body go on full alert as he glanced around.

She glanced around, as well, wondering what had drawn his attention but knew now was not the time to ask. He was in his "ready to act" mode.

"You hear that?" he suddenly asked, quickly coming to his feet and placing his tuna can aside.

She strained her ears. "No, I don't hear anything. What do you hear?"

He looked at her. "Rushing water. Stay here." He quickly walked off.

Rushing water?

She didn't like the sound of that. Suddenly an eerie feeling passed through her. No, she wouldn't stay here. She stood, put her own tuna can aside and went after Mac.

Bane Westmoreland glanced around at what used to be a mining site. It had taken a full two hours to cut through downed trees and plow through all kinds of debris to get there. He appreciated one of Flipper's brothers for having the mind to bring several bulldozers. If it hadn't been for that equipment, they would still be miles away from here.

That tornado had done more damage than they'd thought. Since this was uninhabited land, the devastation in this section of Torchlight hadn't made the news. Nick had decisively pinpointed the mineshaft that Mac was holed up in as the one with the spill-off.

Even though they didn't have concrete proof, they figured he and Teri were together. Getting them out safely from among all this rubble would be a challenge but they intended to do it.

According to Nick, who was monitoring Mac's tracker, he'd been pretty active this morning. From the timing and frequency of Mac's movements they'd concluded he'd been working out. Not surprising, since Mac could be anal when it came to fitness.

"I checked on him twenty minutes ago and he was in a relax mode," Nick was saying to them now.

"That means he hadn't detected anything," Coop surmised.

"That was twenty minutes ago, and he might have figured it out by now," Viper chimed in to say. "We need to get them out. We've seen that lake and the water has to go somewhere. Since it's not flooding aboveground, that means it will be flooding connecting outlets below. Mac has no idea that's going to happen."

"Or no way to stop it when it does," Flipper added.

Bane, like the others, knew the seriousness of what was about to happen. He was about to say something when Nick interrupted. "Hey, guys, I just got a new reading on Mac. He's on the move and his brain waves are signaling trouble."

Bane nodded, his expression serious. "Okay, guys, let's get Mac and Teri out of there and send them home to their girls."

Mac rushed quickly to where the pool was located and got halfway when the sound of rushing water increased. When he got to where the troughs of hay had been, he stopped. There was standing water in that area. "What the hell!"

He quickly moved past the troughs and when he stepped on what had been a solid floor, suddenly the board beneath him collapsed. He broke the fall by grabbing hold of a boulder, the same one he'd sat on that morning. Gripping tightly, he barely held on. There was no doubt in his mind that if he fell he would get swept away in the rushing water below.

"Mac!"

He snatched his head upward and saw Teri coming toward him. Hadn't he told her to stay put?

"Go back, Teri. There's a chance the floor might collapse under you. Water is flooding the mineshaft. You need to go back and find a high place and stay there."

"And leave you here?"

"Yes."

She frowned at him. "Not on your life, Thurston McRoy!"

"Teri…" he said in a warning tone. "Please do as I say."

"Save your breath," she said, glancing around. "Hold on, Mac. I've got an idea."

She had an idea? What kind of idea could she have? Teri needed to get her butt out of there and try to find higher ground, although he didn't recall there being any higher ground. The thought of anything happening to her had him—

Suddenly Mac felt a rope tossed around him. He glanced up and watched Teri reviving her role as a cowgirl. Twirling the rope around the air in perfect precision, she then lassoed him in with a second rope that went around his body perfectly.

Ropes? What in the world? Where did those ropes come from?

"Pull yourself out now, Mac!"

He tugged upward and found it was tight. Where had she tied the end of the rope for it to be as sturdy as it was? Knowing the answer would come soon enough, he used the rope to hoist himself back up on solid ground.

"Mac!" Teri threw herself into his arms and he held on to her tight. "I thought I was going to lose you."

He then pulled back but kept his arms around her waist. "Thanks, but I told you to stay back."

She lifted her chin. "And I disobeyed. Good thing I did."

"Where did the ropes come from?"

"Some troughs are built with a compartment underneath to hold a rope. I checked and they were there. I hadn't lassoed in a while but knew I had to do it. I tied the ends around the trough to take your weight when you pulled yourself up." She glanced around and saw the flooding waters. "What is going on?"

"Looks like the lake is flooding with the spill-off, which means we need to find higher ground."

"Is there higher ground in here?"

He had been afraid she would ask that. He took her hand when more water began flowing in around them at a high rate of speed. "Come on. If there is, we need to find it."

They were trying to outrun the water and Teri saw they couldn't. Already the water was waist-deep and just as she'd feared, there was no higher ground. She wouldn't get hysterical, but they were going to die.

At least the girls were in good hands and she and Mac were together.

He'd stopped and was looking around and she knew without him saying that there was nowhere else to go. They were back where they started, which was at the entrance, but nothing had changed and it was still blocked.

He was still holding her hand and she tightened her hold on his. "Mac, I love you and you've been a good husband, and—"

"We will be rescued, Teri," he interrupted her to say.

She lifted a brow. "By who?"

"The guys."

She knew what guys he was talking about. His teammates. Did he really believe that? Or in their last moments of life was he trying to give her hope? "How will they rescue us, Mac?"

He shrugged as he looked at the blocked opening. "Not sure how, but they will get it done. In the meantime, I need you to stand on my shoulders."

"What? Why?"

"Because that will keep the water from getting to you until they do."

She frowned, knowing that meant the water would get to him first. "And what about you?"

"Don't worry about me. Timing is important. We could tread water, but not for long. If the guys can't save us both, at least they will have more time to save you. Now, let me hoist you up on my shoulders."

She shook her head, imagining the weight of her on his shoulders with water steadily surrounding them. "No, I won't do it."

"Don't argue with me," he said, trying to lift her up.

She pushed his hands away, although already the

water was nearly up to her breasts. However, she didn't care. She would not have him risk his life to save hers. "Mac, please don't ask me to do that. What will I tell the girls?"

He reached out and caressed her cheek. "The same thing we agreed long ago to tell them if I never returned home. That I love them and will always love them. Just so you know, the same applies to their mother, as well. I love you."

Mac leaned down to kiss her. She knew it was supposed to be a brush of his lips against hers but the moment their lips touched, their passions were inflamed. It didn't matter that water was still increasing around them. Nothing mattered but this kiss and she refused to believe this was their last.

Mac finally broke off the kiss and whispered against moist lips, "And if you are pregnant, Teri, please let our son or daughter know I would have welcomed them into our world with all the love a father could give."

She fought back her tears. "Don't do this to me, Mac. You just said that your teammates are coming. Are you now doubting their abilities?"

"No. They are SEALs. They just might not have enough time to save us both and you are more important."

"Says who?"

"Says me." Then, in an unexpected move, he quickly pulled her up to sit upon his shoulders. She tried struggling free and he said, "Stay put or you'll knock me off-balance and we'll both drown."

"Don't do this, Mac. Let me down."

"No."

Mac was six-foot-three and water had already reached

the upper part of his chest. Had she remained standing beside him, it would be up to her neck now.

It seemed the water was coming in faster and when she felt her backside get wet she knew the water was up to Mac's shoulders. Tears she couldn't hold back anymore began to flow.

Then suddenly, when she knew the water was close to Mac's neck, she heard him laugh out loud and say, "About time."

She glanced down from her place perched on Mac's shoulders to see one of his teammates. Flipper. Where had he come from?

"Whatever," Flipper said. "Stop being an unappreciative ass." He then glanced up at her and smiled. "Hi, Teri," he greeted, like it was a normal thing to find them trapped in a mineshaft that was quickly filling with water.

"How did you get in here?" she asked, needing to know. Mac had said they would be coming, but honestly, she truly hadn't believed him.

"We figured it would take longer to remove all the debris from the entrance, so they made an opening large enough for me to swim through," Flipper explained. "We need to hurry up and leave out the same way. Here," he said, handing her a snorkel mask and then giving Mac one, as well.

"Where is yours?" she asked him.

He gave her an arrogant smile, his blue eyes flashing. "I don't need one. Now quickly put it on."

Teri did as he said, remembering Mac's claim that Flipper, master diver, could hold his breath underwater longer than any human he knew.

"You can release Teri off your shoulders now, Mac,

to put on your mask." The water was close to Mac's face and he reluctantly released her to Flipper so he could put on his mask.

"I will lead you guys out. Follow me. We need to be careful. Some of the pieces of debris floating around in the water have jagged edges."

Flipper dived into the water, and Mac motioned for Teri to follow. She dived in behind Flipper, knowing Mac was bringing up the rear.

Chapter 11

"I am so glad to see you guys," Mac said to his friends. He was surprised to see Nick as well as Flipper's four SEAL brothers. "I had no idea that the mine would flood."

"We didn't, either," Bane said, grateful their mission had been accomplished and Mac and Teri were safe.

"Had we known we would have rescued you sooner. We've been here for two days," Coop added.

Mac lifted a brow. "Two days? Then what took you guys so long?" he asked.

Viper's shoulder lifted in a careless shrug. "We assisted the sheriff in finding a little boy. That took an entire day. Besides, your brain waves were signaling you were in a pretty calm state, so we figured you and Teri could use that time to work out a few issues."

"Oh, you did, did you?" Mac said, frowning deeply.

"Yes, we did," Bane replied. "When we talked to you the day you got here you were in a foul mood, already eating nails, shooting fire and ready to give your wife hell. We were hoping the time alone would help. Did it?"

Mac glanced over at his wife, who was being checked by one of the first responders. Damn, he loved that woman. She'd been a real trouper and he could credit her with saving his life. He looked back at his friends. "Yes, but it will be an ongoing process, guys. I admit I'm seeing things in a different light, but…"

"You'll still resort to being an ass when the mood suits you," Viper said, frowning.

Mac gave Viper a daggered look. "You act like I enjoy being difficult."

"Don't you?" Coop asked. "You've had plenty of time to clean up your act and accept Teri as your equal."

"I do accept her as my equal. Damn it, she saved my life in that mine," he snapped out.

Surprise and shock appeared on his friends' faces. "She did?"

"Yes." He then told them what happened.

"Wow," Flipper said. "It's a good thing you married a cowgirl with smarts. Some people would have freaked out."

Mac nodded. "Teri has a level head on her shoulders."

"She just doesn't know how to spend your money, right?"

Instead of waiting for his answer, his friends walked off.

Out of the corner of her eye, Teri had watched Mac talk to his friends. Even across the distance, she could feel the closeness he had with them was unlike what he had with her. Of course, it would be different since they were his friends and she was his wife, but he trusted them unequivocally. He trusted her but with conditions.

She appreciated their time together in the mineshaft. They'd ironed out a number of things that had been eroding their marriage. But they still had work to do. She still had confessions to make. And she believed they would do that work because they loved each other and neither of them wanted what they had to end.

Teri knew she still had to tell him about the ranch. She had been about to tell him when he'd detected something was wrong. Now she had to find time to discuss it with him. Right now, she was just glad they'd been rescued. She was ready to go home to their girls.

First thing she wanted to do was check into a hotel and take a good bath and wash her hair. They'd been told the cabin had been destroyed and they would be allowed to go look through the rubble to recover any of their belongings. Then there was the issue of more clothes, which meant she and Mac needed to go shopping.

For now, she didn't want her husband out of her sight. She'd come close to losing him. They'd come close to losing each other and she was still having a hard time getting beyond that fact.

"You're free to go now, Ms. McRoy."

She glanced up at the first responder, who'd been treating the minor cuts on her arm from a piece of debris. "Thanks."

She stood and glanced back over at Mac. He was now standing alone and looking at her and doing so in such a way she could feel heat stir in the bottom of her stomach. No matter what, they had shared an experience in that mineshaft that would always be there, unifying them, bonding them.

She broke eye contact with him and looked down at herself. She'd been given a blanket. His clothes were still wet and so were hers. They'd also been told the vehicles they'd driven to the ranch had been totaled. More bad news. The main ranch house had sustained a lot of damage and was now uninhabitable. But the good news was that Amsterdam and the other horse had survived the tornado. She'd been glad to hear that.

"Ready to go to the hotel?"

She looked at the man with the deep, husky voice. Her husband. "How will we leave?"

He held up a key fob. "Bane left us his rental. I figured we could go get cleaned up, buy new clothes and then return to the cabin to see what we can recover. However, I have a feeling a lot of the stuff is lost."

She had a similar feeling about that. Luckily, she'd only brought a few things with her. "What about your things?"

He shrugged. "All replaceable. Ready?"

She nodded. "Yes, I'm ready." She had already thanked Mac's teammates but wanted to thank them again. She looked round and didn't see them anywhere. "Where did the guys go?"

"They're on their way back home."

She could understand that. Like Mac they'd returned to their homes only a few days ago from their last operation. Yet they'd left their families to come here to save her and Mac. And they *had* saved them. She and Mac had been just minutes away from drowning.

"I really appreciated what they did, Mac. You are

part of a wonderful team." Teri figured he already knew that but wanted to speak the obvious anyway.

"Yes, I am."

From Mac's expression Teri could tell he, too, was filled with deep gratitude. They knew what the outcome would have been if Mac's SEAL team hadn't arrived when they had. And then for Nick Stovers and Flipper's brothers to be included in the mix was super special. She truly appreciated everyone's help.

"Yes, I'm ready to leave. I need a bath and my hair needs washing."

"I'll take care of both for you. Come on." He took her hand and headed toward the waiting SUV.

Mac glanced over at his wife as he backed the vehicle out of the parking lot. Her eyes were closed and he figured it wouldn't be long before she was asleep. She deserved to rest and he would be the first to say she'd been more than a great trouper. She'd been a real lifesaver. It was something he would never forget. His gut tightened at the thought of how she'd put her own life on the line. She had kept a level head and done what she needed to do.

His friends had given him food for thought. But he'd been doing a lot of thinking long before they'd fed him any words. The problems in his marriage wouldn't disappear with just a few days holed up in a mineshaft. It would take continuous work on their part. Especially on his.

"Mac…"

He glanced over at Teri when she said his name. She'd fallen asleep, so in sleep she was thinking about him. Such a thing touched him deeply. While at the hotel he intended to pamper her. What he hadn't told her was that thanks to the wives of his teammates, certain arrangements had already been made.

A smile touched his lips. He needed more time with his wife and intended to get all the time he could. They would be returning home to Virginia soon.

When he stopped at a traffic light, he turned to look at her and saw how her head was resting against the back of the seat. Hair had fallen in her face and he couldn't resist the temptation to reach out and brush a few dark curls back from her forehead. He didn't stop there. The pad of his finger gently rubbed against her cheek. His action didn't wake her, didn't even make her stir. Instead she continued to sleep.

He had a stop or two to make before they got to the hotel, one place in particular.

"We're here, Teri."

Teri slowly opened her eyes. Yawning, she pulled up in her seat and looked through the car's window. "Where are we?"

"At a hotel in Cheyenne. All the ones in Torchlight were filled to capacity with so many first responders arriving. They still have a lot of people unaccounted for."

"I hope they find them. That first responder who treated me told me how your teammates helped find a little boy. That was special." Easing her seat belt from around her waist, she asked, "Are you sure we can get a room here? The place looks full, if the parking lot is any indication."

"Don't worry, we have a room."

Teri glanced over at him. Something about his words sent heat flowing through her. They had a room? It wasn't what he'd said but how he'd said it that made certain areas within her stir. "Good."

"Stay put. I'll be around to open the door for you, Teri."

Last time he'd given her such an order she'd defied him, but not this time. She was too tired to move just yet. Swimming out of that mine hadn't been easy and she had been grateful for Flipper being in front of her and Mac at the rear. Paramedics had been there to check them over the moment they'd reached solid ground. In less than five minutes after they'd gotten out, the sheriff announced the mineshaft was filled with water from top to bottom and she'd known there was no way she and Mac would have survived.

"Do you need me to carry you inside?"

She glanced up at Mac. He'd come around the side of the car and opened the door for her. He had a store bag in his hand. "No, I can walk. You made a stop somewhere?" she asked. He reached out and circled her wrist with his long fingers. He was wearing another Stetson and she wondered where he'd gotten it when the one he'd purchased the day he'd arrived had been destroyed in the flood.

Mac smiled. "Yes, I made a couple of stops. You slept through them."

"Oh. I guess I was more exhausted than I thought."

"You've been through a lot, Teri."

She glanced over at him as they walked inside the hotel. "We both have."

Teri noted that instead of checking in at the front desk, Mac led her over to the bank of elevators. It was a beautiful hotel, one of the well-known chains. The lobby was filled with a lot of fresh flowers. She didn't know how long they'd driven to get here. This hotel wasn't located in downtown Cheyenne but on the outskirts of town.

"We don't have to check in?"

He looked down at her when they stepped inside the elevator. "No. The guys took care of it."

She wondered what else the guys had taken care of and found out when they reached their hotel room. A bottle of champagne was on ice with a card that said Compliments of Team Six. There was also a huge bag from the hotel's gift shop and another bag from a well-known clothing store in the middle of the king-size bed.

"What's this?" she asked, moving toward the bed. Although the hotel room wasn't a suite, she thought it was larger than most. It even had a small balcony instead of just a window. They were on the tenth floor and the balcony overlooked some of the most beautiful valleys and meadows she'd ever seen.

"Clothes that my teammates' wives ordered for you from a clothing store downtown. I told them what we needed and the sizes. The guys ordered clothes for me from one of those western outfitters in town. They picked everything up and delivered it here before heading out to the airport."

"Who? Your teammates?"

"Yes, thank God for online shopping."

Teri was touched by what everyone had done. His teammates and their wives. Women she'd gotten to know. "That was truly nice of them, Mac."

"Yes, it was." He tossed the bags he was carrying on the bed to join the others. "Now for your bath. You prefer the tub or a shower?"

"The shower will be fine. That way I can wash my

hair." She went through one of the bags and pulled out a pair of jeans and a Western shirt. There were also underthings—bra and panties. She also had more boots and another hat. She looked at the tags on the clothing. Of course they were her size. When it came to her, Mac knew every single physical detail.

She glanced over at him. "You did good in telling them what I needed."

"I try. Now go ahead and get started on your shower. I have an important call to make and I'll be in there in a minute."

He would be in there in a minute? Did that mean he planned to join her in her shower? It wouldn't be the first time if he did, so why did the thought of him doing such a thing arouse her with anticipation?

"Oh, okay." She grabbed the underthings from the bag and quickly headed for the bathroom.

Chapter 12

Mac hung up the phone after ordering room service from the hotel's restaurant to be delivered in a few hours. He and Teri needed to go back to the cabin, search through the rubble to see if they could recover any of their belongings. But not today. They had more urgent and pressing business to attend to.

Going over to the nightstand, he pulled open the drawer to retrieve the bag he'd kept separate from the others. Pulling out one of several condom packets, he headed for the bathroom.

The room was steamy and although he couldn't see her, he knew Teri was somewhere behind the opaque glass wall. He placed the condom on the vanity before stripping off his clothes. Reclaiming the packet, he moved toward the shower door. All he could think of was a naked Teri, that fine body of hers and how much he needed to sink into it.

When he opened the door, she had her back to him with her head under the sprayer as she washed her hair. But the swoosh of air as the door opened must've alerted her that she was no longer alone. He saw her body tense and go still.

"Mac?"

"Who else would it be?" he asked, placing the condom packet in the soap compartment before easing up behind her.

She relaxed her body against his. "Can't ever be too sure. I've watched enough *NCIS* to reach that conclusion."

He started to tell her that was television fabricated for her enjoyment and then decided not to bother. If watching those shows kept her cautious whenever he was gone, then so be it. "Then rest assured it's me, baby," he said, bringing her body back against him and leaning close to whisper in her ear.

"Okay, it's you. I thought we decided we wouldn't do this."

"Because you're not on any birth control," he said, using the tip of his tongue to lick against the side of her ear.

"Yes, and we need to reach an understanding in our marriage."

He pushed the wet hair from her face after he turned her around to look at him. "Taking you or our marriage for granted is something I've never wanted to do, Teri, and if I did do that, then I'm sorry. I do understand your feelings, trust your decisions, respect what you do while I'm gone. I will get better but don't expect me to change overnight. Please accept me as 'work in progress.' I promise to do better but I'm human, I might make mistakes along the way."

"I'm human, too, and I might make mistakes, as well, Mac."

"Good, now we understand each other and agree to work together to improve our marriage."

"Yes, but I need to tell you what I bought while you were gone. You're not going to like it."

"It doesn't matter this time. Considering what you've gone through, what we've both gone through, it doesn't matter to me now. Whatever it is you bought without talking it over with me, I'll forgive you for it this time. Consider it a pardon."

She raised a brow. "A pardon?"

"Yes. Everyone is entitled to at least one during their lifetime."

"But you don't know what I bought or the cost."

He shrugged as he reached above her head for the shampoo. "Doesn't matter. We still have a roof over our head and food to eat, right?"

"Yes."

"Then whatever you bought didn't put us in the poor-house."

"You sure, Mac?"

"Positive. And you can tell me all about it later. Better yet, surprise me."

"Surprise you?"

"Yes. Surprise me. Right now, the only thing I want to think about is doing other things."

"Other things like what?"

"Making love to my wife. And don't worry. I stopped by a store to grab a few condoms." There was no need to tell her he'd gotten the economy pack of a dozen.

She smiled up at him. "Why aren't I surprised?"

"Not sure. Why aren't you?"

Instead of answering him she went up on tiptoe, wrapped her arms around his neck and pressed her mouth against his.

Joy filled Teri.

Mac was giving her a pardon. That meant even if he hadn't agreed with her purchase of the ranch, this time he wouldn't make a big deal out of it. But still, she knew moving forward he had to agree to trust her more to handle things when he was gone. They would both be works in progress and she didn't have a problem with that.

He broke off the kiss and reached up to fill his hands with shampoo from the dispenser. "Turn around. I know you've already lathered your hair but I want to do it again. I love washing your hair."

She turned her back to him and sighed deeply at the feel of his fingers working lather into her scalp. That, coupled with her backside resting against his groin, sent a multitude of sensations all through her.

Teri was convinced nobody could wash her hair the way Mac did. He had the best fingers…for everything. She recalled those same fingers touching every part of her body, especially when he worked those same fingers inside her, making her reach an orgasm of gigantic proportions.

"You like the way that feels, baby?"

"Hmm," she said, not able to say the words, yet knowing he knew what she meant.

"Now for the rinse-out."

He tilted her head back under the spray and she felt

warm water rushing through her hair and down her back. After squeezing excess water from her head, he said, "Now to clean the rest of you."

Then, filling his hands with soap, he used his hands to lather her body. The feel of his hands on her body made her moan because he knew exactly what areas to touch.

"You shouldn't stir me this way, Mac," she said, when he turned her around to face him.

"Why not?"

Did he really have to ask her that? "I can't think straight when you do."

He began lathering her front and said, "It wouldn't bother me in the least if you were to stop thinking at all. Or if you think only about me."

Little did he know she did that anyway. He didn't know how lonely her nights were without him in bed with her. "How can you be so sexy and so annoying at the same time?"

"It's a gift, babe," he leaned in and whispered before placing a kiss across her lips.

Then, using the sprayer, he washed the suds from her body and then ran his hands all over her. "You're squeaky-clean now."

She believed him. He had washed her hair and her body. "Now for me to wash you."

Lathering her hands with soap, she began rubbing them all over his body. Her husband was well-endowed and his erection was showing her how loaded he was. Touching him made sensations flood her insides, made a tingling sensation settle between her thighs. No part of his body missed her care and attention.

When she heard him moan, she glanced up and met

his gaze. Held it and felt desire and love in the very depths of her soul. Holding him in her hand always did this to her, empowered her as a woman.

His woman.

"You're killing me, you know."

She shook her head and smiled. "You're a SEAL. I heard they don't die easily. They're too rough and tough."

"Then why do I feel like putty in your hands?"

Teri threw her head back and laughed as she continued to hold him. "Trust me, this does not feel like putty. Not one single inch of it."

After figuring she'd tortured him enough, she used the sprayer to wash all the suds from his body. No sooner had she done that than he suddenly backed her against the shower stall. "Now I'm going to take care of you, Teri Anne."

"You always take care of me, Thurston."

He smiled and she watched him retrieve the condom packet from where he'd placed it earlier. He made quick work of sheathing himself. Returning to her, he asked, "Now, where was I?"

"If you have to ask, then maybe we—"

He didn't give her a chance to finish. Mac lifted her onto him at the same time he captured her mouth in his. And when he began thrusting hard into her, Teri was convinced that, considering his ferocious sexual appetite, he intended to make up for lost time.

Chapter 13

Mac opened his eyes to find Teri sitting cross-legged in the middle of the bed, staring at him. Seeing her flooded his mind with memories of how they'd spent the last few hours. They had made love in the shower, dried off and made love again in the bed. Dinner had arrived in their room and afterward they'd taken a walk outside only to return to their hotel room to make love again. All night long.

It was morning and the sun was shining brightly through the window shades. It was a beautiful day and he had awakened to the face of an even more beautiful woman. A woman sitting in the middle of the bed with a huge grin on her face. A stunning smile. It was even a mischievous smile. For a minute, she looked like the cat that ate the canary.

"Good morning, Mac."

Instead of responding, he reached out and cupped his hands behind her head to bring her face closer to his. And then he did something that he'd done a lot of lately. He kissed her, getting the feel of her that he definitely needed.

It was strange how things worked out. He'd left Virginia to come after his wife. There began an adventure, one he could certainly have done without, but possibly one that was needed. He couldn't recall when the two of them had spent so much "us" time together. They missed their girls, he knew that, but they were enjoying the time they were spending here with each other. He and Teri would return to the cabin to go through the rubble and sometime later today they would be returning home.

By the time the kiss ended, he was ready to pull her deeper into his arms for another kiss, but she pulled back and said, still smiling brightly, "Today you get your surprise."

He lifted a brow as he reached out and gently rubbed up and down her arm, needing the contact and loving the feel of her smooth skin. "My surprise?"

Her smile got even brighter. "Yes. I've made all the arrangements."

He was trying to keep up with her but failing. "What arrangements, sweetheart?"

"To take you to see your surprise. Mac, please keep up," she said jokingly.

He was trying. He leaned up and kissed her again, this one just as thorough but not as long. "I'm trying. How about you start from the beginning since I'm sure there is something I missed."

She didn't say anything at first. It looked as if his

kiss had left her dazed. He wanted to take advantage of that look and tumble her back into bed with him and make love to her all over again. He was about to do just that when her next words stopped him.

"Your parents have agreed to watch the kids, which works out since they hadn't expected us back until Sunday anyway. I've called the airlines and booked the flight. We leave this evening."

Whoa, things were now moving so fast his head was spinning. He pulled himself up in bed. "Where exactly are we going?"

"Texas."

"Texas?"

"Yes."

He ran a hand down his beard. "Why?"

"To show you what I bought and that's all I'm saying about it. The rest is a surprise. And when you see it, you'll be okay with me buying it because it was a pardon, remember?" she said grinning. "Now I'm going into the bathroom to get ready for our day. We've got a lot to do." Before he could say anything, she'd slid off the bed and rushed into the bathroom.

As soon as the door closed behind Teri, Mac eased to sit on the side of the bed. Damn, he needed a cup of coffee. Black. A little gin in it wouldn't hurt, either.

What on earth had his wife bought in Texas? A purchase he'd pardoned. Had he spoken too soon?

He remembered the smile on her face and how excited she was to share this surprise with him. He wanted to share her happiness, but that feeling of doom wouldn't go away.

Getting out of bed, he went to the coffeepot in the

room and got it started. By the time he was sipping his first cup he'd figured it out. Teri had bought Tia a horse. That had to be it. He recalled her bringing up the subject of doing that last year, saying how well Tia was doing with her riding lessons.

Mac had squashed that idea when he'd made Teri see that not only did they not need a horse but they had no place to keep one. She'd come back to say the stables where Tia's lessons were held kept horses for other owners and for Tia to have her own personal horse to ride would be wonderful and a great ninth birthday present. He hadn't agreed and he had pretty much told her he hadn't wanted to discuss it any further. And they hadn't.

Had she gone behind his back and purchased the horse anyway? Knowing how he'd felt about it? Tia's tenth birthday was coming up in a few months and usually whatever gift they gave their daughter was a joint decision. Had Teri made that decision without him?

Mac pushed back the anger he felt, remembering he'd decided that when it came to Teri and any decisions she made without him, he wouldn't sweat the small stuff. But there was nothing small about owning a horse. Not the boarding of it or the cost of shipping it from Texas to Virginia.

"I'm back."

He turned around. An ache slipped through him and the lower part of his body hardened. She was standing there after having showered, a towel covering her middle. Barely. His wife was definitely acting the part of a seductress this morning. A very happy and elated seductress.

Had buying a horse for their oldest daughter and now

knowing he wouldn't be blowing a gasket about it put her in such a happy mood? At that moment he knew if that was the case, then he would let her play out her surprise. Just seeing that huge smile on her face, something he hadn't seen in a long time, was worth it.

Placing his coffee cup down he slowly crossed the room to her and drew her into his arms. "Had I known you were taking another shower I would have taken it with you."

She laughed. "That shower gets us in trouble, Mac."

"But it's trouble we can handle."

She didn't look too convinced but eased closer to him anyway. "Did you forget we're supposed to go to the cabin today and look around?"

"No, I didn't forget," he said, pulling her closer to his naked body. "We have time and we will still make the flight to Texas."

"In that case…"

She reached up and cupped his face in her hand, leaned up and kissed him. He decided to let her do her thing before taking over. Mac liked the way she was using her tongue to entice him and when he was certain he couldn't handle it any longer, he swept her up into his arms and headed back toward the bed.

Teri squeezed Mac's hand as they stepped off the plane in Dallas, Texas. She glanced over at him. He'd slept on the plane during most of the fight and a part of her wanted to believe she'd worn him out that morning. If so, it would have been a first during the ten-plus years of their marriage.

After making love, they'd dressed and breakfasted downstairs in the hotel restaurant before leaving for the cabin. Seeing the wreckage had nearly broken her heart since she'd liked the cabin and enjoyed the days she'd spent there.

The tornado had flattened it, but Mac's duffel bag was located practically intact in a tree not far away. Most of Teri's stuff had been destroyed but she was happy when Mac had come across her driver's license and her house keys.

They had gone back to the hotel, packed and headed for the airport. Instead of heading for home they had caught a flight to Dallas. It was late and she'd booked reservations at a hotel. It would take an hour to drive to Terrell in the morning.

She still hadn't told Mac where they were going and he seemed okay not to ask questions. He was going to accept the surprise she had in store for him. Now, as they drove to the hotel in the car they'd rented at the airport, she glanced over at him to ask, "You okay?"

"I'm fine. How long will we be in Dallas?"

She chuckled, wondering if he was trying to get her to spill her surprise. "Not long. You'll get your surprise tomorrow, after we get a good night's sleep."

She could tell from the look on his face that a good night's sleep wasn't something either of them would be getting.

"I miss the girls," he then added.

She missed them, too, but she knew what she had to show him and share with him would change their lives forever. And regardless of his so-called "pardon," she wanted to believe that after analyzing the benefits of owning a ranch he would see it was a win-win situation for them.

Once the pressure of having to tell him about the purchase had been lifted from her shoulders, she'd been able to closely examine the advantages of moving the kids from Virginia to Texas. And with Mac retiring in a couple of years, she could see him becoming a rancher. He could handle a horse just as well as she could and he would be his own boss. She couldn't help getting excited at the prospect, and a part of her felt she was insuring their future and their kids' futures.

They arrived at the hotel in Dallas, where she'd been able to get a suite, unlike the one they'd stayed at in Cheyenne. The moment the door closed behind them, he pulled her into his arms. The move surprised her. She had figured that, pardon or no pardon, he would be asking her questions by now, but he hadn't. It seemed as if it was her rodeo and he intended to let her ride it like she wanted.

And speaking of riding…

She liked riding horses but she liked riding her husband even more. Deciding to let him take control for a while, she accepted his kiss with the same hunger that he was showing. And when he broke off the kiss moments later to lift her into his arms and head for the bedroom, she wrapped her arms around his neck and buried her head into his chest. His masculine scent aroused her, made her want him in a way that had all kinds of sensations sweeping through her, rushing through her bloodstream.

And then every so often, he would lean down and devour her mouth with those barely-touch-your-lips kisses that literally curled her toes. When they reached the bedroom, he stood her on her feet and plowed her mouth with another kiss that made the earth feel like it was tilting on its axis.

"Mac…"

"What do you want, baby?"

She wrapped her arms around his neck. "I want to show you what I can do."

He smiled at her. "Then do it."

Having him give her the word emboldened her and she stripped off her clothes while he watched. She wanted him to watch. When she was totally naked, he began removing his own clothes.

"So tell me, Teri. Do you have a plan?"

Oh, boy, did she. Now if she could stop staring at his body long enough to regain her senses and put her plan into action. She followed the movement of his hands as they went to the zipper of his pants. She continued to watch as he removed his jeans to expose a pair of sexy black briefs. It was then that she saw he was every bit as aroused as she was. When he had completely stripped, she drew in a deep breath. Regaining her senses, she pushed him down on the bed on his back. Then she quickly straddled him.

"I'm about to put my plan in action, Mac."

"Baby, go for it."

She did.

Lifting her body, she eased down on his shaft, loving the way it felt inside of her. As soon as he was snugly there, to the hilt, she smiled down at him. She began moving, up and down, withdrawing in a way to set a rhythm that had him moaning, growling her name, as she rocked down on him with an intensity that drove her deeper and deeper with each downward plunge.

She'd become an expert horsewoman at sixteen and

she was showing him just how well she could ride. It wasn't the first time she'd done so and it wouldn't be the last. She loved when she was in control like this, with him beneath her, taking her body while she took his. Just the way she liked and the way he wanted.

She felt so much love and desire. So much need.

From the first, when he'd introduced her to lovemaking for the very first time, she'd never wanted a man the way she did him. That thought rang through her mind every time her body lowered down on him and then lifted up. Her knees ground into his side and it seemed instead of reining him in, it spurred him to lift up the lower part of his body to meet hers.

Her fingers gripped his shoulders and his hands were wrapped around her waist. Suddenly, his hands moved up to the back of her neck to maneuver her head down to capture her lips. His tongue took control of hers and she could feel his heat, every ounce of strength within him and the full throttle of his masculinity.

Suddenly, a bolt of sensation struck her. She pulled her mouth from his to scream as an orgasm tore through her and she could feel the same rip through him. He quickly reclaimed her mouth and switched their positions where she was now beneath him, their limbs entwined, their bodies plastered together.

Moments later, when he broke off the kiss, she slowly opened her eyes and smiled at him. In a voice filled with sexual exhaustion, she said, "Plan accomplished, Mr. McRoy."

Mac woke the next morning to glance down at the beautiful woman in his arms. Their second round of lovemaking had completely worn out his wife—to the point where she'd immediately drifted off to sleep.

Easing out of the bed, he closed the door behind him and went into the sitting area to call his teammates. If he didn't, they would wonder why he hadn't returned home by now.

He told them about his surprise and what he'd guessed it was. Of course, Bane, Viper and Coop were excited at the prospect of Tia getting a horse. They would be, since they owned plenty of horses and the animals had been part of their lives for years. All three owned ranches and Bane had family members—a brother and several cousins—who raised and trained horses for a living. Mac admitted that after thinking about it, he'd decided Tia having a horse wouldn't be so bad. Especially since she did enjoy her riding lessons. Coop, who had a ranch in Laredo, even explained to Mac the best way to ship the horse to Virginia.

Mac recalled the horse that had been kept for him at his grandparents' ranch in Florida. Riding that horse had been the highlight of his summers each year, when he and his sister would leave the city to enjoy their time with their grandparents.

From the bright light coming in through the window, he figured it was about eight, and a glance at the clock on the nightstand confirmed it. He would let Teri sleep. Once she awakened, their day would get started. He figured, at least he hoped, she would take him to see the "surprise" so they could get back home to the girls.

"I love Dallas," Teri said, looking around after the waitress had taken their order.

They had decided to get out of the hotel to dine at

a small café within walking distance. What Mac liked about this particular café was that it was one of those mom-and-pop establishments and wasn't crowded. Only a few of the tables were taken.

He leaned back in his chair while sipping on his coffee as he gazed over at her. He'd drifted back to sleep after his phone call to his teammates and he and Teri had awakened just before noon. Hungry. He hadn't asked her anything other than how soon they could eat since they'd skipped breakfast.

"Do you?" he asked her.

"Yes. Have you forgotten I used to live not far from here?"

She was right. He had forgotten.

He'd never visited her in Terrell, where her grandparents' ranch had been located. But he did recall how hard the decision had been for her to sell it. "Yes, I had forgotten," he admitted. "I guess a lot of things bring back memories for you here."

"Yes," she said wistfully.

He reached across the table and took her hand into his. "I don't have a problem with that, just as long as they don't include an old boyfriend."

She chuckled. "They don't. If you recall, I was too busy trying to juggle both school and the rodeo to have a steady beau."

He did recall her telling him that one of her grandparents' stipulations about her involvement with the rodeo meant she had to also do well in school and college. Since education was important to him, he could see him making a similar stipulation with Tia if she ever decided she wanted to one day compete on the rodeo circuit like her mother had done. He'd long accepted the rodeo might be in his oldest daughter's blood and he was preparing for that day.

"I find that odd," she said suddenly.

He lifted a brow and looked at Teri. "You find what odd?"

"That man and his daughter. Their behavior."

He glanced across the room. The little girl who sat across the man appeared to be about eight. The two were eating breakfast and he didn't see anything the least bit strange about them. They were just two people eating breakfast.

"What's so odd about them?" he asked, looking back at his wife.

"She seems petrified of him."

Mac again glanced at the two. Again, he saw nothing amiss. The man seemed to be enjoying breakfast and the kid was not eating anything. In his opinion, the little girl appeared defiant, not afraid. "He probably laid down the law about something she didn't like. It happens, Teri."

"How would you know?" she asked, grinning.

"What do you mean how would I know?"

"That's what I'm asking. When have you ever laid down the law to your girls?"

He grinned back when he actually couldn't think of one single time. "I have good girls. I don't have to lay down the law. I lay it down to their mother, who I'm sure passes that law on to them when needed."

Teri rolled her eyes. "You come home after I've established the law and let them break it."

"No, I don't."

"Yes, you do."

Mac smiled. Okay, maybe he did. "So, I spoil them

a little whenever I'm home. Is there anything wrong with that?"

"Yes, a lot."

He didn't want to argue with her about it right now and was glad when the waitress delivered their meal.

Teri clicked off her cell phone after talking with Mac's parents to check on the girls. According to them, everything was fine. Mac had gone to the men's room and she was slipping her phone back into her purse when her eyes fell on the table where the man and girl still sat.

She had tried not to stare, but more than once her gaze had been drawn to the two. Regardless of what Mac said, Teri was convinced something wasn't right. She was about to take another sip of her tea when the girl caught her eye while the man talked on the phone. There was a look in the little girl's gaze as they stared at each other. The man noticed the exchange and frowned at Teri, quickly clicking off the phone and saying something to the girl, who looked at him with what Teri felt was fear in her eyes.

Then, as she continued to watch them, the girl intentionally swept her plate and eating utensils to the floor. The man stood and grabbed the girl, nearly snatching her off her feet.

Teri was out of her seat in a flash and had crossed the room. "Turn her loose," she told the man.

He pulled the child behind him. "Do you dare to interrupt me chastising my child?"

"Yes, because if she was yours, you wouldn't handle her that way."

"Get out of my way, lady."

"No, I won't. Prove she's yours." Teri knew they were drawing stares and she didn't care.

"You either get out of my face so I can get my child out of here or I will—"

"You will what?"

Before he could respond the little girl said, "He's not my daddy!"

When the man turned as if he was going to give the child a slap, Teri pushed him and grabbed the child. Now it was the man hollering. "She took my child."

"What the hell is going on here?"

Teri immediately recognized Mac's booming voice. When the man tried to push Teri aside to reclaim the child, Mac intervened to protect her and shoved the man back instead, nearly knocking him to the floor.

"I asked, what the hell is going on?" Mac roared again.

"This woman took my child," the man snapped, straightening on his feet.

Mac looked at his wife, who had a furious expression on her face. There was no doubt in his mind she was ready to fight to shield the child if she had to. Teri Anne McRoy, the mother, was showing her protective colors.

Mac then looked at the little girl hiding behind Teri, who seemed to be holding on to his wife for dear life. He saw the fear in her small eyes. His gaze shifted back to Teri and before he could ask her anything, she got back in the man's face and said, "This child isn't yours. She gave me the signs."

"What signs?" Mac asked, trying to figure out why his wife thought this girl was not the man's child.

Teri glanced at her husband. "The same ones I've told

our daughters to make if they were ever taken against their will."

"She's crazy!" the man shouted. "That is my child."

"Prove it!" Teri snapped at the man.

Mac noticed the man had yet to ask anyone to call for the police. Leaning down to the child, who was still clutching Teri, he asked, "Is he your father?"

The little girl shook her head. "No. He took me from Mommy."

"She lies! She is my daughter!" the man shouted.

"Then prove it," Mac said, backing up Teri by making the same demand she had earlier. He noticed the other customers in the restaurant were evidently suspicious of the man's relationship with the little girl and were taking out their cell phones.

The man reached into his jacket as if he was going to pull out his wallet. Instead he pulled out a revolver and pointed it at them. "Give me the girl!"

Teri knew from the growl she heard from Mac that all hell was about to break loose. Mac could handle himself and would protect her. Teri's main concern was the child. When the man repeated his words, someone in the restaurant shouted, "The police are on their way."

That announcement angered the man. He tried reaching for the girl and Teri snatched back at the same time Mac moved forward, knocking the gun out of the man's hand before giving him a hard blow to the gut, sending him sprawling to the floor. When he made an attempt to get back up, Mac knocked him out cold.

"Teri, you could have gotten killed," Mac said. She heard the anger in his voice.

She smiled up at him before leaning up on tiptoe and

kissing him on the cheek. "Not with my husband stand-ing here protecting me. You're my hero."

She then looked down at the little girl and asked softly, "Are you okay?"

Instead of answering, the little girl threw herself into Teri's arms and cried. Moments later, the police burst into the restaurant.

Chapter 14

Mac sat beside Teri at police headquarters while she gave a statement regarding what had happened in the restaurant.

The little girl had been reported missing that morning, snatched from her mother in broad daylight at a shopping mall. Instead of taking her immediately into hiding, the man had probably figured he had time to enjoy a meal first with her in plain sight. As Teri spoke to the police, explaining why she'd decided to come to the girl's aid, he could see obvious admiration and respect in the officers' eyes.

"His name is Leonard Caper and he has a rap sheet a mile long. This was the first time he tried snatching a child. He's confessed to some guy paying him to do it, pick up any little girl. He's singing like a canary and we're following up all leads," a police detective was saying.

"Well. I'm glad he's off the street and I hope you get everybody who's involved."

"Yes, ma'am, we intend to."

Mac and Teri had met the little girl's parents. They hadn't wasted any time arriving at the police station to get their daughter. He doubted he'd ever met two more thankful individuals. The girl's mother had thrown her arms around Teri and cried profusely. Teri had cried, too. As the father of four girls he understood the father's need to get a piece of the guy, and more than one officer had to hold the man back from doing just that.

"If there's a trial, ma'am, you might be called back to testify," the detective added.

"I don't have a problem doing that if needed."

"Thanks, we appreciate it. And there is a ten-thousand-dollar reward for you, Mrs. McRoy. It was set up by the Dallas Fire Department, where the little girl's father is employed."

Teri shook her head. "I don't want it. Give it to the parents to go toward the little girl's college education."

Even more admiration shone in the officers' eyes. "You will have to sign papers for that to be done."

"Sure, I can do that," Teri said.

Mac raised a brow when Teri turned to him with a worried look on her face.

"What's wrong?" he asked her.

"I hope not keeping that money is fine with you. We didn't discuss it."

"And there's no need. I agree with what you've decided to do. Besides, it was your money to do whatever you want with."

Teri shook her head. "No, it's our money. That's the way it is between us, Mac."

He knew that to be true. That was the way it was between them. Mac sighed deeply. They still had a lot of talking to do, things he needed to find out that he still didn't know. Namely, what she had bought that had her anxious.

One thing he'd discovered today was that his wife was capable of holding her own, even without him.

"Man, do us a favor," Bane said, as he and his teammates talked to Mac on the phone later that day. "You and Teri need to go home as soon as a flight can get you there. Instead of spending quality time together, the two of you are doing nothing but finding trouble to get into."

Mac couldn't help laughing at that, since it certainly seemed that way. They had finished giving their statements to the police but not before the news reporters had gotten there. "I'm just glad Teri picked up on the fact that little girl was in trouble. I hadn't suspected a thing."

"That just goes to show that she has certain skills you don't have, Mac. When will you realize you have a special woman on your hands?" Coop asked. "It's all over the news how she faced that man and took that girl from him."

That part angered Mac. "She could have gotten hurt. That bastard had a gun." Mac didn't think he would ever forget the moment when that man had pulled his weapon out and pointed it at them. Namely, at Teri.

"And you got back in time to take care of business like you were supposed to do," Viper said.

"I'm going to make sure my daughter knows the signs when she grows up. People are messed up these days," Coop tacked on.

"Just the thought of that bastard assuming he could

snatch somebody's kid like that," Flipper said. "It was a good thing you and Teri were there."

Mac nodded. "Well, it was almost too much action for me," he said. "I expect it as a SEAL but as a civilian? What's wrong with coming home to peace and quiet?"

"Nothing is wrong with it, unless you're married to Teri," Bane said, laughing.

Mac chuckled, knowing he wouldn't have it any other way. Moments later, after ending the call with his friends, he left the sitting area to go into the bedroom, where Teri was just clicking off her own phone.

She glanced up at him. "That was the folks. They saw us on television. The girls saw us, as well. They think their parents are heroes."

Mac smiled. "You mean they think their mom is a hero. You're the one who figured the kid was kidnapped. You want to tell me about these signs?"

She smiled over at him. "Keep your fingers on one hand crossed, and when you can, get someone's attention."

"And the kid did that?"

"Yes. She was sitting with her fingers crossed, and after you left, she knocked her dishes off the table, hoping to get someone's attention. But I was already on it."

"Apparently." He had walked out of the restroom to return to his table, only to find Teri confronting the kidnapper, with the child cowering behind her. He was certain that had he not knocked the man out then Teri would have done so herself. After ten years of marriage, he was surprised to be seeing his wife in a new light.

"Her parents told her what to do and she did it. Like I told the police, she was a real trouper. If anyone was a hero, that little girl was."

"Well, more than ever I'm ready to go home," Mac said. "When are we going to see the horse?"

She lifted a brow. "What horse?"

"I figured that was the surprise. Am I right?"

She shook her head. "No, you aren't right."

He didn't say anything for a minute and then he asked, "Then what kind of surprise is there here in Dallas? What on earth could you have bought here?"

"Nothing in Dallas."

He lifted his own brow. "Then where, Teri?"

"In Terrell. I was able to buy back my ranch. So I did."

Mac stared at her, certain he'd heard her wrong. "Could you say that again?"

She nodded. "I got a chance to buy back my grandparents' ranch due to a 'first right of refusal' clause I had included in the contract when I sold it. That meant the current owners had to offer it to me first before they put it on the market."

"And you bought it?" he asked, incredulously.

"Yes."

He stared at her for a minute. "And how did you pay for it?"

She nervously licked her lips and he immediately knew that he wouldn't like her answer. Because he could think of only one way she could have paid for it. "Teri, how did you pay for it?" he repeated.

"I used some of our savings."

"Some of it?"

She shrugged lightly. "A big chunk of it."

He stared at her. "How much, Teri?"

"Not as much as you think."

"How much, Teri?"

"Remember your pardon, Mac."

"How much, Teri?"

She then gave him a figure that made him see red after his head began swimming. He knew how much they'd had in their savings and he now knew how much was left.

He thought about how long and hard he'd saved. How carefully he'd guarded each purchase. Yes, they had enough, but that money belonged to both of them and she hadn't consulted him at all. That money was for their future, for their girls. Generational wealth.

He didn't want them to worry the way he'd had to worry growing up.

He drew in a deep breath and then said, "The pardon is off."

She frowned. "You can't do that."

"I just did." He then walked out of the hotel room.

Teri froze the moment she heard the door slam shut behind Mac. He was mad. Furious was more like it. She had expected his anger days ago but when he'd said he would give her a pardon, she had believed him. He'd said it extended to her last purchase, no matter what she'd bought. Granted, a horse was definitely not as expensive as a ranch, but still…

And now he had left.

His usual mode of operation whenever he came home and discovered she'd purchased something he thought was outrageous would be to put distance between them to cool off. Then he would return in an hour or so but ignore her for a day or two. Next would be the lectures, where he would do all the talking and like a disobedient child she was supposed to listen. Hadn't expressing how she felt over the past few days gotten her anywhere other than back to square one with him?

Okay, she would admit using so much of their savings was something she should have consulted him about since it had been funds set aside not only for emergencies but for the kids' education. Maybe wanting to buy back the ranch had been selfish of her. Had she put her wants ahead of her family's needs? It had been her decision not to keep the ranch years ago and it was a decision she should have accepted. She had for years, but then lately she'd begun regretting that decision, wishing she could offer their kids the same lifestyle that she'd had growing up. And she knew that moving to the ranch would be the right thing for all of them.

Granted, she should have consulted Mac, but he hadn't been available for her to do that. So she'd made the decision for them. He hadn't bothered to find out why. She would have gladly laid out the advantages if he'd given her a chance, but he hadn't. Now they had a ranch house that she wanted but he didn't. And she and the kids wouldn't live there without him. Was it wrong to want it all? The ranch. Mac. She and the girls there with them. A happy family. A marriage that was not filled with arguments. Teri knew she would do whatever it took to keep them together. She would put him and their marriage first.

Getting up off the bed, she knew what she had to do. She grabbed her purse and reached inside for the business card of Jack Polluck, the man who'd handled the sale for her years ago and her recent purchase. Within minutes she was placing a call to him.

"Yes, Mr. Polluck, this is Teri Cantor McRoy. I want

to put my ranch up for sale." She paused and then said, fighting back her tears, "Yes, I'm sure."

Mac tried to cool his anger by walking around a nearby park. He still couldn't wrap his head around the fact that his wife had bought not appliances, a new television or a horse. But a ranch. And she had used most of their savings to do so. What in the world had she been thinking?

And he hadn't bothered to ask her that?

He rubbed a hand down his face in frustration, realizing he was acting just like he usually did whenever he returned home from being gone for a long period of time to find the balance of their savings account less than what it had been when he'd left. He hadn't given her a chance to explain her actions.

He dropped down on a park bench. How could she explain buying a ranch in a state where he'd never lived? But then, she had lived here and evidently liked it enough to want to move back. However, after this morning, would he move to an area where kids could easily be snatched from their parents?

Mac was fully aware that he needed to be fair. He had to admit such a thing could have happened in any city in the United States. Even in Virginia. It was up to parents to prepare their kids and it seemed like Teri had prepared theirs. They knew how to give out signs. Hell, he hadn't even been aware of that. But Teri had.

What was it going to take for him to realize and accept that Teri had never bought anything foolishly? Whatever she did, whatever she bought, was something that would eventually benefit the family. He wasn't sure how a ranch in Texas would benefit them, but he was certain she would have laid it out for him if he had given her the chance.

And hadn't he pretty much acknowledged days ago that the recent problems in their marriage were more than her buying stuff? They included his habit of taking her and what she brought to their marriage for granted. He realized that, yet he was again doing that very thing. He stood up and began heading back toward the hotel. Determined that this time they would handle the situation differently.

When he got back to the hotel it was to find it empty with a note left in the middle of the bed.

Mac,
Sorry. Once again, I blew things. Even though
I'd imagined we could all be happy there at the
ranch, I thought more of my happiness than that
of you and the kids and that wasn't fair. I've called
the real estate agent to put the ranch house back
up for sale and he feels certain he will be able to
sell it for what I paid for it within a month or so.
I'm heading back home to the kids.
Teri

He crumpled the paper up after hearing the defeat in her words. He glanced around. She was gone. For the second time in less than a week his wife had left him.

The key to the car was on the nightstand, which meant she'd taken a cab. He grabbed the key and headed for the door, knowing he was the one who was sorry.

Teri flipped through a magazine. She was on standby but she didn't mind waiting. She would rather sit here than be at the hotel with Mac giving her the silent treatment. There was nothing left to be said. She hoped the note she'd left him explained it all.

Time passed. She was reading an interesting article and barely noticed the person sliding into the seat beside her until he said, "Aren't you tired of running away, Teri?"

She jerked her head up and stared into Mac's face. He wasn't smiling but then neither was she. "Why did you come here?"

He shrugged. "My wife is here and whenever I'm in the States, I like being with my wife."

"The same wife who likes spending your money?"

He chuckled. "Yes, that one. But then, my money is her money."

She rolled her eyes. "Yes, until she buys something. Why did you come here, Mac? I left a note."

"That note wasn't good enough."

"Well, it was for me." She then checked her watch. "Are you on standby, as well?"

"No. I came to get you. Our flight leaves tomorrow and not today. You were supposed to show me my surprise."

She jutted out her chin. "You said my pardon is over. So is the surprise."

He didn't say anything for a minute. "I want to see it."

"See what?"

"This ranch you bought."

"The same one that is now up for sale? Well, I have no desire to show it to you now. It doesn't matter."

He reached out and took her hand in his. "Maybe I need to explain something to you, Teri. Everything you do matters because *you* matter. I'm the one who owes you an apology. I know there're reasons for you to have bought the ranch and I need for you to tell me what they are."

"Why? The reasons won't change anything."

He shrugged. "Maybe not. But this time I'm willing to hear you out before passing judgment."

She lifted a brow. "Why? You've never done that before."

"I know. I'm honestly trying to do better. I told you I was one of those works in progress. Why didn't you take me at my word? Why were you so quick to walk out on me?"

She looked away for a minute and then back at him. "Because I'm tired of fighting."

"We don't fight, Teri. We disagree. All couples do it from time to time. We shouldn't be any different."

"But we are," she implored.

"Then it's definitely something we should be working on correcting." He stood. "Come on. I want to see the place."

She looked up at him. "Do you really?"

"Yes. On the way there you can tell me why buying it was so important to you and how you believe it will benefit us and the girls. That's what it's about, Teri. That's what it's always about with you. What's always in the forefront of your mind. I know that and truly believe you wouldn't do anything that wouldn't be for our best interest."

She fought back her tears. "I want to believe that, Mac. All I'm asking is for you to hear me out. And if you don't agree with my assessment after seeing it, then so be it—we will sell it."

He nodded. "Fair enough."

She then took his hand and stood. He gave her a wry smile and said, "I have a feeling I'm going to like it."

She lifted a brow. "Why do you think that?"

"I just do."

Chapter 15

Mac did like it.

The moment he drove down the long driveway, he knew he was a goner. Probably before that, when she'd persuaded him to take the scenic route lined with large magnolia and oak trees and a number of bluebonnets. Then there were the lush meadows and valleys and the numerous lakes.

At one point he'd pulled to the side of the road, a part that had a beautiful view of the lake. He could see himself riding bicycles with the girls around here or having a picnic with Teri. He had visited Bane's, Viper's and Coop's spreads and he thought this place rivaled theirs in size and could be just as productive.

During the drive, Teri had made her pitch, and a pretty damn good one, too. She told him of the improvements the family that had last owned the ranch had made. They'd been improvements that had been needed but that she hadn't been able to afford, which was one of the reasons she had sold.

There was a spanking new barn and several small outbuildings that could be used as guest cottages whenever anyone visited. Another thing that impressed Mac was the size and style of the ranch house. Each of his daughters could have their own room with no problem. It was spacious and built in the ranch style he preferred.

He'd met the previous owners, who would remain in the house for the next couple of months. He'd done the figures in his head and would admit Teri had been able to buy back her home at a fair price, which showed just what a good negotiator she'd been in making the deal.

And this had been her home. The glow in her voice and the smile on her lips when she talked about it was a strong indicator of just what this home had meant to her. He hadn't known. After she'd sold the place, he had assumed she had walked away without looking back. Although that might have been true, losing her home had been a pain she'd refused to let surface. But it had been there.

She'd never admitted such to him, but it had been revealed in her voice when she'd told him of all the fond memories she had shared here with her grandparents.

Another plus that he hadn't yet shared with her was that his investment in Bane's family land management company, as well as their horse business, had showed a damn good profit last year and that had been passed on to the shareholders. That, along with his bonuses over the last two years, would be enough to replace the money from the girls' college fund, and they'd still have more than enough left over to start a business here. Already he could envision him going into the horse business with Bane's relatives, like Coop had done.

Even though they owned huge spreads, Viper and Coop had hired capable men to run things whenever they were gone. He could see himself doing the same thing.

"So, what do you think?" Teri asked, when they returned to the hotel hours later.

Closing his fingers around her wrists, he reached out and drew her to him. "Do you want me to be truthful?"

She ran a hand through her hair and sighed. "Not want, Mac. I *expect* you to be truthful."

He smiled, remembering when he'd made the same stipulation of her. "I will always be truthful with you."

Pausing a moment, he pulled her over to sit on the sofa. "You did good for your family, Teri. You might have thought of your wants with the purchase of the ranch, but you still considered the needs of your family, as well."

His eyes held hers. "I can see future growth here and generational wealth we can pass on to the girls. That's something I've always worked hard to do. It's why I took it so hard when you made purchases. Well, I can see it now. I can see this being a working ranch, one we can make profitable to pass on to the girls. I'm sure one of the four, maybe all four, would want to continue it like you wanted to do."

He reached out and took her hand in his. "Spending this week with you has opened my eyes to a lot of things, Teri."

She lifted her brow. "Such as?"

"What a lucky man I am. Hell, you saved my life in that mineshaft. I hadn't known a rope was under that trough or about any signs kids are taught in case they're ever snatched. In addition, you're pretty damn smart. I admit there was nothing you've ever bought while I was away that did not benefit us. I know you don't think I trust your judgment, but I do and I intend to do a better job proving it."

He decided to add, "That doesn't mean I won't ever question you about anything, because I might. When I do, please take it as my need to have more clarification versus questioning your judgment."

She nodded. "Thank you."

"No, I want to thank you. You're my wife, my partner, my soul mate and the mother of my kids. I love you, Teri. Don't ever forget that. Although I was upset about how you placed yourself in danger with that guy to get that little girl away from him, for you to have the guts and courage to even do such a thing showed just what a strong, capable woman you are. I am so proud to be your husband."

"Oh, Mac," she said, reaching out and cupping his beard, running her fingers through it.

He reached out and lifted her up to place her into his lap, wrapping his arms tight around her. "And another thing, I do want another baby, Teri. Like you, I didn't know how much I did until you told me about the son we lost. It doesn't matter whether we have a girl or a boy—I want to be a father again."

"Oh, Mac, I do want another baby, too, but what about all your concerns?"

"I believe in you. I know you will always do your best for all our kids."

"Thank you."

He'd entertained the thought of retiring in a few more

years. Now that there was a ranch to run, they would run the ranch and raise their kids together.

"I don't think you know how happy I am right now, Mac. I was so scared and worried. What I haven't told you is that I blamed myself for losing the baby."

"Why?"

"Because I lost the baby two days after I returned home from Terrell. I thought the flight had something to do with it, although the doctor said it didn't."

"And you should believe the doctor and not blame yourself for anything. I don't."

"You don't?"

"No, and you shouldn't, either."

"I love you so much," she said, before burying her face in his chest.

"And I love you." He stood with her in his arms. "And I intend to show you just how much."

He carried her into the bedroom knowing there would always be days when they didn't see eye to eye on everything, but at least they would agree on this one thing. They were a team.

And his wife would always be his to claim, just like he would be hers.

When they reached the bedroom, he placed her on her feet. She reached up and wrapped her arms around his neck and pulled his mouth back down to hers. He had no problem giving her what she undoubtedly wanted. Namely, appeasing the hunger taking control of both of them.

He knew what she wanted and he was right there with her. Stripping his wife out of her clothes, he proceeded to do just that. His hands were busy, unbuttoning her shirt, then taking it off, unsnapping her jeans and letting her lean on him while he slid them down her hips. Her bra and panties followed and before removing his own clothes, he straightened and stared at the beautiful body before him. Her breasts were absolutely gorgeous and her waist small, even after four children.

He recalled that after Tia had been born, Teri had hated the stretch marks left from her pregnancy, but he had convinced her that any marks from giving birth to a child of theirs would be her badge of honor. A badge he appreciated her wearing and one he wanted her to do so proudly. After that, she never mentioned the stretch marks again.

"You know what I think?" he said, still staring at her. He was ready to do more than just look. He was ready to touch.

She smiled up at him. "No, what do you think?"

"That you're the most beautiful woman I know."

His words made Teri smile.

She was fully aware that other women found her husband sexy and could understand them doing so. She was cognizant of walking into rooms where women nearly drooled when they saw him. And she could honestly say she had never felt threatened. Mac made it a point to assure her how much he loved her and how beautiful he thought was. He said he didn't mind if his compliments ever went to her head.

He leaned down close to her ear and whispered, "And you know what else I think?"

"Um, you're on a roll, so you might as well confess all."

He leaned closer. "I think you would look even more beautiful pregnant again."

She fought back tears. For him to say that meant he wanted to see her pregnant again. They had been using a condom for all their sexual encounters after being rescued. Was he hinting that he wanted to have unprotected sex with her again? That he was willing to not only risk her getting pregnant but also was hoping that she would be?

"I'm on board if you are, Mac. It will take two for that to happen."

He cupped her face in his hands. "Then let's get it on, Ms. McRoy."

He leaned down and kissed her breasts and when he did so, she closed her eyes and drew in a deep breath. When he sucked a hardened nipple between his lips she felt her breasts swelling in his mouth, making her moan.

When he pulled his mouth away, he said, "Not sure I'm ready to compete with my baby for these breasts, Teri."

Since she breastfed all her babies, she knew what he was referring to. "Poor baby."

He chuckled. "For some reason I don't think your sympathy is sincere. That means I'm going to have to torture you for a while."

Teri knew all about Thurston McRoy's type of torture. She didn't want to admit it, but she loved it.

"Please don't." Inwardly she hoped that he would.

He bent down and licked his tongue across her stomach. When he did so, every cell inside her body flared to life. And when the tip of his tongue began swirling around her navel, she felt every nerve ending in her stomach flare to life. This was torment, and with every flick of his tongue she felt a pull, a tingling sensation between her legs.

As if he sensed her predicament, he glanced up at her and smiled. "You haven't felt anything yet, baby. Get ready. Here I come."

Getting down on his knees he stared down at the juncture of her thighs, and at that moment her legs began to quiver with the intensity of his gaze. He uttered a growl before leaning in and burying his mouth there.

Mac intended to show no mercy. Just pleasure. With that goal in mind, he used the tip of his tongue to stir a fervor within Teri, widening her thighs to capture the bud of her womanhood.

He took his time and showed no signs of letting up, intending to pleasure her. Even if it took all night. Already she was rocking her body against his mouth. He had no problem with her doing that since the more she rocked, the deeper his tongue intended to go.

Then he felt it, the first sign that she was about to come. Her thighs were quivering around him and when she suddenly threw her head back and screamed his name, he knew a maelstrom of pleasure was engulfing her. He could taste it.

When her trembling ceased, he stood and pulled her into his arms, capturing her at the same time his hand settled right between those legs.

"Now for something else going in here," he said, after breaking off the kiss. Using his fingers, he began stroking her there.

"You're torturing me again, Mac," she accused breathlessly.

"Guilty as charged," he whispered in her ear.

And then he edged her closer to the bed and eased her down on her back and joined her there, sliding on top of her. Teri lifted her hips and Mac knew why and what she wanted.

Deciding he'd teased her enough, he eased inside of her, and instinctively, she opened her legs. Then he began thrusting in and out, back and forth. She moaned his name when he increased his strokes and he felt her body shudder again beneath him.

A growl escaped Mac's throat when he became caught up in the same pleasure he was giving his wife. Over and over, their bodies worked in unison as her hips rose off the bed at the same time his came down on hers.

"Mac!" She screamed his name when they both exploded in an earth-shattering climax that seemed never-ending.

He kissed her, slowly recovering from the effects of one hell of an orgasm and knew that before the night ended, there would be more, and all just as powerful.

Chapter 16

Teri glanced across the table at Mac as they enjoyed breakfast at the hotel's restaurant. "What do you mean we aren't going home today?"

Mac smiled. "That's what I mean. Do you know that of all the days we've spent together this week, not a single one has been relaxing?"

She raised a brow, remembering all the hours spent in his arms making love. "So, you don't consider any of our time together relaxing?"

"I'm not talking about the lovemaking, Teri. I'm talking about just normal, uneventful time with you where we aren't trapped in mineshafts or you're not risking your life saving little girls or you're not showing me our future on the ranch. I want to go out and do something. Together. You like this area? Then show me why. The only time I've been to Dallas is when we came for

Flipper's mom's birthday celebration. I didn't get to see much of it then."

Teri smiled, glad Mac was truly interested in the area she called home. "There's really a lot to do here. I can show you all my favorite places."

"Then let's spend the day together. When we go back up to our room, you can map out places for us to visit."

Teri appreciated Mac's thoughtfulness. Although he'd told her that he was looking forward to moving to Terrell, what he'd just said meant that he truly was. She would include getting together with Flipper and Swan in their plans since they were still in Dallas visiting Flipper's family.

After changing into more comfortable clothes and shoes, they hit the streets. They walked and checked out the Sixth Floor Museum at Dealey Plaza, a museum dedicated to the life and death of President John F. Kennedy. Since she was a history major, she was able to tell Mac a lot of things she figured he hadn't known.

They went to several other museums and the botanical gardens, as well. Holding hands, they walked through the gardens with rows and rows of both flowering and nonflowering plants.

"Do you think the girls will have a problem leaving their friends?" he asked her when they left the gardens to head out to the Reunion Tower.

She was excited about taking him on the high-speed elevator ride that went to the top in sixty-eight seconds. It had always been a fun place for her while growing up.

"I think they will at first, but I also think they'll love it here and make new friends. I can't wait for them to see it," she said.

"Neither can I."

After visiting a number of other sights, they drove into Terrell, and she took him around town. News had traveled fast about her buying back her family farm and everywhere they went people told her how glad they were that she'd decided to move back home. They visited her old high school and she even took him to the rodeo school where she'd learned to rope her first calf.

She knew Mac had an ulterior motive for wanting to meet some of the people in Terrell. He would be gone for long periods of time during covert operations and needed the peace of mind that she would have a similar network of friends in Terrell like she had in Virginia. He soon saw that this was home for her and everyone in the area around the ranch knew her and looked forward to her return. He mentioned that he was glad Flipper's parents lived close by, too, in Dallas.

Teri was happy, too. She was excited to meet Flipper and Swan for lunch. The couple were thrilled to hear that Teri and Mac had bought back the ranch that had been in Teri's family for years. Flipper and Swan had their own good news to share. They were expecting their first child. Teri was happy for them. She would never forget how Flipper had risked his life by swimming into that flooded mineshaft to save them.

Later, on the drive back to the hotel that evening from Terrell, she tried calling Mac's parents to check on the kids. When she didn't get an answer, she turned to Mac. "That's odd."

He looked over at her when he brought the car to a traffic light. "What is?"

"I can't reach the folks."

"What's odd about that? This isn't a school night so they probably took the kids out for pizza or something. You know how the girls wrap them around their fingers."

Teri chuckled. "If anybody knows about their ability to wrap someone around their fingers it would be you. The girls have you wrapped so tight it isn't funny."

"Whatever. And about it being not funny, you don't hear me laughing, do you?"

Teri smiled. "Although I totally enjoyed our time together today, I really miss the kids."

"I do, too, and I enjoyed our time together, as well. We need to do it more often. How does the idea of date night sound?"

"It sounds great and the Wilkersons' daughter turns seventeen this year, and old enough to babysit for us. She's smart and levelheaded."

Once they got back to the hotel, they stopped at the ice-cream shop and enjoyed a bowl of ice cream together. When they reached their hotel room, Mac opened the door and then stepped aside for Teri to walk in ahead of him.

"Mommy! Daddy!"

A surprised Teri shrieked upon seeing the girls and raced across the room to give them hugs. She gave her in-laws hugs, as well. She then turned to Mac. "You arranged this?"

He grinned as he walked across the room to give her a hug, since she was obviously in a huggy mood. "Yes. I knew that although you were enjoying my company, you were missing the girls as much as I was. I called Mom and Dad after you went to sleep last night and made arrangements to get them here."

"That's why you kept me away all day?" she asked, grinning back at him.

"No, I kept you away because I wanted to spend time with you," he said, leaning in and kissing her across the lips.

"Do we really have a ranch, Mommy?"

"Will we have horses?"

"And plant our own food to eat?"

"And make new friends?"

All the questions came at them from the girls seemingly at once. Together Mac and Teri answered each and every one of them to the best of their ability, although the reply to a number of them was "We'll just have to wait and see." It was important to them that their girls looked forward to making the move as much as they did.

"So when can we see this ranch?" Mac's father asked, and Teri could hear the excitement in his voice.

"Tomorrow," Mac said, wrapping his arm around Teri's waist. "I talked to the owners and they are looking forward to showing you around."

"And it's the house where you lived as a little girl, Mommy?" Tia asked her.

Teri smiled down at her daughter. "Yes." She wished she could tell Tia about her and Mac's plan to get her a horse, but she knew it would be a surprise. Tia had a birthday coming up and that would be soon enough to share the news.

School would be out for the summer in three weeks and they intended to put their current home up for sale and begin packing. They hoped to be settled in at the ranch before school started in the fall.

That night when they went to bed, Mac held her in his arms. He had arranged for the girls and his folks to have a hotel room next door with a connecting door. It was hard to deny Tasha when she wanted to stay and sleep with them, and Teri was surprised Mac couldn't be charmed by their youngest daughter. Usually he would give in to her, but this time he didn't. He told Tasha that she needed to stay with her grandparents because Mommy and Daddy needed time by themselves together. Teri could tell Tasha didn't agree, but she left with her grandparents anyway.

"Thanks for bringing them here," she said to Mac when they were alone in bed. She wasn't dumb. At some point during the night Tasha would get out of bed and knock on the connecting door. And when she did, Mac would get out of bed, open the door and let their daughter into their bed to sleep with them.

"You were missing them and so was I. Besides, the folks wanted to see the ranch. It was the perfect time."

"And your parents are perfect with them."

"I have to agree with that," he said. "I have a feeling we'll be seeing a lot of them once we move to the ranch."

"I hope we do. We'll have plenty of space at the house, or they might prefer one of the cabins for privacy. One thing is for certain, we'll have plenty of room."

"We will definitely have that." He then pulled her deeper into his arms.

When he leaned down and kissed her, every part of her yearned for him, aching in a way that had the area between her legs throbbing unmercifully. "I hope you know sooner or later we're going to get a little knock on that door. Tasha never takes 'no' as an answer, especially when it comes from her daddy. You know what that means, right?" she asked Mac.

He grinned. "Yes, I know what that means. We don't have any time to waste."

Mac pulled her to him and kissed her, and she nearly drowned in the masculine essence of him. Something he always said rang through her mind.

She was his to claim. Now. Forever. Always.

Epilogue

Five months later

Bane Westmoreland opened the door and smiled at the couple standing on his doorstep. With the arrival of Mac and Teri, all his team members were accounted for.

"About time you guys got here," Bane said, leaning over to give a very pregnant Teri a kiss.

"Stop complaining," Mac said. "Teri doesn't move as fast these days as she used to."

Teri glanced over at her husband and frowned. "Don't you dare blame me for us being late, Mac, when you refused to move from in front of the television until that football game was over. I tried to get you to leave the hotel an hour ago."

Bane shook his head since it was obvious Teri was in a tiff about it. "I see it's business as usual with you two."

"Not exactly," Mac said, grinning and wrapping an arm around his wife's protruding stomach. "We found out yesterday before leaving home that we're having twins. Both boys."

"Congratulations!" Bane said, happy for his friends. "Now, get inside so everyone can congratulate you two, as well. Six kids. Wow!"

Mac grinned proudly. "Yeah, that's what I say. Wow! The good thing is my folks love the ranch and are crazy about the cabin we're giving them. They will move in soon. Mom's going to be a big help to Teri and our six kids while I'm away."

Bane nodded, smiling. "Sounds like you two have things worked out. After having only three kids I understand how important extra help is."

Mac, Teri and the girls had moved to their ranch in Texas a couple of months ago. Of course the SEAL team members had been there to help. Their ranch would be a horse ranch, and thanks to Bane's family, who owned a horse breeding and training company, already several horses had been added. Like Coop's ranch, Mac's would also serve as a horse depot that housed the animals before they were shipped off to be trained. There was even some discussion about later making Mac's ranch an official horse training site. The partnership was proving to be a financial incentive for Mac and Teri.

Since Mac was still on active duty, one of the Westmorelands' foremen, who wanted to move closer to his son, daughter-in-law and grandkids in Dallas, had accepted the job as Mac's foreman. The McRoys' ranch had been named Timberlake, a joint effort by their daughters.

Mac had surprised his wife last month. On her birthday, he had given Teri a special gift. A horse. Namely, Amsterdam. Upon discovering how much the horse had meant to Teri, Mac had bought it from the owners of the Torchlight Dude Ranch. Mac had also bought horses for each of his daughters.

Tonight they were all gathered to help Bane and Crystal celebrate their move to their new home on "Bane's Ponderosa," his stretch of land in Westmoreland country. Once Mac and Teri were inside, no introductions had to be made. Bane's teammates knew all of his family members, those living in Denver, Atlanta, Texas and Montana. They also knew the Westmorelands from Alaska—who went by the last name of Outlaw.

Also present tonight was the newly elected local sheriff, Peterson Higgins, better known to everyone as Pete. Pete had been best friend to Bane's brother Riley and Bane's cousin Derringer since grade school and was like a member of the Westmoreland family.

Bane and Crystal circulated around the room and Bane couldn't help noticing that the two senators in the family, Reggie Westmoreland and Jess Outlaw, had their heads together discussing a piece of legislation they intended to pass with the help of their colleagues.

A couple of other Outlaws—Garth and Cash—were talking with Bane's brothers Dillon and Canyon and his cousin Riley, hashing out how their two companies, the Outlaw Shipping Company and the Westmoreland Land Management Company, could benefit each other.

In another corner of the room, Teri was getting tips about what to expect with the birth of her multiples from Bane's wife, Crystal, and Nick's wife, Natalie, both mothers of triplets, and Bane's brother Jason's wife, Bella, who had twins.

Bane was happy for Mac and Teri. Mac would be retiring as a SEAL in a couple of years to become a full-time rancher and Bane knew his friend was looking forward to it. With Teri and six kids, Mac would certainly have a lot of help.

The doorbell sounded and Bane wondered who the latecomer could be. With the arrival of Mac and Teri, he'd figured everyone on his and Crystal's guest list had already shown up. Giving Crystal a sign that he would get it, he moved to the door and opened it to find an older couple, who appeared to be in their late sixties or early seventies, standing there with a baby in their arms.

Bane was certain he did not know the couple. "Yes, may I help you?"

The man spoke. "We hate to impose but we were told Peterson Higgins was here tonight. We are the Glosters, his deceased brother's in-laws."

Bane nodded. "Yes, Pete is here. Please come in."

The man shook his head. "We prefer not to, but we would appreciate it if you could tell Peterson we're here. We would like to speak with him. We will wait out here."

Bane nodded again. "Okay, just a minute." He circled around the room before finally finding Pete in a group in the family room, discussing motorcycles with Bane's cousins Thorn, Zane, Derringer and one of the Alaska Westmorelands—Maverick Outlaw.

"Excuse me, guys, but I need to borrow Pete for a minute," Bane said to those in the group. Once he got Pete aside, he told him about the older couple waiting outside. Pete placed his cup of punch aside and quickly moved toward the front door.

Bane wasn't sure how long Pete had been gone, but

when he returned he was carrying a baby in one hand and a diaper bag in the other. Everyone's attention was drawn to Pete when the baby released a huge wail.

It seemed all the mothers in the room hurried toward Pete. "Whose baby?" Bane's cousin Gemma was the first to ask, taking the baby from a flustered-looking Pete.

"This is my nine-month-old niece, Ciara," he said, noticing how quickly the baby girl quieted once Gemma held her. "As most of you know, my brother, Matthew, and his wife, Sherry, were killed in that car crash six months ago. This is their daughter. Sherry's parents were given custody of Ciara when Matt and Sherry died. But they just gave me full custody of her, citing health issues that are preventing them from taking proper care of her. That means I'm now Ciara's legal guardian."

Pete looked around the room at the group he considered family and asked the one question none of them could answer.

"I'm a bachelor, for heaven's sake! What on earth am I going to do with a baby?"

* * * * *

Note from the Author

I want to take this opportunity to thank Kim James for sharing her experiences and challenges as a military wife with me in order to give greater depth to my heroine, Teri McRoy.

And to all military wives everywhere, you are deeply appreciated for serving your country right along with your enlisted spouses. We honor you. Thank you so much!